DIRTY CURVE

USA *TODAY* BESTSELLING AUTHOR

MEAGAN BRANDY

Edited By: My Brother's Editor
Edited by: Fairest Reviews Editing Service
Proofread by: Lisa Salvucci
Photographer: Frank Louis
Formatted by: TalkNerdy2me
www.thetalknerdy.com

My newsletter is the BEST way to stay in contact!
You'll get release dates, titles, and FUN first!
Sign up here: https://geni.us/BMMBNL

Join my FACEBOOK reader group!
—> **Meagan Brandy's Reader Group**

To the one who looks in the mirror and sees only what others speak.
May the fog lift and reveal what you've always hoped but doubted.
That you, my friend, are more than enough.

SYNOPSIS

You know how in college there's that one guy everyone wants to be?

That's me.

I'm the top dog.
The number one.
The big man on campus.

Some say those things are solid wins.
My new tutor would disagree.

My title means nothing to her.
My status lost on her.

And now my mind? That sucker is stuck on her.

She was told to make our sessions priority over all, to drop everything when I need her, and come to me. She does.

But I don't want to steal her time anymore.
I want to earn it.

If anyone can do that, it's me.

I'm Tobias Cruz, the king of the curveball. I don't lose.

Not the game, and surely not the girl.

Little did I know, this girl has herself a secret ... and it's the dirtiest curve yet.

CHAPTER 1

Tobias

Anatomy.

What a fuckin' joke.

This course was supposed to be my free pass, my easy A.

My 'show up late, leave early, do whatever the fuck I want' class.

I mean, come on! It's *anatomy*.

I know everything there is to know about the human body. I know what makes it tick, how to bring it to the edge and keep it there, teetering, shivering, just before it shatters.

I *know* the human body.

This shit, though?

Who the fuck is Vesalius?

If dropping names I've never heard of isn't bad enough, professor 'Kiss My Ass' starts talking positions. Naturally, I perk up at this, sit straighter in my plastic, cramp-inducing chair even.

Positions? I know them well—horizontal, vertical, a ninety-degree angle, bent over a stadium seat. Give me an hour with a gymnast and I'll invent some never before attempted shit, but distal and proximal?

The fuck?

Oh, but I'm getting my A ... in the form of *A* pain in the ass who, as of this morning, was assigned to me, with clear instructions to 'use my head, the one attached to my shoulders.'

I'm pretty sure those were my Coach's exact words.

I miss a few assignments and the man drops the gauntlet on me. Mandatory tutoring to keep my ass on track, as if I fucked off the first three weeks of the semester too bad already to make up the difference. I didn't but fuck it.

Coach always knows best.

Which is why, on this fine Tuesday evening, the one day this week my team's not on the field, I'm forced to make a quick run to meet the chick who's supposed to help me pass.

It's a cold as shit night, so I tug a hoodie over my head, throw on a hat and head out the door.

The athletics center is attached to the front side of our locker rooms and is an easy ten-minute walk from the new pad, so it doesn't take long to get there. Once in the building, I make a hard left and keep heading down the long, tunnel-like hallway, scanning over the two championship banners hanging from the piping.

The first is from 1969 and the second, from last year, my first season as the starting pitcher here at Avix U. I came in freshman year on a redshirt, which meant I was forced to ride the bench and prove I could make the grades required of a college athlete. I was only allowed to practice but not play that first season, so that's what I did.

I practiced every fucking day, three times a day, with and without the team.

Their then main man knew instantly what was coming, so he did what any smart ballplayer would do and transferred out before his spot on the roster shifted from starting to relief pitcher.

I promised Coach the day I signed on I'd get him the title on that banner, and he promised to do whatever he had to do to get me an MLB contract. He got his, and now that I'm a junior, I'll get mine.

Once the season's over, I'll finally be eligible for the draft, and I will be drafted.

No damn doubt.

Which is why this tutoring bull, while extremely nauseating and sure to be a horrible fucking time, not to mention time suck, is annoyingly necessary.

Pretty sure Coach said that, too.

I hop up, tapping the blue and gold tapestry, and keep moving, but my steps slow when hushed arguing echoes off the concrete walls.

"Tell me this is a joke?" a girl hisses.

"Does it sound like I'm joking?" Coach Reid, ever the no-bullshitter, counters in a tone far less concerned than hers.

"I have other students. *I* am a student. I have another job, and I have—"

"Don't bring any of that in here. He's priority," he tells her.

"Priority, wow." The girl's voice drops, a little more

desperate. "This is the last thing I would have expected."

"Why is that? If you ask me, I'd think it's safe to say the concerns you had when transferring to my department no longer exist."

A chortled laugh follows, and it's not a happy one. "I can't tutor Tobias Cruz."

I perk up when my name is dropped, a smile stretching across my face as I lean against the wall to eavesdrop some more.

Let's hear it, girl.

"You can and you will." Coach lays down the law. "As for your time-frame issues, you'll need to figure out how to manage this and your other obligations or I'll have student services pull the contract and seek outside tutors who *can*."

There's a moment's pause, and then she speaks again, "I don't ask *anything* of you, but I'm asking you to assign him to another person. Please."

She keeps going but I tune her out, laughing at how predictable the situation is, and finish her sentence in my head ...

I can't tutor him, he's too good-looking.

I focus in again in time to hear her say, "This is unbelievable."

I laugh again ...

The thought of him drives me wild, it'll be embarrassing to have to sit beside him and—

A gasp yanks me from my thoughts, and I turn to find a chick with a messy ball of hair on her head staring at me, her neck stretched so she can peek out of Coach's office, body still tucked inside.

"Did I say that out loud?"

Grinning, I kick off the wall and step forward, but she doesn't straighten where she stands and serve me her sassiest of smiles. She doesn't slide farther into the hall and wait for me to come closer or make her way to me.

She doesn't do any of those things.

The girl dashes her ass back into the office, leaving me alone in the tunnel.

And I mean, that's kind of fuckin' rude.

With a frown, I head over to tell her so, but before I can reach the entrance, the girl's flying out the door, her chin tucked to her chest.

I put on my best grin and wait for her head to shoot up as she grows closer, for her to peek up at me, flutter her lashes, and apologize for trying to pawn me off, then beg me to let her make it *up* to me by going *down*, but she doesn't do any of those things either.

She walks on by, like nothing.

Doesn't try and rub up on me.

Doesn't linger, hoping I'll grace her with more, be it a quick conversation or impromptu *in*vitation.

The girl doesn't even look my way and then she's gone.

My entire body twists with her speedy exit, now facing the direction she disappeared.

Confused, I subconsciously grip the bill of my hat, lift it an inch, all to pull it right back in place.

The fuck just happened here?

Avix Inquirer:

The spring semester's in full swing, and thanks to our very own Playboy Pitcher, so is the 2021 baseball season.
Let's go, Sharks!

CHAPTER 2

Tobias

"Tobias."

Staring at the now-closed doors, I lick my lips, tempted to follow the girl out, but Coach Reid calls my name again, so I step into his office.

He drops into his chair, tossing his phone onto the desktop with an exasperated huff. "Sorry about that. I was hoping to talk to her before you got here, but I forget your internal clock is like an old man's and you show up a half hour early everywhere you go."

"Yeah." I frown, subconsciously glancing toward the hall again. "It's all good, Coach. She, uh, seems like fun."

When I face forward, I find him frowning in my direction, and my lips pull to one side. "Not my fault you read that wrong. Thinking with the head on my shoulders, swear."

He scoffs, shaking his head. "Yeah, you better be, and don't worry, she'll do what she's told."

"You sure? 'Cause that sounded like a case of

coercion and I didn't catch the submission part."

He chuckles, scrubbing his hands down his face as he leans forward. "Trust me, son. It's handled, and since she took off, go on and head back to whatever it is I'm sure you had planned."

"Why did she take off?"

His eyes snap to mine. "What?"

"Coach, she legit ran the fuck out. Didn't say a word to me."

Coach Reid looks to the side as he grabs his keys from the drawer. "What she lacks in social skills, the girl makes up for in brains. That's all you need to know."

A frown creeps over my face. "All right."

"All right," he echoes. "Now go, but no calling me to clean up any messes," the man jokes.

"Yeah, you look like you could use a couple days of sleep."

"I'll sleep in July when the season's over."

"And I'm on my way to spring training."

"Exactly, son." He laughs, pushing to his feet and leading me out the door. "Go have your fun. I'll send you what you need to know."

Nodding, I spin on my feet, saluting him on my way out. "Thanks, Coach. See you tomorrow."

I head out, and with my head still stuck in no-man's-land, a mythical place where a lowly bun-sporting chick blows me off, I make my way home to join my teammates for some chill time.

Inside, I find my closest friend and roommate Echo, leaning against the wall, chatting up a couple ball babes. Our third and first basemen, Xavier and Neo, brothers in every way that counts, take up most of the space on the couch, a head of bleach-blonde hair I recognize sitting between them.

Our place is nice, low key, and we work hard to keep it that way.

It's a three-bedroom bachelor pad directly across from campus, courtesy of Coach Reid, who happens to be the athletic director here at AU, and the man who gave my life purpose when I had none.

It's a real sweet setup with all-expenses paid and a jacuzzi out back. He hooked me up with the spot when I accidentally got myself in a sticky situation that was against frat house rules—who knew the handbook clearly stated, in big ass bold letters, that bikini-Jell-O wrestling wasn't allowed on campus?

Not me, that's for damn sure.

Now, though, we're in the clear and taking recommendations for this year's contenders at our annual Memorial Day Jell-O Jamboree.

Sure, it's technically against the rules for a school to fund their athletes beyond tuition, but the NCAA made a change to their guidelines this year. Student athletes are now allowed to make money off endorsements and the like, so no one really knows who's paying the bills. The man never *directly* hands me a dollar, so no harm, no foul.

My coach knows my worth, and he made it clear from day one he will do anything to make sure I'm comfortable as well as able to keep my focus where we both want it—on the field, where he needs me.

Having no financial burdens allows me to do that, it's part of the reason he's asked me not to accept any sponsorship offers. He says they always ask for more and what I can give is already limited to near nothing. I can't afford to put my energy anywhere else, and he understands that more than anyone. He'd probably pay someone to do my work for me too if there was a way to go about it that didn't involve bringing someone else in, and that's just too risky.

It's like I said, Coach always knows best.

He also knows without me, his entire program would be fucked.

No joke.

The team ragged on Echo and me when we started packing up, talking shit about how we were becoming two old men ready for domestication. They were just fucking around, mad the party boys, as they liked to call us, would be gone and could no longer be a bargaining tool they could use when inviting the sorority houses over.

We knew every son of a bitch on that team would gladly take the third room we had if we let them. Who would pick one pad with twenty dudes, two to four in a room, depending on clout, over a three-bedroom house that gave them their own space? Nobody, that's fucking who.

Especially when we still have full access to the team house, so when we feel like hopping over for some fun, we do.

Echo spots me as I cross the living room threshold.

"What up, man." He breaks from the girls, joining me in the kitchen. "You're back earlier than I thought you'd be."

"Yeah, it was a bunch of bullshit." I tear the fridge open, reaching in for a Vitamin Water. "You want somethin' to drink?"

"Yeah, a fuckin' beer," he huffs out.

I hear him on that. Coach has a strict no-drinking policy that started after holidays and holds until the end of season. Saturday nights are technically our only free days to get drunk and fuck around, that and the occasional Friday when our games are done for the week, but that's keeping in mind how on those kinds of Fridays, Coach likes to run our asses off at practice as a way to weed out who went too hard the night before. That and the early game film review Saturday mornings.

I mean, *I* drink whenever I want, and I do get bitched at for it, but it's all for show, to make sure Coach is being fair and whatnot.

See, I'm a pitcher. *The* pitcher.

Number one in the country, that is, as far as college ball is concerned. I hold the record for the most consecutive strikes thrown and am one of the few pitchers at the D1-level who doesn't use a designated hitter.

Yeah, my coach tried to fight me on it, but he lost.

They all lose when it comes to what I want, not that Coach Reid put up much of a fight.

Bottom line, the team needs me, the school wants me, and coach fought damn hard to get me, so if there's ever a pass to be given, it's mine.

If you ask the world around me, I'm handed things on a silver fucking platter with a side of ass-kissing.

Guess the day in, day out ache in my muscles from over-exertion means nothing.

People don't care to know about the work that goes into what I do, only the outcome and since I stepped into the starting pitcher spotlight, the team went from late-night reruns to primetime playtime. We have MLB

Network switching over to our live games, looking to catch a few minutes of pristine performance, something they know they can depend on when I'm on the mound. And that's not me being conceited, it's facts. It's why I'm paid to be here rather than *paying* to be here.

It's a lot of fucking pressure, but it's worth it.

Never let 'em see you sweat.

With a heavy inhale, I pull my drink to my lips and glance around the room, noticing E's cousin is MIA. "Where's Drew?"

"Couldn't make it. Some shit for bio." Echo shrugs. "How is it that half the team is stuck in some fucked-up version of science this semester, and we're the odd ones out with nobody else in our classes to share the load with?"

"I don't know, but my anatomy class is trash."

"Try physics, bro."

"Yeah, well, you're some kind of fucking genius. You'll pull an A in the end." With a frown, I pull my phone from my pocket and open up the message Coach sent to me with my tutor's email address, quickly jumping over to the other two messages now lighting up the screen, one from Melanie and the other from Vivian ... who is sitting on the couch in my living room.

I lift my eyes to Echo, showing him my screen, and he chuckles.

"Fuckin' knew she was waiting on you," he says quietly. "Neo's been laying it on thick, but that girl has yet to bite."

"Funny, as far as I remember, she's fond of biting." My mouth lifts in the corner.

"You gonna take her up on her offer?"

I nod, knowing I likely will.

Echo shakes his head, smiling like a dick. "You better be careful with that one or she's gonna think you like her."

"I like her."

His head swivels my way again, but I make him wait a solid ten seconds before I meet his pretty boy smile.

"You mean you like to fuck her."

"One could say it's the other way around."

He grins, facing her way again. "Clearly."

"Trust me, she's cool, sweet and smart, the type who'd fly quick if I went boyfriend mode."

"If you say so," the fucker tries to clown. "So, what happened with the tutor, why you back so quick?"

"It was supposed to be a meet and greet, but we didn't get to the meet part."

Echo looks my way. "Why not?"

"She was in Coach Reid's office when I got there, telling him how she couldn't tutor me and what not."

His brows jump. "For real?"

"For fuckin' real."

"Why?"

"Don't know." I shrug. "But as soon as she realized I was in the tunnel and heard her, she freaked. Grabbed her shit and booked it out the door. And get this, the girl kept her head down the entire time, not so much as a flick of her eyes my way, and trust me, I watched for it. She practically fuckin' ran out the hall."

Echo's eyes tighten, and I'll give his punk ass some credit—he squashes his lips together to at least attempt to keep his laugh in, but it slips. "She sounds like a real headcase."

I lick my lips to hide my grin. "You're a dick."

"And you're a pompous motherfucker." He smiles when I shove his ass in the shoulder and step by him, saying, "she was probably nervous. You can be a handful."

"Two handfuls, if we're being technical."

He scoffs, the corner of his mouth lifting. "When you sitting down with her?"

"Coach said she'd be waiting in the library Friday after practice. Table number two, but I'm about to email her to work something else out." I look at him. "You meet yours today?"

He bobs his chin. "It's the same chick I had last semester. I don't mind hangin' with her and we know how each other works so it should be pretty smooth."

"You ever make a move on her?"

"Nah, man." His eyes widen. "Bringing her into this would be a cruel kind of torture. No way she'd enjoy our crew."

I nod, pushing a long breath out of my nostrils when Vivian shoots a sly smile over her shoulder.

"Looks like my time has come."

Echo laughs, pushing my shoulder as he walks away, and I collect the blonde from the couch.

I wrap my arm around her shoulder. "You waitin' for me, gorgeous?"

"You know I am." She smiles, steering us toward my bedroom without pause.

"Sweet dreams, Cruz!" Neo singsongs, so I sing right back.

"Fuck off, Calavera!"

"Oh, I will, son. Twice! Maybe even right here on your couch!"

Vivian laughs, kicking her shoes off as I poke my head out into the hallway.

"TMI, motherfucker!" I shout, closing and locking the door. "TMI."

I spin to find Vivian already helping herself out of her dress, not requiring or desiring my help. Not interested in pregaming. No flirty fun or fired-up foreplay.

I swallow a heavy sigh, toss my hat, and tug my hoodie over my head.

Typical fucking Tuesday.

Meyer

"Your screen's black."

I blink, refocusing on my open computer in my lap, and sure enough, it's gone to sleep, like I wish I could. I must have read over Avix University's "star pitcher's"—as he labeled the thread—email a dozen times since it came through.

Does he seriously think my tutoring him means he sends me his work and I do it for him?

I plaster on a small smile and turn toward my best friend. "Hey."

Bianca stands in the bathroom doorway in a pair

of my pajamas with a towel on her head. "When did you get back?"

"Maybe ten minutes ago, loved your version of 'Work It' by the way."

"I'm telling you, how *The Voice* turned down my audition tape, I don't even know." She jokes and steps from the doorway, instantly in the living room.

This place is literally a square.

When you cross the threshold of the front door, it's left, into the single-counter kitchen, with just enough room to turn from the sink to the stove or right, where two doors sit. One leads to the bathless bathroom, the other to a tiny room that's hardly bigger than a standard closet, and if you don't turn, but step straight, you're in the living room, also known as my bedroom.

I have a dresser turned TV stand and a couch that pulls into a bed—my one chosen expense.

Thank God for Rent-A-Center.

The place is miniature, and sometimes, after really hot days or when there's no airflow, it smells a little stale, the old mats beneath the carpet making themselves known. I have to wipe the windows down constantly to help keep out the mold, but it's warm, safe, and not too far from campus.

Bianca comes to sit beside me on the 'bed,' takes my laptop from my hands, and places it on the far side of her.

"I would have voted for you, you know." I look to her with a nod, and both of us laugh.

Bianca is a horrible singer, something she finds hilarious being that her grandfather is a living legend, and both her parents sang backup for him for years.

She doesn't let it stop her from hopping on the stage at random karaoke nights at Trivies, one of the local pubs within walking distance from campus.

"You and no one else, chica, but enough deflecting. Talk to me. Why were you zoning out? Your little fingers are never not typing away on that thing."

Bianca is my biggest confidant and the only person who knows some of the troubles I face, keyword being *some*.

I've shared with her what I could never tell anyone else, but where she holds nothing back from me, I have had to keep a couple details to myself. I love and trust her, but when you're at war with your own decisions, it's not smart to share your sword.

"I don't know how I'll get through this year, let alone another one." I swallow my sigh. "I'm already exhausted and we're still in the first part of the semester. It's only going to get worse."

With a potential catastrophic nightmare to follow.

I close my eyes, taking a deep breath as Bianca falls beside me.

"You're so close," she softly says. "So close, but you definitely need a break. I'm taking us on a month-long vacation in paradise. We'll leave the minute we finish finals. Bikinis and Bailey all day long!"

I turn to her with a small smile, and she slips her hand into mine. "I'm so holding you to that."

"Bitch, I'm holding *you* to that." She laughs.

Bianca and I are similar in some ways and polar opposites in others.

She's tall and thin while I'm short and currently a good twenty-something pounds past my norm, which is still heavier than she could ever be. I'm on the quieter side and keep to myself, more so now than ever, where she can have a bit of a wild side sometimes. She's confident, outgoing, and, inadvertently, the life of the party.

She and I were assigned the same room freshman year, and at first, I didn't think we would become more than roommates, but I was wrong. We were fast friends and have been ever since.

She's the most genuine person I know, and the only one who truly stuck around when my life shifted.

"Thank you for helping me out in the evenings. I would be so screwed without you."

"Seriously, stop thanking me. I told you, being here works out for me just as much as it does for you. I need the downtime away from all the sorority drama. This is about the only place I can smile anymore."

"Awe, is this your happy place?" I tease, but with a grateful rasp, one she picks up on.

Bianca winks when a soft hum calls for me.

I pull myself up, walk toward that tiny room in the corner, and slowly push the door the rest of the way open.

My gloomy mood disappears instantly, and I step inside with a smile that matches the one staring back at me. "Hi, baby girl."

DIRTY CURVE

CHAPTER 3

Tobias

Today, I'm feeling fan-fucking-tastic. I woke up at a quarter to five, as usual, went for a run and did my morning workout routine. After that, I hit the town grocery store and because of my grand mood, decided to make my mom's famous homemade chorizo for breakfast. Instead of using the leftovers to meal prep for the next few days like I normally would, I leave it all out for the boys to eat when they finally decide to open their eyes.

I'm not a miserable, downer kind of guy, more a smiley, whistle when you walk fucker most days, but there's something about coming off a two-game shutout that takes you from a seven to a ten.

So, yeah. I'm feeling good ... that is until I've reached the top step of the stairs leading to the library, and no messy-looking bun is in sight.

Stuffing the last bite of my breakfast burrito into my mouth, I look at my watch, and a frown builds along my forehead.

Okay, to be fair, it's seven fifteen as of this second.

Technically, I'm exactly on time when I should have been earlier, but my body felt good this morning, so I went for those two extra miles.

Either way, I'm not late, but where the hell is she?

I have class in forty-five minutes, and sure, the science building is a short stretch from here, but I don't do late, and neither should she, especially when she's on the job.

Now I'll have to rush there, having no time to stop and chat with friends along the way, or give the ball babes the attention they pay Dr. Double-D-Maker good money for.

That's just inconsiderate.

I look at the time again.

No way would she be more than a minute or two late, right? Maybe she's here somewhere and I didn't spot her at first glance?

I try rewinding my brain, to remember what she looks like, come up with nothing past the bun but a faded gray sweatshirt. The kind your grandma buys you from Kmart for Christmas every year, baggy and boring and itchy on the inside after one wash.

To my left are several girls, each hunkered over some papers and shit, but they don't seem to be waiting for anyone, and to my left there's ... well, we'll go with a group lost on their way to a rodeo, or members of the Future Farmers of America. Pretty sure there's dry horse shit on at least a handful of their big-ass boots.

Is that snakeskin?

With a huff, I look around again.

Where is this chick?

I walk into the library, and right up to a desk that

looks like it's for people who know shit in here—as a team, we have our own study hall area, so this is foreign territory for me.

I flash a big, bright grin at the little thing sitting behind it. "I'm hoping you can help me out."

The girl's cheeks turn cherry red and my lips curve higher.

The teeth always get 'em.

"I need to find a girl."

She nods, her eyes wide.

They're actually kind of scary, the *I'll stab you in your sleep, then hold you all night as you bleed out*, scary. Maybe hide under your bed like some urban legends shit.

"She's a tutor."

"Okay. Sure." She clears her throat and pulls out a little clipboard with a bunch of names signed on it. "What's her name?"

"Don't know." I shrug.

"Right." She blows out a breath and her bangs fly in the air. "Well, it looks like we only have four girls in this morning, so it shouldn't be too hard to figure it out. What does she look like?"

When I don't respond, her serial killer eyes lock back on mine. "You don't know her name or what she looks like?"

"I've only ever had a view of the top of her head." I lean my forearms on the counter with a smile, knowing she's reading into my statement the dirtiest way possible. "Her head's about to my chin, brown or blonde hair, maybe." I shrug. "I'm not so hot with random details."

She nods slowly, her lips pinching slightly.

I know that face, she's getting a sour taste in her mouth. This always happens when I don't drop a line and offer the chance for them to sink their teeth into the bait.

She's about to pawn me off now, uninterested in helping me out since I'm uninterested in helping *her* out of her clothes.

The girl's face scrunches, and she drops against the seat. "Go to the tutoring center next to the child development building. They should be able to tell you who was assigned to you, but make sure you take your student ID."

A low laugh slips from me, and I tap the counter as I slide away. "Cute, that's cute, girl, but thanks."

Spinning around, I grin and head straight where she directed.

The tutoring center is two buildings over, so I shouldn't lose much more time, but I am down to twenty minutes until my first class of the day, which stresses me the fuck out.

I need to get my assignments from this chick and get my ass in gear.

More forceful than intended, I yank the door open, causing it to slam closed at my back, making the dude behind the counter's head jerk up.

"Hi. I need the name of my tutor."

He does a double take, knocking over a stack of papers he must have just pulled from the printer.

Yeah, even dudes dig me.

I grin. "My tutor. Who is she? Where is she? She was supposed to meet me a half hour ago at the library."

Before I'm even done talking, his fingers begin blindly flying across the keyboard.

I'd need my ID, she said. Ha!

"That can't be right." Looking up, the dude sits tall in his rolling chair, and I take note of the change in his expression. His face is a little tenser, a bit more focused, and a lot more *tell me she's not spending hours alone with this god of a guy.*

It all becomes clear right then and there.

He shakes his head. "She never works before twelve and she would never miss an appointment."

My left brow lifts slightly, and I grin. "She your girl?"

His white skin turns as pink as his polo, and he defends, "no!"

"But you want her to be."

"She's my friend, that's all," he swears, as if it really matters.

"I bet you've got your *friend's* number." I cock my head and I think he might be ready to hyperventilate. "Can you tell her to come here, now? I need—" Shit. I can't tell him and risk my eligibility. "I need to talk to her. Quick."

The guy speaks with a hard-fought swallow. "Sorry, Tobias, but you'll need to come back this afternoon, and even then, it might be hard. She doesn't work in the office, only comes in to print and grab things. I can email her and ask her to get in touch with you, but that's all I can do."

"Yeah." I shake my head slowly. "That's not gonna work for me, my man. Can you write her number down for me?"

He stumbles over his own words. "I can't give out her personal information. Her preference is set as email. I can offer you that, but like I said, her mornings are blocked out. No tutoring. No—"

I tsk with my tongue. "Look" —I glance at his name badge, reading Jonny— "Jonny Boy, I *need* that number," I tell him as I text the man who makes it all happen.

The response comes before I even look up, and when it does, I smile, lean my body against the counter and wait.

The kid stares at me, unsure, but it doesn't take long for his phone to ring. With a weary expression, he answers, and three, two, one ...

"Yes, sir. I'll take care of it." He squeezes his eyes shut, nodding as if the person on the other end, aka Coach Reid, can see him through the line. "Will do, thank you, sir." After he hangs up, he abuses his poor keyboard some more, and a paper pops out. Rolling backward, he snags it and rolls right back, smacking it down in front of me.

And Tobias Cruz wins again.

I snatch it up, pointing on my way out. "Thanks, Jonny Boy."

Outside, I send a text to my tutor.

Me: It's Tobias. I've been waiting, Tutor Girl. Where you at?

I stare at my phone and then stare some more.

I scroll up, make sure it was sent, double-check the number, and then lift my phone in the air just in case.

Nothing happens.

A full minute passes and still, no text back.

What's that about?

Did I pay my phone bill?

Yup, I did. Coach responded instantly, like he's

supposed to.

Like they *all* do.

With a frown, I suck it up and call the man, knowing I don't have my assignments to turn in, so class isn't an option.

He answers on the first ring. "You get that number, son?"

I grin, nodding at a girl who walks by in a pink jumpsuit thing. Love those. Real easy to take off.

"Cruz."

"Yeah, sorry." I face forward. "I got it, but I think it's the wrong number."

There's some shifting before he speaks again. "Why do you say that?"

"She didn't respond and it's been ..." I look to my screen. "Almost five minutes. Weird, right?"

"Five whole minutes, huh, kid?" He chuckles. "Why'd you need her so early, you have a test today or something?"

"Nah, no test." I run my fingertips over my fade. "She sorta ... has my work."

"... what do you mean she has your work?" When I don't respond, he sighs into the line. "Damn it, Tobias."

A sour tang coats my mouth, and I squint at the sun. "Sorry, Coach."

Should have just sucked it up and did it, dumbass.

"All right." I imagine him dropping against his chair and tossing his hat on the desk. "I'll handle this and get a hold of your professor, but Tobias ... no more last-minute shit, understood?"

I nod. "Yes, Coach."

"Good. Now get off campus for a few hours so I can make an excuse. See you on the field."

"I'll be the one in white." I grin at my own joke—everyone hates our home jerseys.

I hang up and walk off with an extra pep in my giant ass step.

I knew Coach would have my back.

He always does.

Strike one, little tutor.

Meyer

Carrying the cup back into the kitchen after refilling the humidifier for what must be the fifth time today, I take a second to lean against the laminate countertop. I close my eyes for a single deep breath, wishing for a moment of calm, but the twenty seconds of silence I've had in the last thirty hours is interrupted by a buzzing sound.

With a sigh, I set the pouring cup in the sink, and slide over to where my phone is plugged into the charger. There are dozens of missed calls and texts, several from Tobias, one from Bianca, and another from Garret Jones.

I read Bianca's first and pull in a breath as I go through Tobias's.

It's easy to see where he went from semi-normal human to egomaniac—four minutes and three texts in.

I definitely can't handle the heavy that comes along

with him right now, not when I'm running on no sleep and a few spoonfuls of peanut butter.

I respond to B first, letting her know she can come over like she asked, and I'll love her forever if she grabs something along the way.

Next, I pull up Garret's message, but right as I start typing, the phone rings and I accidentally answer, freezing when a deep voice begins to speak.

Crapola!

Squeezing my eyes shut, I lift it to my ear.

"Are you trying to lose this job, Meyer? Because as you know, I can make that happen."

I hate when he threatens my position like this, as if I didn't get this tutoring job on my own merit, but being he pulled me into his department, he *does* now have complete control over my main source of income.

Keep your claws sharp but hidden.

"I only had two appointments today and both were rescheduled last night."

"Cut the shit, Meyer, all right? You know exactly what I'm talking about. You listen good, when Tobias Cruz calls, answer. If he texts, respond. Wants an impromptu session, make it happen."

"You act like I'm the one who canceled our first session, and I didn't even know he tried to call until five minutes ago." I won't even mention the giant misstep of him being given my number. "I turned my phone off last night because Bailey's—" I swallow. "I just had a long night."

"This is your job. Do it or I'll find someone else who can."

I do my best to fight the overwhelming sensations

threatening to take over, but moisture pools in my eyes anyway, and I blame it on my state of exhaustion. What I don't allow is for my sniffles to be heard through the line. I won't give him that.

"Do we hear each other?"

I flick my gaze to the ceiling. "Yes, *Coach*."

He's silent a moment before speaking again. "Good."

"I'll call him and tell him you're ill, just this once, and *you* will get a hold of him tomorrow."

I don't know if he was waiting for a thank you, but he doesn't get one.

"Understood, but be sure to let your protégé know that I won't be doing anyone's work. Ever."

He doesn't respond but I know he heard me.

He hangs up and I hang my head in defeat, not bothering to lift it as I read the text that comes through seconds later, a threatening warning from the man to *never force him to have to call me again.*

Because he wouldn't call if he didn't have to.

The tears I held off fall onto my bare feet, soaking back into my skin as if to remind me it's no one else's job to catch them.

Bailey wheezes from the living room, a cry from the pain her barky little cough causes her inflamed airway following.

My sick baby girl.

I push off the counter, quickly splash my face with some cold water and dry it on my shirt as I walk into the living room.

I ease myself onto the bed beside where she lies

and lift her into my arms, rocking her as she cries into my ear. She's barely able to keep her eyes open, she's so restless. Poor thing can't stop coughing long enough to truly sleep.

I hug her to me and take a deep breath.

School and work can wait.

She's all that matters.

Exhaustion be damned.

CHAPTER 4

Tobias

"Aw, shit. What are you doing here, Cruz?" Neo shouts the second I walk into the gym.

Dropping my bag, I lift a brow and start peeling off clothes so I can slip into my workout gear. "Just put your sister on a bus back home. She said I need to work on my breathing, so here I am."

Xavier shakes his head, but Neo hops off the cable so fast I'm surprised his ass doesn't trip over his own feet.

"Don't be an ass."

"Then get off mine."

We look to each other at the same exact time, both of us grinning.

Echo sits up on the leg press, trailing my every step, while the others go back to their midmorning workout routines. I opt to hop on a treadmill to get my heart pumping strongly. Echo does exactly what I knew he would and makes his way to the one beside me.

He cuts a quick look around before flicking his eyes

my way. "What's goin' on, you get out early or somethin'?"

"Never made it to class." I meet his narrowed gaze. "That little tutor of mine? She didn't show up with my shit today."

His head tugs back. "For real?"

I nod, pressing the arrow button to increase the speed on this thing. "I wasn't early, but I was on time, and she wasn't there. I went to the tutoring center and everything, but couldn't track her ass down, so I had to call Coach."

Echo whistles beside me. "You tell him she was doing your work for you?"

"I told him she had it." I shrug. "So, I guess I left it up for interpretation."

He scoffs and matches my pace. "You're a dick, gettin' some poor chick in trouble. You should have just sat down with her and knocked it out."

"Yeah, I'm gettin' that now." I frown ahead.

"Did you even ask her to do your shit for you or did you tell her to?"

"Same shit, man. It's her job to make sure I pass, and I won't pass without my work." I chuckle, but Echo doesn't follow, so I turn off my treadmill and face him.

Of course, he does the same.

The creases between his eyes are enough to know he's in an off mood again today, some shit he's not ready to talk about eating him up.

He likes to take it out on me, and I like to let him because if it ain't me, it's someone else, and if it's someone else, well, then we end up in a two-on-two brawl. He can hold his own, but he's my boy, so he'll never have to. Not when I'm around.

"That was a dick move." He glares.

"Don't act innocent. You're as much of an asshole as I am."

"I know, but fuck man, we'll qualify for the draft after this season. Don't fuck us both by dropping the ball in class."

"It's being handled, and as far as the draft, we're fuckin' golden." I step closer, widening my eyes. "We got years of this shit ahead of us, on the same team, if these scouts know what's good for them. Dynamic fucking duo, bro. It's me and you." I nod, my grin growing, but he's not biting on my chill pill and pops off again.

"That's the shit I'm talking about, Cruz." He shakes his head, stuck in his. "Anything can happen today, tomorrow—nothing's for fucking certain. Nothing. It's time to get shit straight and at least pretend baseball might not be around forever." He backs away, grabs his shit and heads for the exit, but not before he adds, "The season is all we have right now, so don't fuck it up."

The second he walks out the door, I subconsciously rub at my elbow.

He doesn't know what he's talking about.

Baseball's all there is.

All that matters.

I'm Tobias motherfucking Cruz, the best goddamn pitcher college ball has ever seen. I hold the record for consecutive strikes thrown at this level, and last season I became the first to ever pitch back-to-back no-hitters in a college championship game.

I'll be traveling across the country this time next year without a thing holding me back, living it up like a damn god.

I will make it because failing isn't an option.

Fuck school.

And fuck the little tutor who blew me off like she could.

I'll do what I'm supposed to do without her help because, like I said, failing isn't an option.

I managed to keep my head in the game, my dick wrapped in the finest of rubber, and my grades up to par the last two-and-a-half years.

What's one more semester to get me to the draft? I never planned on staying past my junior year anyway.

I've got this.

I won't fucking fail.

"You're failing." Coach Reid glares.

Fuck.

"I wouldn't say I'm failing." I grin. "I might be behind by a week or two, but Coach—"

"You're sitting Friday's game."

A laugh flies from me, but when Coach keeps a straight face, I tip my head to the side and take another step into his office.

"Come again, Coach? Shower must have gotten water in my ears or something, 'cause no way I heard you right." I shake my head, adding to my own bullshit and sending the remnant droplets from my hair flying all over.

He leans forward, unfazed. "It's been two weeks and you haven't met with that tutor of yours yet. Why?"

"Haven't needed to."

He nods. "Interesting, because I got an email from your professor that says you never made up the assignments you missed. You know, the ones that *I* promised him you would when I covered for your ass two weeks ago?"

"I'm playing on Friday, Coach."

He lifts his chin, clicking and unclicking his pen. "Your grade's at a sixty-six percent, you have to have at least a seventy to hit the field. You know this. My team, my standards."

It's my team we both know this, but I'll play along.

There's no fucking way he'd sit me, but he's in the mood to wear his authoritative hat today, so I ask rather than plainly state the fact we're both aware of.

"You'd sit me, Coach?"

He hesitates a second, then narrows his eyes. "Get the shit done, son, and get it in so you can be on that field."

"It's Wednesday."

"I'm aware."

"That only gives me tonight to do it, and tomorrow to turn 'em in."

"That's right." He nods. "Don't worry. I've made it clear your professors are to grade everything immediately and make the necessary updates. All you gotta do is get the work in by noon."

"You said professors."

"I did." He glares. "Says here not only are you struggling in anatomy, but you're failing history and you bombed your English essay."

"Don't plan on becoming a teacher."

"You plan on finishing the season on the field or the bench?" he counters. "You know, once you get below a certain point, my hands are tied."

I run my tongue along the backs of my teeth.

Fuck!

All right, it's good. I'm good. I have two days, that's what he said.

I blow out a deep breath, nodding. "I'll get it done, but maybe next time start with that, huh?" I chuckle.

"I like messing with you, it keeps your fire burning." He sits back with a grin. "You got it all, son. Keep this last bit of school straight, your life will be set, and I'll officially have a legend grown straight from my program."

I nod and knock my knuckles on his desk.

What most people don't know is Coach Reid saved my ass the same way I saved his. He was getting screwed left and right. While most of the sports here at Avix continued to boom, his baseball program was failing. They cut funding due to lack of progression and failed seasons, but every couple years, he would do the work himself, track down a solid stud on the field, and within a season, some big-time school would smell the success, come in and swoop the bastard away. Coach Reid was getting ready to lose his job, just like I was getting ready to lose my last chance.

My senior year of high school, my parents dropped a bomb; they decided they wouldn't allow me to use the college savings they set up for me a decade earlier if I went as an athlete. They knew that was all I wanted, and my grades wouldn't get me a scholarship, so that was how they intended to trap me into a life they wanted for me.

I started getting into pointless fights when I was always more of a defend the weaker kind of guy, got myself kicked off my high school team, ruining their chances of a winning season. Everything in my life had fallen apart. The schools that showed interest in me cut me from their prospects list, and to top it off, I was on the brink of expulsion, at risk of failing my senior year.

That's when Coach Reid showed up.

He offered me a branch no one else was willing to give me, not even my parents, and I grabbed onto that bitch at the root.

He had my back when everyone in my life had turned theirs, my parents included, and he's been here for me ever since, even when I didn't deserve him to be.

It makes me sick to think about it, but I made mistakes here at Avix, too, some the same as back home. Instead of sending me on my way, he sat me down, letting me know he understands, reminding me nobody changes overnight, and to keep working.

No matter what it was, he was there to bail me out, literally on one occasion of drunken celebration.

The school paper really had a heyday with that one.

They always do when it comes to the negative parts of who I am.

Bottom line, I'd do anything for the man in front of me, just like he would for me.

"I won't let you down, Coach." I nod. "I got this for the both of us."

"No doubt in my mind, son." His smile is easy, but brief, as he brings us to the next step. "Suck it up and call the tutor. Get both these grades above seventy by Friday, and above eighty by Boston."

"I can do that."

"Yes, you can. Use the damn girl, that's why she's there. Take up every fucking minute she's got if you have to. That's what she's paid for."

"What if she doesn't have the time?"

"You're my top athlete, she's the school's top tutor."

"What kind of qualifications does such a title entail?" I joke.

Coach chuckles. "She has a premier passing rate and is the most requested, smart-ass. The girls had a continuous waiting list a mile long. It took a lot to get her over here, but she's exclusive to athletes now. Her job is making sure they get and stay where they need to be."

"Sounds good, Coach." I nod.

"Listen, every session she has with you, she makes three times what she does with any other student." He pins me with a pointed expression. "Don't ever tell her you're aware of this but know it's something she can't refuse."

My brows pull in slightly, but Coach dismisses me as he answers his phone, so I head back to the locker room to finish getting dressed, thinking about what he's just said.

So, Tutor Girl gets paid the big bucks to help me out?

It's no wonder she didn't do my work. She knows I have to call eventually, and when I do, she'll be making a grip off our time together.

Grabbing my phone off the shelf, I plant my ass on the bench and send her a text.

Me: Hola, Tutor Girl. I require your services. Tonight. A good two hours of it.

I grin at my choice of words and consider adding a money sign, but Coach said not to tell her I know, so I'll be a good boy and just wait for her to respond.

And then I wait a little bit more.

I pull up TikTok, scroll through a couple videos I was tagged in from last night's game, and then go back to the message thread. I can see she's read it now; it's got a little thing at the bottom that tells me so, yet still, she doesn't respond.

I take a screenshot of the "seen" and circle it in red, even add a little smirk face next to it and send it her way.

I grab my bag from my locker and toss it over my shoulder right as the power ranger theme song peeps, letting me know a message has come through.

I grin, making her wait until I'm outside to open it up and read it.

That grin of mine disappears the second my eyes land on my screen.

Tutor Girl: Please contact the student resource center if you'd like to schedule an appointment for tutoring. An email with my office hours will follow this message.

Oh, she wants to play pinky up, huh?

Yeah ... no.

I text her again.

Me: This kind sir shall call his trusty coach and share thy screenshot.

I chuckle to myself and send another.

Me: I believe he's asked you to "service" me when needed.

Grinning, I make my way toward the library. She just needed a little push and now that I brought her boss into it, she'll remember that helping me puts more dough in her pocket.

The three little lines show up at the bottom, disappearing twice before a message finally pops up.

Tutor girl: What time did you have in mind? I'll see what I can do.

Me: Now.

Tutor girl: I need at least 40 minutes.

Forty minutes, she says.

With a grin, I shake my head. Guess she has to get primped for our little session.

Stuffing my phone in my pocket, I nod to myself, feeling a little lighter, knowing I've done the first part of what Coach has asked of me.

I make my way into the library, and what do you know, table number two is free, so I take a seat and wait.

Still in college and others are already making money off my name.

I smile to myself.

Yeah, going pro is going to be the shit.

CHAPTER 5

Meyer

In a rush, I blindly tie my hair back, grab the cereal bowl off the floor and drop it in the sink—Cornflakes, dinner of champions.

"You all right over there, girl?" Bianca teases. "I know you're always channeling your inner Barry Allen, but you've been looking at the clock every five seconds with a whole new kind of dread, more than the usual."

I swallow past the itchiness creeping up my throat and smile. "I hate last-minute sessions. I like to have everything ready so we can jump right in and waste no time, but I don't even have time to go to the tutoring center or athletic department to print what I need. I'll have to split my screens, look at things one at a time, and that's annoying."

"I hear you." She yawns.

"Bailey ate about an hour ago, and she's been down for about twenty minutes now."

"Are you still running the humidifier even though she's better?"

"Only through the night, so don't worry about it. I'll turn it on later." I tug my sweater over a tank top, not bothering to change out of my leggings. "Thanks for getting here so fast."

"Of course, I was planning on coming over before work anyway."

"You sure you won't be too tired later?"

"Not as tired as you. Besides, they're lucky I'm coming in to help them close when I just got moved to mornings." She shrugs. "So, who is it tonight? Quarterback? Point Guard?"

"I wish," I mumble. "Pitcher."

Her brows jump. "Ah, the tall, tan, tasty-looking Tobias Cruz?"

I turn, frowning at my fuzzy boots as I slip them on, and quickly retie my hair on the top of my head. "That would be him."

"Does every college athlete suck at school, or what?" She drops back on the couch bed I never had a chance to fold up this morning, and I follow.

"Not even close."

"So why do they so desperately call on you, dear friend?"

"Because I have something they all want and can't get enough of ..." I play along, and Bianca and I look to each other.

She wags her brows while I tap at my temple.

"Ugh, of course!" She teasingly groans, nudging my leg with hers. "A genius swimming in a pool of powdered protein."

"Blended, not stirred," I add with a low laugh,

shrugging against the cushion. "Honestly, I never have too much of a problem with my students. Some do struggle pretty bad, so I help them find ways to connect. Then there're the ones who use me for a second eye on papers and things. It's always a mix, but for every bag of apples I'm thrown, there's always one with a rotten core."

"I met Tobias a couple times when I was with Cooper." She fake vomits at the mention of her ex. "It wasn't enough to have an opinion outside of the boy is fine, but are we thinking Avix U's *Playboy Pitcher* is rotten at his core?"

A choppy sigh escapes, and I push myself to my feet, shoving my laptop into my bag. As I zip it up, my phone vibrates from its place on the charger.

I don't have to look at the screen to know who the message is from, but I do so as I pick it up.

Student T. Cruz: I'm here, Tutor Girl. Prompt enough for you?

I stare at the name I've programmed him under, trying to keep my frown hidden as I look at Bianca. "I have no idea what to think."

"Well." Bianca laughs. "I guess you're fated to find out."

Am I?

Tobias

My head snaps up when a bulky ass bag is slowly set onto the tabletop.

I follow the pasty hand that hesitates to let the thing go to find a pale-skinned brunette with bed head and that oversized sweater I remembered sliding into the seat across from me.

Ever the patient guy, I wait for her to say hi, make eye contact or acknowledge my presence in some way, but she doesn't. Instead, she pours her attention into pulling out a bunch of shit—pens, papers, notepad, fuckin' *highlighters*. Let's not forget the busted-ass laptop.

I focus on her face again, and while she has yet to bring her eyes to mine, the girl's fully aware mine are locked onto hers. A tinge of color brightens her fair cheeks.

Grinning, I sink a little farther in my chair.

Chick's nervous, and rightfully so.

It's like Echo was getting at, I'm kind of intimidating—dark hair with eyes that rival the Pacific Ocean, as the Avix Inquirer likes to put it. I've got what my ma says would be a million-dollar smile if it weren't so crooked. Little does she know that works in my favor.

I may not be Hulk huge, but I am cut like the captain, lean and fit with little to no body fat to speak of.

I dress clean and drive a nice ride, thanks to Coach.

I'm a fucking catch.

Not that I want to be caught—*no, fuck no*—but I understand the attraction women have toward me, and I do my best to give them the attention they wish for, even if it's not the kind they're hoping for. Sometimes, though, a smile goes a long way.

"Okay, so I'm not as prepared as I should be. I don't have your assignment list on hand, so if your professor hasn't had a chance to input recent work, I'll need you to tell me what it is we need to work on today." She opens her laptop and begins typing. "I'm a little tight on time tonight, so we have to stop right at the two-hour mark."

She wants to cut to the chase.

I get it, get in, get out, right?

But the girl still hasn't looked up and now I'm getting pissed.

"Tutor Girl ..." I drag out, cocking my head to the side. "Look at me."

Her shoulders stiffen and she gives herself an extra second by running her tongue across her rust-colored lips before sitting back in the chair. She tucks her chin in and a little to the right, slowly lifting her eyes to mine.

It's as if she's afraid to meet my gaze head-on, but now that she's forced herself to make the move, she doesn't cower or quickly flick them away.

She stares, pretty sure without breathing, and I stare right back.

Girls got a soft-looking face, like she uses lotion or something on it, and her eyes, they're a strange brown, like a rainy day, postponed game, mud brown.

A rusty red-brown, kind of like her lips.

She could use a couple days of sleep with the dark circles under her eyes and maybe a burger or some sun. Her body's hidden, so I can't tell if she's bones under all that mess or if she has curve appeal.

She fidgets, and unable to maintain eye contact, glances away, but I keep staring, watching her grow more on edge, more uneasy, and it hits me.

Oh, hell no.

"Are you a tweaker?"

Her eyes slice to mine. "*What?*"

"You heard me."

Her mouth is agape, but quickly twists in anger. "Are you freaking kidding me right now?" she hisses in a whisper.

I lift my hands. "Look, I get you're hired through the university, but I can't have a drug addict around me. Bad press and all that. I deal with enough bullshit from the school paper as it is."

"I assure you." She holds my gaze strongly now. "I am *not* on drugs."

"Not even a little phentermine to get ya goin'?" I raise a dark brow. Her cheeks are kind of hollow ...

Her lips pinch into a tight line and she fights a glare, putting on her professional cap when, visually speaking, she looks anything but. "Thanks for your interest in whether or not I eat highly addictive diet pills like candy, but if you're done with your passive aggressive way of pointing out I'm not a size four, can we move along?"

"Whoa." I jolt forward in my chair. "That is *not* what I meant. I was only saying—"

"I don't care," she cuts me off. "Can we get started or not?"

Tapping my palm on the tabletop, I frown. I didn't mean to offend the girl. It was a legit question that, okay, I probably could have worded differently, but I can tell from the small interaction we've had, she's not interested in an apology. To be honest, I'm not convinced I'm off the mark here, but I have a game to play in two days, so ...

"Yeah, all right." I lean forward, resting my forearms on the fake wood. "We'll start, but real quick, let's get this outta the way, yeah?" The pull in her brows tells me she's paying attention and maybe even a little more nervous than before.

"I really gotta get this shit done, so can you try to keep this 'I'd rather shit Flamin' Hot Cheetos than be here with you' act you got going until we're at least halfway done? Not sure I could say no right now—game days amp me up and I could use the release."

She stares, eyes wide, and then a quick, unexpected laugh bubbles out of her.

And you know what? It ain't a bad laugh.

I grin.

Suddenly, she stops, her fingers flying to her mouth as if to keep the sound inside.

Her eyes cut to her screen as she clears her throat and starts typing away.

"Okay, so I have the class syllabus, but I was right, and can't see what's missing. I'd need to sign in at the tutoring or athletic center, but they're closed this time of night."

"It's six."

"And they closed at five."

"Maybe you're not as good of a tutor as you think if you can't fly when given wings."

Her eyes pop up to mine, and she opens her mouth to speak but slowly closes it.

"Nah, nah, Tutor Girl." I drop my head to the side with a small grin. "Speak."

She hesitates a moment, but only for a moment. "I

schedule ahead so I can come up with a game plan and make sure I'm giving you my all. So that you feel you have someone in your corner through every stage of the process and never failing you. That way, in the end, if you never set foot on that baseball field again, you have no one to blame but yourself."

This girl's either really taking this tutor stuff seriously, or a damn good bluffer—neither are important. All I need is to skate by enough to play ball.

"That sounds … textbook great, but so you know, I'm not interested in studying. I need to get my work done and turned in, that's it."

"And when you have a test? Midterms? Your finals?"

"We worry about it then."

She drops back in her seat. "That's working backward. I can teach you to learn as you go, so it won't be so overwhelming on either of us when exams come up."

"I have a lot on my plate, Tutor Girl, and it might sound shitty, but what overwhelms you isn't something I can afford to worry about."

"I'm aware," instantly flies from her mouth. It's not harsh or damning; in fact, it's soft and nearly whispered, but by the way her eyes widen the slightest bit, I think she wishes she hadn't said a word.

We keep eye contact, but I can't read what's going on behind hers, they're too guarded, so to move us along, I reach forward and push my assignment list toward her. At first, she doesn't look at it, and small creases form along her brows as her eyes travel along my face, maybe without her realizing. With every shift of her gaze, the lines along her forehead deepen until she finally blinks and when her eyes reopen, they're on the paper in front of her.

She scans over it and quickly looks to me. "There's two courses on here."

"Oh! Right." I bend, snag my bag from the ground and pull out the third, slapping it on top of the other.

She blinks. "Three classes."

"Three classes."

Double-checking something on her screen, she says, "I have you down for one. I don't think I have space for such a heavy workload."

"That makes no sense, Tutor Girl. We're here, let's get the shit done."

She shakes her head. "I have to work in two-hour increments, each credit is two hours of study time. Each class is four credits, on average, which is eight hours and that translates to—"

"Four sessions a week. I got it. Math's not my problem area."

She sits straighter in her seat, and for the first time since she arrived, I see an outline of breast. It appears there may be something hiding under that ugly ass sweater, after all.

"This is serious. If I take you on" —when I grin, she scowls at me— "I'll have to drop another student and that's not fair. We'll just ... we'll have to work on the class you have the lowest grade in."

"Not gonna work for me."

She drops back and I can tell she's about to argue, so I Aladdin her ass, and say the magic words, forcing her to play Genie.

"Coach's orders." That right there sets her straight. Literally.

Her spine squares as her entire body grows rigid, and all signs of stress vanish from her face. In fact, any sign of life vanishes from her altogether. "He told you I'd tutor you in both?"

My smirk is slow. "He told me to take up every spare minute you had, Tutor Girl. Starting right this second and ending the moment the bell rings on the last day of the semester, metaphorically speaking, of course."

The girl quickly pushes to her feet, excusing herself for the restrooms.

And she doesn't invite me to join her.

"Okay, time's up for today."

I look up from my laptop screen with a frown, quickly glancing at the time on my phone.

It's 8:03 on the dot, three minutes past her two-hour mark. "But I'm not done."

She ignores me and begins rushing to pack up her things. "We finished all the overdue anatomy assignments, and two for history. All you have left is a page of section questions for that class and English has no new assignments listed yet. You should be able to finish up at home."

"That won't work."

"Why is that?" she asks, without looking at me. She's only looked at me a handful of times since we've been here. It's annoying.

"Because it's due tomorrow."

"And you have the rest of the evening."

"I live with another dude who, by now, has guests, so as soon as I get home, all the blood in my brain is gonna drop to my dick, and my shit won't get done."

Her cheeks color once again. "Sorry, but I can't stay."

"Again, not gonna work—"

"Look." The chick finally makes the conscious decision to look at me, her brown eyes on the frustrated side. "I understand why you think you make all the decisions, considering most people allow you to, but I *have* to leave right now. You can stay all you want if going home is distracting. I'll even review your paper for you sometime tonight if you email it to me, I promise, but I *really* have to go."

There's a plea in her eyes, even if it's not heard in her practiced tone.

Now I'm curious. "Why the rush?"

Her lips smash together, and she quickly finishes shoving shit into her bag.

What is *with* this chick?

Here I am, doing what girls wait for me to do and initiating conversation, yet she's still pretending not to be interested.

Not that *I'm* interested, but she should be.

Putting my own things away, I tell her, "You need to meet me tomorrow."

"Fine. Tomorrow at three. Same spot."

"Nope." I make sure to pop the P like a dick. "I

have to have all this in before noon, or this was pointless. Tomorrow at ten."

Her shoulders drop and she shakes her head. "I can't. I can't be here before twelve thirty."

"Not my problem, Tutor Girl. Better tell whoever it is you save your mornings for their happy days are on pause until June." On my feet now, I shrug and step past her, forcing her to turn and follow. I shove open the door, allowing her to walk through it first, but only so I can turn my back on her and call out, "I'm priority number one, remember?"

And then I'm gone.

Tutor Girl thinks she can dictate when we meet?

That's not going to happen. I'll make sure of it.

Her morning dude can suck it.

I wonder who it is?

And now I'm wondering why the fuck I'm wondering.

DIRTY CURVE

Avix Inquirer:

Spotted, The Playboy Pitcher charging
up the steps to the library. We know
he's not grinding the books, so maybe
'grinding' something else? I'd bet
five fins he's discovered the dusty,
dark corner we call Romp-her Row. Poor
Librarians.

CHAPTER 6

Tobias

Right on time, a bag is slammed onto the desk, and not with gentle hesitation like before.

"Good morning to you too." I grin, lifting my eyes to her, and frowning when I do.

She looks worse than she did last night. Wet hair in an ungroomed ball on her head and even darker circles beneath her eyes, but this time, they seem slightly swollen and red, like not only did she not sleep much but maybe cried a bit. She's wearing the same garbage sweater again, and this time, there's a stain, probably spilled beer, right along her right breast that wasn't there yesterday.

"Rough night?"

She tenses, a blush creeping up her porcelain cheeks, but says nothing.

There has to be something wrong with this girl, and as much as I want to call her out on it, I have class soon, so time to get moving.

Apparently, she thinks so, too, 'cause she gets right

to it. "Did you happen to get anything down last night?"

"Sorry to disappoint, but I don't go down."

Her hands freeze over her keyboard a moment, but again, no response comes.

Man, she's no fun. Not a laugh or a flirty "oh, but I do" comment meant as a not-so-subtle offer.

Nada, nothin'.

A frown builds. "I did the first couple questions before I got distracted."

Last night, when I got home, Echo and Drew had company, like I knew they would, and like good teammates, they made sure there were extras.

I was hoping for a reaction, it's really the only reason I told her, to tease her a bit. To make her anxious or nervous or fuck, I don't know, blush. Show signs of the real-life girl that's got to be in there, and cut back a bit of the robot mode she's stuck in.

Of course, I get nothing.

"That's good." She nods. "A little effort is better than none."

Little effort?

Little effort?

I sit forward and knock my knuckles on the tabletop right in front of her.

Her eyes dart up to find mine angry and annoyed.

"Clearly, I hate school, hate classwork, but I *did* manage the past three and half years of it *on my own.* I'm not some unmotivated asshole. I get up by five every morning to work out *before* working out with my team. I practice my craft, in some way, every fucking day. Watch game film, study stats. Every. Single. Day. I hold records for the shit I've accomplished because I work my ass off and am now that fucking good as a result of that *effort*. Despite what you read in the paper, princess, that ain't me. So, don't treat me like some frat boy fuckup."

Her brows snap together, her fingers curling into her palm. It's as if she's trying to figure something out, but what is lost on me. I can't gauge this chick for nothing.

Finally, she nods. It's slow, small, but it's there.

I'm sure that's all there will be of that, but then her eyes meet mine, and the shine in them has my anger fading.

"I didn't mean it that way," she nearly whispers, not once looking away like she did every five seconds last night. "I know how much work you put into your craft; I didn't mean to insult you." Her features pull, as if she's struggling in some way, with what I don't know. "Being an athlete is life consuming and I'm supposed to be here to help, not stress you out or add any new problems, so if it's okay, let's get started. I don't have too much time this morning."

Funny. She's sorry for her comment, but no retraction of the statement, huh?

"I've got you for two hours."

"It won't take us that long. I expected—" She stops herself and speaks again. "I've printed all the pages we need, and highlighted the key terms from the questions, so all we have to do is read and paraphrase."

"I've got you for two hours."

"You have to turn these in, in two hours."

"Don't much care right now."

She sighs and drops her head, rubbing her temples with her fingertips. "Could you please just start the work?"

"What's your problem?" I cross my arms and drop back against my chair. "I never met you before our first session, but you act like you've got me pegged and can't stand the thought of helping me out."

A strange, tangled expression sweeps over her, as if she's at battle with her own mind and has no idea what she's even thinking, making it impossible for me to guess.

And I'm kinda feeling like being a dick.

Tutor Girl wants me to hurry, huh?

I scoot my chair back to stand and her eyes follow my every move. "I'm gettin' a coffee. Be back."

She begins to say something, but I don't wait around to hear it. I walk toward the front of the library, where a coffee bar sits.

Unfortunately, it doesn't take as long as I hoped, and I'm back to our dreaded table in minutes.

I set coffee in front of her, and she stares at it like it's the best and worst thing she's ever seen.

Her brows pinch and she drags out her next words. "I really shouldn't..."

"You askin' or tellin'?"

"Definitely not asking," she says with a soft chuckle, looking to me as she wraps her hands around the paper cup. "Thank you. That was ... thoughtful of you."

Thoughtful? Me? I'm not sure anyone's ever called me that. I'm not even sure why I bought her a coffee in the first place, but she was on my nerves, so when I got to the counter I said, "two fancy coffees that taste good" instead of one. Weird, since I'm not exactly a coffee drinker.

Yeah, I know, that makes zero sense, her pissing me off and trying to get rid of me shouldn't make me wanna buy her shit, but I did, and it's done.

Maybe now she'll thaw a bit.

She takes a few small sips, her eyes closing as she does and when she opens them, it's with a small twitch to her lips. We go over the questions and highlight the key points of each one and then she sits back in her chair. "Okay, why don't you get started while I check my emails and I'll review as you go."

Or maybe not, and now I'm irritated again.

"So, tutoring consists of you doing shit on your computer and supervising while the student does their work alone?"

I don't know why I'm arguing. I don't want to be here any more than she does, right? She's the one who didn't want to tutor me, and sure, I could have done this shit at home, avoided this entire session, but why should I?

I expect her to snap at me, but she doesn't.

Instead, she offers a small smile and gently closes her laptop. "Maybe we haven't worked together enough for that yet."

"So, when you get comfortable, you just do your own thing and count the dollars coming in?" Why am I being such a dick?

The girl pulls a breath in through her nose. "I'm not trying to make this easier on me, I swear." She shakes her head. "But we did go over the prompts already. The next step is to read and that's independent work. I'll be reading over each answer to make sure you have all you need and help you get there if you don't. You will get full credit for this, I swear, but it's up to you to read the passage."

My frown deepens, but she keeps going. "When you have an exam or an essay, things will be a lot different.

We'll have to be extremely collaborative, but this isn't that type of assignment."

"Whatever." I set my coffee down after a single sip and start the damn questions.

Despite her earlier claim, she's completely involved throughout the entire assignment. I'm no idiot, but I can admit I have a hard time focusing on schoolwork when the subject holds no interest to me, something she seems to understand.

"This is good and should put you above the mark to play tomorrow. It might even allow you a tiny bit of leeway on the exam coming up, but that will depend on your professor. You might want to remind your teachers you need it graded stat."

"Oh, they know. Coach Reid made sure of it; the man always has our backs."

"When it's convenient," she mutters to herself, but I've been known to have supersonic hearing.

"You realize you only have this job because of him, right? He's the athletic director. You tutor athletes."

She shoots to her feet, a bit of sass I didn't expect following.

"I've been working for the school since my freshman year. I came in as a student tutor, in fact, long before I was moved to the athletic department. So yeah, now I work strictly with athletes because their passing somehow became more important than the guy trying to make grades to keep his scholarship or a single mom who can't afford to fail because she hardly has the time to be here in the first place."

"And athletes don't have those same problems?"

"Some do, yeah." She tosses her bag over her

shoulder. "Just like some don't, and I don't see how an athlete, who has no desire to do anything other than go pro after college, meaning they throw away all their years of learning here, some who are here at no cost to them, is priority over those of us who want more in life. But sports are heaven and Coach Reid is God, so who cares about us poor peasants."

With that, she storms off, and I find my ass on my feet, trailing hers.

"Yo! Wait a minute." I move to catch up with her, which only takes a few steps since my legs are twice the size of hers. "I said hang on now."

She stops on the second step, and I place myself in front of her, moving down a couple spots, so we're eye level.

I gently grab her arm to hold her there, but when her eyes shoot to mine with undeniable concern, I quickly let go.

"Look, sorry I said all that, all right? But I don't appreciate you bad-mouthing someone who's like family to me."

Her jaw sets, her lips pressing tight. "I can ... respect that." She swallows. "We'll avoid the topic to cut out the problem." She speaks quietly, gives a tight-lipped grin, and walks on past.

I turn and watch her walk away, which is a total waste of time, since I can't make out the shape of her ass hidden by all that cotton.

It's maddening, and you know what? So is she.

Swear she does all this to irk my nerves.

Speaks but says virtually nothing.

Stares but hides her every emotion.

Wears that stupid fucking sweater.

It's almost as if the girl lives in some sort of invisible box, one she keeps locked tight around her, and if I were to try to punch past it, I'd be met with a triple layer of bulletproof fucking glass. My knuckles would be reduced to fractured fragments first try.

Not that I'd try.

If I did, though, I already know she'd simply keep doing what she annoyingly does.

The exact opposite of what I expect her to.

Meyer

I hustle away from Tobias as quickly as possible, biting the inside of my cheek to keep my emotions in check. Emotions that seem to be all over the place.

Having to sit and listen to him praise his beloved coach isn't something I factored in, nor is it something I can stomach.

It was clear, right there in those blue eyes of his. His coach means a lot to him. The man is obviously an important part of his life.

I bet he's supportive and uplifting, maybe even a father figure for him, like a good coach would be.

Like a good man would be.

I wonder what he'd say if he knew, if his opinion would change.

Not that it matters.

Reality is as sad as it is serene.

Speaking of the devil, a text comes through demanding my presence at the man's office, so off I go.

Of course, he's on the phone when I get in, and leaves me to wait there for several minutes without so much as acknowledging I've entered the space

I stand several feet away from the wooden desk, fighting a frown as I stare at the plaque proudly displayed at the edge of it.

Coach Thomas Reid it reads in bold, golden letters, *Coach of the Year* printed in cursive just beneath it.

The sole qualification must have been having a winning season.

"Meyer," he snaps, and my head jerks up.

"What?"

"Are you hearing me?" he asks, but he's not looking for a response, his obnoxious sigh quickly follows. "I said I've pulled a few of your guys and gave them to that other girl."

My muscles clench and I take a step closer. "What do you mean you pulled a few of my guys?"

"I mean, I pulled some of your 'students' and assigned them to the girl you recommended."

"You said you needed another person dedicated to your department. I never would have introduced her if I had known she would be taking from my schedule."

"I did need someone, and now I have her, and I'll give her whoever the hell I wish."

I take a deep breath, look at the one and only potential bright side here and hope that just maybe ...

"Tobias will take precedence." He kills my thought quickly. "The others you can fit in wherever so long as they pass their classes and can play, but you had too many blocked out days for the hours my pitcher requires." He tosses a paper my way.

It falls to my feet, so I bend to pick it up, noting Tobias is slotted Monday through Saturday now, doubling our time together.

"This ..." Anxiety begins to build, making my skin warm and itchy. "This isn't normal. This is more time than the students with learning disabilities are allotted."

He shrugs, daring me to object.

I quickly scan along the page, my head shaking frantically.

"You took four." My eyes dart up to his. "I'm being cut four students to accommodate one?"

"The time has been filled in."

"Time?! I'm paid per student. If I have him six days a week, I'm losing a quarter of my income. I'll have to find another job and—" I stop abruptly.

He leans forward, his light blue eyes hard and disgusted. "Not my problem, is it? Your job is to tutor the boys I need you to, that's what you signed up for, and I need you to tutor Tobias Cruz. Our schedule is getting tougher, we have Cal Poly coming up in three weeks, and I need to know school won't be a stress for him."

"This is beyond your usual lack of caution."

The corner of his mouth lifts in a nasty smirk. "There is no risk here because you are who you are, and *he* is who he is. You'll never be on his radar without the beer it takes to get there, honey, and he'll continuously have his hands full of something better."

Wow.

I want to scream and cry, to demand he apologize and start over from scratch.

But mostly, stupidly, I wish he'd look at me like he used to.

Even if I could *never* do the same.

It's with that thought in mind that I go home, open my computer, and do what I should have done months ago.

I submit my transfer application to the University of Florida.

CHAPTER 7

Tobias

"Okay, that was the last question. Now we can get a head start on your research essay for history. You have a few weeks, but if we can narrow down what you plan to write about and get the materials mapped out, we might be able to drop one of our sessions."

I stare at her, waiting for her to glance up, but of course, she doesn't.

She *never* does.

We've met for two weeks now, eight sessions in total, and this chick is still holding on to her 'I'm stronger than thou' act. I mean, she's a damn good actress. I'd almost believe she truly didn't want to be here if it weren't for those big brown eyes of hers.

See, every now and again, she *has* to look up, has to make sure I'm paying attention and what not. When she does, the second her gaze locks onto mine, her lips part, but just a tad, and she sucks in a tiny little breath.

It's like my eyes pull at something in her, probably her pussy strings. I dig it.

Just last night, the ball babe waiting for me after class said she wanted my night to be hers, all so she could see the shade of blue my eyes take on when they take me on.

It's a thing, girls talk about it all the time.

So yeah, my dick's big and my eyes hold the vaginal verdict—to screw or not to screw, that is the question ... that only holds one answer.

Not that I took the chick up on her offer.

This girl, though, I give it to her, she's good at hiding her lack of control.

I bet it's buried under that sweater.

"Are you even listening?" Her head lifts.

See? If I don't answer, she has to look at me.

Lips part, tiny gasp ...

I don't answer. I tilt my head in an attempt to get under her skin and make her wonder what I'm thinking, but she looks away, back at her fucking books.

What the hell?

It's not like I *want* her to want me, but it's damn weird that she doesn't.

I just want to fuck with her, to tease her, to have the upper hand like I'm supposed to. But she just keeps ... schooling me.

"Okay, so I'm emailing you a list of options now. Pull it up and we'll eliminate based—"

"I'm hungry."

"You just ate."

"I had a sandwich."

"You had *two* sandwiches and a bag of jerky. And a Vitamin Water."

"I'm hungry."

She huffs, pushing to her feet without verbal complaint, so I hop up and start packing my stuff as she packs hers.

"Chinese or Mexican?" I ask, glancing over to her, staring with a deep-set frown. She says nothing, so I repeat myself in case she's in awe at my invite and needs reassurance she didn't imagine it. "Chinese or Mexican?"

She pulls her bag over her shoulder, turning away. "The list is in your email. Try and look it over before Thursday if you have a chance, okay?"

Thursday.

This chick pisses me off.

I cross my arms, widen my stance, and stare at her.

She looks from me to my feet and back. "Don't be difficult."

A slow smirk spreads across my face, and *yet another* deep sigh escapes her. Her shoulders drop an inch.

The girl knows already what I'm about to say.

We've only been here for an hour and ten minutes. I got her for another fifty.

"Chinese or pizza?"

"I'm not hungry."

"Pizza or pasta?"

"I'm not hungry."

"You're a damn liar. Your stomach's been growling for twenty minutes. Did you eat at all today?" She's still that pale girl she was, but sometimes she looks like she's rested and other times she looks like she was partying all night, and hell, maybe she is.

"Not that it's your business, but yes, I ate."

"What?"

"What?"

"What did you eat?"

Her cheeks grow slightly pink, and she avoids my gaze, like normal. "I had a peanut butter sandwich."

My eyes narrow. "No jelly?"

She pulls fake lint off her jeans. "No jelly."

"Why not?"

"Oh, my god." She turns and walks past me, but, of course, I keep up. "Mind your own business."

"Well, I should know if my tutor is starving herself because she thinks she's fat." She gasps. "You're not, by the way, so if my shitty, insensitive phentermine comment has you cutting meals. Don't. You need to eat."

She scowls. "I said I ate."

"I don't believe you."

"I don't care."

"You need Chinese."

"I don't *want* Chinese."

"Well, you're eat—"

"Stop!" She turns to me, resolve in her eyes, but something deeper behind them. "Please, just ... I'm walking out the door now. I'll see you Thursday."

Slowly, cautiously, she leaves.

And I follow.

No one tells me to get lost or whatever it is she's doing. I do that. Not her.

I give her a small head start, let her think she's in the clear, and then step in line beside her.

"Will you go?" she whispers, glancing around as we strike it across the grass.

It takes a second to register, but when she looks to the side for the millionth time, sweeping the vicinity with jerky movements, it's clear as damn day she's making sure no one's eyeing us.

No fucking way she's trying to avoid being seen with me.

Reaching out, I catch her upper arm and quickly jump in front of her.

She doesn't expect it, and she takes a step the exact moment my feet plant, bringing her right against me. All fucking on me and yeah, there's some major miracles under this fucked-up rag she wears.

I wonder if they're real? They're on the firmer side, full, but still offer that natural squish against my body, like I could grab 'em good and hard and she'd like it.

Would she like it?

Her eyes widen, and her hands come up to push off my chest, but I grab ahold of her other arm, keeping her right there, right where she is.

She inhales through her narrow little nose, causing her tits to press harder into me. Those big, sandy brown eyes of hers, begging me to let go.

Don't want to.

Someone bumps her with their backpack as they walk by and she stumbles closer, her hip brushing against the hard-on that came out of fucking nowhere, uninvited, yet painfully present.

Her chin slowly lowers, and while she tries her hardest not to allow it, her eyes then follow. She's looking at my jeans, and with the new angle, the scent of her freshly washed hair assaults my nose.

Fuuuck, this girl smells like vanilla ice cream. I happen to *love* me some vanilla ice cream.

"Tobias," she whispers, looking away.

"That's the first time you've said my name."

Her brows crash. "What?"

"Uh, huh." *Oh, it's that spicy vanilla, too.* "Thought maybe you were afraid of it."

Her head turns, and I realize I've reached up to hold a fallen strand of her golden-brown hair.

"What are you doing?" she worries.

"What am I doing?" I push even closer. "I'm wondering why I want to fuck you all of a sudden, and *why* all you ever do is try real hard to get away from me." She gulps, but I ignore it. "Why you worried about being seen with me, Tutor Girl? Women beg for me. Being around me might be good for a girl like you. Get you noticed more."

Why would I want that?

Why wouldn't *I want that?*

Something makes her sassy after that and she steels her spine.

"Yeah, well. I've never felt a need to be noticed. Now if you'll excuse me, I need to go." She yanks herself free of my grip, but I catch her around the waist because she's pissing me off.

"You didn't answer the question."

"Let go," she whispers.

"Why you tryin' not to be seen with me?"

"I'm not—"

"Don't lie."

She sighs and finally meets my gaze again. "We

aren't friends."

"And?"

"We live different lives."

"*And*?"

"Why are you asking me questions that you don't really want the answers to?"

"What the fuck does that even mean?" I glare at this frustrating little thing in front of me.

"What's my name?"

I open my mouth to respond, but I'm forced to pause a second and her brows lift as if she's proving a point. "Well, what is it?"

She clears her throat. "It's Meyer."

"I like it." I nod.

A tight laugh leaves her and she nods, frowning at the ground.

"We're strangers, Tobias." A hint of dejection crosses her face. "You're here because you have to be. I'm tutoring you because it's my job, and I'm obligated. That's it."

"For the hundredth time ... and?" I prompt, irritation crawling up my skin. I know there's more.

I know where this is going, and her next words confirm it.

"And I can't afford rumors being spread about me."

"Cause I'm a rumor waiting to happen, right?"

She makes it a point to lead my eyes the way hers point, where a stack of Avix Inquirer sits, a photo of me stepping out of the locker room after Tuesday's game printed across it. "Don't pretend you're not."

I can't control what they write, but what's the point

of telling her this?

She probably thinks I ate that shit up. That I wanted the pathetic bad boy label and press that came with it.

I didn't, but the papers created him anyway, and once I realized they'd never stop, I did the only thing I could: I accepted the role.

They could say whatever the hell they wanted, it didn't matter, because on game day, their mouths were clamped shut or hanging open. There wasn't a negative fucking thing they could say about my game, and my game is all that matters.

Not the girls I do or don't bring home or the assholes I've knocked out. It's all about the fastball, the slider, and my filthy fucking curve.

Meyer clears her throat, hesitating briefly. "I should ... go."

"Why do I get the feeling that's the opposite of what you want to do?"

Instantly, her chin falls to her chest. "Message me if you need me before Thursday and I'll do what I can."

My hand twitches against her back. "And if I said I need you now?"

"You'd be lying."

"I'm not a liar."

"Then I guess you won't say it," she whispers, her eyes lifting to mine.

She gently pulls from my hold and, this time, I let her because this entire situation makes no sense to me.

Offering a small, anxious smile, she walks away, leaving me and my hard-on to fend for ourselves.

Not that I wanted her to handle it.

Not even a little bit.

I look down, frowning at the obvious bulge in my jeans.

Yup, dick begs to differ.

"What crawled up your ass?"

I spit a seed out of the corner of my mouth and lean forward to rest my forearms on my knees, watching these fucking idiots attempt to look like a baseball team that's worth a shit. "Nothin'."

"Right." Echo wipes the sweat from his brow with a rag and then tosses it to the side. "'Cause your hats in your hand and your ball and glove are on the floor 'cause nothin's wrong. Fuckin' liar." He throws a few seeds at me.

"Fuck off."

The asshole chuckles, wincing when a ball is hit, barely hops past short, and bloops into center field.

"Damn." Echo shakes his head.

"Right?" I drop back against the bench. "Gavin can't hit for shit, Shea can't fuckin' catch a ball to save his life and fuckface playing center didn't even run up on that. How do they expect playing time when they play like pussies?"

"That what it is?"

Confused, I look to Echo.

He raises a brow. "You not gettin' any pussy playtime, my man?"

I scoff and turn back to the game. "Like our walls are thick, my man."

"Oh, I hear your grunts... of frustration." He laughs, sliding down the bench when I whip my arm out to smack him.

"Imma kick your ass, Ech."

"For real, though. What's got you all chafed?"

I glance past Echo to see no one's paying attention, and he leans in.

"Shit's gettin' busy, bro. Games are getting deeper, the tougher part of our schedule is damn near here and with it, fuckin' midterms are creepin' up" I shake my head. "It's like shit's piling up from every direction and it's frustrating."

"You failin'?"

"Not yet, but I need all my focus to be out here on the field."

"If only it worked that way."

"Fuckin' right?" I huff. "Thank god this is the last year of this shit."

We face the field when the crack of wood echoes around us, watching as the ball floats by center field, an easy out missed, and look back to each other. "Your tutor not helping?"

I frown at the thought of her. "She gets on my nerves, all serious all the time, and it's boring, never wants to flirt to make things less miserable. She won't do shit for me and she leaves the second we're done."

When Echo doesn't say anything, I turn to him.

"You mean she ain't bending over backward to meet your every need?" The bastard grins.

"Shit, I wish she would. And if there was a girl who could meet my every need, my man, I'd beg to be her bitch." I laugh, snatch my mitt off the seat and push to my feet. "Don't pretend you wouldn't do the same."

I slap Echo's shoulder with it when Coach Leon, one of Coach Reid's assistants, gives the signal for us to rotate in.

"Let's get out there and show these fools what baseball's supposed to look like."

Together, we walk out of the dugout, knocking gloves as we part, and take our positions.

He stares me down, just the line of his eyes visible through his catcher's mask, and I give him my full attention.

Right here is the only place guys like us are in control, worthy of more than meets the eye.

Here I'm not the *Playboy Pitcher*, the fame-seeking party boy people view me as. I'm not Friday night's good time or a story to share with friends down the road. I'm not a prize that'll lose its shine or a worthless memory that'll fade into nothing.

Here, I'm not the man the tabloids have decided I am, an egotistical jackass looking to score in more ways than one.

Here, I'm Tobias Cruz, the *real* Tobias Cruz.

The twelve-year-old boy who got up before dawn to run four miles before school. The fifteen-year-old kid who tied an old Honda tire to his waste and drug it up and down the street to gain speed. The seventeen-year-old kid who missed out on school activities because I was busy throwing pitch after pitch into a taped-up tent I bought at Goodwill. The eighteen-year-old young man, who was still trying to learn to be one, but both worried and disappointed his parents regularly because I had no time for friends and one single goal in life.

To be the best at what I did.

To get to where I'm standing now, on this field.

I'm a man who knows what he wants and works his ass off to get it. Who understands there are no handouts when it comes to perfecting your craft, no shortcuts, no half-assing.

Who knows, there's no way but the hard way. The grind. The focus. The sacrifice.

And yeah, sometimes that includes allowing the people on the outside to look at you and see a fool because the energy it takes to change their mind isn't worth the time, not when yours is needed elsewhere.

Here, with me on the mound and Echo in his position behind the batter's box, not a damn thing else matters. We know who and what we are.

Echo's the guy who makes the call and I'm the guy who makes it happen.

DIRTY CURVE

CHAPTER 8

Tobias

I was right. I knew I would be.

The season is moving along, we're killing it and breaking school records.

It's intense, fucking awesome, but we're deep into the semester and shit's hard.

History isn't kicking my ass by much, but anatomy is tanking my GPA.

Anatomy!

Fucking ridiculous.

We won't talk about English.

I fold my palms around the back of my neck, leaning forward with a heavy groan. "This makes no fucking sense."

"You'll get it, it just takes time."

"I don't have time, Tutor Girl. The test is in two days. My grade is a sixty-seven percent right now. If I fail this, shit, if I get less than a fucking B, I'll be in hot water. My coach will have my ass."

"You're putting too much pressure on yourself." She scrunches up her little nose, judgment bleeding from her next words. "Stop thinking about baseball and what someone else wants of you and think about what *you* need to do."

"I *need* to play in that damn game," I tell her with a scowl.

"No. You *need* to pass this test."

"Fine. I *need* to pass this test" —my brows lift as my eyes widen— "so I can play in the game."

With a sigh, Meyer drops back against her chair.

We've been studying for this anatomy test for three sessions now and still, I can't fucking grasp 'the anatomy of the heart.'

Her focus falls to the tabletop and she chews on that bottom lip of hers. She does that when she's thinking real hard.

It's distracting as fuck.

"Spill it."

Her eyes jolt to mine and she stares at me for a moment before slowly standing from her chair.

"Whoa, whoa, *whoa*." I jump from my seat, irritated. "We're not done. In fact, we just started. I—"

"Relax." I'm pretty sure I hear a smile in her tone, but she never lets it touch her lips. "I have an idea. Let's go."

"Go?" I gauge her.

"Yeah." Her dark brows lift slightly, almost persuading me she's capable of humor. "Go. Grab your stuff, this will take the rest of our time."

I'm not convinced, but I have shit else for choices,

so I do as the girl says and pack up.

This week, her location of choice is the garden picnic tables behind the science hall. She's silent the entire time, leading me along the fencing, around the math building, and only then do I realize exactly where it is she's headed.

"The field?" I complain, dropping my head back to look at the sky. "Seriously?"

She, for real, doesn't understand the way an athlete's mind works.

Meyer approaches the gate, so I reach over her and push it open for her to walk through.

"Look, I know you want to help, but now I *really* won't be able to focus."

"You don't even know why we're here."

"Doesn't matter." I look around, Tuesday's game already playing out in my vision.

Meyer drops her bag and heads to the mound, *my* mound.

"Careful, Tutor Girl. That's a precious piece of dirt you're standin' on."

I start toward her.

Her hand shoots up, and she points. "Go to home plate."

I frown. "But that mound you're standing on is my spot."

"Come on." She rolls her eyes. "Just go with it."

Waste of fucking time.

But I do as she says.

"All right," she calls out. "We're going to call home plate a base."

"That's like calling cupcakes, cake, sounds right but technically it ain't."

She crosses her arms, her little hip cocking to the side.

Okay, little mama means business ... and has a personality.

Who knew?

Widening my feet, I tip my chin. "Okay, Tutor Girl, I'll humor you. We've got four bases."

Her muddy eyes meet mine and she nods. "Four bases."

"That's what I said."

Aaand that hip pops out a bit more.

Wonder if she's double jointed?

"The heart has how many chambers?"

"No fucking idea, why you think I said this was a waste—" I cut myself short.

Well, holy shit.

A slow grin spreads across my face and she can't hold hers in this time. I watch as those thick lips of hers pull to one side.

"Four. The heart has four chambers."

She nods. "*Four* bases, four chambers. Good." She steps off my mound and motions for me to take her place.

Smirk in full effect, I make my way to her, slipping past and onto the dirt-caked clay. I lift my arms out wide, and she shakes her head, quickly giving me her back.

I think she does it to hide a smile.

I feel like she's smiling right now.

"Okay." She spins, walking backward now. "Who, loosely speaking, has control of the game?"

"Me."

"*Who.*"

"Pitcher."

"Right, the pitcher has control of the game. So, if we think of your position as the core, as what keeps the game alive, we can take the others and their jobs, and connect—"

"The four chambers of the heart and the roles they play." I scan the field, running through the setup she's just given me.

"Good, so say the pitch is thrown and the ball is hit—"

"*If.* If the ball is hit."

She sighs, but it's a different kind, a playful kind. She's softening. "Work with me here, Mr. Perfect."

I grin. "Ok, fine. Pitch is thrown, ball is hit."

"So, the batter runs to first base ..." She nods encouragingly.

I pull my bottom lip between my teeth, squinting at the first baseline. "To the right, so ... the pulmonary valve sends blood to the right ventricle?"

"Yes!" Meyer's mouth curves, a wide, proud smile forming and fuck me ...

I kinda want to be right again.

We work through the next few steps, each answer coming easier than the last and then we're at the final step. "To your lungs."

"Yes." She stomps her foot, excited. "Exactly. Great job!"

In my head, I repeat the steps again, glancing from one position to the next, without having to pause and think. She just taught me this in a matter of minutes, brought me here and worked her little ass off to speak my language, on my level.

I turn to her with a smile and she stares back a moment, but a look I can't explain slowly sweeps over her.

She spins away from me. "Okay, time's up today. I think you'll do great."

"Not so fast." I jog past her and pull out my keys, mitt, and ball from my backpack—always keep one on me.

Curious, she tracks my every move, but I wink, hustling to unlock and step into the dugout. Pulling open the orange bin, I grab a bat and run back, shoving it into her hand without giving her a chance to say no.

"You taught me something, let me teach you something."

She holds my gaze a moment and then drops hers to the hardwood in her hand. "Tobias..."

"Come on, try. I'll go easy on you."

She scoffs, making me grin, and when she hesitates, I add, "Don't be afraid to get schooled, Tutor Girl."

Meyer licks her lips, glances over her shoulder, and back at me before taking position at home plate.

I'm about to instruct her on how to stand when she does it on her own, lining her feet up with the plate, her stance even with the width of her shoulders, bat raised high in the air.

Okay, so she's shown no interest in what I do, but has good form?

Hmm ...

I cock my head, but the girl simply stares me down, clearly aware I've got questions, but not wanting to divulge, so I show her the ball, letting her know it's coming and lightly toss it to her.

Meyer stands to her full height—all five foot something of it—and again, cocks that hip out.

"What?" My shoulders rise innocently.

"You have me standing here with a bat, the least you could do is give me something to hit."

"Okay, hotshot," I tease. "You want some heat?"

Her face flushes slightly, but she doesn't back down and readies herself once more.

I throw the ball with a bit more power.

She swings and misses, a small grunt escaping her, but I don't say a word, and she picks up the ball, throwing it back to me.

The next pitch she nails, sending it sailing past short and into midfield. I watch it go, then turn back to her with my brow raised expectantly, but the girl just shrugs, rests the bat on her shoulder, and waits.

A low chuckle leaves me, and I hustle for the ball and back.

"Again."

We continue for a good ten minutes, both of us working up a sweat despite the chilled March evening.

When Meyer tosses the bat, my shoulders drop.

I'll admit I was having fun. Then again, I always do when a baseball's in my hands.

I guess the fun's over.

Or maybe not ...

My eyes hold on Meyer as she walks over to the short gate in front of the dugout, opposite of where she set her backpack. She begins to lift that hideous sweater, revealing her figure for the very first time and god*damn*. It's like opening up my gramp's old Cracker Jack box and finding a Mickey Mantle rookie card.

Girl's been hiding some treasures.

Far from skin and bones, as her slender face leads you to believe.

Lucky for me, she's looking the other way, her round, perky, and completely unexpected, ass taunting me without her knowledge. Torturing me might be a better way to put it.

My fingers instantly twitch, begging to squeeze and smack it, to hold it in my palms and watch the way it moves when touched and teased, but I don't get to envision it for long, 'cause the girl shifts the slightest bit, sharing even more.

Hips, wide and thick, made for holding on to.

The thick, cheap cotton finally reaches her chest, and I run my tongue along the backs of my teeth in sudden anticipation.

She tugs the thing over her head and fuck me ...

So plump, so ... full. They're ready to spill, not far from toppling out of the tank she's wearing, but as I could have guessed, that's not her style. She pulls the top up as much as the material allows.

I'd pout if I was a lesser man.

I do try and get a good look, though, but she's only half facing me, and then she tries to kill me.

Meyer tugs her hair tie from her head, and lets it fall from its usual mess.

Ass for days and long, tuggable hair is my sweet spot, and hers reaches her midback.

It's mostly brown, but there's a hint of copper catching the sun, kind of like the golden hint of her eyes.

She runs her fingers through it before her little hands wrap around the length, twisting and twirling it up again, and my eyes follow the windup, zeroing in on her chest as it rises with my own inhale.

To see if I'm caught, I look up quickly, but she's not paying me any mind, just staring off, lost in her own thoughts, so I sneak another peek.

Still can't tell if they're fake or not, not that it matters. I love them all.

Big ones, small ones, real ones, fake ones, call me Dr. Fuckin' Suess, and right now, the doctor wants to play, are they or aren't they?

I want to touch 'em, lick 'em, suck 'em, fuck 'em, and then do it all over again.

The second I force my eyes up, Meyer's jump to meet mine, and I don't look away. Can't.

Don't want to.

She does, though, and I know. Meyer's suddenly unsure of what she's doing and why she's here. It's all right there, written along her brow.

It's weird and I don't get it, but she's weird and I don't really get her, so fuck it.

I get ready to throw.

Meyer grabs the bat and we go at it a few more times. One comes flying right back at me, and I snag it with a grin, tossing it up and catching it in my palm.

"You must be a frequent flyer at the batting cages, and you don't want to tell me." I spin the ball in my palm, lining my middle finger up with the right seam to serve her a slow curve as she gets ready for it. "We should go."

I wind up, but before I can let it go, her face falls, and the bat follows.

She rushes to her bag, tearing her phone from the front pocket.

This time, I know we're done for real, so I move to put everything back in the container, lock it up, and make my way to where she's standing. "You know, you did pretty damn—"

"I have to go," she cuts me off, runs to grab her sweater from the fence, and tugs it over her head before lifting her bag off the ground.

Trips me out how she dropped it right there without a care. I've never known a girl who didn't mind the dirt like that.

Backpack on one shoulder, she shoves her phone in the pocket of her hoodie and begins to walk away. "I think you've got it, just remember the positions and plug in the correct terms."

Oh, I'm being dismissed, brushed off and forgotten until next time, like we weren't having fun five seconds ago?

Was this not chill and relaxing for her?

Did this not get her out of that dark box of depression, also known as the library, and out for some vitamin D, something she's in desperate need of?

Why do I care?

"Man, Tutor Girl, you're a whole other girl outside the library," I pop off, falling back to the guy she looks at me and sees because why not? She's done with me anyway, the time slot she penciled me into exceeded, and reinstating my need to get under her skin extreme, if only to remind her I didn't want to be here anyway. That it's whatever. That I'm forced to be around her just as much as she's forced to be around me. "First strippin' for me, then talking plugging and positions? What would Coach Reid have to say about such behavior?"

Her face smooths out completely, her true thoughts hidden, and she gives me that robotic tone of hers I hate. "Go over your study guide one more time tonight, but don't look at it again after that. Not even right before the test. I'll email you the breakdown of today's session later tonight."

She turns and walks away, straight out of the gate.

And like the merry-go-round we seem stuck on, I'm the dick that follows her when I should just let the girl go.

But what the fuck's her problem?

"So, this is where slightly cool and less uptight Tutor Girl turns back into the killjoy, noted."

She gives no reaction and I'm pretty sure that's what I'm after. It must be because I keep going.

"To think, you almost seemed normal there for a second."

Her pace quickens.

"So, what is it, huh? Can't handle being around me this long, gets the juices flowin'?"

She doesn't slow or look back at me, but there's a small frown now marring her face.

Good, almost there.

I want her to snap, to yell or scream. To give me something.

She gives me nothing.

"Yeah, I noticed. You know, you really should take

some of the money you're makin' off me and invest in a thicker pair of them tights you wear like pants, some that will hide the wet spots better."

She gasps, her head jerking in my direction, a broken glare blanketing her features.

I smirk, cock my head and stare right into those brown eyes of hers.

Yeah, I know, it's sweat coating the inside of her thighs—she's thick in the best fucking places and the sun makes you pay for nature's kindness in providing perfect curves.

Was I a dick to call her out on her worn-out leggings and unavoidable perspiration? Of course, I was, and later tonight, I'll feel like a dick for embarrassing her, but I don't yet.

I don't because she's stopped in her tracks and her eyes are on mine. Staring, searching, contemplating ...

Her eyes are on mine.

Why do I want to keep them there?

She swallows, whispering, "I need to go."

"Need to or want to?"

Her lips press together, and her head begins to turn away, but my hand decides to fly up and hold it right where it is, facing me.

My gaze falls to where my skin touches hers and heat builds in my groin. "Why don't you try to get in my bed?"

She nearly chokes, tries to escape, but I block her, and her brows cave. "I'm your tutor."

"That's not an answer." I lick my lips. "I can give you whatever it is you want, do whatever you like. I'm a generous man. I'd be good to you, I promise." I don't realize I'm slipping closer until she's pulling back, a tangled thought flashing in her eyes.

"See you Friday, Tobias." Quicker than I'd have thought her capable, she's gone.

And I'm hard as a fucking rock.

For my messy, prudey, annoyingly pretty eyed, *goddess-shaped* tutor.

The one girl seemingly immune to my charm.

I don't get it, but I want to.

I want to know her. Understand her.

I kind of just want to talk to her for a while.

What kind of warped world is this?

CHAPTER 9

Tobias

With a curt nod, I give my okay, settle my shoulders, lift my knee to my waist and swing my arm around with the power of a lightning bolt. The ball came and went, hit my man's hand with a force that could break a weaker fucker's palm, but not Echo's.

The crowd goes crazy, even before the ump has a chance to make his official call, because there's not a person here who could misread or disagree about that pitch, shit was pure perfection.

Strike three, bitch. I smirk.

Get outta my house, my zone.

As we knew it would be, it's called in my favor and the pouty fucker, with a sad size seven cleat, throws his bat in the dirt, stomping his sorry ass to the visitors' dugout.

I didn't even throw him a changeup. Three strikes, right down the middle, and *still* this guy, who didn't strike out a single at bat last season, didn't hit shit off me today.

None of them did.

"Yeeeaah, boi!" Echo pops up, tossing his catcher's mask in the dirt, and charges me.

When he's a foot or so away, I hop into the air, as does he, and we bump shoulders before hitting mitts in celebration.

"And another one!" he shouts with a grin. "This is our fucking year, Cruz!"

More hollers come and we turn to accept the fist bumps and back slaps from our teammates, but I slide through the rowdy, grinning fuckers, straight to the man who has yet to doubt me.

Coach Reid smiles widely, tipping his chin in a prideful nod.

I toss him the ball with a smile of my own. "How was that for showing up to the game, eh, Coach?"

He nods, clamping my shoulder in a tight grip. "Great fucking job tonight, son. Couldn't ask for more than that. Take your boys to Trivies, tell 'em I sent you. Tabs on me tonight."

When my grin widens, his eyes narrow. "Practice is still at seven a.m. Don't push it. And get in a couple interview questions with the school reporter before you take off, that girl is persistent as all hell."

With a light chuckle, I pat him on the arm, give him a salute in thanks, then hustle into the tunnel with the rest of my team.

It doesn't take long to get fresh and clean. The reporter, Kari, Karley, or something of the like, was all too willing to ask her questions from inside the locker room. Pretty sure the swinging and hangin' dicks persuaded her—girl asked me two questions before the slow rockin' of our center fielder's shlong caught her eye on his deliberate, leisurely stride past us in nothing but his birthday suit, towel hanging around his neck.

Yeah, a men's locker room is not for the weak.

Takes a strong man to stand next to another whose dick is out dicking his own—poor, girthless fuckers.

"Yo!" I bang the metal closest to me as I head for the door, gaining the others' attention. "Head to Trivies from here, boys, foods covered. You wanna drink? Pay for that shit yourself or Coach'll know about it." Some grunt, some agree, some flip me off with a grin.

With that, I walk out, Echo at my side.

He pulls his keys from his pocket, tossing them in the air. "So, we payin' for our own beer?"

"Nope."

"Gotta love Coach." Sharing a laugh, we hop into his 'Stang. "We gettin' fucked up tonight?"

"We're gettin' fucked up."

"I can feel you through your jeans."

I bring my beer to my lips, giving the ball babe a side-glance. "Course you can, you've been scratching your nails across my zipper for the last ten minutes." Tipping my head back, I finish off the bottle and look back to the girl. "If it ain't hard yet, it ain't gonna be, babe. Better luck next time."

She takes a second, deciding if she's going to be offended or not, but when my boys at the table to our left start laughing, she sets eyes on her next target of the night, and happily skips her fine ass over there—bit skinny for my taste, but fine nonetheless.

But my dick didn't agree and he knows best.

On to the next.

I bob my head to the music, skimming the room for the perfect figure for tonight. I need something soft to play with.

To be as productive as possible in my pursuit of pleasure, I follow the length of the wall, passing some cheap, ancient booths and an old wooden bar. They don't update much here but the liquor and the music. Being one of the two bars we have within walking distance from campus, my guess is it's because they know the crowd they're getting—a bunch of rowdy students lookin' to bury stress and blow off steam.

The foods good, and beers cold, though, so the look of the place doesn't matter.

A chick with a killer smile winks my way and I sit up a little straighter when she angles her body to show me her profile. She's got thick thighs, just the way I like 'em, like she's played softball all her life, but she's not on the team. Those girls won't come here.

Nothing but trouble if we mix our competitive edge with theirs. They usually take up at Screwed Over Rocks with the football team. Apparently, we baseball guys are over the top and hard to handle.

The girl waves her fingers my way, and slowly, purposefully, licks her full lips. That alone should have me solid, but my boy ain't even twitching, and this is beauty number two.

Today's game was intense. I guess I need to wind

down more, slow the adrenaline before I speed it up again, so I signal for the bartender to bring me another, and the girl turns back to her friends.

The third beer does nothing, so I push to my feet, but not wanting to give in so soon, I scan the room once more. As expected, not a damn thing piques my interest, just like nothing did last night or the night before or the week be-fucking-fore.

I'm off my game.

My dick game, that is. The poor fucker hasn't seen the sun in a hot minute.

It's sad ass shit, like a bad BJ where there's no fire above my groin and no curling of my toes in my Timbs.

Yeah, guys' toes curl just the same as girls' do.

If a dude's toes don't curve when his dicks down a nice warm throat, he's getting eighty percent and needs to ask for more dedication.

It'll work, in time, but it won't satisfy.

Even if I did find a girl to get me going, I'd still have to go home and handle myself or go to bed aching.

Nothing satisfies anymore.

The perfect shade of golden brown flashes in my mind, and if I wasn't keenly aware of where I am, I'd swear I could smell a very specific hint of vanilla. A spicy, baggy-sweater-wearing kind.

I swallow a frustrated sigh, my eyes narrowing in on nothing.

I need to get a fucking grip.

Echo and Xavier are headed for the exit as I reach them, and together, we make our way out front.

"Once again, my man's leaving empty-handed."

Echo grins.

I flip him off and he chuckles.

"We're going to the team house, you coming?"

"Why the fuck not." I shrug. "Nothing better to do."

"I'm touched, asshole." X chuckles, stuffing his phone in his pocket and pulling out his keys.

"By who, Neo?" I tease. "I knew you two were more than besties."

Xavier comes out with a grin, wrapping his arms around my middle in an attempt to bring me down, but I quickly spin out of it.

It's bullshit, everybody knows he's hot for his boy's little sister, even if nobody says it out loud. I just like to give him a hard time.

"Shit, I forgot to get my card back from the bartender." Echo dashes back inside.

"Yeah, I need to take a piss real quick," X says, on his tail through the door.

I walk over to Echo's ride, lean my ass against it, and wait.

Closing my eyes, I drop my head back with a heavy exhale, the long day catching up with me, but soon as I quiet my mind, something has my eyes popping open again.

A shadow catches my attention just beyond the parking lot, and I squint, attempting to see better.

Hustling across the street with both hands full is Meyer.

Something falls from her bags, and she bends, rushing to grab the item before continuing to cross the dark road, only to drop down on an empty bus stop bench.

At eleven thirty at fucking night.

Across the street from a bar.

A bar full of young dumbasses.

What kind of shit is that?

I make my way across the street.

Before I reach the divider, Meyer pushes to her feet, lifts her bags, and begins walking toward the school.

"What the hell are you doing?!"

She yelps, jumping a good two feet, her crap spilling onto the ground again.

Her eyes fly to mine, wide with alarm, but they quickly narrow once she realizes it's me.

She quickly disregards my presence, retrieving her fallen items once more.

Oookay. No hello, I guess.

"Nice to see you, too. Again, what the hell are you doing?"

She stands tall and pushes forward. "Going home."

"Uh-huh." I hurry to reach her side and keep in step with her. "And why exactly are you walking around by yourself late at night?"

"Why are *you* walking by *your*self?" she counters.

"I'm a dude."

She picks up her pace and I swear the girl rolls her eyes, but it's dark, so I can't say for sure.

I feel like she did.

"Man, you're in a hurry. What, Jonny Boy send you out for some condoms and now you gotta rush back before the Viagra wears off?"

"Oh yeah, you hit the nail on the head." She shakes

her head.

My brows snap together. "Wait, really?"

She stops in her tracks, whipping around to face me. "No, not really!"

I try to take her bags from her hand, but she tears them away, so I lift my palms into the air and start walking when she does. "I mean, if you were, you should know that there's condom vending machines on campus. Unless you're coming back from the dude's house ..." I turn toward her with a frown. "And you know what, if a man's making you walk home—"

"Stop."

"I'm serious. You should kick his ass."

"Tobias, enough."

"Okay, okay." I face forward. "But for real, what kind of dude—"

"There is no dude, Jesus!" She nearly groans.

That shouldn't make me grin.

Why am I grinning?

"All right, fine. No dude." I nod to myself, then peek at her from the side. "Not even a shitty one?"

"Oh my god, Tobias!" she shouts, cutting her head my way. "Stop talking," she says, but there's a slight bit of something in her usually crisp tone.

"Hold up." I angle my head playfully. "Was that ... are you amused by me?"

"No."

"I think you are."

"I definitely am not."

"Oh, yes, you are." I jump in front of her, walking backward so we can face each other. "It was tiny, I'm talking statue cock tiny, but it was there."

Her lips curve into a smile, but she pulls them together to try and hide it.

"Ha!" I shout, calling her out, but then I stumble over a curb she didn't warn me was coming and fall onto my ass. And it's not because of my semi sort of buzz I've got going on.

Now, though, there's no denying.

The girl's laughing at me.

Full-on laughing and you know what?

I ain't mad about it.

She's cute when she laughs.

I stretch my arms over my bent knees, playing cool for a second before I hop to my feet.

"You chose not to warn me, didn't you?"

Her shrug is coy, but she drops her eyes to the grass soon after and when she looks back up, a hint of dejection creeps over her.

She straightens, switches the bags from one hand to the next, and starts walking again.

We walk in silence for a solid two minutes before her eyes flick to mine. "You should go back to your friends—"

"Look, Tutor Girl," I cut her off with a grin. "It's late, it's dark, you're not walking by yourself."

She's quiet a moment before she speaks again.

"I don't want to walk with you," she whispers, her frown is focused forward.

Just like that, the bit of fun is fucked off into the night.

"Yeah, well. Too bad." I don't look her way, unsure

why a flare of disappointment washes over me. "I'm walking home just the same now, so only makes sense I walk with you. Which dorm do you live in?"

"I don't live in the dorms."

"Okay, what housing are you in?" I take off ahead of her this time, ignoring the small huff she lets out. "Front side or back side?"

"I'm not in housing either."

I glance back. "All right, so then where do you live?"

"Let's not talk, okay?"

Man, I don't get this chick.

I offer to walk her home and she basically tells me to fuck right off, or that's what I heard anyway.

How does one even respond to that?

I have no fucking clue, so all she gets is a mumbled 'whatever' and we walk the last few blocks in silence. I continue past campus, and she pauses to ask the security patrol what I'm assuming is something random for the sole purpose of breaking away from me, so I leave her to him.

Home now, I take a quick shower, and flop onto my bed in nothing but my birthday suit, my sleepwear of choice.

That's when it hits me and I chuckle to myself.

Of course.

It's obvious now.

Tutor Girl got upset, maybe even insulted, at my offer to walk her home because I didn't offer to take her back to mine.

Maybe the poor girl felt rejected.

Yeah, that could be it.

Maybe.

It's also the reason I text her an hour later to make sure she got home safe.

When she doesn't respond, I decide I don't give a shit.

I frown at the spackled ceiling.

Sleep can take over anytime now.

CHAPTER 10

Tobias

"I don't know how you guys get up before the roosters every day." Vivian drops into the booth across from us, having spotted Echo and me when she drug her hungover ass through the doors.

"Cruz is the only fucker up before the sun, and I hate to break it to you girl, but it's almost eleven." Echo looks up from his textbook, teasing her.

She stares at the barista, making her drink with stars in her eyes. "And somehow it still feels too early."

"That's 'cause you have no routine." I shrug. "Get up at the same time every day and after a while, it'll be nothing."

She rolls her head my way, last night's makeup smeared beneath her eyes. "You're like my dad. He's been retired for like ten years and he still gets up at the ass crack of dawn every day, makes his coffee, watches the news, listens to birds, and for what? To play old westerns or reruns of CSI?"

I laugh, bringing my protein shake to my lips.

"Sounds like the good life."

She scoffs. "Yeah, except for when you're trying to sneak back in the house at four in the morning and he's sitting on your bed."

My head snaps her way and I grin, but the chick behind the counter calls out her name and she hops up, flipping us a peace sign as she grabs her coffee. Out the door she goes.

The second she's gone; I turn to Echo. "See, told you she's chill."

"You know she's fucking Neo now, right?"

"You know I don't give two fucks, right?" I grin.

Echo chuckles, pushing to his feet. "Let's get out of here, man, I need to run into the student center for some graph sheets."

We head over to the center, but before we reach it, a familiar ball of hair catches my eye.

Tutor Girl and my boy Coop's ex-girl, Bianca, are walking up the steps to the math building, laughing about something on their phones.

I grin.

She has friends and is capable of smiling without hiding it like normal people do. Who knew?

I chuckle when Bianca squeezes her cheeks and plants one where her hand just was before shimmying into the building.

Quickly breaking away from Echo, I jog up the steps to where Meyer holds back.

She's leaning against the rock wall, so I sneak up behind her.

"What up, Tutor Girl, I see you're still alive and

breathing."

Her upper body spins to face me and she pulls her phone into her chest.

"Didn't know you knew Bianca." I grin at the large stone building. "Your next class in here?"

"Tobias, hey," she says in a hushed rush, putting on a tight, fake smile for the assholes who slip by us. "What ... can I do for you?"

"Wow, it's like that?" I cross my arms, scowling down at her. "All business, huh?"

Her brows pull in and she quickly glances around.

Again, with this hideaway shit?

Fuck that.

I put on a smirk. I'm talking full blown, *gonna get me some* smirk, and take a small step forward, internally laughing as her features grow tense.

Her head pulls back slightly, her eyes tightening in suspicion, and rightfully so.

"Come on, baby," I purr, laying it on thick and a bit louder than necessary. "Just last night you were calling me *Daddy*, and now today I'm already back to Tobias?" I tsk, taking another step until her back meets the wall. She tries to get away, but there's no escape.

"Stop," she hisses, turning to avoid sharing the same air as me.

Too bad for her, I crouch to meet her height.

"I believe your words were *don't stop*."

"Oh my god," she whispers, dropping her chin to her chest as the others around us pretend not to be circling, hoping to catch some dirt flying.

"I think I need a redo, Tutor Girl." I run the back of

my pointer finger down her arm, but that fucker freezes right where it's at, on the soft underside just above her elbow.

Meyer's eyes briefly close at my touch, and my brows snap together. Again, with that little mouth part small gasp she tends to give, but hold on ...

I look where my touch rests.

Are those ... *goose bumps*?

No fucking way.

I prepare to do it again, tugging my head back slightly so I can catch every little move she might just make, but before I get the chance, she rolls her shoulder back and my hand falls to my side.

"Go." She shakes her head, refusing to look at me.

She wants to brush me off, as if she's not responding to my touch when she so clearly is.

I don't get it and I don't know what to do with her blatant disregard for me as a person, so I do what I'm used to. What I know.

What everyone expects.

I play with her some more.

"Yeah, a redo's what I need ..." I keep going, step more into her, and speak even louder. "Maybe I didn't quite leave my mark, huh?"

Her eyes squeeze shut, quickly flicking open and narrowing in on me. There's a heaviness behind them that has me slowly easing up.

Unsure of what's happened and why she's caging up even more, I'm about to call a truce. Despite what she's likely convinced herself of, I'm not trying to hurt her. I'm just playing with her.

But Tutor Girl does what not a lot of girls can. She surprises me.

Meyer pushes off the wall, the little ball on her head bouncing with the sudden jolt and erases the space I gave back to her. She lines her body up with mine, a sudden hint of anger tightening her features.

"Don't worry, *Daddy*," she says with conviction and a dash of sultry taunting, but I got a feeling that's for show. "I couldn't forget our night together if I tried."

She shoves past. Gone is the flirty sexiness her posture and voice held for a whole five seconds and in its place is a resolute chick ready to dish it.

Tutor Girl whips around, and volcanic eyes sear mine. "And believe me, I've tried."

At that, the people around can no longer pretend they weren't eavesdropping, and laughter quickly follows.

I smirk and shrug it off, because who the fuck is she and what the fuck was that?

A fake performance I basically pulled from her.

I try not to stare as she storms across the yard, those hips swaying in wrath, that ass, that I can't see but can picture just fucking fine, taunting me as she heads who the hell knows where, but I can't help it. My attention's fucking glued to her.

She's not even supposed to be here. No tutoring or classes in the morning, that's what I was told. That's what she keeps saying. It's probably lies.

Meyer stops to adjust her bag, so I pretend not to be staring at her, waiting for her to find a reason to glance back and see if I'm still standing in the doorway where she left me, but she doesn't.

It's fucking weird. Irritating.

Downright frustrating.

The girl always looks back, right? And who the hell is she to flip the rule book and the game I was playing with her?

And why the *fuck* are these douchebags staring in the same direction as me?

This is bullshit.

Twice.

I called Tutor Girl *twice* today.

Yeah, *called,* not texted. Who does that? No fucking body, that's who, but when she didn't respond or bother to open the four or five messages I sent her—I know, 'cause there's no check mark—what was I supposed to do?

I have work to do in anatomy and she needs to help me.

Who cares if it's a page or two of weak ass vocabulary words. Why should I quiz myself when she can do it for me? It's her job. She gets paid to help me, more than she does anyone else. So, I called the girl, once when I pulled up at the stadium, and again after my post game shower. She didn't answer either time.

It's fucked up.

I'm done with class for the day, and the team met early this morning for film, so I've got shit else to do today but homework.

A heavy sigh escapes as I push to my feet and hop

off of the picnic table I've been sitting on top of for the last forty minutes, the table that happens to be right across from the tutoring center that a certain brown-eyed girl has yet to come in or out of.

Sure, the door says they closed at five, but it's only seven and I can make out the shape of bodies through the window, none that could even begin to rival hers, but still. She could have been in the back or something.

She'll call eventually. I think.

Probably not, since she never does what I expect her to do.

Maybe if I think she won't, she will?

Fuck me, I'm confusing my own damn self.

Annoyed as shit, I head to the only place outside of the field that allows me an escape, the gym.

"Oh man, is that Tobias Cruz I see?!" my boy Noah shouts as I walk into the gym.

Chuckling, I make my way over to where he's working hand weights and resistance bands.

Noah's the starting quarterback here at Avix. He's a fucking god and humble as shit. In the off-season we see each other in here a lot, but when one of us is in season, it's hit or miss. I haven't seen the man since before the holidays.

"How you been, bro? Fuck your way through the dance team yet?" I grin.

He shakes his head, an easy smile on his face. "Not quite, Cruz. Not quite."

See, Noah ain't like me, so I give him shit when I can.

He doesn't sleep around or eat up attention, and

he gets plenty. Honestly, I don't think he's comfortable with any of it, the attention and never-ending skirts who believe they're entitled to your time since they're willing to hand over their own.

I wasn't either, at first, but once I realized any good I did would be spun negatively by the school papers, I went ahead and gave them something else to talk about, the only other thing they chose to print when it came to me.

The Playboy Pitcher living up to his name.

I'm sure Noah gets his, but I'd bet it's with one chick, a girl who is in the same boat as him, someone focused on school and not interested in the frat boy lifestyle.

He's a damn good guy.

I take the space beside him.

"You killin' it out there, starving those scouts." He grins.

"Hey, I'm trying to keep up with the season you had." I whistle. "Damn, Noah. Your ass is gonna burn a fat hole in some rich fuckers' pockets next year, my man. You're going first round, no question."

He looks away with a low chuckle but says nothing.

See? Humble as fuck.

Good dude, great student.

Bet Tutor Girl would like someone like him.

I freeze, halfway extended, to pick up a dumbbell.

What the fuck was that?

No, no.

I don't give a damn who or what she does in her spare time, so long as my work is solid, and I get to play ball.

But! If she is ignoring my calls because she's with some fuckface, that ain't cool.

Son of a bitch, I *sound* like a bitch.

With a groan, I yank my bag off the ground and ignore Noah's raised brow.

I storm right back out the way I entered, my phone already at my ear, ready to snitch her out like a damn toddler 'cause yeah, I've apparently reached that level of ... I don't know, spite? Annoyance.

Disappointment?

"Hey, kid," he answers on the first ring.

I glare at the clearing campus. "Coach."

"Yo, Cruz," is shouted from my left right as Coach Reid asks, "What's going on?"

I turn to find Neo and Gavin, nodding my chin.

"We're picking up X and headed to Trivies. You in?" he calls, his hands cupped around his mouth.

I stop in my tracks.

Huh. It's a long shot, but it's a shot.

"Sorry, Coach. Misdialed." I grin, end the call, and shout back to my boys, "I'm in."

I head their way.

Let's see if Tutor Girl's made a habit out of walking alone in the dark.

A few hours later, and there she is, crossing the dimly lit street.

I want to call out her name, slam her for her reckless choice, and do it again when she rolls those eyes at my rant.

But then she shifts, and the shitty streetlight catches something small on the inside of her jacket. A name badge. She shifts again and I make out the logo on her top, but it's not a top.

It's an apron from the burger place down the road.

She was at work.

She's walking home alone, late as shit at night, from *work*.

Not for fun and escapades, but because she must have to. Walk and work, I mean.

She wouldn't do either if she didn't need to, right?

Wait, she has two jobs?

Instead of doing any of the things I was about to, I step farther into the shadows, follow at a distance from my side of the road and once she's safe and crossing campus grounds, the security guard rolling along in his golfcart at her side, I head home.

I don't know why, but I do the same exact thing the very next day.

DIRTY CURVE

CHAPTER 11

Tobias

"No freaking lie?!" Meyer's lips curve up as she snags the paper I'm holding up in front of her. She scans over it and that smile of hers grows.

Laughing, I repeat her words. "No lie."

"That's killer for a pop quiz."

"I've got a 'killer' tutor."

Finally, her eyes come up to mine and she pulls her mouth to one side. "We didn't go over this section. You read this one on the bus on the way back from your Arizona game. This is all you, Tobias Cruz." Again, with that smile. "Be proud."

Are you?

Meyer clears her throat and looks around, a small frown building along her brows. "Where's your bag?" she asks, tucking a loose strand of hair behind her ear.

"I didn't get a chance to eat after practice, cool if we grab a pizza? There's a patio we can work on."

Her face smooths out and she looks out across the

grass. "Um."

"You won't be sorry. They've got the best sauce around."

With her head down, she timidly says, "I only have two hours."

"I know." I'm no fool. She's here because she's required, but that doesn't mean it has to stay that way, right? I pull my keys from my pocket and walk backward toward the parking lot. "It's only a couple miles from here, I have my truck." My eyes roam across her makeup-less face. "I'll get you back in good time, Tutor Girl. Promise."

She begins to nibble on that lower lip of hers and I pull in a slow breath, willing my cock to behave itself.

I get it, my man, you're fucking starved.

Meyer's brown eyes come back to mine and she says, "Okay."

"Wait, for real?" My head tugs back.

"I said okay." She chuckles, flicking her gaze to the sky.

"Well, okay. Right this way, Tutor Girl." I hop off the curb, unlocking and opening the door to my Dodge Ram for her. "Hop on in George."

She looks to me with a goofy expression. "George?"

"That's right."

"That's odd."

"You ever met a George who wasn't a reliable son of a bitch?" I lift a brow, walking around the hood to my own door. "Bet not."

She pulls her lips in as she climbs inside the cab, and a few seconds later, I'm turning out onto the main road.

Pizza here we come.

Meyer runs her fingers along the doorframe, looking up at the ceiling and down at the stereo system I've yet to turn on. "This is really nice."

I grin. "Perks of a pitcher."

She nods, turning her head toward her window. "Of course."

I cut her a quick glance, but she doesn't face forward again, not until we're parked and climbing out.

She looks over the little hole-in-the-wall, a mom-and-pop restaurant I found my first week here freshman year. It's old and needs a fresh coat of paint, could use a new parking lot and sign, too, but the food is delicious, the sauce homemade, and the couple, kind as shit.

Inside, Franny, the mom of the place, greets us with a weathered smile and a wave. "How you doing, honey, get over here, and you brought a friend!" She quickly turns her head, shouting, "Joe, get out here, Tobias is here and he brought a friend!"

Meyer lifts her hand, disguising her laugh as a low cough.

I give Franny a hug and shake Joe's hand when he steps from behind the swinging door a moment later.

Joe pats my back. "Been a couple weeks, huh? Thought you pissed on us for that new joint down the road."

I laugh. "Not me, Joe, not me." I turn to Meyer. "This is Meyer, she goes to school at Avix, too."

"Well look at you." The old man grins at her. "You don't have all that shit on your face and you're still prettier than this one." He jerks his head toward me, kisses his wife and disappears behind the door once more.

Franny laughs, introduces herself and gets us seated on the back patio.

Meyer shakes her head as Franny leaves, and then turns to me. "They're so cute."

"Yeah, I want to be them when I grow up." I smile.

She eyes me, a look of surprise crossing her face. "What?"

"I guess that's not something I'd expect you to say."

"I wonder why?" I tease, knowing exactly where she's coming from. "You know you can't believe everything you hear ... or read."

Her laughter is light, and while her head lowers, those eyes hold on to mine.

"You okay with pepperoni? It sounds boring but Joe's is fire, swear."

"Don't worry about me."

"You're eating with me."

Her smile is sheepish. "I didn't know you wanted to go eat. I like to leave my wallet at home so I don't spontaneously spend."

A quick meal is spending spontaneously for her?

As I think that, a sense of aversion washes over me.

Twenty bucks didn't always come so easy for me either. My parents lived paycheck to paycheck all our lives, and the little extra they did have, they saved. Maybe I need to remember that next time I pop into the grocery store.

I shake off my thoughts.

"Contrary to what you may believe, or the shitty impression I gave with the whole 'be my schoolwork slave,' I'm not a complete dickhead." I lean forward. "I wouldn't invite you, order a pizza, and expect you to pay for any of it."

"I guess I'll have to take your word for it."

A chuckle leaves me, and she grins at her joke, but hides it by focusing on pulling her laptop from her bag.

"Pepperoni isn't boring, by the way." She looks to me and pops a brow with a playful grin. "It's a classic."

Damn straight it is.

A little over an hour and a large pizza in, my assignments are done. We've already gone over a few ideas for my next English essay, and I officially have no pressing work that needs handled ... but she hasn't asked to leave yet.

In fact, she stood up and chatted with Franny for several minutes about plants and how to keep them alive, while I watched on, finishing up the last of the breadsticks.

She's back in her seat now, though, has shed that awful sweater, and even let a flip-flop fall to the floor beneath the table, one of her legs now folded up in the chair.

And right this second, she's accepting a refill of iced tea, only after making sure it's not an extra fee.

Meyer sighs, smiling into her glass as she looks at me. "We got through a lot today. If you do your reading tonight and your professors stick to their schedules tomorrow, you won't have any work while you're away the next two days."

I nod, staring at her, and while I think she wants to look away, she doesn't.

"We still have a good half hour before we have to head back."

For the first time today, she pulls her phone from her bag. "It looks like we do."

"Read to me."

Her eyes pop up. "What?"

"The sections I have left? Read them to me."

Her chest heats, a soft red changing the color of her fair skin, and I want to reach out, run my knuckle over the spot to see if it's warm to the touch.

I bet it is.

Something tells me she's not capable of half-assing anything, not even a sudden, uncontrollable dose of adrenaline that causes one to flush.

She's fire, I know it, and call me a fuckin' pyro 'cause, goddamn if I don't crave the flame.

To be honest, I'm not sure what to do about this girl. She's so hot and cold.

Okay, maybe she's never hot, but she definitely gets to that lukewarm level, like the half empty water bottle you dig out of your back seat when you're dying of thirst.

But I guess she could say the same about me. The hot and cold part, I mean.

I'm as good as whiplash when it comes to her, I know that, but she does that to me. She confuses my mind and sends shock waves through my brain that don't quite compute the way I'm used to. My initial reaction is always to do what's expected, to *be* who they expect when things around me begin to feel sour or new. Unexpected.

But maybe that's the wrong way to go about it where she's concerned.

Maybe she doesn't expect a thing from me at all.

That's an unrivaled, terrifying, *electrifying* ideal.

Licking my lips, I tip my head the slightest bit. "Please?"

At first, I think she's going to decline, but Meyer reaches over, slowly dragging my history textbook toward her and flips open the page with the next little green tab she added for me last week.

She takes a small sip of her sweet tea and then starts at line one.

She reads to me without pause and I watch her all the while.

The way she tucks her hair every couple paragraphs and how she smiles to herself when she gets to a part that interests her. The way her voice elevates the slightest bit when she feels she's come to a concept of importance and wants to make sure I'm engaged.

Both her feet are now bare and perched on the chair. Her knees pressed against the table's edge, and she has the book laying across her thighs. With every turn of the page, her head tips from left to right, and every five minutes or so, she blindly dips her chin to pull the straw between her lips from the glass she has tucked to her chest.

Only when a loud slurping sound is made does she lose focus.

Her eyes fly up to mine, embarrassed, and right back down to the now empty glass.

A low chuckle leaves me, and I sit back in my chair, quickly sneaking a look at the clock. "I'm not sure we have time for another glass, but I bet Franny will get you one to go?"

"Of course, I will!" Franny shouts from wherever it is she's eavesdropping from.

Meyer smiles sheepishly as she slides her feet back into her sandals and stands, beginning to pack her things into her backpack, so I do the same.

Before I can, Meyer picks my book back up, and I don't say a word but lead us toward the front of the restaurant. Franny steps up, passing two large foam cups to me and hands a to-go bag to Meyer.

"What's this?" Meyer smiles, peeking inside.

"That's a half dozen cinnamon knots and they're not to be shared with this one." Franny slaps my chest. "Come back and see us, will you?"

"I will," she promises, thanking her again. "And don't worry, I'm not sharing these with him. My friend's coming over tonight for a movie and she's a sucker for sweets. You just made her night and she doesn't even know it yet."

Franny winks, running off to answer the phone.

"You'll be back in a few weeks to help me finish the deck, huh, Tobias?" Joe calls from somewhere in the back. "We're almost done with her!"

"Yes, sir, I will. Let me know once it's delivered."

"You know I will, and bring that girl with you when you come, huh? Franny likes her!"

Chuckling, I glance at Meyer. "Later, Joe!"

"Yep!"

We step outside and she turns to me. "You're building them a deck?"

"Helping."

"Like a patio or...?"

"Yeah, like a patio deck." Turning, I point at the side of the building. "You can't tell from inside the restaurant, but their little house is attached to the back. If you go around here, that's where their front door is. They have a nice little table set and some comfy chairs out there, but it's down a handful of steps. By the end of their day in the restaurant, their knees are hurting, but they don't care, they go out there every single night, at least for a little while."

"It's their quiet time together."

Nodding, I look to Meyer. "One of the times I came in, they asked if I wanted to visit for a bit, so I did. Next thing I knew we were at the hardware store," I say with a laugh and Meyer smiles, clipping her seat belt into place. "I helped my dad put in a new fence years ago, so I halfway knew what I was doing. YouTube helped a fuck-ton, though."

"I bet it means a lot to them, having your company and your help."

"Does to me too. There're not a lot of places I can go around here and take my hat off, so to speak." I glance her way briefly, and her lips twitch. "That makes me sound like a bitch?"

Meyer laughs, shaking her head. "No, it doesn't."

I grin and head back to campus.

I'm about to strike up a random conversation in an effort to keep her talking, but then Meyer grabs her tea from the cup holder and opens up my book once more.

She picks up where she left off, so I slow my speed and take the long way home.

Meyer

I've been trying to work my way through a single section of my sociology book for the last hour, but every few minutes, I realize I'm staring blankly at the page, my mind on something else completely.

More like someone else.

And to think I sat there completely engrossed in reading his book to him for nearly an hour. Something tells me it had nothing to do with the words themselves, and that's a scary revelation.

An unwelcome revelation?

If I'm being honest with myself, today was nice. Dare I say, needed.

It's been weeks since I've been off campus for any reason other than obligation, and this afternoon, while technically on the clock, felt like a small break I didn't know I was dying for. I can't pinpoint when exactly my life became a hamster wheel, but for a long time now it's been wake up, climb into this circle, wash, rinse, and repeat.

I didn't feel that way today. Today, my mind wasn't already two tasks ahead, and I have Tobias to thank for that.

The short conversation with Franny was soothing in a way I've missed. She has that natural mother's nature about her, but the photos lining the homey walls gave me the impression she may have never been blessed with the role she would have loved.

It's easy to see she's taken with Tobias, which is as equally surprising as it is expected.

He's more than charming and completely over the top, but I'm beginning to realize some of that isn't him. Most of it is, but not all.

Yes, he's extremely cocky, but he's kind of earned the right. He really is at the top of the game, so it's not like his ego's inflated where baseball is concerned. And the rest ... I don't know.

The Playboy Pitcher is said to be an egomaniac. A bad boy with an eye for trouble, bound by air too heavenly for others to breathe.

He is trouble, that's for sure, but I get the sense he didn't inflate the bubble people claim surrounds him. I think he wants someone to step a little closer, to look a little deeper.

He wants someone to open their eyes and look into his without prejudgment.

Or maybe he just doesn't care what others think, and he does the only thing he can.

He accepts the misconceptions for what they are – beyond his control.

If he cared to uphold some sort of image, if he *fit* said image, Franny and Joe's is the last place we'd have ended up today.

They care for him, that much was obvious, but what was surprising, at least at first, was that the man cares for them too. An adorable, hardworking old couple with no ties to him.

No tie, but a common felt emotion, one I know all too well.

Loneliness.

Sighing, I close my textbook and tug the blanket up to my chin.

I'm not so sure it was a good thing to see this side of Tobias Cruz, but I'm also not so sure I regret it.

CHAPTER 12

Tobias

How these sons of bitches let me get up to bat, I don't know.

Maybe the long-haired pretty boy wants to try and prove a point, to be the sole fucker who could say he struck out your boy, but what a dumb shit he is.

He walked Xavier, the fastest fucker on the team, and now we've got one on third and first. We're only up by one right now, but all I've got to do is make it to first and X is coming home, no doubt.

So, when *Winner by Jamie Foxx* comes on and the crowd goes wild—yeah, even the home team fans love me—I swing my bat around and make my way into the batter's box.

"How you doing, cocksucker?" I say to the catcher while keeping my eye on the man on the mound.

"Fuck you, Cruz."

"After your girl, yeah, Hanson?"

"Dick."

"Thick and long, my man. Now tell yours to hit me with that fastball he seems to favor. Watch me make a fool out of 'em."

The ump gives his okay, the pitcher jerks his chin and here we fucking go.

I could almost laugh the second before it leaves his hand.

He's really serving the king of the curve, a motherfuckin' curve?

Screw first base, this ball is going to the wall.

The clash of cork and rubber against metal pings with contact and the ball flies exactly where it's intended, too fucking far to catch.

X comes in and I round to third, clapping like an asshole as I pop up, dusting my knees off like the obnoxious fucker I become on the field.

The pitcher comes off the mound, so I hold my arms out with a grin, but his coach shouts something from the dugout, and the punk turns back.

He knows he can't win now, not when we're up by three with two out and back to the four spot on our batting roster. Not when they're at the bottom of theirs and I'm still set to take the mound.

He knows I never reach my max pitch count. When I start a game, I finish the fucking thing, unless we're up by a fuck-ton, then I'll swap out and let the number two finish out.

This game is ours, just like we knew it would be.

Like they knew it would be, and tomorrow morning, we'll win again, sweeping the series.

My third base coach, who happens to be Cooper today, the brown-nosing fucker, steps closer. "You think they're sour now, wait 'til we show at their clubhouse tonight and get first pick over their ball babes."

I chuckle. "Poor bastards are about to develop mad hate for Tuesdays."

Our shortstop comes up to bat, hitting a line drive past second and I come in, but he gets caught at first, so we're headed back on the field.

Two strikeouts and one infield fly later, we're headed for the locker room, another win under our blue belts.

Coach Reid steps inside grinning with bright red lipstick on his cheek. "There's a Kardashian lookalike waiting in the tunnel for number eleven." He shakes my shoulder as he steps by. "Told her you'd be leading the first group out the door, son."

I chuckle, tugging my jersey over my head. "Good looking out, Coach."

"She have her sisters with her, Coach?" Echo shouts, whipping my hip with his towel.

The boys start planning the night, down to their pick of nonexistent Kardashian sisters waiting on the winning team. We plan to head over to the campus bar to start off the night. We can't drink and we only get a couple hours before it's lights out, early game tomorrow and all, but sometimes that's all you need. One solid hour.

Like Coach said, the girls are waiting at the end of the tunnel and waste no time coming up to introduce themselves. I look out at the now empty field with a smirk, but as I do, the parking lot lights kick on in the distance, and an instant frown takes over.

It's getting dark out. I'm a good five hundred miles from Oceanside, and there's a girl that might be walking alone in the dark tonight.

Fuck.

I break from the giggly group, grab my phone from my pocket, and scroll to Meyer's number, but my fingers pause there.

I narrow my eyes, looking out at the people piling into their cars and heading off.

She has no clue I followed her home those few nights, so what the hell am I supposed to say? Yesterday, I didn't trip on it because I heard her tell Franny her friend was coming over, so I knew she wouldn't be working. Once I heard that, I forgot to remember I'd be gone today, too.

Sure, Oceanside is a safe enough town, but there's crime everywhere, and a girl alone, in the dark near a bar, is a situation that shouldn't exist. Especially if that girl is her. Period.

"Cruz, let's roll out!"

I turn when Echo calls me, one of his arms draped around a blonde, the other a brunette.

Brunette.

Fuck.

I look to my phone and hit the call button.

Fully expecting her to ignore it, as she usually does, I walk toward the group, but then the line stops ringing, and a soft little 'hello' fills my ear.

I stop in my tracks, satisfaction curling my lips.

"What's this fool grinning at?" Neo teases, tossing his hat in the air and catching it on his head in an attempt to impress.

I flip him off and spin away.

"Tobias?"

"Hi."

"Hi." Her tone is teasing.

"Uh, I'm in Arizona."

What the fuck? No shit, I'm in Arizona. She knows this.

"We won." I nod. "Not that there was a chance we wouldn't but ..."

"Of course not." She laughs quietly. "But congratulations anyway. Jonny had the game on at the center today. Nice pitching."

"Jonny, huh?" I frown. That pink polo wearing bastard.

She hesitates a moment, and there's some shuffling around in the background. "Did you, I mean, is there something you need? I'm with someone, so I only have—"

"Like a student?"

"What?"

I lift my hat a little, glancing over my shoulder at my crew.

X throws his arms up, but I spin back around.

"You're tutoring someone right now?"

"For the next couple hours, yeah."

"Who?"

Bro, chill. What the fuck is wrong with you?

I lick my lips. "You know what, it's all good. I had a question but I can, uh, figure it out."

"Are you sure?" she asks. "My student's in line for a book rental. I have maybe five minutes before he gets back ..."

He.

Of course, it's a he. They're probably all he's and she's a she and fuck, dude. Shut up, you whiny ass bitch.

"If I call you later, you free?"

"I don't usually pay attention to my phone when I'm at home, but since you're telling me now, I can at least keep it near and try."

There, she said home. That's all I was after.

Right?

"Tobias motherfucking Cruz, get your ass over here. These girls are thirsty, if you know what I mean!" Gavin shouts from behind me.

I shake my head, flipping him off.

"I'll let you go," she says, a hint of hesitation in her tone.

"Is your dude back?"

"He's not."

"Then why hang up?"

"Cruz!" another asshole screams, louder than the rest.

"Bye, Tobias."

I frown at the sky. "Later, Tutor Girl."

I hope you have the opposite of fun.

I know I will.

Curfew comes quick and I'm thankful for it.

I'm exhausted. The crew was rowdy tonight, and

the girls more scandalous than ever. It was too much, and I'm ready for the perks of being the main man—my own fucking room.

"So, which one you sneaking in tonight? The Brazilian beauty with the accent or the Barbie doll with lips like a blowfish?" Echo knocks his elbow into mine as we climb from the Uber. "Mine's the captain of the volleyball team. Ass for days, son!"

Chuckling, I pull the key card out and we slip through the back doors. "None for me tonight, my man."

"For real? What's going on, suffering from some more DDLY?" We look to each other. "Some Dick Don't Like You?"

Laughing, I shove his ass and step onto the elevator first.

He comes in next, blocking the door with a grin. "Sorry, fuckheads. Catch the next one."

Our teammates groan, cussing us out as the metal doors close in their faces.

"You're an ass."

"I know." He smirks, turning to me with questioning eyes. "You ain't been hooking up lately."

I shrug. "Not in the mood."

"You not being in the mood is like meeting a chef who hates cooking. Not so sure such a thing exists."

The elevator doors open and we step off on the ninth floor, cutting a left toward our block of rooms.

"So, what's really going on?" he asks.

"I want her."

"Who, my volleyball captain?"

I scoff a laugh. "Nah, man." With a sigh, I swing my

eyes to his. "My fucking tutor."

His brows jump, amusement quickly following. "Well, there it the fuck it is, son. I called that shit when she stunned your ass by walking away from you without giving you the time of day."

I chuckle when he bumps his shoulder into mine. "Yeah, fucker. You did."

We enter my room, and he leans against the frame. "I take it she's yet to bite?"

"It's like she's got no teeth."

His head tugs back in shock. "Damn, maybe she has a man?"

I drop onto the edge of the bed, shaking my head.

"You asked ..." he guesses.

I look to him, and he pushes off the wall, his eyes narrowing.

"You pussy-whipped fucker." His grin is slow. "You asked her."

"You have to be getting pussy to be pussy-whipped, asshole."

"That's debatable, my friend." He laughs. "So, which is it? She free or taken?"

Running my tongue along my teeth, I let out a heaving breath and turn to face him once more. "She definitely ain't free."

Echo gets what I'm saying, and his lips slowly begin to curve.

Tutor Girl doesn't have a man, but she ain't free.

She's mine.

Or she will be.

She just doesn't know it yet.

DIRTY CURVE

CHAPTER 13

Tobias

"Okay, one more time." Meyer hops off the cement wall and comes closer. "The basic system that makes up the human body include ...?"

"A list longer than Neo's sexual history."

She laughs and Neo flips me off from the dugout.

We've been taking our study sessions to the field the last couple days because my times been limited and cutting her out of it is something I don't want to do. That, and if I fail, I'm fucked.

This is the last section test before the midterm and can bump or bust my grade. If I tank it, I have to get a ninety or higher on the midterm and that sounds damn near impossible.

Neo was out here running drills when we got here yesterday, and then popped up again today for some quick sprints, but he's already swapping out his cleats for the ridiculous Crocs he swears by.

I throw another one into the netting, nodding my

chin at Neo as he says goodbye.

"Bye, Meyer," he singsongs, giving her his best grin and earning one back.

I spin, pretending to throw a ball at his ass and his hands fly up, an embarrassed laugh following.

My lips curve into a smirk.

Asshole.

"Come on, name the first three, at least."

"I'm never going to remember these." I turn back to the netting.

"Yes, you can. You said you study stats, right?"

My eyes fly to hers, narrowing, and a hint of a grin finds her lush lips.

I want to bite them.

"You're onto something, Tutor Girl. I watch twenty-minutes of game film a day."

She pops both brows. "And we study for two hours almost every single day. You got this. Name the first three."

Squaring my shoulders, I send the ball flying, and it smacks the little square made of red tape perfectly. I bend to pick up another, frowning when I find the bucket empty, but then Meyer steps up. She's got a paper in one hand, a ball in the other.

She tosses it up, catching it on its way back down without taking her eyes off me, a small smirk on her lips. "Name three and it's yours."

I turn my body so I'm fully facing hers and she squares her shoulders in triumph, as if I couldn't simply walk my ass over to the net and refill the bucket with the thirty balls waiting there, like I have once already.

She tips her pretty little head as she tosses the

thing in the air, but I'm quick, and dart my hand out to catch it.

Meyer jerks forward with a little growl, playfully shoving at my chest, but before she can pull back, I grip her hand with my own.

I expect her to pull away, but she doesn't. She stares at the contact, so I lace my fingers with hers, and she allows it, coming closer when I give a little tug.

Her eyes find mine and stay there.

They stay there until she whips her other hand out, snagging the ball from mine.

My shoulders fall and she tugs free, a triumphant smile spreading across her lips.

"So easily distracted, Mr. Cruz."

"Girl, I'm telling you, you could breathe near me and I'd be fucking distracted."

She blushes, squashing her lips to the side to fight away her grin. "Unless you're on the field, right?"

I open my mouth, but all that comes out is a laugh. "There's one way to find out ..."

She rolls her eyes and a few minutes later, we're packing up our things.

Later that night, I'm lying in bed, and I can't stop thinking about her, but it's not that same frustrated feeling like before. At least not tonight.

I saw the way she smiled at me today, it was different. I'm not sure in what way, but it was. So, tonight, I'm gonna sleep good, 'cause I know without a fucking doubt that Tutor Girl is going to bed thinking about me, too.

Chuckling, I flip onto my stomach, close my eyes,

and fall asleep.

Meyer

Bianca lets herself in, a bag hanging from each hand. "Okay, I've got two subs, one ham, one turkey, both split right down the middle and every candy the mini mart had to offer."

"Any chance you brought a bottle of, god, anything?"

"Shut up, are you done breastfeeding?!" She practically beams.

I laugh, but my shoulders fall, and my intuitive best friend drops the bags where she stands, hopping up onto the bed in the next second.

She crosses her legs, so her knees are touching mine. "Talk to me."

"I have a problem."

Worry frames her eyes, and she nods. "Okay, what kind of problem?"

I squinch my nose. "A tall, tan, tasty-looking one..."

Bianca blinks, and then she blinks again. And then she laughs, falling back onto her back and reaching out to yank me with her.

"Oh my god, you little bitch, you scared me!" She buries her face in my shoulder, popping up onto her elbow just as fast with a widespread grin. "I take it he's *not* a rotten apple?"

"He's not a rotten apple." I chew on my inner lip. "He's ... a Sour Patch Kid, mixed with those white, mystery Skittles."

We look to each other and laugh.

"Okay, this I have to hear." She flips onto her stomach, waiting for more.

"He's exactly what meets the eye on the outside: gorgeous, charming, and magnetic. Athletic. But it's ... it's like there's this hard shell of expectation he has to fill because his exterior packaging says it's the one he belongs in, like the epitome of stereotypes."

"That's shitty but makes sense."

"Yeah." I nod. "But the filling inside the shell isn't made up of the same things." I pause, thinking of his cocky ways, and fight a smile. "Okay, some of that's on the inside too, but it's the honest parts. He is cocky, but that's because he's good at what he does and he's unapologetic about it. It's oddly endearing." I chuckle. "And he is charming, but it comes from how he communicates. He's direct, straightforward, and unafraid to let on to what he's thinking." My palm falls to my stomach when an airy sensation begins to swirl. "It's strange though, because you'd think someone who is all those things would be able to brush off what others say, and it seems like he does as far as the school papers and campus jerks go, but I can tell when I've insulted him."

"Hold up, what?" She pushes up onto her butt, frowning at me. "You don't insult anyone. Not even people you should." She pops a brow. "So, what the hell are you talking about?"

I throw my arm over my face with a low groan. "I know, I don't know, but I swear I do. I can sense it. Doubt he'd ever admit it, but I *know* he gets his feelings hurt sometimes, and his defense mechanism is to pretend he doesn't, and that's when his inner Sour Patch comes out. It's like he feels categorized or snubbed or something and so he pops off, acting the way he thinks he's being treated."

"Meyer." I look to her. "If he feels 'snubbed' ... that means he likes you and he just wants you to like him back. Right now, it seems like he's not so sure."

I swallow. "Yeah. I know."

That much is obvious too. At first, it was in his eyes when he'd look at me, now, it's in his touch, and he always finds a way to touch me. A brush of his arm or hand, a grab of the wrist. Or like today, when he threaded his fingers into mine and pulled me a little closer.

Today, I let him.

Today, I forgot how complicated the situation truly is.

"But you do ..." Bianca pulls me back into the conversation, her eyes narrowing. "You like him, right? That's the tall, tanned, tasty-looking problem here?"

I do.

But I can't, shouldn't.

It's selfish and wrong and a disaster waiting to happen.

I could never be honest with him, not now.

Bianca senses my thoughts, and a knowing, saddened smile spreads across her lips. "M—"

Tears fill my eyes and I look to the ceiling, willing them to go away.

The situation is complicated, more so than she even knows, but I think it's time to tell her the truth. The *whole* truth.

So I do.

But by the end, there is no revelation, no resolve because it changes nothing.

I can't simply cut the cord, walk away before it gets worse, because I'm contracted to spend six-to-eight hours a week with the man, ten when exams are close.

So basically, I'm screwed.

I'm no fool, I know it's going to get worse, deeper, just like I know it's up to me to keep the barrier between us in place. It won't be easy, but it's more than necessary.

I can't fall for Tobias Cruz, a little voice in the back of my head whispers, but a wiser, louder one replies with, *you already have.*

CHAPTER 14

Tobias

I roll my shoulder clockwise, and then counterclockwise, stretching through the slight ache before pulling some Tiger Balm from my bag.

Meyer looks up from the packet she printed out at the tutoring center this morning, watching as I dig two of my fingers into the little container. "What is that?" she wonders.

"Ever heard of Icy Hot?"

She nods.

"Kind of like that. It's an all-natural pain reliever, calms my joints."

"Does your shoulder hurt a lot?"

"My legs, my arms, shoulders." I chuckle when her brows shoot up. "It's nothing past normal. I don't really give my muscles a break much, but this helps."

She stares as I glide the thick Vaseline-like ointment over my right bicep and shoulder, and my lips twitch when her lips part the tiniest bit. I'm thinking she realized it too, because she then darts her eyes to the paper again. "Um, okay, that's the last of the questions for anatomy. I highlighted the ones you need to add to your flash cards before the next session."

I nod, accepting the paper when she hands it to me and push to my feet.

"You know, you're really good at what you do."

Her eyes fly to mine, and the surprise in her expression tells me she didn't expect such a compliment from me.

"I'm serious, you've got a knack for what you do."

A hint of pink colors her cheeks and she looks down. "Thank you."

"Is that what you want to do?" I ask her, suddenly curious. "Be a teacher, college professor maybe?"

A hesitant laugh escapes her, and she stands, beginning to pack her bag as I do. "I do, yeah. I think people would reach a little higher, believe in themselves more if more people care to help them understand. I'd like to do that for someone."

"You do that now."

Again, her gaze flashes to mine, small creases forming along her forehead, as if she's confused, but she shouldn't be.

"You do."

"I don't know about that, but ..."

I step closer to her. "You do. You work hard. You care and it shows."

She stares at me a long moment, and then she forces a small shrug. "Nah, I just want to have the summer and holidays off work," she mocks herself.

I laugh and hers follows.

Glancing over at the mound, I turn back to her. "You want to learn how to throw a curve?"

"What?" she chuckles.

"Let me show you."

She crosses her arms, her lips pinching to one side. "You want to show me how to execute your secret weapon?"

"Ah, so you do know a little about my game."

She rolls her eyes, but it's playful. "I'd have to be blind, deaf, and basically never step foot on campus not to."

"Or you low-key stalk me."

She laughs, shouldering past me with a lively glint in her brown eyes, and she doesn't stop until she's on the mound. "Okay, Playboy. School me."

With a smirk too deep to hide, I grab the ball from the dirt and head her way, keenly aware that our mandated time together ended exactly seventeen minutes ago.

And the girl's still here.

Meyer might know how to hit, but the girl can't throw a ball for shit.

Grinning, I hop to my feet and jog the five steps up and over to pick up the ball where it fell.

"I told you I was no good."

"I believe you now."

She laughs, dropping her head back, and my eyes fly to the slender length of her neck.

I bet it's smooth and soft, a spot that fires her up.

Right then, her hand lifts, gently encasing it as if to rub the heat beaming down from above away. She's facing forward right as I reach her, and as her eyes lock on mine, the ball falls from my hand.

With a small frown, she bends to pick it up, and as she stands, I can't stop myself, I dart a hand out, catch her around the wrist.

She tenses, her gaze snapping to mine, and while she swallows, she doesn't pull away. So, I tug her into me. I'm talking right on me.

Her copper eyes are wide and unsure, a little uneasy but a little more intrigued.

I shift a little closer and she chases a choppy breath.

Gliding my thumb a little higher on her wrist, I press right over her pounding pulse, not missing how it begins to knock a little harder.

Her fingers tighten around the ball and heat builds in my gut.

I want to feel her tighten around me.

Tense under me.

Moan *for* me.

She swallows. "I should go."

"I should kiss you."

"Tobias—"

"I might fucking kiss you."

"Please don't," she begs, and now all I can think about is driving her mad, fucking wild, until she begs for something else.

My eyes flick to her lips, my tongue coming out to drag along my own. "Make me a promise and I won't."

Her feet shuffle nervously. "What kind of promise?"

"That when you want to kiss me, you will."

"I ..." She looks down, but I use my knuckle to bring her focus right back.

"Promise me, and if you never want to, it won't matter."

But you'll want to. I'm thinking you already do ...

She nibbles on her lower lip and my chest rumbles against hers.

I want to pull it in my mouth, apologize to it for the torture she's inflicting, and then cause some of my own. I want to taste her so fucking bad.

Meyer's features pull, and her answer is nothing more than a harrowing whisper. "Okay."

My muscles flex. "Okay?"

"Yeah, okay." She nods, attempting to pull free, but I'm not quite ready to let go, not even when she tries and fails to change the subject with her next breath. "You know, if you pass this exam and your midterm next week, you'll have your eighty percent in this class."

"Kinda want the girl more."

She cuts her eyes away, chastising herself. "You were supposed to be an asshole."

My chuckle is heady, and my palm slides into her hair. "Did I disappoint?"

Reluctantly, she smiles up at me, but it holds that hint of heavy she always seems to carry, and I know.

"You have to go."

"Yeah," she murmurs, her fingers twitching beneath mine. "I really do."

I hate it and it takes a fuck-ton of strength, but I force my hand to fall from hers and take a single step away.

"See you on Thursday, Tutor Girl."

At first, she hesitates, as if maybe she doesn't want or can't bring herself to go, and I wonder if she might just stay, but she doesn't.

She takes slow, backward steps away from me, and then spins to grab her things.

I pack up as she does, trying to ignore how she leaves without another word, but just as I get the last ball in the bucket, she calls out.

"You didn't, by the way."

My head lifts, finding her just outside the fence, maybe thirty feet away.

I rest my arm on the net, nodding my chin. "Didn't what, Tutor Girl?"

"Disappoint." Her smile is hidden, but her words are strong. "Quite the opposite, in fact."

My grin is instant, but she turns away before giving me hers.

I know it's there, though.

I can feel it.

I had to cancel on Meyer tonight due to a mandatory film session with the team, and our next session isn't until

Sunday. I could wait, but I'd rather not, so instead of hiding out in the dark tonight and silently making sure she gets home safe, I decide the burger joint is where I'll be eating dinner.

I spot her through the painted glass the second I pull into the parking lot, that forever bun on top of her head.

She's got a pitcher in one hand and a tray in the other, and the second I walk through the door, her eyes pop up to mine.

At first, she freezes, but slowly, a smile spreads along her lips and she walks over with a single brow raised. "Table for one or is your date coming?"

"Nah, she couldn't make it." I shrug, bringing myself closer to her. "She's working at this little burger joint in town."

Playfully flicking her eyes to the ceiling, she leads me to the bar top in front of the cooks, so I plant my ass on one of the round stools, leaning forward as she steps around the counter.

"What can I get you to drink, Mr. Cruz?"

"What time you get off, Miss ... wait. What's your last name?"

Her eyes dart to the coffeepot she's reaching for and lifts it up from its base. "It's Sanders and I get off at ten."

She heads down the aisle, refilling an elderly couple's glasses before moving to the opposite side of the room.

Well okay then.

Looks like I'm here until ten.

Deciding to wait in the truck after I get my order,

I must have fallen asleep because the next thing I know, she's knocking on the window.

I roll it down and her hands come up to grip around the frame.

"You didn't need to wait for me." She looks toward the road and back.

"Get in." I turn the key over.

It takes her a moment, but then she comes around the truck and slips inside. "You knew I worked here, didn't you?"

"I might have seen you in your apron one night."

"Seen me ... where?"

"Headed home."

"Headed home..." She trails off with suspicion. "Tobias?"

At the stop sign, I meet her big brown, uneasy eyes. "I went back to the bar a couple times, not once with the intention of stepping foot inside it."

Her chest rises with a full breath.

"Why?" she wonders, so I tell her.

"I don't like the idea of you being out at night alone, so I made sure you weren't."

"Lots of people walk home alone at night."

"I don't want you to be one of them."

She opens her mouth but closes it just as quickly.

"I'll pick you up every night I can, if you let me." A grin slips over me. "And if you don't, it'll be like the first night, and I'll follow you anyway."

She lets out a small laugh, but tension quickly builds along her brows, and she looks away. "So, you know where I live then?"

"Nope." I shake my head and in my peripheral, I spot hers turn toward me. "Once you were safe and with the campus security, I went home." After I answer her question, I realize something, so I put her mind at ease. "If you don't want me to know where you live, I can take you to campus, or you can walk from my house, which is just across the street on the far-left end."

She doesn't say anything but begins tugging at the hem of her long-sleeved shirt, so I turn onto the main road that leads to the front of the campus, but just as we pass the park side, she tells me to turn, bringing me down a narrow street about as big as an alleyway that's lined with small rows of apartments. They're the kind that look like they might have been a motel at one point but were broken up and sold in chunks. Some are nicer than others, but they're all sort of jammed together.

"You can stop here," she says, unbuckling her seat belt and turning to me. "Thank you, for tonight and for ... the nights I didn't know you were there."

"You mean I didn't just win a gold medal in the art of stalker mode?"

A laugh spurts from her and the strain in her shoulders disappears.

"No, you didn't. Bronze maybe, but you know." She lifts a shoulder, a small smirk playing at her lips.

"Hey now. I haven't been reduced to bronze in years. Okay, maybe I should have followed you home."

Her smile is wide, but she turns away, looking back with only her eyes. "Seriously, thanks. Sometimes it is kind of scar—"

Meyer's head snaps up, her eyes narrowing out the front window, and then in a rush, throws the door open and jumps from the cab.

"Hey, what—?!" I shout, quickly rushing out after her.

What the hell?

She pretty much runs forward.

"It's okay, let me get you settled, okay?" someone says, half their body sticking out an old green Camry.

"Bianca!" Meyer shouts. "What happened?" she panics.

The girl, who I can now see *is* Bianca, whips out in alarm, but swiftly settles when she realizes it's Meyer approaching what must be her car.

"Oh, thank god!" She steps from the door. "I think Bay's mimi is in your bag, and I can't for the life of me find the spare. I was going to run out and get one."

"Oh shit." Meyer's words are stressed, but her body seems to relax with Bianca's answer, and she starts digging through her purse, pulling out and holding up something in her palm.

Bianca throws her hands up in a praising motion as Meyer slips past her, poking her head into the back seat.

That's when Bianca spots me, a shrill shriek leaving her. "What the fuck!"

I chuckle, lifting my hat from my head and flipping it backward. "Sorry, didn't mean to scare you."

At my voice, Meyer freezes, half her body stuck inside the vehicle, as if she forgot I was here, or didn't realize I got out of the truck when she did.

Slowly, the knee on the back seat extends, her left foot planting back on the ground with her right and she comes out of the car, a ball of blanket in her hands.

Her eyes flick to mine and she steps from under the carport, back into the light.

A small cry fills the air, but then Meyer begins to bounce her arms, and the soft sound fades away.

Not a ball of blanket, a baby.

"You should go." Meyer nods, turning toward what must be her apartment, but she pauses, cautiously facing me once more when my feet shuffle a little closer.

Meyer keeps her straining eyes on mine as I approach and they stay there when I reach her, but mine fall to the fluffy white blanket.

I peek through the small opening near her chest to find a teeny, tiny little thing. A baby girl, if the pink pacifier tucked into her mouth tells me anything.

The little one's eyes are closed and the blanket's pulled tight, so I can't see much else, so I step back, looking to her mama.

"I'll see you Sunday?"

She stares a long moment, sort of frozen and unsure, but then she gives a small nod.

So, I turn, walk back to my truck, and as I climb inside, it all clicks.

This is why Meyer runs on fumes most of the time. She's not out partying or doing whatever the fuck it is most of us here do. The girl's out working herself to death with assholes like me all afternoon, and at the burger joint into the night. When she's not, she's got her own classes to manage and taking care of a baby.

Her baby.

Trip. The fuck. *Out.*

I don't know how the hell a college student can

have a baby and still get shit done. Hell, I don't know how anyone can get shit done with a kid, but she seems to do it like a boss.

She's structured, organized, and on top of her tutor game.

It's no wonder she tries to keep her mornings for herself.

Here I am, the dick who basically threatened her into adding me anytime I've needed her to by using my tightknit relationship with her boss. I realize now that shit worked too well.

She never complains, is always available for me, and goes out of her way to be where I need her to. I've taken her mornings, afternoons, and nights. Weekdays and weekends and even others' study times when necessary. I know because I've seen her calendar book lying open before, scratches through other last names and mine scribbled in below or beside it.

Honestly, I'm with her more than I need to be because I fucking like to be.

I want to be.

But she's with me out of obligation.

In my driveway, I pull my phone from the cup holder and bring up her name. I type out a text canceling the Sunday session I just confirmed, but before I can hit send, I remember what my coach told me.

She makes more when she works with me, so maybe if I fall behind again, just by a little, I can get more hours with her. Maybe then she can breathe a bit easier, take fewer shifts at her second job, and have more time at home with her baby.

I delete the text and send a new one.

And then I stare at my phone, an unexpected anxiousness in my gut as I wait for her response.

CHAPTER 15

Meyer

The baby monitor beeps at my side, letting me know Bailey's beginning to stir, ready for her early morning feeding. I sit up, wiping the sleep from my eyes and tap on my screen to check the time.

My ribs constrict instantly, the text notification that came through not ten minutes after Tobias pulled away last night still sitting on my screen.

I knew when it beeped it would be him, since the only other person who would call me that late was still here when it came through, and sure enough, a half hour later when I dared to peek, it was his name I found.

I didn't open it.

I don't know if it made me more anxious or afraid, but either way, his message sits waiting.

And it's going to have to wait a little longer.

Climbing from bed, I step into Bailey's room right as her soft little cry comes.

"Come here, baby girl," I whisper, lifting her into

my arms, grabbing her Binky and blanket and bringing it with me.

She fusses as I prop my arm pillow up against the back cushion of the couch bed and sit. Tucking my comforter high in my lap, I lower Bailey and begin feeding her.

Her eyes come up to mine and I smile down at her, brushing my fingertips over the little bit of dark hair she has.

"Hi, Bae, are you looking at mama?" I run my finger down her nose, and her little hand wobbles up, so I give her mine.

She wraps her fingers around my thumb, grinning around me.

"My strong girl." A low laugh leaves me as I lower my head to kiss hers. "You're getting so big."

Tomorrow she'll be four months old, and the time has flown by so fast it's almost terrifying.

She smiles, laughs, and rolls over with ease. Her back is getting stronger by the day, so she'll be sitting up with a little help in no time.

I hope I'm with her when she does.

Bailey's eyes roam my face and hair, and then the area around me, but it's not long before her little grip loosens. She's falling asleep again, so I lift her to my shoulder, gently patting her back until she's settled, and slide myself a little lower on the arm pillow.

My eyes slide to my phone once more, a frown taking over.

I pick it up, hovering over the notification.

My lungs fill with a heavy inhale, and as I read what the man had to say, the pit in my stomach deepens.

I think I expected him to cancel on me.

I might have thought he'd question me.

One thing is for sure, though.

I most definitely didn't anticipate his text would hold an offer, asking if I wanted to have our Sunday session over Zoom so I could stay home with my little, as he called her.

He must have felt compelled to suggest a change in the routine we have going and that's not fair to him.

So, I politely decline, and only after I hit send do I remember it's only five in the morning.

Huffing, I let my phone fall beside me.

It's whatever, there's nothing I can do about it now, he probably won't even notice when it was sent by the time he sees it.

A yawn pushes past my lips, so I close my eyes.

My alarm is going to buzz, very quietly, in about fifteen minutes, and after that I'll have about two hours, if I'm lucky, to get through some of my own coursework before she wakes up ready to play. So, I drop my arm to the bed and close my eyes for the last few minutes of calm I'll have for the entirety of the day.

Before I've had a chance to take a full breath, my phone vibrates in my palm.

Oh my god, I woke him up.

Tobias: why not?

I frown and respond.

Me: I'm so sorry, go back to sleep.

Tobias: cute, Tutor Girl.

Cute? What's cute.

Ten seconds later, a picture pops up and my eyes pop with it.

Okay, so I didn't wake the man up.

It's a quick shot of the camera turned toward him. His shirt's off, hat's backward and his tongue is sticking out of his mouth. He's holding his fist in front of his chest to show the two-mile distance stamp on his watch. It's dark, nothing but the stadium lights lighting the track behind him.

He's not trying to be sexy and there isn't a hint of cockiness to be found. It's just a playful shot he took on the fly, and I like it.

It's him.

Happy-go-lucky, confident.

I trace the shape of his jaw, neck, and the deep cuts of his broad shoulder. I follow the muscles of his arm and then move back to the way his lips curve, full and flushed by nature.

I jerk when my phone vibrates again, and Bailey jumps.

Shit.

Tobias: I already made breakfast, ran the bleachers, and I'm coming up on my third mile.

Me: You're insane.

Tobias: Guess that makes two of us. I'm not the

one texting before dawn.

My lips curve into a small grin. Touché. Granted, my alarm isn't set to go off until five thirty.

Me: You know what they say. The early bird gets the worm.

Tobias: And the hot water, Tutor Girl! That's gold right there.

My lips pull into a grin.

Tobias: I'm gonna finish my run and later I'm gonna call you to talk about Sunday. Tell me you'll answer.

Guilt and indecision swell in my throat.

We've been around each other plenty of times now, so if he were going to remember me, it would have happened already, and he is only asking for a phone call.

There's no risk, right?

A little voice in the back of my mind screams wrong, that something about his asking feels intimate, but apparently that voice isn't loud enough, because I agree, and then I get up and get my day started.

Who knows, maybe he'll forget.

My boss at the diner called and asked me to swap shifts, and since Bianca came over with breakfast, she convinced me to take the offer so I could get it over with.

I hate leaving when Bailey is awake, but I'm glad I did today. Now I'm free until Monday when the cycle repeats itself all over again. Well, free other than the two-hour window set aside for Tobias on Sunday.

Speaking of ...

I pull my phone from my bag, finding several missed calls and texts.

Tobias: That right there is strike number two, Tutor Girl. Careful, the third might just come with some heat.

He follows his message up with a smirk-face emoji and an airy sensation whirls through me.

He's playful, but I knew that.

The man literally can't help the flirty way he approaches everything. It's simply what happens when you're attractive, athletic, and charming without trying. He couldn't tone it down if he wanted to. Not that he wants to.

On the walk home, I go back and forth on how to respond, but as I reach my alleyway, I come to a decision.

I'm simply not going to. Message him back, that is.

We'll meet on Sunday, like normal, and he can ask

me about it then. Unless he continues to call.

Last time he thought I was ignoring him, he let my email go unanswered for weeks, fell behind on his work, and only reached out again when his play time was at risk. I don't think he'll do that again, but I also don't know that he's the type to keep calling.

"There she is."

I shriek, my hands flying to my chest as I whip my head to the left.

Tobias sits on the open liftgate of his truck bed with a mini ice chest beside him and half empty lime-flavored Jarritos in both hands.

My pulse jumps when he stands, his shoes crunching against the loose gravel with his every step.

"And with her phone in her hand." He stops directly in front of me.

His grin is crooked, hat's backward, and eyes a playful blue.

Jesus, he's handsome.

"Hi, Tutor Girl."

"Tobias." My voice comes out thick, and those lips of his curve even higher.

As discreetly as possible, I swallow. "What are you doing here?"

"You told me you'd answer." He slides a half foot closer. "You didn't, so I had to break out the big guns and make a call."

My face falls, dread punching me in the gut, but then Tobias reveals what I didn't even notice was hidden behind his back ... a large Styrofoam cup.

"What is that?"

"It *was* a giant cup of sweet iced tea from Franny's, but the ice is all melted and the sugar's probably settled at the bottom now."

"You brought me tea?"

"And a pizza, but I ate half of it while I was waiting so ..." He shrugs.

A light laugh escapes and his grin deepens.

"Bianca didn't tell you what time I got off?"

"My nephew was born right before Christmas break, and when I went home, there was a little label above the doorbell warning people not to wake him," he shares, opening a straw on his jeans with his free hand, and poking it through the slot on the lid. His eyes meet mine. "I didn't knock in case your little was sleepin'."

Something thwacks behind my ribs, and I shift on my feet. "That was thoughtful of you."

"That's the second time you've told me that."

I'm not sure what to say, so I'm glad when he pushes the cup toward me. "Try it out, Tutor Girl. Tell me if it's no good no more."

Reaching for the cup, I wrap my hand around the thick Styrofoam and his is so large, my fingers slightly overlap his. He shows no sign of letting go, so I lean forward, taking a small drink, and then another long, full one.

Tobias chuckles, and I look to him, my palm quickly coming up when a drop of liquid rolls over my lips. "Still to your liking?"

I grin, accepting the cup when he finally does pass it over. "I'm not picky."

"Good to know." His smirk is deep.

I shake my head, sneaking a quick look at my front door.

"You need to go in?"

I nod. "Saturdays are my only full day at home, or usually, I should say. Normally I work at night when Bailey goes to bed, but I swapped today."

"Bailey," he repeats. "That's her name?"

My stomach muscles clench and I nod. I don't know why I told him any of that. It's not like he cares.

"That's good you swapped, one less day you'll try walking home alone after dark." He flashes his perfect teeth and I can't help but laugh.

"Do you usually get up as early as you were up today?" I ask what I've been wondering.

He nods, unable to hide his grin and I know exactly why.

I just admitted to thinking of him.

"Every day like clockwork. My days are seventeen hours of grinding, Tutor Girl."

"That's tiring."

"So is a baby, I imagine."

I lick my lips, fighting off the warmth sweeping through me. "Yeah, it is sometimes." I look to my front door and back to him. "I should go."

"Yeah, you should," he agrees, running back to his truck and coming back with what he said, a half-eaten pizza. "For you, Miss Sanders."

My frown is instant, but I smile through it. "Thank you, Tobias."

"Anytime, Tutor Girl."

He climbs into his truck, and as he slowly rolls

backward, he leans on his arm out the window.

His blue eyes shine in the sun, and he slips his hat off his head, tossing it in the seat beside him. "See you tomorrow."

"Two o'clock sharp."

He grins, shifts into drive, and says, "I'll be here" and then he takes off.

It's after he's gone and I'm digging my keys from my bag that I realize what he said.

Here.

Tomorrow at two o'clock sharp, Tobias Cruz will be *here*.

My stomach flips and I have a feeling it's not only nerves.

Not good.

DIRTY CURVE

CHAPTER 16

Bianca called at seven this morning to tell me she woke up sick and didn't want to risk passing it on to Bailey. She said she'd be here if I needed her, but it was up to me.

The last thing I want is for Bailey to get sick again, or for Bianca to have to care for her when she feels like death, as she put it, so it was a no-brainer.

I told her not to worry, that I'd be fine, and then I remembered Tobias.

Now it's one thirty-five and I'm anxious.

He'll be here in twenty-ish minutes and I'm considering waking Bailey up, putting her in the stroller and walking who knows where. Park, maybe?

Or we could go to the farmer's market downtown? It's gorgeous out so that could be relaxing.

My phone goes off and I'm half hoping it's Tobias canceling.

It is Tobias, but he's not canceling.

He's here.

Crapola.

Tobias

Stepping out of the truck, I meet Meyer at her front door.

She's uneasy, that's obvious, and I kind of figured she would be. So, I drop my bag at my feet, and pull out the lawn blanket I stuffed inside. "It's nice out, want to sit out here on the grass?"

She stares a long moment, and then her chin falls with a soft laugh. "There's a small patio in the back, I think we'll be more comfortable out there."

"I think you're right." I grin.

She shuffles back, her lips twitching nervously as I slip by.

I know she's waiting for me to look around and scope the place out, so I make it a point not to, and instead glance over my shoulder while pointing at the sliding glass door.

She nods, so I glide the thing open, wincing when it squeals. My eyes fly to hers.

"She's not *that* light of a sleeper," she teases, walking over to push it the rest of the way.

Grinning, I step out onto the patio.

The ground is cement and the wood enclosure is old, but it's high so nobody can see over, which is good to know. She has two mismatched sofa chairs pushed against each other, and a round table in front of them, an old coffee cup sitting on top.

"Oh." She squeezes her body by mine, quickly grabbing it and dusting off a couple stray leaves from the overhanging tree. "Sorry," she mumbles, and when she looks up, she gasps.

It's low and unintentional, but the good kind always are.

She's close and she didn't realize it, but she likes it, even if she hasn't grasped that little fact yet.

She will.

"We can move the chairs. I push them together sometimes."

She spins, nudging one back with her knee, but I reach past her, holding it still, and her eyes meet mine over her shoulder.

"Leave it. Might make it easier to work together."

She stands frozen, only moving when a door is slammed somewhere close by and jolts her from what I hope was an X-rated thought of yours truly.

She clears her throat, stretching her body as straight as she's able in an attempt to slip by without brushing against me, but she's only half successful. Her chest's too full to be hidden in any way, so it glides along mine with her escape.

I drop into one of the seats, pulling my laptop out and it's not long before she's falling in the chair beside me, her computer in hand.

She drags the table in the middle more and opens up my course lists. "You coming over worked out for me today," she says, and we look to each other. "Bianca woke up sick, so I wouldn't have been able to meet you. I would have had to cancel."

My eyes narrow, and I lean forward on my elbows. "You almost did, didn't you?"

She nods.

"Why?"

"If she wakes up from her nap while you're here, your time will be cut short."

"You'd make me leave?"

Her frown is instant, as if she's confused by my question. "You'd want to stay?"

"My calendars clear, Tutor Girl. You're all that's on it today."

At first, I think she might grow uneasy, put her professional cap back on, but she doesn't.

She kicks off her slippers, folds her legs in the chair, and turns to her computer screen, but it only takes her a total of two minutes to realize all my work is already done.

She looks to me with a single brow raised and a side squashed smile.

I can't help but laugh. "To be fair, I finished it after our last session so I could focus on the game."

"Well, don't think you're getting off that easy, you still have tests we can study for."

I playfully groan, sinking farther in the chair, and she knocks her elbow into mine.

"Come on, hotshot. You may know all there is to know about baseball, but you've got a lot to learn about vessels and veins." She hides her smile, pulling out the notes she tucked neatly into my binder last week, and begins going over it from back to front.

A half hour in the walkie-talkie thing she brought out beeps.

Meyer's eyes slice to mine, tension building behind them as a quiet little croon follows.

To make it easy on her, I go to stand, but her hand comes up, hesitantly covering mine on the armchair, and my blood runs warm under her soft touch.

Without thinking, I flip my wrist, so her palm is lying in mine.

"I ..." She trails off, now focused on the contact. "She'll want to eat right away."

"Sounds like me when I wake up." She looks to me once more. "Can I help?"

"When I'm home, she won't take a bottle." Meyer fights a grin, and my eyes fall to her chest.

Not fake, but full. *Literally.*

"Right."

She laughs, her muscles loosening before me. "Sometimes it takes a little while."

"I've got nowhere to be."

With a deep breath, she nods and pushes to her feet.

I want her to be at ease, comfortable and here with her little one. That's why I came over today instead of meeting her at the library, so I try to think of something.

"I could make us something while you feed her?"

"There's not much in there right now." A hint of pink colors her cheeks and she averts her gaze. "I haven't gone to the store in a while."

"So, I'll run home." I shrug. "I've got chicken out

already and a jar of my mom's salsa verde. You got a stove in there?" I jerk my head.

She nods.

"Then we're good. I'll go to my house and you ..." I stand as she has. "Will you answer the door when I get back?"

"I'll consider it," she teases, a flash of delight in her eyes.

"Nah." I step closer, and her slender neck stretches, allowing her to keep those eyes on mine. "You'll do it, wanna know why?"

"Why?"

"Cause I'm gonna ring the doorbell over and over until you do."

"Good luck with that," she plays in a whisper. "Because it doesn't work."

A laugh slips from me and I curl my body around hers, taking backward steps toward the door. Right as I reach it, that soft croon turns into a cackled little cry. "Go feed your girl, little mama."

I spin and walk out.

I'll be back to feed mine.

And I am.

Exactly forty minutes later, I'm on her front porch.

I go to ring the doorbell, to see if she was messing with me or not, but before I can, the door is slowly tugged open. Meyer stands there, her baggy sweater gone, and arms full.

Her eyes meet mine, a hint of nervousness surrounding her, but she offers a side smile. She slides back, giving me space to enter, and nods her head toward the kitchen, but I don't move ahead.

I pause a foot in the door, set my bags by my feet and take a step closer to her.

She stands perfectly still, the palm on her little's back gliding higher with my advance.

I hold her gaze as I lift my hand, and when it meets soft skin, my eyes fall to her daughter.

She's yet to lift her head from her mama's chest, but the moment she feels my fingers brush against her own, she blindly wraps hers around mine. She instantly waves our hands up and down.

A grin builds on my face, a low chuckle following. "She's quick."

I briefly look to Meyer, but only for a moment because the sound of my voice startles the little one, and her tiny body flails.

She seeks out the source of the sound.

Right then, bright blue eyes framed in long dark lashes meet mine and they don't look away. She stares right at me.

"What's up, little one?"

Bailey buries her face in her mama's chest, but as quickly as she does, she brings those baby blues back, and this time with a gummy smile.

My laugh is low and when Meyer's follows, my gaze lifts to meet hers.

"She's cute as hell," I tell her, grabbing my bags off the ground. Licking my lips, I pull my bottom one between my teeth, but my grin sets it free. "Just like her mama."

Meyer looks down and I hit the kitchen.

Pulling everything out of the bag, I glance over my

shoulder, knowing Meyer is still standing in the doorway, watching.

"You good with a little spice, or should I go easy on the sauce?"

"You cooked it already?" Bailey's hand comes up, tapping against Meyer's chin.

"I did."

Her smile softens, but she kisses Bailey's forehead to hide it. "I like a lot of spice." She tells me as she walks away.

Tell me fucking more ...

I squeeze my eyes shut and give my head a little shake.

Not the time.

Serving us up a heavy plate, I step from the kitchen into the living room.

I didn't allow myself a look at her place before, but this time I peek around.

The space is small, just big enough for a loveseat and TV stand, but there's a few doors on the left wall that must be bedrooms of some sort since there's no bed or crib in here. She's got a little play mat set up on the carpet in front of the couch, little toys hanging from the bendy things on top of it and that's it. It's clean and neat and she's done with it what she's able.

"Do you mind eating out here?" Meyer asks.

There was no table or even room for one in the kitchen, and I'm betting she doesn't want to call attention to that by us taking a seat inside, not that I'd argue against eating outdoors.

I prefer the sun any day, so I tell her that, dropping

into the free chair at her side, Bailey propped up on her bent knees.

She thanks me and we eat in silence for a few minutes. "You cooked at home to give me time with her."

I drop my grin to my bowl, taking another bite.

It's true.

When I got home, I changed into some sweats and a sleeveless, grabbed everything I needed, but only twelve minutes had passed, so yeah. I decided to cook there instead to kill time in case she needed it.

The baby makes a gurgling sound and Meyer gives her a big, cheesy smile; her fork held halfway to her mouth. She turns to me mid-chew. "You said your mom made the sauce?"

I nod. "She's a hell of a cook."

"I was going to say, this is really good." She takes another bite. "Are you ... is this where you're from or does she mail you things?"

I clear my throat, glancing up at the fading sun. "Nah, I'm from San Luis Obispo, a good four hours away. I've only been home a couple times since freshman year, but when I do, I never come back empty-handed."

"That's sweet."

"Yeah." My limbs tighten, but I stretch through it and turn the conversation to her. "How about you? Where you from?"

"Uh." She looks away. "Here originally, but I was raised in a little dirt town in Nevada. The kind where everyone knows everyone, and nobody gets out."

My bowl cleared, I set it down and lean back in the chair. "Looks like you did."

A sense of sorrow washes over her and she looks to Bailey, who bites on her little fingers in her lap. "It doesn't count until real life begins."

"Real life," I repeat, leaning forward to gain the baby's attention. Her blue eyes meet mine and her arms lift, all to slap back onto Meyer's legs. I chuckle, tapping my fingertips on her belly and earning another little grin.

"I think she's as real as it gets, Tutor Girl."

Meyer and I look at each other.

Her eyes move between mine, but she quickly drops them to her daughter, so I shift the subject.

"Bianca, she helps you out a lot?"

"God yes." She nods. "The child development center does have a day care I take her to when I'm tutoring, which is amazing. The program here is one of the best in the area, so I guess I lucked out there, but they close at six. After hours is when Bianca comes over and stays with her. I'd be screwed without her." A soft cry leaves Bailey and so Meyer lifts her, laying her across her shoulder.

I watch as she gently begins to pat her back, rubbing small circles after every few taps.

"So ... no other family around to help out or ..."

Meyer's hand freezes mid-pat, her body tensing slightly, but slowly, she eases once more.

Her eyes move to mine and I know she knows what I was thinking.

Does her baby girl have a man in her life, a father? Someone else who loves and lives for her like her mother does?

I want to know.

"I have a brother," is what she whispers.

It takes effort not to frown, but I manage to hold it back.

"A brother." I nod, lifting a brow. "Now the batting makes sense."

A nervous chuckle escapes her. "Yeah, he plays for a smaller school a few hours away, but just for fun. He tries to help, but I don't let him. He's in school too, and that's what he needs to focus on. He'd kill me if he heard me say that, though." She laughs again. "You said you have a brother?"

My frown is instant and I look away. "Yeah. He's ... what men are made of, I guess."

"And what's that?"

I shrug, flipping my phone in my lap. "Good at everything he does. Not a bad bone in his body, not a selfish or egotistical one either." Dropping my head back, I squash a sigh. "The kind that goes out of his way to please but not for notoriety, but because his conscience meter is set to perfection."

"Kind of like what you're doing for Joe and Franny?"

My lips curve the smallest bit, and I move my eyes to hers.

Her smile is small, as if she gets it, as if she understands what it's like to work toward one thing but forever being seen as another.

Less than.

Or maybe I'm being a bitch and am making up the curiosity that's softened her eyes.

Bailey begins rubbing at her eyes, and I wonder, "Is she getting tired?"

Meyer nods. "Normally she's up for another hour but she didn't nap long today so who knows how the night will go now."

As I look over again, Bailey's eyes find mine, growing heavier by the second, but she doesn't fuss or cry. She tucks her hands in and lets them close, and something inside me grows warm.

Every couple minutes, they pop back open, but eventually her little fingers relax and her breathing grows steady.

"I think she's sleeping," I whisper.

When Meyer doesn't respond, I look up to find her watching me, a distant look in her eyes. "Meyer."

She blinks, refocusing. "Hm?"

"She's asleep."

Meyer nods, slowly pushing to her feet as she mouths, 'be right back.'

I use the time to put our bowls back into my bag, while grabbing my other one and making my way back out to the patio, but when I round the corner, Meyer is standing at the foot of the couch, preparing to sit.

"I had to put the monitor on the charger and it's getting a little too cold to keep the door open." Her lips tighten, and she holds a hand out. "The heater's kind of pathetic, so ..."

I'm nodding before she finishes and drop down with my bag in my hand before she does herself.

"Right," she whispers, reaching for her laptop, but I dart a hand out to keep her from grabbing it, and her eyes fly to mine.

I pull out the book I borrowed from Echo's collection, placing it into her hands instead.

Slowly, she takes it, confusion blanketing her face.

"I hear it's not good to overstudy."

She chuckles, glancing at the cover once more. I think she's trying to decide how she's supposed to feel or react, but what she doesn't realize is her mind's decided for her.

The girl's already settled more into her seat, and the grin on her face is one of anticipation. "This book's been read before." She looks to me expectantly.

"Stole it from my roommate, he's got a good two dozen where that came from." My eyes roam over her profile. "When's the last time you read for fun?"

Meyer shrugs.

"Read to me, Tutor Girl."

She scoffs a laugh, but when I don't follow, she pauses to study me. I want to grab her by the waist and pull her into me, feel her ass against my lap while staring into her eyes as they come closer. Grow darker.

Watch her come undone and be the one to make it happen.

But I can't, at least not yet, so I say it again, "Read to me, Tutor Girl."

She chews on that lower lip of hers, and in the next moment, cracks the thing open. "Chapter One."

Avix Inquirer:

Trusted Readers, we need your help!
Word on the street is our Playboy
Pitcher is 'playing' a little less,
but we're not buying it.
Find him, Sharks ... I dare you.

CHAPTER 17

Tobias

"Now that was a fucking game!" Neo shouts, banging his hands against the metal lockers. "You served them their ass, Cruz!"

I smirk, tossing my jersey into the laundry bucket. "You thought not?"

Neo laughs, turning to X.

"And my boy here with that hard ninety!" He lifts him onto his shoulder. "We're gonna show them Cal Poly boys how real coastal boys play ball!"

The team grows rowdy, shouting while stomping the ground and slapping the metal in front of them.

"Let's get through this next series, then we pity the poor punks who have us coming at 'em next."

"Don't shit on our parade, Cruz, just 'cause you're bailing on it again."

"Have one for me, huh?"

"I'll have two for you, my man."

Echo steps up then, leisurely tugging his jersey

over his head. "You really not coming out with us again tonight?"

"Nah, man. Can't."

He raises a brow. "Can't or don't want to?"

"Both?"

He laughs, shoving at me. "Just be careful, my man. For your sake and hers."

"Heard, my man."

He jerks his chin, heading off toward the showers, and I'm out.

I round the corner, digging my phone from my pocket.

"Where you running off to in such a hurry?"

My shoes squeak against the freshly polished floor, and I jerk my head right to find Coach leaning against the door to the equipment room. "Tutoring, Coach."

He looks to the clock on the wall, slowly sliding back to mine. "You know your grades fell in two classes according to Friday's check-in, but the books show you had double the sessions last week ... you sure you're getting your times' worth?"

"Yes, Coach, I am."

Squinting, he nods. "I take it Meyer's not giving you any more problems?"

"Nah." My lips curve. "She's coming around."

Slowly, but more and more every time.

"She must have, being it's after nine and you two have an appointment." He tips his head, eyeing me.

"Hey" —I toss my keys up in the air, catching them in my open palm— "you said take all the time I want, right?"

"I said take all the time you *need*."

My forehead pinches with a slight frown, but I laugh it off when his grin slips, and he pushes off the wall.

"Glad you're dedicated, son." His hand comes up, clamping onto my shoulder. "After UNR, we've got a tough team coming, and midterms will follow."

A thought hits and I spin to face him. "About that ..."

Meyer

Tobias gets set, sending the ball flying into the fence that's just over sixty feet away before bending to pick up another. He cuts me a glance over his shoulder, grinning when he catches me watching. "How much longer do we have?"

I tug my fingers free from Bailey's and tap on my phone screen. "Ten minutes to pack up, twenty until I have to be at the school."

He nods, goes back to throwing the ball a few more times before rushing to clean up his mess.

My hands holding hers, Bailey stands in my lap, jumping lightly on her feet and making little screaming sounds just to hear her own voice.

As Tobias comes back, he dusts his hands on his jeans and reaches over, lifting her into his arms and up over his head. He carries her over to his bag, bending to reach inside, and pulls out a ball. Holding it out in front of her, he says something I can't hear, and her little hands find their way to it. Straight into her mouth it goes.

Tobias laughs, but his head quickly snaps my way. "It's a toy one, can't hurt her," he rushes out.

My smile is slow, but I quickly turn away, pouring my focus into packing up my things.

A tingling sensation sweeps through my arms and legs.

He thought of her when he wasn't with me, as he did when he knew she existed for a whole five seconds. As he did last week when he went out in search of this park. It's a few miles from campus, full of shaded trees and an empty field, a place he can get some practice that allows me quiet time with her, and a little schoolwork mixed in, as he put it.

And then there was last night.

He insisted on picking me up from work, and when he did, he had a pizza from Franny and Joe's with him, hoping to get to stick around for a little while. I couldn't, didn't want to tell him no, but when we got there, Bailey heard me come in and woke up. He knew my time was short with her earlier that day, so without my saying a word, he walked back out the door. It took some convincing, but I got him to agree to take his pizza with him. Of course, he texted me ten minutes later and told me he left it on the porch and Franny would be upset if I let it go to waste.

All I could do was smile at the screen, as I find myself doing every time I think of him.

My body grows weighted and warm.

To the others on campus and every other person who bet on what the media claims, he's the Playboy Pitcher with a one-track mind, loose belt and looser morals. The egomaniac who thrives on press and publicity, and yeah, he might be some of those things.

He might be all of those things, Meyer.

My throat grows thick, and I swallow past the offset tethering of dread and hope.

He might be all of those things.

He might go out, taking all he's offered, and he's offered a lot. It's no secret girls chase bragging rights. A gold mine.

A good time.

I did.

He might be everything people say.

Glancing over my shoulder, my eyes find him and Bailey.

He's got her in one arm, his glove and ball bucket in the other as he walks to his truck. He sets his things in the back, and then his free hand goes right back to her.

He lets her push the ball toward his mouth and plays along as she wants, fake biting it and tapping her head with the bill of his hat.

She lets go of the ball, forcing him to catch it before it falls and her hand flies up to his hat, slapping it down and into his eyes.

His laugh is loud, and I feel it in my stomach.

He might be those things.

He might be mine.

Tobias spins his hat, so it now sits on his head backward, and then that perfectly crooked grin is pointed at me.

I'm not sure what my face looks like, but suddenly his grin loosens, his body turning so it's parallel to mine, and he keeps moving forward.

His steps are slow and as he grows closer, he gently lowers Bailey onto the blanket we left sitting on the grass before I moved us up here to feed her.

He hops over the railing with ease, staying one row in front of the one I chose, and when he pulls his bottom lip between his teeth, every nerve ending in my body fires off.

His bicep flexes as he reaches forward, gliding my hair from my eyes with his pinky.

"Come to my game."

I swallow and he lifts his left knee, placing it on the plastic seat in front of me.

"That's not a good idea."

His body leans over, his hands coming down to grip the bleacher chair at my sides, and after a brief glance back at Bailey, he brings his face within inches of mine.

"I wanna look up from my place on the mound and see you sitting there, watching me ... rooting for me." His focus falls to my lips and his tongue comes out to lick his own. His blue eyes flick up to mine. "Come to my game, Tutor Girl."

My stomach hollows, my grip tightening on the armrest. "I'm sorry, I can't."

He tries not to show it, but creases form along his brow and he gives a curt nod. "Yeah," he pushes up, bending to grab my bag and Bailey's car seat, "just thought if you had extra time or something. It's all good. You can't get paid during a game, right?"

My brows crash. "That's not it."

"It's all good, Tutor Girl." He cuts me a quick grin, but it's fake and his eyes are empty. "Let's get you to the school, huh?"

Left with nothing else to do, I nod, pick up Bailey and strap her into her seat while he shoves the blanket on the floorboard.

We're back at the school in minutes, and he's gone just as fast.

Tobias doesn't call me that night.

The next evening rolls around, and I'm leaving a late session at the library when I find myself passing a group of girls who must have just come from the game ... the game he asked me to go to. They're decked out from head to toe in Avix baseball attire, numbers painted on their cheeks, and ribbons curled into their hair. They're smiling and laughing, having enjoyed their Friday night under the stadium lights.

I keep past them, but slow when one of the girls asks, "think Tobias will be there tonight?"

"He'll go if Vivian tells him to," another teases.

The tall, long-legged blonde laughs. "That ship has sailed, honey."

"Please, all you have to do is call him."

"Yeah, do it for the greater good," another girl jokes.

"You guys, we've never been about date nights," Vivian jokes.

Her friends laugh and suddenly the air feels thick, so I quicken my steps home.

Bianca has a date tonight, so she's kissing my cheek and running out the door only minutes after I walk through it.

Bailey is asleep and Bianca said she woke to eat no more than an hour ago, so she won't be up again until three or four in the morning, depending.

I have no schoolwork to do since I stayed up most of the night jamming through it, and I've already arranged my schedule for next week. Quickly glancing at the clock, I decide to try my brother since I missed his call, not only this morning, but last night too, unfortunately, once again we play phone tag, and his voice mail is all I get.

A long sigh pushes past my lips and I drag myself to my feet. Baby monitor and blanket in hand, I step out onto the back patio, fall into the chair, and peek up at the darkening sky.

Friday nights look a lot different than they used to, not that I was ever much for partying, but I would go out on occasion, and sometimes it was fun.

I wonder if that Vivian girl did what her friends wanted and called Tobias.

I wonder if they did, too.

There's nothing that says he didn't go out on his own.

I flip my phone over in my hand, wiping at the smear on the screen.

My fingers are itching to text him, an annoying need to know what he's up to making my skin itch. I could always text him a quick congratulation on yet another win, see what he says ...

Screw it.

I text him, and the moment I hit send, I shrink in my chair, my hands coming up to cover my face.

God, Meyer. Pathetic.

It's not like a text will tell me if he's out and so what if he is! He can be.

I don't want him to be.

Covering my mouth with the blanket, I groan, squeezing my eyes shut.

"What the hell are you doing, Meyer?" I chastise myself.

Don't be dumb—

My phone beeps and a breath lodges in my throat.

My chest grows warm with unease and excitement, things that don't go together but are equally felt.

Chewing on my lip, I grab my phone, opening it to read his message.

Tobias: I'm a beast, Tutor Girl. You should know this by now.

A laugh leaves me, and I fall back into the chair as a second message comes through.

Tobias: What you don't know is I have a giant bag of caramel corn the vendor lady stashed for me and the password to my boy's Netflix.

Anticipation swirls low in my stomach, creating an unsteady sensation as I wait for more, unwilling to dare and read between the lines because I know I don't have to. Tobias never beats around the bush and his next text proves it.

Tobias: What do you say, Tutor Girl? Will you open the door for me?

My skin tingles and I text him back a quick yes, and

not ten seconds later, my phone rings, his name flashing across the screen.

I answer, but he speaks before I can.

"Open up, Tutor Girl."

I dart up in my seat, my head snapping around to stare at the front door. "You're here?"

"I'm here."

He's here.

He was already on his way.

Standing, I head for the door, pulling it open with the phone still held to my ear, and when I do, my pulse flips.

He's still in his uniform, black eye paint still drawn along his cheekbones, hat still pointed forward and hiding half his face, but his eyes shine regardless.

"You can hang up now," he says into his phone, that is also still held to his ear.

A nervous laugh leaves me and I drop it, stepping back to allow him inside.

"Mind if I change real fast? I left quick to beat out the news crew. Figured if I stayed, you'd be sleeping by the time I got here."

"Not if you had told me you were coming."

"Didn't want to give you a chance to tell me no." He grins, disappears into the bathroom, and steps out not two minutes later.

"Think we can pull out the bed so we have more room?" He looks to me as he picks the remote up from the side table. "You do that and I'll get us all signed in?"

I nod, doing as he suggested and not five minutes later, we're pressing play.

I must have fallen asleep at some point, because when I wake, it's to Bailey's soft cries. The clock reads three thirty, and the space beside me is empty.

Tobias went home.

Pulling myself into a sitting position, I wipe my hands down my face and toss the blanket I don't remember covering myself with, but then I hear him.

My head snaps left to right as Tobias steps into the hall. Bailey held tight against his bare chest.

My heart beats double time as he comes closer, a tired smile on his handsome face.

"Someone woke up," he whispers, his focus on her. "Ain't that right, Bailey Bay?"

My heart pounds against my rib cage and I can't look away from him.

Not as he reaches me, still fixated on her, and not as he climbs onto the bed beside me. He gently places her in my arms, and only once she's secure does he look up.

"Was that okay?" he worries, his blue eyes roaming my face.

I don't trust myself to speak, so I nod, and he settles into his spot, but he doesn't look away.

He knows why she's woken, and he's silently begging I don't ask him to go.

I don't want him to go.

I shift my baby girl in my arms and lift my shirt up over my left breast so she can latch on. Once she does, her hand comes up, as it always does, so I tug my hair free of the scrunchie and allow it to fall the way she likes it. Instantly, her little fingers glide into it, holding on with gentle ease.

Tobias's soft chuckle heats my neck, and my skin flushes.

With a deep breath, I face Tobias, and our eyes lock once more.

Completely in sync, both of our heads lower onto the couch cushions we're sitting up against.

A few moments pass, his blinks grow heavier, and then his fingers fold into mine.

Tobias falls back asleep and I sit there, tracing over his every feature.

At first glance, he looks the part of the rough and rugged ball player.

His hair is kept short and he's never past the point of stubble. His smirk is ever present, his walk is more of a lazy strut, and his body a testament to long hours of hard work. He's tall and confident, with flirty eyes and a cocky smile, but what you don't see by simply looking is the softness he holds. Tobias has a kind heart he can't deny, but doesn't allow others to take advantage of. He doesn't give the media the attention they crave, he brushes everything off one shoulder and squares the other.

He focuses on nothing but what he needs to advance in the areas in his life he feels are worthy of his efforts and he doesn't let anything get in his way.

It's admirable.

He is admirable and hardworking.

I've met my fair share of athletes now and while they all have a varying degree of commitment to their craft, his is unmatched.

He's constantly working to get better, pushing himself harder, and taking every step he's capable of to grow.

He's up before dawn, working out and tossing the ball around, all to do it again once his team is there to join him, and he repeats it later in the day in the form of a game or two-a-day practices. If he's not doing that, he's watching film and studying his opponents, pinpointing their weaknesses, and forming a game plan to use against them. He memorizes their every twist and turn, the way they point their toes or grip their bat, the degree in which they swing off every pitch along with their hit to miss ratio.

How he has room in his head for school I'll never know, but he gets done what he needs to and steps out onto the field strong every game.

It's true what they say on the news.

Tobias is baseball.

It's his life and it will continue to be, just as he deserves.

Come this time next year, he'll be gone, that's no secret, so what's the point of spilling mine?

CHAPTER 18

Meyer

The moment I step from the child development center, I jolt to a stop.

"Jesus." My hand flies to my chest, and I glare. "What are you doing here?"

"Not even a hello for me, hm?"

"Hello, boss." I fold my arms. "What are you doing here?"

He eyes me a long moment, before his chin lifts. "I moved all your appointments for the next two days around."

I frown. "Why? I don't have any of your players until Thursday evening."

"Because we don't get back until Wednesday night, but it's midterms for them straight away.

"I don't get it."

"Go home, pack your bag, be at the athletic department by four tonight. You'll ride with the equipment team to Cal Poly."

My face falls. "What ride?"

"My star player has requested his tutor to join him on the road this week since his grades are barely hanging on, says he needs all the extra help he can get before midterms." His eyes narrow. "Wonder why he thinks you would agree to that?"

My head throbs instantly. "Maybe he knows the choices aren't technically mine ... but you told him, no," I add, sure. Of course, he did.

He sticks his hands in his pocket, his frown deepening. "While you're on the road, your sessions will be virtual. I've already let the students know."

"What ... no. I can't."

"Why not?"

I gape at him. "Are you serious? Just because you're ashamed of me and my life doesn't mean I don't have one to manage."

His gaze darts away but comes right back, and I get the sense this isn't something he's okay with, but baseball trumps all, as usual. "You'll get a travel bonus, one for you, and one to cover your sitter while you're gone."

A laugh bubbles out of me, but it's mocking.

He really thinks I would leave my daughter behind and travel hours away for two, three days?!

I don't say it out loud, but something has his eyes narrowing, searching mine.

I hate the way he looks at me.

Clearing my throat, I stand tall. "I can't just pick up and go. I have another job I need to be at tomorrow night. Thanks to you, I can't afford to lose it by calling out."

"At that diner, right?"

My head tugs back. "It's not your concern."

He scoffs and begins to walk away. "Call your boss and make it happen. Full details are in your inbox."

I look to the screen on my phone with a growl, and shout back, "I didn't get an email!"

He glances over his shoulder, his eyes meeting mine. "Might have sent it to your personal one by mistake."

My chest weighs heavy, but I don't show it.

I unlock my phone and plan to send a text to Tobias, telling him to be prepared for me to chew him out, but I pause, going to my emails instead.

I skim the information, my eyes bulging when I get to the bonus information listed.

They're offering a thousand dollars a day, plus room and meal vouchers at the hotel. On top of that, another twenty-five hundred for childcare.

Suddenly I no longer feel the need to argue, so I hit ignore when Tobias calls not two minutes later, likely having already heard, his beloved coach delivering the news.

This will cover me and leave me with a little extra for the next few months.

With a deep breath and a smile on my face, I walk right back into the day care center to sign out my baby girl.

I'm back home within thirty minutes, packing for the trip I was coerced into taking when there's a knock at my door.

I'm expecting Bianca, but right behind her is Tobias, in all his sweatpants and sleeveless glory, with a box of bagels in his hand.

"Be warned, there's a naughty man in Nike coming in hot," she singsongs as she pushes through the door. "And he comes with carbs."

Behind her, Tobias wiggles his brows, but I shake my head, running back into the living room to pick up the dirty clothes off the floor.

On my way home, I called Bianca to tell her about the trip and the bonus and like I knew she would, she asked if she could stay at the apartment for some downtime and told me to claim that sitter fee for myself. So, I am. Bailey won't be staying behind, but the school doesn't have to know that.

Bianca tosses her bags on the floor and hops right up on the bed, crawling up to Bailey. "Auntie B is here, baby B!" She smiles down at her and Bailey grins, sticking her fingers in her mouth. "Tell your mama to let you stay with me."

Bailey makes a cooing sound and Bianca laughs.

"Tell your auntie B she's lost her mind."

Bianca and Tobias both chuckle and as if she recognizes his voice, Bailey's head snaps to the left.

She searches the room and when he gets closer, his knees hitting the metal of the fold-out bed, she lets out a little squeal. Her legs start to kick, and her arms begin to wiggle.

"Well at least someone's excited to see me," he teases as he drops his fist onto the bed and lowers his upper body, letting her reach up for his hat with fumbled movements. "Hi Bailey Bay, you ready for a road trip?"

My stomach muscles clench and I go back to stacking onesies in the diaper bag.

Sensing Bianca's eyes on me, I cut her a quick

glance. She gives nothing away, but I know her. She wants to smile as much as she wants to scowl.

Same girl. This, whatever it is, is scary.

Tobias picks up on something and looks from her to me as he stands, but Bianca makes sure no tension is created by reaching over to snag the box he set on the arm of the couch. "So he comes unannounced and bearing gifts." She bites into a blueberry bagel, speaking with her mouth full. "My guess is he has something to say."

"He should have a whole lot to say, considering I'm packing a bag for a trip I didn't know I was going on."

Tobias chuckles, looking to me with a giant grin. "Sorry about that."

"Uh-huh." My eyes narrow. "Your smile is too big. Spill."

It grows deeper. "Bus driver owes me a favor, team coordinator, too."

"K..."

"They're counting me on my bus, counting you on your bus, and *we* are driving up together tonight. I got a rental."

My face falls and Tobias's excitement dwindles.

"Tobias, Coach Reid won't—"

"Fuck him," Bianca snaps, catching herself mid eye roll. "I mean ... who cares, right?"

Tobias frowns but keeps his attention on me. "He won't know. Him and Doc fly out tomorrow at noon, team leaves at eight. You'll be at check-in tonight; I'll meet them at the field mañana at two."

"So, you think you'll be staying in her room tonight, do you?" Bianca raises a brow.

His smirk is slow. "Like I said, the team coordinator owes me one."

"That's not a no." Bianca fights a smile and Tobias's grows.

I toss a diaper at her, and she tosses it into the bag with the others as she drags herself to her feet. "Hurry up and get out of here. I'm ready to have this place to myself, plus or minus one."

"The one better be Coop," Tobias teases.

She pauses at the bathroom door, spinning to face him with her hands on the frame. "Coop will be with you, four hours away." She smirks, closing herself in the bathroom.

Tobias turns to me.

"She told you that on purpose."

He chuckles, but his expression grows an anxious kind of excited.

"What?"

"Nothing."

"That was a quick nothing." My eyes narrow with suspicion, but Tobias only grins wider, spinning to my giant pile of 'must haves' it takes to travel with an infant.

He claps his hands and then starts loading us up. "Road trip here we come!"

"Okay, known for their materialistic society, the Lycurgus founded *who* around 800 BC?"

"AC/DC."

I laugh, falling back against the headboard.

"'Highway to Hell', 'Let There Be Rock', 'Back in Black'." He grins.

"Come on! That's the third one in a row you've missed. No more rock star knowledge! You have to get a ninety or better."

"Maybe I don't want to."

I roll my eyes, playing a quick game of peekaboo with Bailey as she tries to tug her foot to her mouth.

"For reals." He looks over. "Maybe I want as much Meyer time as I can get."

I shove him and he grins, pulling himself up beside me.

"We're already studying a ridiculous number of hours."

"Who said anything about studying?" he says in a light roar, lifting Bailey up so she can push off on her tiptoes.

"Right." I laugh. "Well, this little trip you forced me into did manage to give me my first full weekday off in forever."

"Oh, yeah? Does that mean you're coming to my game?" He smirks, but his tone is painfully hopeful.

I shake my head, and he looks away, but not before his frown takes over.

"I'm on the clock both days we're here, but I guess the school's required to give a twenty-four-hour leave after staff travel, so Thursday I'm free and I can't wait."

"Guess you should thank me for making this happen," Tobias jokes, teasing Bailey with the bill of his hat, and then tears it off quickly, but she doesn't care. Her hands still go right for his head, her little palms rubbing across the dark strands, and not a second later, she dips forward, attempting to bite him.

Tobias grins, pulling her back, and her eyes dart my way, going straight to the bun on top of my head. She jolts in again, ready to grab at it, but I lean back.

"Awe, come on, she wants yours now." He makes a pouty face, shimmying Bailey a bit. "Is she being mean, Bailey Bay?"

With a playful sigh, I pull my hair free, letting it fall around me, and Tobias wastes no time, blindly grabbing a long strand and holding it up, tickling and teasing her with it.

She tries to grab it, but he moves it just fast enough that she can't quite get it, and she begins jumping in his hold, smiling and giggling like crazy.

His chuckle is warm, and when my head turns to look at him, his follows. His blue eyes meet mine, a tenderness written within them. His mouth curves a little higher, but it's different than his usual grin, expressive in a way that makes my throat run dry.

But everyone gets in their feelings when an infant's smiling at them, and Bailey hasn't stopped.

She lets out a squeaky scream and a laugh leaves me.

My lips pull to one side. "She wants your attention back."

Tobias's eyes move between mine, and now his grin is full of conceit.

"Of course, she does." He gives her what she wants, focusing on her. "They all do." He leans forward, making ridiculous faces she seems to enjoy. "All but your ma, Bailey Bay."

My stomach leaps into my chest and he knows it, a mischievous chuckle escaping him.

I push his shoulder with mine before climbing off the bed as an excuse to face away, and walk over to my bag, pulling out a hairbrush. I sit on the vanity chair, brushing the tangles out of my hair since I just tore the hair tie from it. As I grab it all in my palms again, twisting to throw it right back up, my eyes shift in the mirror.

Tobias is propped against the pillows, half lying down and half sitting up, Bailey's chest on his. He's looking at something on his phone, his other arm wrapped around her lower back to make sure she doesn't roll off.

Bailey pats his jaw, squeezes his nose, and drags her hands down his face to pinch at his mouth. Tobias tips his chin, allowing her to explore the shape of him however she wishes, but that's not even the part that creates the ache in my chest. It's the way his lips pucker the slightest bit, as if he's pecking her fingers adoringly, if he even realizes it.

I don't think he does.

I think it's natural.

He likes her.

Right then, his eyes fly my way, instantly finding mine in the mirror, and my stomach dips.

He doesn't look away, and I'm not sure how long my hand stays frozen in the air, my hair half twisted up, but neither of us snaps out of it until Bailey begins to fuss.

Her bow slips off when she buries her head in his neck, and she begins rubbing her eyes as a fake little cry leaves her.

"I think someone's hungry, mama."

I nod, allowing my hair to fall back down, and his gaze follows the movements.

Tobias pushes to his feet and I spin on the vanity chair.

When he's taking his last step toward me, I finally remember to stand, reminding myself to breathe as I do.

He passes Bailey to me, but his hands don't fall to his side, but instantly reach forward, pushing my hair over my shoulder, his fingers lingering near my exposed collarbone.

His jaw flexes, his eyes lifting to mine as he brings one strand back, handing it to Bailey. "She likes to hold it when you feed her, right?"

Pressure falls on my ribs, but I manage to bob my head a little.

He's silent another moment, and then he steps back, jerking his chin toward his room. "I'm gonna take a shower, maybe order some room service after ..."

"K," I whisper.

I think he wants me to say more, to confirm I'm not going to bed or ask him to order me something too, but I can't bring myself to say another word, and so he heads into his room, pulling my conjoining door closed, but not all the way.

I settle onto the bed to feed Bailey, wondering what the hell I'm doing and fully aware I'm at the edge of no return.

I don't know what to do, but I know what I want to do, and it's not the morally correct option.

It's the selfish, lonely, hopeless one.

Tobias

"If she wakes up, we'll hear her. If not because she's ten feet away, then because of this." Meyer lifts the monitor up, shaking it.

I glare at the connecting door. "How effective are those things? 'Cause this is a giant hotel and there's another door that leads to that room."

"Two if you count the other side door."

My head swoops toward hers and Meyer laughs.

"Oh my god, the door is literally half open." She fights a grin when my glare deepens. "Okay, fine. I can turn this on, walk all the way to my garbage cans in the alley, and hear her on this just fine. I don't ... but I can. I tested it with Bianca's awful singing voice." She grins.

I lean back on the bed, peeking through the gap of the door.

"What are you doing?" she teases.

"If I lean back a little more" —my back stretches, my hands gripping the edge of the mattress— "I think I can see the edge of the playpen—oh shit!"

I slip off the edge of the fucking bed, my chips falling and spilling around me.

Meyer starts laughing her ass off, her hand coming up to cover her mouth.

"You better quit," I warn, but the girl laughs even

harder.

"Oh, you think it's funny, huh?" I grin.

She shakes her head, trying to get out an 'I'm sorry' but she can't stop laughing. Her palm drops to the comforter, so I quickly pull my shoulders off the ground, gripping her by the wrist.

I tug her toward me, catching her other wrist as she falls right on top of me. Her palms flatten on my chest, and she chuckles, nearly choking, but then her head lifts, her hair still loose and falling in front of her.

Her laughter dies on her lips, and she clears her throat.

I can see it in her eyes. She wants to flirt, but more than that, she wants to be flirted with.

And then she wants what follows.

The pull in her core, the heat between her legs, the kind that only burns deep with the touch of a man.

A man who wants her just as much.

What's holding you back, baby?

Her chin dips, and she peeks up at me through her lashes. "Mind if I use your shower, I don't want to wake her after the long ride today."

I nod, the idea of her naked in my room sending a jolt through me.

My dick thickens, hardening beneath her, so I quickly roll her onto her back, lifting my hips so they're no longer touching hers and before she can feel me grow.

I jump up, offering her my hand and smirking at the way her lips have parted. "Put your hand in mine, Tutor Girl."

A heady laugh leaves her and she does as I ask,

allowing me to tug her to her feet.

"Shower's all yours, Tutor Girl," I rasp, letting her go.

She slips into her room, quietly returning with some clothes and a grocery bag with her soaps in it. Her eyes slide to mine as she reaches the bathroom door, but she quickly pushes it open, closing herself inside.

The shower turns on, and I blow out a long breath, flopping onto my bed, looking up at the ceiling.

Fuck me, this girl.

I bang my head against the pillow, chuckling at the irony of the situation.

Me, Tobias Cruz, the tabloid playboy, shacked up in a hotel room with a girl I can't even beg to touch me. Of course she's the one I want to touch me.

I want her to step into that shower, and then call me in to join her, allowing me the pleasure of taking her dripping wet, of *making her* drip, I'd have her so wet.

So fired up.

She'd burn from the inside out, the way I do.

My gaze falls with my exhale, freezing when my eyes meet the long mirror on the wall ... directly across from the bathroom door, the *frosted* bathroom door.

Slowly, I push up as Meyer, on the other side of it, slips from her clothes.

I can't see her body, but the shape of her is clear, a perfect silhouette.

She's curvy and smooth and a perfect fucking woman.

And that woman stops moving, hesitating where she stands for who the hell knows what reason, and my body plays games on me, tenses and flexes and aches, anticipation fucking burning me at my core.

It only lasts for a moment though, and then the squeak of the shower door sounds, her figure disappearing as she steps inside.

My eyes close, and I tune into the sound of the water falling, to the way it pours harder and then softer, allowing me to create a visual of her exact movements in my head. Before I realize what I'm doing, my muscles lock up on me, my eyelids popping open to find my dick hard and in my hand.

My chest rises and falls rapidly, and I squeeze my shaft, desperate to ease the ache the mere thought of Meyer has created. I groan, pumping myself in my hand once, twice, and my head falls back.

I picture the hollow of her breasts and the width of her hips, of her perky ass and imagine the silky soft feeling of sliding between it.

My dick throbs, my breath hitching as I thrust into my hand, but then my body freezes and I jolt up, my hands flying to my head and rubbing along my face.

Too mortified to spin my body, I cut my eyes toward that second room where a little one sleeps.

Shame washes over me, and I dart toward the small, second sink, quickly splashing water on my face.

I smack my forehead as I grip the countertop, bending at the waist.

Dragging in a deep breath, I stand, spinning on my feet. Right as I do, the bathroom door swings open, and Meyer steps out.

And fuck me, an old T-shirt never looked so good. One that's too long for me to know what, if anything, is underneath.

Her hair is down and slung to one side over her chest, the tips dripping wet, right where her nipples are peeking through.

She jerks to a stop when she realizes I'm right here, no more than two feet in front of her, and those brown eyes of hers rise.

A nervous little laugh follows. "You scared me."

My fingers ache to touch her, to pull her closer, and I think she knows it, because the corner of her eyes crease the smallest bit.

She's afraid, but not of me, of what might happen next.

Her tongue pokes out, anxiously swiping across her lips, and suddenly I'm hard again.

"It's getting late, we should really get to bed," she barely whispers.

She has no idea the effectiveness her accidental tone holds, it's rich and throaty, sexy. An unintentional hint of her not so well-hidden desire.

She's feelin' me, and I want her to give in.

To take, 'cause, fuck me, I'm ready to give.

I'll give her anything she wants if she lays those lips on mine.

I'll do all the work. I just need her to make the move.

Make the move, baby...

She doesn't. Instead, turning her body so she can slip past me without so much as brushing me. But before she can disappear into her room, I spin, darting my hand out to grab ahold of her wrist, keeping her there.

I can't bring myself to turn toward her, not if dismissal is what I'll find, so while staring at the place she was, I say, "Tell me you like me."

When her wrist twitches in my palm, my eyes snap to meet hers, though my body remains facing away.

"Tobias ..." Her shoulders pinch.

"Just ..." Fuck. Now I do spin toward her, stepping in but not over the threshold of our connecting doors. "At least tell me you don't hate being here."

She softens before me. At her side, her hand begins reaching out for me, maybe even subconsciously, because at the last second she realizes it, lowering it right back to her side.

"I don't hate being here," she murmurs, her chin lowering as her eyes hold mine.

I don't miss the hint of color that's risen along her neck, or the way her toes begin to curl into the carpet beneath her feet.

My smirk is slow. "You *like* being here, don't you?"

Her laugh is husky and low, and a small grin now plays at her lips. "Good night, Hotshot."

I bite at mine, unwilling to take my eyes off of her. "'Night, Tutor Girl."

You'll be the star of my show tonight.

DIRTY CURVE

CHAPTER 19

Tobias

"Okay, what's wrong?" Meyer sets the textbook face down, careful not to lose the page we're on.

"It's almost eight."

"I know, I'm sorry, she usually falls back asleep by now." She glances over at her playpen, and little mama's eyes are just beginning to close. "Once she's out, this will go a little faster. We should have a least an hour uninterrupted."

"What, no." I pin her with a fixed expression. "That's not at all why I said that. If anything, she's keeping me from passing out from boredom."

A short laugh leaves Meyer. "Okay ..."

Fuck. Okay. "Any chance she'll be okay to sleep in her car seat again today, just for a short twenty-minute drive?"

She tips her head, suspicious.

"I don't have to be at the field for a few hours."

"I'm aware."

"Are you also aware that Poly is in San Luis Obispo?"

"Am I aware of what town I'm in right now? That would be a yes." She fights a grin. "What's up with you?"

I hold her gaze, and after a moment, hers widens.

She starts shaking her head, but I'm already nodding mine.

"Tobias, no."

"Come on."

"No way."

"Please, you just said you were hungry, but room service sucks. This is free breakfast."

"I don't—"

"I need a reason to leave soon after arriving," flies from my mouth before I can even fucking think, and now Meyer's looking at me warily. I shrug. "Help me out, Tutor Girl?"

She chews on her lip, looking to Bailey, and when her eyes come back to mine, I know I've got her.

To my parents we go.

God fucking speed.

Meyer

As we pull up in front of a quaint little home just a mile up from the ocean, nerves begin to prickle my skin.

This isn't a good idea. In fact, it's horrible.

They're going to get the wrong idea.

I have a child and I'm coming here with their son, a man who's a few months away from no less than a million-dollar contract, and that's being insanely humble. If the simple sight of me doesn't scream gold digger, I don't know what does.

"Maybe this is a bad idea." I turn to him, but I'm a little taken aback when I find the same tense expression written along his brows. "Tobias?"

"We could find a diner somewhere instead?" he says, looking from the home to me. "I could tell her that I ran out of time or ..." He sighs, dropping his head back against the seat.

I don't get the chance to say anything else and our window to pull away is gone as right then the front door opens and a dark-haired woman, maybe late fifties, reveals herself on the other side.

Tobias looks to me, anxiousness drawing creases along his forehead.

As I said, this is likely an awful idea, but it's not like we're a couple and this is a big step.

It's not like there's a deeper purpose to my coming here with him today.

It just so happens I'm on the road with him, as his tutor, and he's being kind by including me.

If they know their son, and I'm sure they do, they should see that for what it is.

So, I unbuckle my seat belt, and those creases along Tobias's forehead grow, but he does the same. And then he shakes them off.

Outside of the truck, I unclip Bailey's car seat from its base and pull her to the edge of the seat, but Tobias is suddenly there, easing me out of the way. He gently grabs her, reaching over to get the diaper bag as well.

We're greeted at the door by his mom, who smiles brightly at her son and pulls him into her arms.

"Hey, Mom."

"Look at you, so big and strong." She squeezes his arms, and he laughs. Her eyes then fall to the car seat in his hands, and she smiles. "Oh my, my, who might this be?" Her palm falls to her chest.

My eyes dart to Tobias, realizing he didn't tell her we were coming, but he, too, is looking at Bailey. She's sound asleep, her pink bow still held in place, a perfect match to her watermelon dress and booties.

"So tiny," his mom croons before turning to me and waving me over. "She must be yours?"

"She is." I smile, offering his mom my hand, but she pulls me in for a quick hug. I laugh nervously, and step by her when she ushers us inside, but not before I spot the little sign over the doorbell Tobias had told me about.

The place is bright and welcoming, the walls a soft gray and blinds a blinding white, all open to let in the little bit of sun the day has to offer.

His mom shouts for her husband, and quickly points her smile toward me. "He's watching the stove."

Tobias clears his throat. "Mom, this is—"

"His tutor," I rush, just in case.

His mom looks from me to her son.

"My tutor," he repeats slowly, and I can feel the weight of his stare, though I ignore it. "Whose name is Meyer, and this little sleepyhead is Bailey, her daughter."

His mom smiles. "I'm Olivia, and this is my husband, Garro." She waves a hand toward the gentleman who joins us.

He's just as handsome as his son, tall with the same strong jawline, but his hair, while as dark as his son's, is peppered with gray and his eyes a deep brown.

The blue comes from his mother.

"It's nice to meet you both."

"Likewise, and breakfast is ready." Olivia nods. "I just need to finish up some more tortillas."

"Can I help with anything?"

"No, no, hun. Come to the table when you're ready." She smiles, disappearing into the kitchen.

Her husband steps in to hug his son, mentioning something that I don't catch, and I run my hands over my leggings, turning to grab Bailey for an excuse to do something.

Tobias, of course, doesn't release the car seat, but tells his dad we'll be right in and leads me over to the living room corner, where he gently sets her seat down.

"I didn't want her grilling me and—"

"Shh," I cut him off, digging into the diaper bag for the baby monitors, and placing one on the small table beside Bailey. "I don't want to sound like we're being gossipy."

"My mom loves gossip, just ask her."

I grin, and with one to match, he jerks his head toward the door his mother passed through. Following behind him, we ease into the next room, and I choose a seat across from him on the picnic-style table.

In the center of it sits bowls of fresh cut onion, cilantro, and a few different kinds of salsa. His dad lowers the proteins in front of us while his mom brings a container full of warm tortillas.

"I hope you like breakfast burritos." She smiles.

"I do, thank you."

Everyone gets settled, and served and we begin to eat, Tobias and his parents catching up on things they've missed.

They laugh about something that happened over their last visit and his mom tells him about the projects his dad has going at home as well as sharing updates about his nephew.

Tobias eats up every minute of it, smiling and asking questions as they pop into his head while I enjoy the food in front of me.

"You know your brother will be finishing up his residency this winter, isn't that exciting?" his mom says, catching my attention.

"Wow, that's amazing."

Tobias's eyes snap up to mine, and his elbows come up on the table as he refocuses on his plate.

"Isn't it?" Olivia beams, reaching for the bowl of fried potatoes. "Tobias, did you hear me?"

"Yeah, Mom. I heard. Badass."

Olivia's eyes seem to narrow. "So, when do you think you'll—"

"Honey." His dad gently interjects.

"I was only going to ask when he thinks it'll be time to stop playing a child's game and take school seriously."

My breath lodges in my throat at her breezy tone. She spoke as if it's the most innocent question.

As if it's not a complete and total insult to the man across from me, who refuses to look up and engage in the conversation, who must have sensed where it was going the moment his brother was mentioned.

I'm pretty sure my eyes are bugging out of my head.

"I mean you don't even come see us, you're so busy jumping from city to city, missing class while you're at it, and for what? To throw a ball around, pick fights with people like in high school?" She shakes her head. "If your brother hadn't called me to tell me you were going to be in town, I probably wouldn't have seen you until Christmas, if you even came down. I know you only made the trip this past year because you wanted to meet your nephew."

"I'll come for Christmas, Mom." He takes a drink, his head still hung.

And then the worst thing happens. Olivia turns to me.

"Meyer." Tobias tenses as I do. "You understand the importance of school, right? You're a student as well?"

I nod, wishing she'd stop talking

"Meyer holds a 4.0, has since freshman year," Tobias shares, his eyes popping up to mine briefly, happy to shift the conversation away from himself.

But I think it only fuels his mother's point further.

Her hands lift into the air, and he gives a curt nod. "Of course, you do, because you know what it takes to be successful in life. Hard work and dedication." She looks to Tobias. "Your brother knew that too. He worked hard and got into medical school. You saw the time he put into his studies, and you would think you'd learn something from witnessing that."

"Mom, please."

"Tobias, I'm serious, honey." What's sad is her tone holds true concern. "We didn't do all we could to make sure you could go to college—"

"You're right, Mom," he cuts her off with a firm, but respectful, tone. "You didn't. If you remember right, I worked it out with the help of someone who actually believed in me."

The baby monitor beeps, and before I can even attempt to stand, Tobias does. Since his need for an escape is greater, I remain seated, offering him a tight grin when I really want to glare.

He wastes no time, stomping away, but he lets it all go as he reaches Bailey, his voice nothing but tender and patient through the monitor. "I've got you, baby girl."

His mother's eyes fall to the tabletop and it's only moments later that the sound of the front door reaches us.

"I bet he took her out to see the chickens." His dad's grin is troubled as he rises to his feet. "I'll go keep him company."

His mom stands and begins carrying the dishes over to the counter, so I push myself up to help.

She's quiet for several minutes, and I'm more than happy to follow in her footsteps, so I work beside her in silence.

Once everything is put away, Olivia grabs a tray of cinnamon crisps and I follow her into the living room.

"You know my husband coached him when he was young. Well, up until Tobias was too stubborn to listen to a word his dad had to say." Her lips twitch, but she quickly shakes off the sentiment. "Come high school, he was three times the trouble Talon was. So hardheaded and he couldn't care less about the things that didn't interest him. Fight after fight, little to no effort where effort was due. If it wasn't baseball, it wasn't even a thought."

I force a tight-lipped smile, uncrossing and crossing my legs as anxiousness works up my throat.

"Oh, I forget who I'm talking to." She shakes her head, breaking off a corner of a treat. "You're his tutor, right?"

I nod, not trusting myself to speak in this moment.

"Then you know firsthand what I mean."

My legs begin to bounce and I look away, but my head is shaking before I can stop it. And then words are spilling from my mouth without permission.

"No, actually." My voice is quiet, but it's heard.

Shocked, she looks up from her cup. "I beg your pardon?"

I've already spoken, so I can't pull it back now. I do all I can, offer a tight smile and continue.

"I'm sorry, but I don't know what you mean."

Her eyes narrow the slightest bit, and she sits back in her chair.

"Tobias struggles with school, sure, but not in every class and never to the point of failure. He works really hard to sustain his GPA and if it starts to slip, he does what he needs to do to get it back up."

"Yes, honey, to sustain his GPA." She nods. "So, he can remain on that godforsaken team, not to set up his future."

"Baseball is his future."

"Baseball is a game, a pastime, not a life." She pushes to the edge of her seat, a hint of insult in her tone.

"I'm sorry, Mrs. Cruz, but you're wrong."

Tobias

Stepping through the back door, I find the kitchen table is now empty.

They must have settled into the living room.

Patting Bailey's back, we head their way, but then my mom's voice travels through the baby monitor that didn't get turned off, and I pause where I stand as Meyer says, "I'm sorry, but I don't know what you mean."

I swallow, bouncing slightly when Bailey begins to wiggle, wondering what she means by that, but I don't have to wonder long.

"Tobias struggles with school, yes," she tells her. "But not in every class and not to the point of failure. He works really hard and he sustains his GPA and if it starts to slip, he does what he needs to do to get it back up."

My lips twitch.

"Yes, honey, to sustain his GPA." My mom pretty much mocks. "So he can remain on that godforsaken team, not to set up his future."

"Baseball is his future." Meyer responds instantly.

"Baseball is a game, a pastime, not a life."

A sharp sting spears my chest.

Damn, Mom.

"I'm sorry, Mrs. Cruz, but you're wrong," Meyer tells her, and my muscles grow warm.

"My son refuses to look at the future as a man

should. He had a role model in his father and then in Talon. His brother is going to be a doctor, for Christ's sake. That's something to celebrate."

I shake my head, pushing through the door, but a hand on my shoulder halts me, and I look to find my dad standing there.

"Tobias." My dad's smile is one of regret, silently asking me not to hold it against her, but before he can say another word, Meyer does.

"Can you not see that Tobias is what legends are made of?" Meyer eases with the softest of tones, and I subconsciously lean closer to the door. "He's the definition of hard work and determination. He pushes, not only his mind, but his body beyond natural limits, nearly to its breaking point sometimes, and he does this with a smile because he loves it. He's passionate about his abilities. What he's doing for the sport today will be remembered for years to come, and that will only double when he moves up. And he will move up."

My pulse kicks, and I swallow past the lump in my throat.

"Mrs. Cruz, Tobias is expected to go first round in this year's draft, and in case you don't fully understand what that means, please let me tell you—"

"I understand that my son was lucky enough to get a second chance, got into a school with a push from that man, and instead of working hard like his brother, he's throwing it all away."

"I don't want to take away from what your other son has accomplished," she quickly comes back. "Because it's amazing what he's doing, but over twenty-one thousand students are *accepted* into medical school every year. Accepted. I don't know if you know this, but just over twelve hundred athletes are drafted into the majors every season. Twelve hundred out of fifty-two *thousand* hopefuls and *your son* is expected to be chosen *first*. One in fifty-two thousand, or one in twelve hundred, depending on how you want to look at it."

There's a long pause, and my chest tightens as my hand does on Bailey's back.

"That's something to celebrate. *That*... is something to be proud of," Meyer nearly whispers.

A moment passes and then the door is tugged open, and Meyer and I come face-to-face. She jolts to a stop, and I swear her eyes are clouded.

She swallows and I want to reach out and touch her, drag her closer and keep her there, but she reaches for Bailey before I make a move, gently pulling her into her arms.

"Do you mind taking me back to the hotel? I have a call I need to be there for and Bailey will be getting hungry soon."

All I can do is nod.

Meyer quietly thanks my parents before walking out the front door, and I'm not far behind.

The ride to the hotel is a silent one, but my mind is screaming.

Back in the room, she sets Bailey in her playpen and attempts to slip past into the bathroom, but I block her path before she can.

"Tobias—"

"Did you mean all you said?"

She looks down, but using my knuckles, I bring those brown eyes back to mine. "Did you mean what you said?"

"I didn't say anything."

"You said a fuck-ton, Meyer, by saying anything at all." My chest burns, my blood hot and flowing double time.

"Your brother's always the one who lets them know when you're coming to town, isn't he?"

A frown falls over me, and I look away. "My parents don't follow my career, but it's all good."

"And you don't tell them when you're in town because every conversation leads to the same place ..."

"You mean the domain of dreary disappointment? Yeah." I hide the sting in my shoulder blades by lifting one. "But I'm used to that."

"You shouldn't be," she whispers, a gentle softness in her voice I'm not sure she's aware of.

"It follows me everywhere I go, Tutor Girl," I tell her, forcing the corner of my mouth to curve up. "I do something good, something I can be proud of and someone else comes to tear it down, to make me rethink every fucking step I take."

Realization dawns on her and a sadness clouds her eyes. "You deal with it at home and at school."

"I don't know what it is, but I can't escape it." I shrug. "I thought it would be different at Avix, new town, new team. New crowd. Older, wiser and all that. But then the paper got wind of my situation, teen with a track record a mile long who just got a full ride, after being cut from the prospect list of every other D1 in the country, and instantly I was *The Playboy Pitcher*, the bad boy on campus. It's like they were thirsty for someone to focus on and that focus became me. I do something shitty; they expose it. I do something good; they twist it."

"Last year I helped a girl move out of her apartment after her roommates ditched her with all the rent, and the paper blasts a story about how I ruined some poor girl's dreams, driving her to drop out of college." I scoff, shaking my head. "You know the shittiest part of that? I broke a school record that same week, and for some reason I was excited, like fuck yeah, now they have to say something good. Something I could show my parents, but they didn't print a damn thing about that."

Meyer's hand falls to my chest, her fingers spanning out as she tips her head back farther, her eyes tight and on mine. "I'm sorry you have to deal with that," she whispers. "If they knew who you really were ..." She shakes her head.

"I don't care what anyone else thinks, not anymore. Not if you see me the way I heard it." I reach out, pushing the hair from her face, every muscle in my body straining, tightening as her eyes darken before me. "All you said before. Are those really the things you think of when you think of me ... *do you* think of me?"

The hand on my chest twitches, her pupils growing larger, stirring me deep to my core.

I'm fucking aching.

For her.

For this.

For us.

She takes a small step forward, but I dart my hand out, catching her by the bicep, and hold her right where she stands.

She gasps and a low rumble works its way up my chest.

"Come any closer, baby, and you'll feel the proof of

what you do to me."

Her throat bobs, creases forming along her brow, and I admit, it stings when her feet shuffle back, away from me.

I drop my chin. The thought of facing her rejection way too fucking much, but then her little hand glides down.

My pulse jumps behind my ribs, hard and fast and instant as my eyes slice up to hers.

I walk her backward, through our joining doors and don't stop until her shoulders meet the wall in my room. When she swallows, I slip my foot between hers, moving in until her chest is brushing mine.

I'm rock hard for you.

Her thighs clench, and a low groan slips from me, my muscles flexing as her little hand dares farther south.

I hiss when it passes my abs, slipping beneath my shirt to meet the edge of my briefs.

Her head falls to my pecs, and her hand begins to tremble in need.

"I want you," I tell her and swear to God, she whimpers. "I know you can sense it, feel it." I lean forward, brushing her loose strands of hair from her face with the tip of my nose, my lips grazing along her ear. "I bet you've known it now for weeks, but I've ached for even longer."

She shivers, and my dick twitches again.

"Don't be afraid, Tutor Girl," I rasp, lightly grinding against her.

Instantly, Meyer's head falls back to meet the wall, her eyes hooded and eager. I run my thumb along the plumpness beneath her bottom lip, dying to bite on it the way I've watched her do so many times.

"Take from me, Tutor Girl, swear to God anything you could possibly want, I want more."

Her fingers curl over the elastic of my boxers, and she gives a gentle tug, her heated breath fanning over my neck and driving me mad. "I have a call and you ... you have to go ..."

A deep rumble rises from my chest as her fingertips curve, digging into my pecs as she fists my shirt. She tried to reason with herself, but it's no use. Her need is taking over.

You're so close, baby ... come on...

"You made me a promise, Tutor Girl, and I know you want to keep it right now," I whisper, allowing my hand to fall to her hips. I grip her there, squeezing and she inhales sharply. "*Take.*"

Her eyes close, her chin lifting, but then my phone begins to ring, and it's a tone reserved for one person.

"*Fuck.*" I pant, blindly pulling my phone from my pocket.

"Son," Coach Reid's voice fills the air.

Instantly, Meyer's eyes snap open, and she turns to stone in front of me.

I jolt with silent laughter, bringing my finger to my lips, but she's already torn herself from me, and I spin, my phone to my ear as I watch her disappear into her room.

"Here, Coach." I clear my throat, adjusting my junk in my jeans and quickly move to toss my travel bag onto my bed.

I tear my slides from the side pocket, shoving them into my game bag and make sure my eye black stick was put back where it goes after the last game.

"I don't want you warming up until thirty minutes

to game time today. I already went over this with the rest of the staff, but to cover all the bases, I'm telling you, too."

"Heard, Coach."

"We're stepping out of the airport now. See you in a few."

I hang up, a low laugh following.

Thank fuck he didn't ask to talk to anyone. Not that he'd announce if he became aware I wasn't on the bus anyway. If he did that, he would have to acknowledge the rule that says athletes must travel to away games together. That would end with my ass on the bench and that's just not a fucking option.

I need to get there before the bus to play it safe.

But first, I need five minutes with the brunette next door.

Smiling, I slip inside her room, but I find her sitting on the bed, her laptop open, a dude appearing on the screen a moment later.

My frown builds.

"Hey," I call.

"Okay, Matt, let's start with physics. Do you have your worksheet?" she asks.

The dude lifts what she's asked, so I slowly back away.

In the rental, I send her a quick text, and then head to the field.

The smirk on my face doesn't leave, and for the first time in maybe ever, I'm more excited for the end of a game than I am the start of it.

I look down at my aching dick with a sigh.

Sorry, bro, it's a massive blue balls kind of day.

CHAPTER 20

Tobias

The ball slaps into Echo's glove with a loud thwack, and my mouth curves high.

The team's on the field in seconds, but they got an earful from Coach the last time they hopped up on my back, so it's nothing but shouts and muscle flexes, a couple back pats and some fucker snags the hat off my head.

Echo, though, he doesn't give a shit if he gets chewed out.

"That was a hell of a yakker, son!" He bends his big ass down and hoists me up on his shoulders, spinning to face Cal Poly's top hitter ... who didn't make contact with a single ball today.

The redheaded dude flips me off, spitting on the dirt, and we laugh.

"Damn, Rogers, spitting on your own field?" Echo chuckles. "That's rough, my man. Better luck tomorrow, huh?"

"Fuck you, stay away from our clubhouse tonight,

assholes." He glares, bumping into his teammate as he backs away.

"Eight o'clock sharp?" Echo nods, lowering me to my feet before wrapping his arms around my neck and yanking me to him. "Heard, son. Heard."

"You're a dick." I laugh, catching my glove as Coach tosses it to me.

Echo makes his way into the dugout as Coach steps in front of me. He grips my shoulder a moment and keeps his eyes on mine as he tips his chin the slightest bit. The gesture may seem small to some, but it's not to me. A sense of pride swells in my chest and I nod back.

"For you, Coach."

"No, not today. This team hasn't lost to our program in twenty years, son, and not only did they lose at home, but they didn't bring a single bastard across the plate." He gives my shoulder a short squeeze. "This one's for you."

My jaw clenches as my mother's words from this morning come crashing into my mind, as does the way my father sat back and said nothing. But Meyer didn't.

She spoke up when I couldn't, when my father wouldn't.

Just like Coach did the night I begged my parents to allow him over for dinner.

"Come talk to me after showers," he says as he walks away.

Echo jogs over, his gear now off and jumps up, attempting to catch me in a headlock, but I tear myself free, snagging my hat from his hand.

"You're coming out with us tonight."

"Nah, man." I put my hat on my head, moving my eyes his way.

"*Yeah, man.*" Echo shoves me. "This is your hometown; you need to let these Cal Poly boys know it."

"After today, you think there's a question?"

"Okay, there's my cocky boy."

"Fuck you." I chuckle.

"No, Cruz." He makes a show of biting his knuckles. "Fuck *that*. On the floor, on a chair, against the motherfucking tunnel walls ..."

I laugh, eyeing the prize he's pointed out, and what do you know, she starts walking over.

It's not until she's within earshot that the hand behind her back becomes visible, a microphone tucked tightly inside it.

Echo's head falls with a full groan. "We know who she's after. I'll take the friend," he teases, escaping a whole two seconds before the brunette's cameraman is front and center.

She lifts a brow, but I laugh it off, and her smirk turns into a smile.

I spot Coach looking this way. He signals with a small nod for me to entertain the girl, so as her hand comes down on my bicep, I put on my best grin.

She switches into sassy secretary mode as she slips closer, looking back and forth between the camera and myself. "I'm here with the man everyone is dying to get their hands on, the one and only Tobias Cruz."

My grin turns into a smirk, and I think the girl is pleased.

Time to kick the charm up to ten.

It's like Coach says, exposure is key and personality wins every time.

Meyer

Bailey was up for my entire last session, but she was in a happy, playful mood, so I was able to swap out her hanging toys a few times and get through the lesson without any interruptions.

My earlier call I wasn't so lucky, but thankfully Freya, the swim team captain, was able to hop on again once she went down for her nap. Overall, the day wasn't as difficult as I expected it to be having her with me.

Wanting to make use of my time away with Bailey, I take her down to the hotel restaurant for a quick bite to eat with the room credit the school allotted, ordering a few things to take back to the room so I get the full benefit. We take the cookies and things back once I'm done, and I changed us into something we can wear into the water.

I try to ignore the fact that Tobias still isn't back when I saw several familiar uniforms file in on the walk here.

Setting our things down, I carefully step us into the water, and at first, Bailey's stiffens, her body jerking as her muscles lock and I smile at her, holding her away from my body slightly. She heaves forward, quickly clinging on to me and a low laugh escapes me.

A little slower, I step farther out, bending at the knee to bring her more under the water.

She starts to loosen, so I bounce a bit and her

fingers fly into her mouth, her lips curving into a smile around them.

"See, Bay. It's fun." I grab her little hand and pat at the water.

She squeals, jerking her upper body, and I laugh, making sure my hold is tight as she tries to push away from me.

She starts slapping at the water, giggling like crazy, and my smile couldn't be wider. Her blue eyes light up every time the water sprinkles against her face and she looks to me with her toothless grin, as if to say, 'did you see, Mama?'

"Look at you playing in the water." I lean over to kiss her temple. "Such a big girl, Bay."

Tears fill my eyes, it's such a bittersweet moment.

She's having so much fun, experiencing something for the very first time, and there's no one to share it with.

There's never anyone to share anything with.

As I think it, guilt weighs in my chest.

That's not true.

Bianca is always there, and if she isn't, she's reachable, at least when it comes to me. I know she goes out of her way to make sure she's only a call away when it comes to me, because she knows I'm on my own.

My brother is busy, and I hate bothering him, though he'd be upset to hear this, but he's trying to create a life and will drop everything if I ask.

I refuse to let him in on my struggles for that very reason.

When our mom passed, he was still in high school. If it weren't for his best friend's family, I would have had to defer college, and we'd have had to move to stay afloat since the only person who cared for us had nothing to leave behind. She worked hard all her life for the little we did have.

Thankfully, Milo's friend gave him a home and I didn't have to pass on my scholarship. At first, I was going to do it anyway; it didn't feel right to leave him, but when he found out, he promised to never speak to me again if I did, he knew as well as I did if I let it slip from my fingertips, another would likely never come. He never would have cut me out, but I trusted my baby brother to trust me. If he couldn't make a life for himself when his time came, I would make sure I made one for the both of us.

It was really hard on us both, being away from the only member that gave a damn. And then Bailey blessed our lives. Even though Milo's not here, it's obvious the peace she brings me is mirrored in him.

Bailey begins rubbing at her eyes, so I step from the water.

At first, she cries, as if she wants to get back in, but once I get her wet onesie off, and wrap her in a little cocoon white plush towel I brought from the room, she settles long enough for me to wrap one around myself.

As I get back to the hotel and I'm opening up the app to access the key card, a shadow falls over me.

My cheeks heat, knowing I'm a mess of knotted hair and dripping clothes, but a smile still plays at my lips as I spin.

It falls flat instantly as I find a completely different man standing there.

He looks from me to the ball of towel in my hand. "If my memory serves me correctly, I believe I received an email with payment information for childcare for this trip."

"Guess you're not as old as you're beginning to look." I shrug. "Your memory is still intact. I decided to bring my sitter along," I lie.

He scoffs, his eyes falling to my arms again, but I spin, keeping my daughter out of his sight. He doesn't deserve to look at her. His gaze snaps back to mine, a flicker of something I can't and don't care to read racing through them.

"Imagine my surprise when I looked at my log to find this was your room."

"You're the one who booked it."

His nod is calculated, and he slides his hands into his khaki pockets. "I believe my pitcher's room ended up being the one directly beside yours."

"Is it?" I keep my face blank.

He cocks his head, staring for several seconds. "Have you seen my boy, Meyer?"

Vomit threatens to rise in my throat, but I refuse to swallow. "Have you tried knocking on his door?"

"He's not in there." His eyes narrow, flicking to my window and back.

"Well, I don't know what to tell you." I push my door open more, using my back to keep it from slamming shut.

"Team says he left the bar an hour ago."

Bar.

My stomach curls.

Of course, I almost forgot about the stories that follow the players home after away games.

It's the same for every sport, according to the few students of mine that are prone to overshare.

"Figured he'd be back by now." He runs his fingers over the bill of his hat. "Oh well, he'll call me when he's ... done." A low snicker leaves him. "Guess old habits never die."

I look away, refusing to fall into whatever it is this is.

The truth.

A trap.

A pit of lava with my name on it, also known as reality.

Coach Reid begins to walk away, but jerks to a stop, gazing at me curiously. "Shouldn't you be on a call or something?"

"All my calls are done for the day, so I figured I'd take in all the hotel has to offer before I return to my chic little shed." My voice is more bitter than intended.

His nod is slow, eyes narrowed, but before he goes, he says one more thing. "If you're bored, you can catch his interview, should be up on the school website by now." He walks away.

I quietly close the door and focus on what I need to do rather than the questions now threatening to cloud my mind. Placing Bailey in her playpen, I take the towel off of her so she doesn't get herself tangled up, and she instantly begins to cry, the cool air now hitting her chilled skin.

"Just a minute, Bay." I jog over and fill the sink with lukewarm water, quickly rushing back to her and lifting her into my arms once more.

"Hey, Bay, it's okay. Here we go." I gently lower her

into the water, using a rolled-up hand towel as a pillow behind her head. "There we are. Here, want your mimi?"

She fusses a little more, but quiets in the warmth once the Binky is in her mouth. She rubs at her eyes so I bathe her as quickly as I can, thankful when she settles in the playpen after long enough for me to quickly wash myself off and free my hair of the chlorine.

She's humming and fake cackling when I get out, so I throw my hair in the towel and get us both settled on the bed for her feeding.

She gets angry when she can't play with my hair, but I run my fingers over hers a few times and a heavy exhale slips from her nose, making me smile.

"There we go, Bay," I whisper.

She doesn't eat much, too tired from her evening playtime to stay awake long enough, so I know she'll wake again soon.

I should brush my hair out and get some of my own work done while I can, but instead, I open my computer, click on the school webpage and scroll down until I find the link for the Avix Inquirer.

The headline and time stamp that reads nearly four hours earlier makes my throat burn, but I click through anyway.

Avix Inquirer: Does the Playboy Pitcher have a plaything back home?

I push the ache creeping up my ribs down as I look to the placeholder image on the interview video, a dirt-stained Tobias standing beside a gorgeous reporter. He looks as handsome as ever.

Hat backward, smirk deep, and eyes playful.

I start the video and the woman speaks first.

"I'm here with the man everyone is just dying to get their hands on, the number one prospect this year, Tobias Cruz."

Her innuendo is clear, and Tobias grins, letting her know he picked up on it.

"Tobias, tell us about tonight's game. What was going through your head when that last batter stepped into the box?"

He licks his lips, drawing her *and everyone watching at home's* attention to his mouth. *"I was thinking about what I was going to order from room service when I got back to my hotel."*

A low laugh leaves me.

"Okay, so you were confident you were getting out of this game without a single run scored?"

Pride warms me, and I hope his parents felt compelled to tune in.

"It's not the first in the season, and it won't be the last. I'm just happy to have a kick-ass team behind me."

"Was it a different kind of sweet to come to your hometown and dominate against the coach who didn't offer a spot to you three years ago?"

"No, it was sweet to add another W to my coach's record. And for the record, even if Cal Poly had wanted me, they wouldn't have gotten me. Coach Reid is the reason I've become the player that I am, and I'll forever be in his debt."

My pulse quickens and I pull my knees up, unsure if I want to hear more.

"We love to hear a player such as yourself give credit

where it's due." The young woman smiles, opening and closing her fingers against the microphone. *"So, how will you celebrate this win tonight, Mr. Cruz."* She smiles coyly.

Tobias's chuckle is low, his lips curved to one side as his tongue comes out again to wet them. *"Just so happens I've got someone waiting on me tonight."* The woman widens her eyes playfully, looking to the camera and Tobias grins wider, adding, *"It's good to be home."*

My gut sinks and I look back to the heading again.

Four hours since the game ended.

Of course.

This is his hometown, where he grew up all his life. No duh, he has people waiting around to see him. Old friends and old flames, old hopefuls hoping for a second shot.

And there's nothing standing in their way because Tobias is a single man. A successful, charismatic, single man with the world at his fingertips.

I don't want to be here should he stumble in, especially if when he does, he's not alone, so I pull out my phone to see if my paycheck has been deposited yet, finding that it has.

I call the airport only to be let down when I find out the ticket costs more than my monthly rent because only private planes leave from the local airstrip. So instead, I do the only thing I can.

I close and lock the connecting door while wishing against everything I truly want, that Tobias doesn't come back tonight.

I need time to get myself in check.

To remember my role and his.

To cry where no one will see, like the senseless girl

I've allowed myself to become.

But then the worst thing happens.

Laughter fills the hall outside my room, growing louder and louder until it's no longer seeping through the crack beneath the front door, but coming from the wall behind my head.

And it's not a man who's laughing.

It's a woman.

DIRTY CURVE

CHAPTER 21

Tobias

Heat spreads through my body, sending beads of sweat rolling down my bare chest.

I groan, my slick palms gliding along satin as my muscles clench, releasing a moment later.

Licking my lips, I twist my torso, and it takes mad effort to peel my eyes open, all for them to snap closed in the same second, the beat of the sun too damn bright above me.

Where the fuck?

I bend my neck to look behind me, spotting a sliding door I don't recognize, and when I look down, I realize I'm on a lounger I've never seen, a sheet thrown over the top of it.

My temples throb, beating like an amateur drummer, too hard, too loud, and with no real rhyme or rhythm. It takes everything in me to throw my legs over the side, pushing up into a sitting position.

My forearms fall to my thighs in an effort to hold

me up, and then the squeak of a door sounds behind me.

I keep my head down, not wanting to know whoever the hell is behind me, but then a Vitamin Water is held out in front of me, a familiar watch tied around that person's wrist.

My chin drops in relief. "Fuck, Coach." I squint up at him, wincing as I do.

He blows a long breath out of his nose. "Drink this, take these, and hit the sauna. You've got a couple hours to sweat this shit out and then it's game time."

Nodding, I look to the giant ass horse pills, and push to my feet.

"What the fuck happened last night? How'd I get here?" I look around, rolling my shoulder a few times to ease some of the tension from yesterday's game. "Where the fuck is *here*?"

"This is my suite; it comes with a deck view." He chuckles, a small shrug following. "And you got here like you always do, son. You called me after you had your fun. I sent an Uber after you and had them drop you here."

My frown falls to the grass. Not a single image from last night popping into my mind.

"Last I remember we went to the bar to meet those A's scouts you said were coming to talk to me on the DL, but I don't remember them showing up."

"You're lucky I was able to get a hold of them to let them know you retired to your hotel room." He lifts a brow.

I nod, and then every muscle in my body locks.

My hotel room.

My motherfucking hotel room.

My girl.

My girl, who has no clue she's my girl ...

Oh fuck.

Fuck, fuck, fuck.

Last night I didn't ... fuck me, did I?

Setting the water and pills down, I run my hands over my hair, scrubbing them down my face. I dart past Coach, rushing around in search of my shirt and shoes, both folded neatly on the armchair inside.

Tossing some pillows, I hunt for my phone, but it doesn't show up. "You see my phone?"

"No, maybe you left it somewhere last night?" Coach Reid watches me from the patio.

"Fuck!" I hiss.

"You need to hit the sauna," he says again.

"I'll be good, Coach." I dash for the door, tearing it open.

"Tobias, wait!" Coach Reid shouts behind me, but I'm already gone.

And when I get back to my room, Meyer is stepping from hers.

There's a chair propping her door open, and she has Bailey's car seat in one hand, diaper bag in the other.

She's leaving?

I skid to a stop, her eyes popping up to mine the second my feet are planted.

She gasps, her lips parting. "Tobias."

I wince.

The way she whispers my name, as if her body aches but her mind has reached acceptance, makes my throat burn.

"Hey." I approach her, and when she shifts, subconsciously twisting until Bailey is shielded from my view, my hand darts out, seeking the stability of the wall beside me.

As I grow closer, I find her eyes rimmed with red, cheeks stained nearly the same exact color.

She's been crying and the realization knocks the air from my lungs, but at the same time, something settles within me, allowing another full breath to take the last's place.

She thinks I fucked up, and that means, in her perfect little mind, there's something to be fucked up. On the other, for her to assume what her gorgeous eyes are telling me makes my stomach ache, but why wouldn't she?

It's what the school paper loves to focus on, my shit off the field. It doesn't matter if you read it or not, it's damn near impossible not to prejudge off of the quick glimpses you can't get away from. They plaster the things in the halls of every building and post on every social media site in existence. But that's not the worse part. That's understandable, something I can't and haven't been able to get away from.

What's twisting my insides is the fact that she could possibly believe, even for a second, that she meant so little to me after the time we've spent together, but again, I can understand it. I hate it, but I understand it.

How could she possibly know to the full extent what she means to me, when I've yet to spell it out for her? She knows I want her, but she could easily, subconsciously, translate that back to the headlines she reads over time.

Tobias Cruz, The Playboy Pitcher strikes again ...

No.

Not this time.

I dart forward, gently taking her face in my hand. She turns away, but I push closer, and she holds her breath as if the thought of breathing me in is too much.

"Meyer, look at me," I rasp, my hand sinking into her hair. "Baby, please ..."

She licks her lips, blinking hard, and when she finally meets my gaze with her own, an emptiness lurches in my chest.

Her eyes are desolate, and they serve as a punch to the gut.

We didn't exactly make plans for last night, but in my head, we didn't need to. We had plans and our plans consisted of us, together. End of fucking story.

I don't know what happened last night, but I didn't do anything I'd regret.

There's no way.

I wouldn't.

Not to her.

Not to them.

I don't even care to look at another girl anymore, let alone touch one, and it's been that way for weeks now, long before her smile shifted.

It *has* shifted.

We have shifted.

My head begins to shake. "Listen—"

"I didn't mean to assume anything and you don't owe me an explanation." Meyer's tone is pleading, as if she's begging me not to speak. "We're—"

"Say friends, I dare you."

Her eyes squeeze shut, a single teardrop sneaks its

way out as she does, and serves as a rope around my neck, cutting off my supply of oxygen and leaving my lungs starved.

Her nostrils flare and she straightens her spine. That's when she opens her eyes.

If they weren't clouded, the void expression within them might just kill me on the spot, but the moisture lets me know I'm in there. You have to care about someone for them to have the ability to hurt you.

"I'm a mother." She nods. "I'm a mother and I've been irresponsible."

"No."

"Coming here was a bad idea, I knew that. It was reckless and ..."

"Don't say it."

"I should have never been assigned to you." She swallows, resolve slipping over her and making my fingers numb. "I shouldn't be here, and I really shouldn't have brought my little girl. I made a mistake." She swallows, the honesty in her tone just about burning my skin from my bones. "I knew the life you lived and I never should—"

Her words halt on her lips when the door she's standing in front of opens, the door that leads into my hotel room.

Both our heads snap that way, watching as Neo backs out, a chick latched on to his body.

His foot bumps the diaper bag and he jerks to a stop, both their gazes slicing our way.

"Well, good morning." Neo chuckles and the chick's face, who I now realize is the reporter from yesterday's game, turns pink. The girl slowly lowers her feet to the floor, glancing between the three of us, and Neo smirks, tossing something into the air.

My hand flies up on instinct, catching it in my palm.

It's the spare key card to my hotel room, the one our team coordinator handed me when he passed them out to the team after yesterday's game. His way of covering his own ass should someone see him skip over me and wonder why.

I glare and Neo's smirk deepens.

"Hey, you passed out at the grill. It took three of us to get your ass into the car and out into Coach's room last night. I loaned you a shoulder and you happily loaned me your room so I didn't have to keep X up all night in mine."

I fucking knew it.

My pulse quickens, my eyes snapping back to Meyer, but hers are frozen on my room door.

Neo grabs the girl by her hand and rushes down the hall, throwing a salute as he rounds the corner. "Hi, Meyer!"

But Meyer doesn't say a word, she's stuck, unmoving with the same open mouth expression she had on moments ago, her words lodged in her throat.

Slowly, she blinks, her shoulders falling as her muscles begin to give, and the base of Bailey's car seat gently meets the floor.

Her eyes come back to mine, a sorrow building within them.

She shakes her head, at a loss for what to say. "Tobias, I—"

I jerk forward, take her neck in my palm, and smash my lips into hers.

Meyer's muscles lock up, but only for a moment,

and then every bit of her melts against me. She kisses me back.

It's deep and distressed, as is the long, choppy inhale that follows, but when I push my tongue inside, she opens up for me, *loosens* up for me.

It's like I can finally fucking breathe, her air providing whatever it is mine's been missing.

She pushes up on her toes to get more of me, her arms wrapping around my neck in an attempt to get closer, so I help my baby out. I glide my palms from her ribs to her back, and when I tug her flush to me, she gasps.

I fumble with the diaper bag at her feet, not taking my mouth off hers as I toss it through her open door, and I bring my right hand to her back again, using caution as I grab Bailey's car seat with my left. I lead us into Meyer's room.

Nudging the chair out of the way, I set Bailey down, making sure the sleeping princess is facing away, and then drive my fingers into Meyer's hair. I bend, lifting her legs up and set her on top of the small desk, and yank her to the edge so her hips are aligned with mine. My dick's so hard it throbs, and I attempt to ease the pain by pressing it against what I know is a sweet, soft center.

A whimper tears from her throat and I'm ready to shred her shirt from her body, to reveal the skin I've fantasized about more times than I care to count.

"*Fuck*," I pant, and her husky chuckle draws me right back.

I take her mouth again, biting at her lower lip, demanding my tongue's entrance once more, and god*damn* I could come just by fucking kissing her.

She's silky and smooth and tastes like mine.

She *is* mine.

"Let me taste your skin, Tutor Girl." I lean in and one of her palms slaps onto the wood beneath her, her head falling back with compliance, and when my heated breath fans along the underside of her jaw, a sharp gasp pushes past her lips.

A gasp that turns into a moan when my mouth falls to her neck, but I don't kiss her right away.

I push the tip of my tongue out, flicking it against her. "You gonna shake for me, baby?"

Her thighs twitch and I know I've found my first sweet spot, a spot I'll torture her with when she's shaking and desperate and needy. For me. For more. For fucking all.

I kiss her there again and her back arches, pushing her chest into mine.

My dick throbs in my jeans. I'm a fucking rod, so solid I'm in literal fucking pain. I wince, seeking out the arc of her pussy, and she knows what I need. She shifts her hips, pushing as close as she can and rubbing along my hard cock.

Her legs come up then, wrapping around me in search of more.

Fuck me, I need more.

I swoop her up, spin and drop us onto the bed, my palm gliding down to her ass and pushing her into me.

"This ass," I groan, my left hand gliding up to tap at the edge of her ass cheek. "I've fucking dreamed about it, fucked myself fantasizing about it." I bite at her lips and her eyes practically roll back in her head.

"Mine," I whisper, forcing my tongue into her mouth and rolling into her, my muscles clenching.

All fucking mine.

Both of them.

My muscles freeze and I push up on one hand, darting my eyes toward the door, toward the little gray car seat, pink flowers dusting the top, a frilly white lace trimming the edges.

Slowly, I ease into a sitting position, Meyer's pants loud and heavy at my side.

I push to my feet and make my way over to her and when I peek over the edge, Bailey's blue eyes come up to mine.

And baby girl smiles, her little hands slapping at her sides in excitement, and when they come back up, she's got a baseball in her hand, the toy one I bought for her a while ago.

My eyes go back to her mama, who sits up in the bed, lips swollen from my kiss and curved to one side.

Meyer gave her the little toy I bought her daughter, even when she was angry with me, because really, she wasn't mad at me, she was mad at herself for daring to hope we were more than what she felt last night when sounds of another woman came from my room.

She said so herself, she didn't mean to hope, and I understand what she was trying to say now.

Carefully unbuckling Bailey's seat, I lift her into my arms and make my way back to Meyer.

Her eyes remain locked with mine as I lower the two of us onto the bed, gently setting Bailey in the middle of us. She instantly rolls over, pushing up on her hands and drooling all over the pillow, a high-pitched squeal following.

Meyer and I both laugh and look to each other once

more.

Sorrow shines in her deep brown eyes, but I shake my head.

"You were right to assume," I tell her, taking her face in my palm. "Because we aren't just student and tutor, haven't been for a long ass time as far as I'm concerned."

She nibbles at the inside of her lip, eyes on me.

"I don't know how the fuck last night turned into what it did, but it never should have happened. I wanted to get back here, and I was the first out the door, but then this thing with scouts popped up and ... I should have called you. I should have left when an hour went by and they never showed, but it didn't and that won't happen again."

"I don't expect you to—"

"Expect it," I cut her off. "Whatever it is, expect it, want it, demand it even. There's only one other person in this fucking world I allow to get in my head, but baby, you didn't ask permission." My lips curl into a smile. "Girl, you didn't even want the spot, the way I remember it, but you stole it regardless."

Her chuckle is soft and while her chin lowers, those eyes of hers stay on mine.

"Even if you didn't, I'd have given it to you." My eyes move between hers. "Let me be someone that matters to you, 'cause, you matter to me, Tutor Girl. Both of you do."

"You do matter, Tobias," she whispers. "And that's one of the hardest parts of this."

Something warm spreads through my chest and I can't fight the smirk that takes over.

"I put a ticket in your name yesterday for today's game. Come. Watch me pitch." I run my thumb along her jaw, my pulse punching against my ribs when she leans into my touch. "Be the reason I win today."

Something flashes in her eyes, but she blinks it away, a light nod following. "Okay."

My brows jump, my smile fucking wide. "Yeah?"

"Yeah."

"You'll be there?"

"I said yes." She laughs. "That means I'm coming."

I groan, hop up and over the bed until I'm on my knees on the ground at her opposite side. I tug her toward me, take her lips again and nip at her when she playfully denies my tongue entrance. Tearing away, I grip my cock with my fist and raise a dark brow. "Next time you say *I'm coming* ... you will be, so careful with your choice of words, Tutor Girl, or don't be if you're ready to jump right to it."

I stand, and her attention snaps from where I'm fisting myself to my eyes, following me as I take backward steps away from her, my eyes clenched tight.

"What are you doing?"

"Replaying the taste of you, so when I step into that shower right now, I can get there quick."

"Tobias!" She chuckles, but I'm not playing.

I climb into her shower with one thing on my mind.

Her naked and under me.

Works like a fucking charm.

DIRTY CURVE

CHAPTER 22

Meyer

I put Bailey in the best outfit I brought along, a red and blue striped dress Bianca bought her for the Fourth of July, but she's grown so much in the past few weeks, it already fits her perfectly. The little jean shorts have white stars stamped along the butt and her sandals are sparkly silver. As I'm finishing the final touch, gliding a red bow over her head, the phone in the room rings.

With a frown, I pick up.

"Hello, miss, I have a guest at the front desk asking for you."

Slowly lowering onto the edge of the bed, I ask, "Who is it?"

"It's a woman, miss, but she doesn't seem to wish to give her name."

I nod. "I'll be right there, thank you."

What the heck?

Grabbing my phone, I push it into my back pocket and check my hair in the mirror.

I left it down for the first time in what must be months. I didn't think to bring a curling iron, but I used my brush and the hotel blow dryer to straighten it. It looks nice. Pretty actually.

That and the blush and mascara I put on, again for the first time in forever, and I can't help but smile at my reflection.

I'm still heavier than I'm comfortable with, but Bailey's only five months old and I hear that's normal. Still, I pull my sweater over my head to hide the extra weight and lift Bay into my arms, heading down to the lobby.

As I walk in, I look around, but I don't spot anyone, and then my name is called.

I spin, my eyes widening when they land on a pair of blue ones.

"Hi, Meyer."

"Mrs. Cruz ... hi." I slip my fingers into Bailey's hand. "Tobias isn't here."

"I came to see you."

My face falls. "Oh ... um, is everything okay?"

She nods, reaching out to brush her fingers along Bailey's arm. "Yeah, but I'd like to chat if you have time? Can I buy you a coffee, maybe? I saw they had a small café when I walked in ..."

I must hesitate because she holds her palms up. "Please, just for a few minutes."

"Yeah, okay." I offer a smile, falling in line beside her as we walk to the café.

"She looks adorable," she says, holding the door open for the two of us to slip through. "How old is she?"

"Almost six months."

Mrs. Cruz smiles, lowering into one of the bistro seats near the fountain's edge. "And how long have you known my son?"

My stomach flips. "Mrs. Cruz."

"It's just a question, honey, I'm sorry." She sighs. "I'm all over the place. Please, sit down."

Hesitantly, I take the seat across from her, waiting for her to be the one to ask more questions so I don't have to.

She doesn't make me wait long. "Is she trying to crawl?"

"She scoots herself backward, but she hasn't figured out the whole knees forward thing yet."

She laughs, making a wide smiley face at Bay and opening and closing her fingers in a wave.

Bailey kicks her feet, jumping up and down on my thigh as she reaches toward her.

"May I?" Her voice is quiet, a hint of desperation woven in, and I know she not only wants to hold Bay. She needs to.

There's just something about an infant, they have the ability to soothe aches and erase pain with a simple smile or touch, so I nod, passing her off and the grin that takes over her face reminds me so much of the ones I've witnessed on her son.

"Tobias was such a happy baby," she says after a moment. "He learned so much faster than Talon did, skipped over crawling altogether, and started taking steps while holding on to things at seven months old. He talked early, walked early, he did everything early." She remembers. "It's like he was competing with his brother from day one, and every single time, he fell a little short.

Talon was older, so he was taller faster, shaved first, had a girlfriend first. Normal life stuff, you know? And then his freshman year of high school, Tobias hit a growth spurt. Suddenly he was taller, faster, had more girlfriends." She laughs lightly, but it's hollow.

"He thought he had finally done it, and then Talon was advanced into the AP program. It was like the cycle started all over. Tobias tried to beat him. He asked to go to study hall and stayed late with his teachers. He watched documentaries and tried those listening books the libraries used to have ..."

"He did?" I swallow. The sorrow that's taken over her tone makes it hard to listen. He tried to be a better student and didn't understand why he couldn't grasp things the way others could. It's so hard to find the kind of learning that works for you. That must have made him feel less capable when I know that to be false.

"Oh, yeah." She sighs. "He did."

"Mrs. Cruz—"

Her sad smile comes up to mine. "Please, call me Olivia."

Nodding, I continue, "Olivia, those are good things."

"They are, but I never really stopped to wonder why he did it, and now I understand." Her eyes mist over, but she looks back to Bay, seeking that warmth, and Bailey doesn't disappoint.

Her little palms come up, gently tapping at Olivia's face, pulling a tender laugh from the woman.

"Tobias was working for something he thought he'd find if he achieved what his brother had." Her blue eyes curve my way. "Recognition."

Unsure of what to say, I simply sit and listen for

more.

"We'd have barbecues and neighbors, or my husband's coworkers would come over, and we'd tell them how Talon's English essay won an award, but we never thought to mention how that same month, Tobias tried out for the freshman baseball team, and how thirty minutes into the very first day of tryouts, the varsity coach came over to watch him, offering him a spot on his roster that very same day."

A reminiscent smile covers her lips. "He was so excited, kept saying how he was the only freshman on the team and there hadn't been anyone his age on the varsity team in years. He had the biggest smile, so excited to tell us all about it, and you know what I did?" Her nostrils flare as she fights her emotions, and I'm almost nervous for her to share.

She swallows, her gaze falling to her lap in shame. "I told him to keep his voice down, that Talon was busy writing his admissions essay in the other room and couldn't be disturbed. I-I gave him a twenty-dollar bill and told him to go for Mangonada's, but not to spoil his dinner." Her tears come then, but she quickly looks to the sky to blink them away. "I didn't even say, 'here, go celebrate, I'm proud, son.' I just pushed him out the door and went and peeked in on Talon."

My chest aches for the boy she's describing, not unlike the man I've come to know.

I judged him wrong at first. It's not that he didn't care about school, because he does. He just struggles no matter the approach he takes and it seems he's tried many. When he felt as if he failed, he pushed his main focus into his passion, something he knew he was great at.

But does it really matter?

If he's driven to do well in school in order to do what he loves on the field, is it even important to remember *why* he works hard to keep his grades up? He does keep them up and that's what counts. He's not failing. He's not on the verge of dropping out.

He does what he has to do. Period.

I assumed he didn't care, but now I know that's false. It's like he shared with me yesterday. Avix took his hotshot title and did what they could to spin him into a hot mess. He simply accepted what he couldn't change, that the world would see him how they wished and no achievement of his would change that.

It didn't at home, with the two people who loved him most in the world, so why would it here, on a campus with thousands upon thousands of strangers?

Honestly, it's almost as if he doesn't take himself seriously at times, like he laughs when others do because that's his role as placed upon him by outsiders who don't really know him.

He is Tobias Cruz, 'The Playboy Pitcher.' An all-star athlete with the dirtiest curve in the game, future MLB gold and a hall of fame legend.

He is baseball.

God, he is so much more.

Olivia clears her throat, taking a moment to tickle Bailey's belly while I nod and thank the waitress as she fills two mugs with hot coffee.

Adding a load of creamer, I sit back in my chair, enjoying the warm beverage before Bailey is ready to come back into my arms.

"The fighting started not long after that," his mother

shares next. "I realize now that was only for attention too, but every time we had to pick him up at school or the park or take him home early from a tournament because he got kicked off the field for something or another, the first thing that would fly out of my mouth would be something along the lines of 'why can't you behave like your brother did ...'"

"Your son loves you, Olivia," I whisper, unsure of what else to say. "He talks about your cooking and even makes what he calls your 'famous recipes' sometimes. You know he's helping an older couple in town build a deck at their home?"

Her smile is pleased. "Is he?"

I nod. "He said if his dad hadn't shown him how, he wouldn't know what to do."

Olivia's muscles seem to ease a bit and I'm grateful for it.

I can't imagine the pain it causes a mother when she realizes she's let her child down. Just thinking about doing wrong by Bailey makes my heart ache.

"He loves you and to be honest, I'm not sure he holds any of this against you," I tell her before cautiously adding, "He just wants to feel like you're proud, and maybe not of what he's doing as a pitcher, but of the man he's trying to be. Someone who works hard and doesn't give up. Who is there for his friends and teammates when they need him, who goes out of his way for a girl he hardly knows."

Secretly walking me home in the dark to make sure I was safe when he didn't know more than my name and hair color. How, once he did, he started to pick me up without my asking. Suggesting he bring dinner to me when he sees my fridge empty while making sure not to acknowledge that fact as he does it, because he was raised better than that.

I smile at Olivia and a long sigh leaves her.

"Maybe I was wrong about that man," she says softly, allowing Bailey to take her hands and using hers to help hold her up. "I just thought he was trying to take advantage of my son, but maybe he really did save him."

My brows pull in and I tip my head slightly, but then realization dawns on me.

My son was lucky enough to get a second chance, got into a school with a push from that man ...

Olivia's words from our last conversation come back to me, followed by what Tobias said to me today.

There's only one other person in this fucking world I allow to get in my head ...

"Coach Reid."

Olivia nods. "Tobias came home one day with all these ideas in his head, and to be honest, we didn't believe any of it. I was so angry. He was a senior, his grades were up and down, and he had just been kicked off the baseball team."

He was kicked off his team?

"Then here came this man in a blue polo, putting the fire we'd come to miss right back into his blue eyes, and I was terrified the man would disappear, making the fall ten times harder the second time around. One day, he packed all his things, and off he went the next. He called us from school, showed us his room, and introduced us to some of his new teammates. You know, on video call?" She lifts Bailey to her shoulder, patting her butt and bouncing her lightly as her cloudy eyes come to mine. "He was happy and smiling and ... he *is* happy, isn't he?"

I nod. "He is ... and it doesn't hurt that the school paints him as a god."

A loud laugh spurts from Olivia.

"I'm serious, there're giant posters of him in the halls, and this banner the size of a billboard outside of the athletic department. I mean, talk about giving someone a big head, right?" I tease, and her laughter continues.

"I bet he loves it."

"Oh yeah."

She sighs, a thankful smile on her lips. "He's lucky to have you, Meyer." She tips her head. "You're not just his tutor, are you?"

My mouth opens, but nothing comes out, and I look to my lap with a chuckle.

When my eyes meet hers, I find a knowing gleam within them.

"He's ... I like being around him and when I'm not I ... want to be."

Olivia fights a grin. Not well either. "But?"

My lips twitch and I look to Bailey. "*But* ... things are a lot more complicated. My life and his ..." I shake my head, unsure of what else to say.

"My husband was a butcher when I met him. Want to know what I was?" She raises a brow, answering before I have time to say a word, "A vegetarian."

A laugh leaves me, and she winks.

Touché.

Olivia looks to the water fountain beside us, smiling when a dove comes down to sit on a rock, as if a new sense of calm has settled over her. "Man, first-round pick, huh?"

Her lips curl even higher. "My baby boy."

My nose burns as my emotions get the best of me and when Olivia looks to me, both our laughs crack.

Setting my mug down on the table, I lean across it. "Will you do something for me?"

Olivia tips her head, and to my surprise, she says, "name it."

DIRTY CURVE

CHAPTER 23

Tobias

Echo pops to his feet, holding a hand out to the umpire as he jogs over to me on the mound.

I wipe my brow on my sleeve, staring down the next batter as he makes his way toward the plate, but I shift my attention to E when he puts himself in front of me.

He spits, lifting his glove up to cover his mouth, so no dickheads can read his lips while he bitches me out. "Bro, what the fuck are you doin'?" he hisses. "That's the third motherfucker you've hit."

"He's talking shit."

"Newsflash asshole, they all do. Don't forget who's got their dick swinging in his face every at bat." If the cameras weren't on him, he'd be glaring at me right now. "I don't know what's going on, but suck it up, bitch. You want to be pissed at something, be pissed at the fucker who hit a double off you and leave his ass stuck on that base."

"Fuck you."

"That's right, fuck me." He punches his glove with his closed fist. "Right here, baby. Hard and fast, just the way I like it."

I can't help but laugh and Echo's grin slips.

He hits my left arm with his glove, pointing my way as he gets in position behind the plate. Echo tugs his catcher's mask back in place, and the umpire gives us the go.

So, I force my anger back into its true form, a burning sense of disappointment, and do what my boy asks, what my team needs.

I do my fucking job and strike out the next two batters, allowing the third to hit out of spite, knowing Coop will make the out in center. And he does.

In my peripheral, Coach crosses his arms, spitting to the side as he eyes me, but mine move to the seat two spaces left of home plate, still empty two innings in.

It fucking stings.

Thankfully, I'm the next at bat, so when Coach tries to approach me, I have an excuse to push past him, grab my shit and get right back onto the field.

'Cause I'm a glutton for punishment, my eyes cut right back to the seat, the one my girls are supposed to be sitting in, and my heart drops to my feet, nearly knocking me over on its way back up.

The seats are no longer empty, but my girls, they aren't sitting there ... my mom is.

My mom is at my game.

I walk to the fence, slapping my palm against the warm metal, and I couldn't stop the smile on my face if I tried.

My mom smiles sheepishly, slipping Bailey's bow

into her hair.

Tutor Girl.

Fuck me, that girl. She wanted me to know she sent her.

With the confidence of a shark in a fishpond, I step up to the plate, spinning to point at my mom before I get into my stance.

I wiggle my fingers, wrapping them tightly around the grip and lift my hands high above my right ear.

I know what he's about to serve me, and I'll let him have his glory ... 'cause after that I'm going to make a fool out of him.

I take the strike, and then I nail his slider, taking first base.

When I look up in the stands, my mom's on her feet, her hands folded in front of her and I see it. For the first time in a long time I feel it, my mother's pride.

My lungs inflate and I clench my teeth together, 'cause goddamn, it's a lot.

She's here, at my game in our hometown. It's more than I'd ever expected and until this fucking moment, I had no idea how much I wanted this.

I have one person to thank for it, and I've got a feeling she's watching me right now from her hotel room, so I look into the camera along the first base line, knowing they'll zoom in as I do and say something only she'll understand.

"No lie."

From there, I rock the fuck out of the rest of the game, showing my mom exactly what I'm capable of.

And when I get back to the girl waiting on me, I

might just beg her to let me do the same.

After the game, I try to talk to my mom, but the bus is set to head back to Avix in an hour and to keep up my charade of being on it, I have to stick with the team.

My mom asks me to call her when I get in so we can chat, and after a quick promise to her, I run into the locker room.

I take a hurried shower and bag my shit up to make the equipment manager's life easier, and make my way toward the exit, but as I step from the locker room and into the hall, Coach is there.

He's leaning against the wall, his hands in his pockets. Turning his head my way, he grabs the toothpick between his lips. "First out, as always."

"Yes, Coach." I nod, mentally noting it's a quarter to three, and the hotel's latest checkout time is four o'clock.

"What happened out there today, son? You wasted pitches, added to your count, that's two fewer batters I can give you at Friday's game."

Licking my lips, I look off. "Sorry, Coach."

"Sorry," he muses. "That what you'd tell the scouts if they asked?"

"You mean the ones that didn't exist?" I look back to him, unsure of why I threw that out just now.

The creases at the corner of his eyes deepen slightly. "I told you, I called them off."

"You also told me I was out fucking off, but I was with the boys. And you, the way they tell it."

His brows cave. "I didn't say you were doing anything other than what you just repeated. It's not my problem if you read into it differently."

Unease stirs in my gut, and I nod.

Maybe he's right. Maybe I'm so used to doing stupid shit that I jumped to conclusions my own damn self.

His features tighten, and he licks his lips. "You got something to say, son, say it."

"Last night and this morning felt off." I shrug. "I meant to be back to my hotel early. I didn't plan on getting fucked up."

His eyes narrow farther. "Then I guess it was no different from every other night for you, huh?" I pinch my lips together, unsure if the indignation I'm picking up in his tone is real or in my head. "You go out and get fucked up, break all the rules *I* set, and then you call me to clean up your mess. And then you repeat yourself. I've done it more times than you remember, but all of the sudden, you're upset with me for wording things the way I did when I was helping *you* out?" He kicks off the wall, his arms crossing over his chest as he studies me.

Guilt and a nasty sense of embarrassment sweeps over me. I haven't gone off like that in a while, but it's not his fault he's unaware of the changes I've made in myself. He can only base my behavior on what he's seen, and he's seen a lot of bullshit from me over the years.

"Sorry, Coach," I tell him, meeting his eyes with the respect that he deserves and hoping he can read my honesty for what it is. He is there for me and has had my back more times than I can count. I can always depend on him to do what's right by me and I shouldn't have let my emotions get to me today when I thought Meyer bailed on me.

Same goes for last night. I never should have allowed any of that to happen, and that's on me, not the man that gave me a place to sleep it off. I would have been angrier with myself had I gone back to Meyer like that, loud and unaware of what the fuck I was doing.

After a second, the man pulls me into him and pats my back.

As he steps away, he squints. "You know you can tell me if there's something going on, something you're worried about ... maybe someone?"

My lips curl, but I drop my eyes to the ground before looking back up. "I'm good, Coach."

He raises a brow, but I shake my head.

I'm not ready to share anything with anyone, not yet. She tripped out at the thought of being caught up in the media before, so it'll only get worse.

Xavier steps out of the locker room, Neo and Echo right behind him.

They slow as they pass us, nodding their chins and saying bye to Coach.

"I need to get to the airport," he says, a small frown written across his forehead as he digs into his pocket, pulling out two more of the pills he gave me this morning, the ones I must have forgotten in his room. "Here, take these, now, get some electrolytes back into your body and get some rest on the ride home."

I toss them in my mouth, washing them down with half of my Vitamin Water.

He nods, scowls, and then pats my shoulder as he

begins to walk away, but he pauses after a couple steps, turning back to me with a grin. "Hey, uh, what's 'no lie'?"

A laugh leaves me, and I lick my lips. "A message for a friend."

"Right ..." His mouth twitches. "Check in with me after your exam on Thursday, huh?"

"Yes, Coach."

Damn near bouncing on two feet, I wait for the man to hit the exit, and then I cut in the opposite direction.

A half hour later, I'm walking through the hotel lobby, and out into the garden that leads to our rooms, but as I'm making my way over, my eyes are called to the left.

I pause where I stand, and something in my chest tightens.

Meyer sits on a towel in the grass, Bailey lying on her back in front of her. She leans over her, making it easier for Bay to play with the length of her mama's hair.

Her hair.

It's down, maybe even curled a little.

For me?

It seems longer somehow, and Bailey's enjoying it.

I don't realize I'm walking closer to them until Meyer's eyes lift to mine.

I'm not sure what she sees on my face, but her chest rises with a full inhale, and the softest of smiles curls her lips.

Taking the last few steps to get to her, I bend and grab her by the hand, hauling her to her feet.

She gazes up at me, worry pulling at her forehead as her eyes move between mine. She opens her mouth, but she doesn't get the chance to speak because I cover her lips with my own.

My hands glide into her hair and at first, I kiss her slowly, before pressing my mouth against hers more firmly. The sweet scent of cinnamon and vanilla fills my lungs, conquering my mind, and pushing me forward. I take her long hair in my free hand, wrapping it around my palm as I pull her bottom lip between my own, giving both little tugs. Opening my eyes, I lean back to look at her.

Her cheeks are flushed in a way that has my body heating and me dying to see more of it, but it's her eyes that I can't look away from.

They're bright and open, the deep brown shining with an added copper glow, but more than that, it's what I can't see that has my muscles flexing. There's no tension in sight, no pull between her brows and no hesitation in her touch. It's as if she's with me right now, fully. Completely. Her fears and anxiety tucked away, at least for now, and this time, when my hand falls, freeing her hair, it's her who pushes forward, reaches up, and pulls my lips back down to meet hers.

All I can think is *fucking finally.*

Finally, she's doing what I wanted by taking what *she* wants.

And it seems my Tutor Girl wants more of me.

Thank fuck, too, because I'm not sure I could ever get enough.

Avix Inquirer:

Pink balloons or blue?
Does The Playboy Pitcher have some
explaining to do?

CHAPTER 24

Tobias

Pushing out the double doors of the lecture hall, I take the steps two at a time and start the small trek across campus toward Meyer's apartment. But as I pass the student center, a photo catches my eye and I jerk to a stop, squinting

No...

Tearing my new phone from my pocket, I pull up the school app and scroll down to the newspaper section.

Sure as fuck, there it is.

I zoom in on the image that was published in the school paper this morning and a low curse leaves me. It's of Meyer and myself, standing right outside our hotel room doors, Bailey's car seat at our feet. My hand is midair and Meyer's anxious eyes are on me. The photo must have been snapped seconds before I grabbed ahold of her face and claimed her lips that first time.

The reporter that Neo hooked up with had to have crept back into the hall to take this and sold it to our staff here, knowing she'd get paid a fuck-ton more from them than she would her own school.

It's one thing to throw a shirtless photo of me on the cover of the school newspaper to help up their sales and online views, but it's another to exploit Meyer and Bailey.

I'll have to talk to Coach about this later, see if there's anything he can do.

So much for keeping a low profile until she was ready.

Rather than talking to her about it over the phone, I keep toward her place, but when I knock, it's Bianca who answers.

Her eyes widen and she tugs the door closed behind her. "Uh ... hi."

"Hi." I squint with a laugh. "Meyer in there?"

"She's not actually. She left earlier."

"She's off today."

Bianca nods. "Yeah, she is."

I frown. "Where'd she go?"

She opens her mouth, and then closes it, her cheeks filling up with air as she shrugs. "Call her and see?"

"All right ..." My eyes narrow. "You know if she saw the school paper today?"

"She hasn't been on campus, so I doubt it." She crosses her arms, leaning against the doorframe. "Why?"

Pulling my phone from my pocket, I lift it up and she leans in.

She darts forward, snagging the thing from my hand, hers shooting up to cover her mouth, a muffled, 'oh fuck' following. Her strained gaze lifts to mine. "She definitely has not seen this. Don't tell her about it!"

My head tugs back.

"I mean, just wait until you see her to tell her, or show her, and if she sees it first, fine, but don't like ... send it to her or anything. Let her have the day without adding a new worry." Bianca bites at her fingernails. "It's out there, so there isn't jack you could do about it anyway, you know?"

With a frown, I nod. "Right. You think she'll be upset?"

A laugh bubbles out of her throat, but it's mocking, not to mention a little anxious. "Yeah, she's gonna, might have a mini breakdown to go with. It fucking sucks, I'll tell you that much."

"Where is she?"

Her eyes fly up to mine. "Call her and ask," she repeats. "I have to go, I'm supposed to be on a Zoom call, but I blacked out my screen when you knocked so they could be trying to talk to me this whole time."

Nodding, I step away, heading toward campus as I try Meyer's cell, but she doesn't answer.

We got home late last night, and she was supposed to call me this morning, but when she didn't, I figured I'd wait until after my exam to try her in case she was able to sleep in.

Guess she didn't sleep in since she's already up and out the door before ten-thirty.

I start to text her, but then my phone flashes with Xavier's name.

"What up, man?"

"Bro, where you at? We said we wanted to leave by ten."

Wait, what? "Leave where? I just got out of my

exam."

"Us too, dipshit, but we're going to MiraCosta's game, remember? Check out the third baseman that's trying to take my spot on the team next year?"

Fuck.

"Yeah, yeah, I'll be there in ten. I'm on campus." I hang up, and with a sigh, make my way home, texting Meyer on my way.

Me: I want to see you today, Tutor Girl. Let me make you dinner.

Three little bubbles pop up, letting me know she's responding, but they disappear a couple times before a message finally comes through.

My Tutor Girl: Hey, I'm sorry, but I'm not going to be home tonight.

My feet freeze in place, an instant frown building. Before I realize what I'm doing, I've typed out *well where the fuck are you going to be,* but quickly delete it and go with something that hides the possessiveness burning inside when every bone in my body is screaming to show it.

Me: Oh, yeah?

I don't want to sound like a whiny bitch, so I quickly send something else, so she doesn't have to respond to that.

Me: How about breakfast?

My Tutor Girl: I would say yes, but I don't want to say yes and have to cancel. Today was a little unplanned, but I'll call you tonight when I have a chance.

My jaw clenches, and I want to ask her where she's at and where she'll be, why she might not be home. She doesn't have a car and Bianca is at her house, so what other option is there and why didn't she invite me to tag along?

Now that my exam is over, I'm free and since we're both off, something that likely won't happen again, since she's only off because of the trip to Bispo, I wanted to take her somewhere, get off campus so I could have her to myself again.

Two days wasn't enough, but maybe it was enough for her?

She didn't even ask me about my—

My thoughts are cut off when my phone beeps.

My Tutor Girl: By the way, I checked your scores ... I KNEW YOU WOULD ACE THAT EXAM!

My mouth hooks to one side, and I lick my lips, getting my ass moving toward my house again.

That right there was all I needed, just a little something from her.

She said she'll call me tonight, and I'll be answering

on the first fucking ring.

Xavier and Neo are waiting outside for me when I get there, and we load into X's ride, headed for the game.

I pull up the article in the school paper once more and scroll down to the comments section where people are placing bets on who Meyer is and if the baby in the car seat is mine. There're the usual haters filling the thread, but it's the heart-eyes emojis and 'lucky him' comments that I focus on.

"What are you smiling at back there, fucker?" Neo teases.

"Your sister sent me nudes," I joke, looking up in time to dodge his backhand and watch as Xavier shakes his head.

I tuck my phone back in my pocket, smacking the back of the seat. "So, how are we gonna do this? Slide in quietly, sit back and watch this team attempt to look like a team?"

"Nah, we had a better idea." X laughs, nodding at Neo.

Neo lifts a bag from the floorboard, tossing it my way.

The contents spill in my lap and I can't help but laugh.

Well, all right then.

It's the second inning by the time we're changed

and making our way down the main aisle that leads to the bucket seats above their dugouts.

The crowd starts to laugh and shout and just as my boys wanted, we gain the attention of the home team in our shark costumes. The camera crew zooms in on us, putting us up on the big screen. So, we do the little dance our mascot does at the home games and jiggle our shark tales in circles.

The coaches shake their heads, and a few of the players who don't have their boxers in a bunch laugh, dancing along.

We take the field-level seats Coach hooked us up with and kick back to watch the game, but a half hour in, these fucking things are killing us, so we step out of them, passing them off to some drunk frat boys a few rows back.

By the fourth inning, Xavier has seen all he came to see, and to his frustration, the kid's not half bad. He has the ability to give X a run for his money next year if Coach decides to take him on, and he just might. If he looks this clean out here, he'll only look better when he's playing up a level and against worthy opponents.

X takes off up the steps, and Neo sighs beside me, turning his head to me.

Concern lines his eyes, but he nods, and I know what he's thinking.

He and his boy will figure it out, he'll be out there with him day and night, helping him bust his ass, and pushing him like only a good friend would.

"Come on, man. Our boy's gonna need a beer or five." Neo pushes to his feet, offering me a hand, but as I stand, something draws my eyes left, and every muscle in my body locks up.

Two sections up and four seats to the right, a familiar messy ball of hair shines in the sun.

Unsure I'm seeing things right, I squeeze my eyes shut, giving my head a little shake, and when they open, nothing's changed. It's her.

"Cruz," Neo snaps, and I reluctantly look to him.

"Go. I'm gonna hang back, get a ride."

"You sure, bro? 'Cause once we hit the party, there'll be no driving for us."

I nod, pushing him off as I lower back into the seat. "I'm good, man," I say, unsure he's even still there to hear it.

All I know is Meyer *is* here, at a junior college baseball game twenty miles away from campus when I couldn't even get the girl to come to mine, a D fucking 1 University game that *I* play in. Sure, she'd have been at my last one had she not found the opportunity to send my mom instead, but that's not the fucking point.

She's here and as I stare at the girl across the field, I realize she's not only here ... she's here with someone, that or the guy to her left has decided to get friendly, attempting to chat her up and waiting to see if she bites.

I think she's biting.

She leans over, stealing the blond fucker's popcorn, and laughs when he tosses a small handful at her. Blindly taking my phone from my pocket, I call her, my knee bouncing as I wait to see what she does.

I sit forward when she starts digging in her bag, but it goes to voice mail before she can pull it out, so I quickly redial, and then her phone is in her hands.

My pulse thumps and then it fucking knocks when she slowly tosses the thing back down, my call not even being ignored but disregarded completely.

Then it gets worse.

Meyer shifts in her seat, and suddenly Bailey is there, in her lap, but she doesn't stay there long.

The dude at her side snags her, bringing her in to kiss her cheek.

The way I like to.

He holds her against him.

The way I've done, too.

Anger and confusion swim in my gut, and it's followed by a searing sense of jealousy, all that mixed with the heat, and I might just fucking vomit.

Who the hell is this dude?

I've never seen him and from here, he looks like a tall, decent-looking fucker.

He's wearing a hat like a hat's meant to be worn and his tattoos are showing under the sleeves of his T-shirt. It's not tight like some gym junkie, but it's easy to see he's fit.

And that my girl is comfortable with him, maybe too comfortable.

Another thought hits, stinging my insides in ways I can't explain.

Is this Bailey's dad?

We've never talked about that, her having one or not. Who he is or what he's like.

If he was a good man or a bad man, or worthy of being called a *man* at all.

He must be, if this is him, because he's holding one of my girls and the other sitting beside him would never let him close if he weren't.

Either way, the girl to his right isn't his to touch.

She's mine.

I fly from my seat and walk my ass all the way around the stadium, posting up on the tunnel they'll be forced to exit through come the end of this game.

Time seems to tick by slowly, but eventually her laughter assaults me, and my fingers begin to twitch. As they step around, the guy throws an arm around her, pulling her to him as she pushes Bailey along in her stroller.

I kick off the wall, jumping right in front of them and blocking their way.

Meyer jerks, her head popping up with a gasp.

Her brows snap together. "Tobias."

"Tobias?" the guy repeats, his head jerking toward me. "Holy shit! You're Tobias Cruz—"

His words are cut off when my fist connects with his jaw, sending his neck snapping back, and he drops.

"Oh my god!" Meyer shouts.

I jump on him, rearing back to hit him again, but she shoves at my shoulder.

"Stop!" She forces her body between ours, gently touching the busted skin of the asshole's cheek. "Are you okay?"

I spit over her shoulder, right into the guy's face and she jerks around, her eyes wild with anger.

"What the hell is wrong with you?!" she screams, shoving at me, so I push to my feet and she follows.

"What's wrong with you? Huh?" I throw a hand out. "What the fuck am I?"

Nothing, like I've been to my family for years.

Like I'd be without ball.

Like I was before Coach gave me more.

Like I was before she came into my life.

I don't realize I'm backing up, until my shoulder hits the concrete wall opposite of where she stands, her face wrenched tight.

"You know what?" I shake my head. "Fuck this. Fuck you."

"Watch your fucking mouth, man!" the dude shouts as he pushes to his feet.

My lips curl and I dart forward again, but then Meyer is in my way. In my face.

Stepping fucking closer and my body starts to shake.

Baby ...

"He's my brother."

I blink. And then I blink again, slowly cocking my head as I stare at her, searching for a sign of deceit but coming up empty.

So, I use her own words, seeking a truth I need more than fucking air. "No lie."

Her shoulders fall and she shakes her head, whispering, "No lie."

"He's your brother?"

"He's my brother."

I nod, looking off to the side as I blow out a long, strangled breath and when I face forward, I grab her by the wrist, yanking her to me. "And I'm what?"

"Tobias ..."

"Nuh-uh." I tip my chin, my heart still slamming against my ribs. I need to hear it. Now. I need to fucking feel it. "Tell me, baby ... I'm *what*?"

Her smile is soft, but a fire roars behind her eyes as she says, "More."

I don't wait, the need too strong.

I crash my lips to hers and my baby melts against me, kissing me right back.

"Cover your eyes, Bay," is mock whispered behind us, and Meyer laughs as she pulls away.

It doesn't take her long to remember I just laid her brother on his ass, and her eyes narrow expectantly, but it's unnecessary.

I know when I've fucked up, and I can approach it like a man.

Holding my palm out, I offer it to the guy and while his eyes narrow, I can spot the hidden smirk on his lips as he slaps his hand into mine, allowing me to pull him to his feet.

His grip is strong and purposeful and when he lets go, he stands to his full height, that isn't so far off from mine.

I'm still taller.

"My bad, man. I didn't know you were her family."

He lifts a blond brow, his knuckles coming up to dab at the blood dripping down his cheek. "So, if I wasn't, you'd have no problem knocking me on my ass?"

"None at all."

Meyer drops her face into her hands, but her brother laughs, his other hand coming around to pat at my bicep.

"Then I take it this 'more' she called you means you're good to my sister."

"When she lets me be. She's stubborn as shit."

He laughs, and Meyer shakes her head, flicking her eyes to the sky.

"Sounds about right." He looks to his sister, who begins to shake her head fervently.

"Milo. No," she says pointedly.

His grin spreads wider. "So can we skip all this and get to the part where Tobias fucking Cruz is standing in front of me?"

Meyer groans, grabs the stroller, and walks away, leaving her grinning, *bleeding* brother before me.

CHAPTER 25

Tobias

Meyer sits beside me on the sofa, Milo and Bianca on the floor arguing about who made Bailey laugh louder. They continuously look to Meyer to settle the argument, but she keeps shrugging the decision away.

"Ugh!" Bianca tosses herself back on the beanbag. "She's just being nice because she never sees your ass."

"No, she's just trying not to offend your *bratty* ass."

Her mouth falls open. "I don't get offended!"

"No, you just get butt hurt and hold it against people for weeks."

I expect Bianca to shout back, but she simply laughs, rolls over to grab Bailey and set her on her stomach. "Tell your uncle Milo he's a lying bastard, Bay."

Meyer rolls her eyes, dropping her head back.

The fiasco at the field today left me feeling like a jackass, so when Meyer invited me to tag along with them to lunch, I passed. I didn't want to cut into any more of their time together, but when Milo realized I had no plans and was headed home, the guy begged me to come. I'm talking, prayer hands and the whole thing.

It didn't take much. I wanted to go from the start, and knowing he was more than cool with the idea was all I needed.

Bianca met us at the park after that, but Bailey started to fuss and rather than all of us going back to Milo's hotel room, as Meyer had planned to do, we came back to her house.

Bailey starts rubbing her eyes and lowers her head onto Bianca's chest, so Milo snags a pillow from beside Meyer and stuffs it under Bianca's head. He scoots closer, patting at her butt while quietly singing a lullaby I've never heard.

From here, I can't see Bailey's face, but her little cheeks squish with what I know is a smile, and my own curves my lips.

Sensing Meyer's eyes on me, I glance over, and sure enough, they are, but this time, she doesn't look away. So, I twist my body to face hers, lifting my left arm onto the back of the sofa.

I stare right back.

"What's on your mind, baby?"

Her cheeks tint a perfect pink and it takes a second, but then her soft little smirk lifts. "You were jealous today," she whispers.

"Fuck yeah, I was."

A quiet laugh leaves her, and she drops her head back onto the cushion, but not once do those intoxicating brown eyes move.

I want to lean over and put my lips on hers, but I won't. Not in front of her family. That would have to be her move.

And they must think so too, 'cause Bianca says, "Just kiss him already."

Meyer's blush creeps up her neck and she slowly looks to her best friend.

"I'm dying to see what happens when gas is poured over fire, so please, get on with it." Bianca grins.

Milo rolls his eyes, but then pops up on his elbow. "Why don't you guys go out? I know my school goes buck wild Thursday nights since close to no one has classes tomorrow. This place is likely ten times what mine is. There's got to be somewhere to let loose."

"Yeah right. Bailey's—"

"Asleep, chica." Bianca gives me an unrelenting expression. "I know what to do if she wakes up. I know you won't stay out all night, just like you know you could if you wanted, because we'll be here."

Milo nods, looking from me to his sister.

Meyer opens her mouth, but he shakes his head, stopping her from saying exactly what he knew she was about to.

"I'll be here all day tomorrow. We had all day today. Let me do this. I never get to help you out."

"You help me out all the time." She frowns.

"Phone calls aren't the same thing," he tells her.

"It's the perfect thing," she argues.

Milo's shoulders lower an inch. "Let me be here in a different way. Go, have some fun. Tobias'll watch out for you and we'll be here when you get back." They share a look I can't explain.

While unease still tugs at her muscles, Meyer turns

to me.

I tip my head, gauging her. "They're partying at the team house tonight. We could go by there for a bit? They've been on my ass lately, asking where I've been." I grin, dragging my knuckles along her shoulder. "Let me show them."

Please, baby ...

Anticipation has my abdomen clenching.

Meyer searches for something in my expression, and hers begins to soften. But there's a slight pull at the edges of her eyes, as if she's wrestling with something on the inside and whatever it is, it might just win over, make the decision for her, one that won't end in my favor.

And I get it, I do.

She's a busy woman with school and work and Bailey. Her downtime isn't really downtime because she's exhausted, understandably so. I have no fucking clue how she manages all she does, and she does it like a damn queen. All I know is I like being part of it.

That, and I want her to keep letting me.

My lips curve to one side, letting her know it's okay if she's not up for it. I'm good with exactly what we're doing now. I just want to be near her, so it's more than surprising when she whispers, "Okay."

My eyes narrow. "Okay?"

She chuckles, pulling herself to her feet, and my eyes follow. "Yeah, okay."

I shoot up beside her, my grin fucking ridiculous, but I don't care. I've been dying to have her at my side and under my arm.

To show she's mine.

The others laugh and Meyer chews at her lip. "Let me put Bailey in her crib, and we'll go."

"Whenever you're ready, ma."

I watch her walk over, bend to grab Bailey, and disappear into her room before turning back to her brother and best friend. "Should I feel guilty as fuck right now?"

Bianca laughs, dragging herself to her feet. She plants her hands on my shoulders and gives a curt nod. "Yes, you should," she whispers. "That means you respect her as a mother."

"I think it means he loves her."

My head snaps toward Milo and I frown, but it quickly turns into a laugh when Bianca swiftly spins, slapping him with a pillow I didn't even see her snag. "Make yourself useful and go get us some ice cream or something."

Milo smirks, salutes me, and walks out the door.

"He always listen to you like that?"

Bianca grins. "The smart ones do."

Both of us look down the hall when the squeak of Bailey's door sounds. Meyer steps from the room, anxiously running her hands along her jeans.

I walk up to her, grab her by the hands and pull her to me. "You sure you want to go? We can put a movie on instead."

"I think we finished Netflix," she jokes with a smile. "Let's go before I change my mind."

We're out the door in five seconds flat.

I love how she didn't pause to look in the mirror or take the time to change.

I love how she's comfortable in her own skin and has stopped hiding her body under her baggy sweater.

I think that means he loves her...

I look to the girl at my side, and before she can reach for the door handle of my truck, I'm spinning her against it, leaning in and taking her lips with mine.

Meyer responds instantly, kissing me back with as much need as I'm feeling, but when her hands begin to glide along my skin, I pull away. I drop my forehead to hers. "Get in the truck, Meyer, or we might not make it out at all."

"I think I'm okay with that," she pants.

My laugh turns into a groan, and I free myself from her wandering hands. "Not a chance. I'm ready to show you off."

She pulls her bottom lip between her teeth and my chest rumbles. I rip away, practically running around the damn hood. "In the truck, Tutor Girl. Now."

She laughs and climbs right in.

Walking into the house, Cooper is the first person to spot me, and he throws his hands into the air, beer sloshing from his cup onto the floor at his feet. "Ohh! Your royal fucking highness, you've graced us with your presence!" He mock bows.

Grinning, I clap my palm into his.

"What up, fuckhead?" He grins. "Finally get your

head out of your ass, or what?"

My fingers tighten around Meyer's and I tug her forward, placing her a space ahead of me and Coop's eyes fly to hers.

He's shocked, that's for sure, but his smile stays in place. "Meyer!" He flies forward, hugging her, and the beer splashes again.

I grab him by the collar, hauling him back, but Meyer simply smiles, kicking her foot to get the droplets of beer off her toes.

"Hey, Coop." She glances from him to me and back.

Coop does the same. "You and Cruz?" He whistles. "That's ..."

I lift a brow, but it's Meyer who finishes his sentence for him.

"Unexpected?" Meyer gives me a sly smile before returning his attention to Cooper. "Trust me, I know."

Cooper grins, shrugging his shoulders. "Well, hey, rock it out, girl."

Meyer laughs and I wiggle my brows, dragging us farther into the house, saying quick hellos to people we pass, but without stopping.

It's when we get into the main room that people really get rowdy.

Neo's eyes hit mine and he starts barking, jumping up on the pool table in the middle of someone's game. He cups his mouth with his hands, gaining as much attention as possible. "Fellas, tip your hats and pull out them handcuffs. Time to lock a woman up or watch her go, 'cause Tobias motherfucking Cruz has returned to the hothouse!"

The team shouts like they're in a fucking nightclub,

and I catch Neo's eyes again, gliding my fingers past my throat as if to say cut the shit.

He frowns, but then he spots Meyer at my side and winces.

Then the fuckhead shouts again. "And to all you lovely ladies, keep your clothes on, and steer clear of my boy ..." His grin is slow, and he shifts all his attention to Meyer. "'Cause he's got a woman now and trust me when I say, she's first-string material. You don't stand a chance."

He follows it up with a wink, hopping down to head our way, but we're already bombarded by the rest of the boys, each dying to get closer and find out more about the girl on my arm.

They've seen me leave with more girls than I care to admit, something I'm pretty fuckin' embarrassed by now, but they've never seen me come with one.

"You're literally a celebrity to your own team," Meyer mumbles through clenched teeth.

"You proud?" I joke, and her lips pull to one side.

She thinks I'm fucking adorable.

It's odd I love that she does.

Nobody wants to be adorable, but if she likes it, I want to be it.

Daniel Rojas, one of my relief pitchers, steps up first.

"Rojas, this—"

"Hey, Meyer." He focuses on her, nodding his chin my way. "Cruz."

I frown, my eyes moving between the two.

Meyer gives a single wave. "Hey, Danny, how's it going?"

"Good, good." He grins, but he's pushed to the side when Allen, our shortstop's younger brother, steps up.

Allen smiles. "Meyer, what's up?"

"Hey!" Her lips curve and she leans forward, giving him a half hug. "Did you get my email yesterday?"

"Hell yeah, I did."

Meyer laughs. "Well earned. I bet your coach was ready to throw you a party after that."

"My body owes you for that one."

"What the fuck, bro?" I snap and both their heads snap to me.

Along with a few others around us too.

"Your *body* owes her?" I step in front of him. "Are you for real right now? You're gonna come into this house and say some shit like that? To my girl?"

"Tobias," Meyer whispers.

His palms lift in the air. "Aye, I was referring to the ass kicking my coach would give me in the gym and on the stairs, man. Legit my body, my muscles ... I didn't mean anything else by it." His eyes flick past my shoulders briefly. "She's a badass tutor, that's all."

Tutor.

She's a badass tutor, he said.

Of course.

Here I am excited to introduce my girl to all these assholes, but most of them already know her. She tutors for the athletic department and is their top tutor at that. Tutoring athletes is her job. Spending time with athletes is what she's paid to do.

There's a flicker of heat in my abdomen, a nasty flare of jealousy.

But then Meyer's fingers flex alongside my own, reminding me that her hand's still tucked *in* mine, and the stormy sensation is smothered.

With a calm I don't quite feel, but confidence I do, I look to my girl. "That she is, my man."

There's an anxiousness I'm sensing from her, but she smiles, and I imagine she's got that whole angel-devil thing going on.

It's a fucked-up quality, possessiveness, but it is a quality.

And I think she kind of likes it.

Either way, I didn't bring her here to have a shitty night, though, so I swallow the part of me I'm still working on and lift our joined hands, kissing her knuckles as I lead us the final steps to my teammates.

It turns out she only knows two more people here, and the rest take turns stepping in front of us to say hello. The plus side is they like her, but of course they do.

What's not to like?

As a group, we hang around the kitchen, spending the next hour laughing. They make jokes, flirt, and try to get under my skin, but it doesn't work.

It might have sixty minutes ago, but not now. Not after witnessing her with my crew. There's a respect between them and her, one they earned on their own time, and knowing that feels pretty fucking good.

They see her as a person, not a toy, and I'm loving the look in these asshole's eyes as they realize she's mine. Mine, mine. As in not just a date for the night.

"So, Meyer, how'd you get stuck with this guy?" My buddy Franky drops down beside her, throwing his arm over her shoulder. "Everyone knows I'm the one who swings harder south."

I knock his arm away, pulling my girl in front of me, and curling my hands around her waist. "Yeah, bro, you swing heavy ... but you also stay swinging."

Franky shoots to his feet, a drunken grin on his face. "One time I couldn't make a moment count, and to be fucking fair, I was a half a bottle of Jose in!"

The boys laugh and Meyer hides her smile by dropping her chin to her chest.

"You know how it goes, Franky, Jose, no lay."

"That's the last time I tell you guys shit!" he shouts with a smile, spinning away when his name is called.

Neo turns to the group and starts telling them some story about him and X in high school, so I lean forward, putting my lips to Meyer's ear.

"For the record, my southern region is impressive as shit, I'm talking north pole status."

Meyer's shoulders shake with her laughter, and she tips her head back, but as her brown eyes meet mine, a weight slips into them, shadowing the golden rims from my view.

The moment her lips move, they're all I see. Plump, full and intoxicating. I take them with my own, playfully nipping at her when she pulls away.

"I'm going to step outside and call Bianca to check on Bailey," she whispers.

"I'll go with you."

"Stay." She spins in my arms. "I'll be right back."

If it wasn't policy to leave a freshman outside the door to keep track of who comes in, I would have followed, but since we do, I stay planted where I am, keeping one eye on the front door, the other on my boys.

Meyer

Out front, I walk to the edge of the driveway, keeping myself in view of the safety guy at the door, and plop onto the grass.

I text Bianca so I don't risk waking Bailey and then look along the road.

This is 'Ruckus Row' here on campus, every house on the block owned and affiliated with campus. The boys' team and frat houses line this side of the street, while the other is made up of sorority and female squads.

Both sides are well lit tonight, LEDs glowing all around, music flowing from most, but there are a few quiet ones. Come tomorrow, the yards will be full and people will be going from house to house on the hunt for whatever it is they're searching for that night.

Some will be looking for a good time, others will be looking for a good way to forget...

Last time I was here, it was for all the wrong reasons, a night I've regretted for far too long, but somewhere along the way, that regret faded into something else, something a little more dangerous.

It transformed into hope.

It's completely reckless, at least where my heart's concerned. I know myself and I won't allow my life to be thrown off course. I can't. I have Bailey to think about, but

I'd be lying if I said it won't break another piece of me to watch the man I've come to know walk away ... like the one I thought I knew before did.

Like all the men in my life have, outside of my brother.

If he does, it will be my fault.

When he does, it will be my fault ...

I'm the one who allowed things to get this far.

"Now this is familiar."

My head snaps right and I shoot to my feet. "What are you doing here?"

His eyes narrow and he goes to speak, but a couple guys step out the door, spotting him.

"What's up, Coach!" One salutes him, while the other nods his chin.

"Boys." He gives a curt nod, watching as they slip behind the wheel of a blue Chevy before turning back to me. "I went by your house today."

My face falls, tension swimming in my stomach. "Why?"

He scoffs, malice driving the sound from his throat. "I wonder, Meyer." He steps closer. "Why would I come by, hmm?"

I swallow, shaking my head. "I don't know."

"Where were you today?"

"That's none of your business."

"No?" He sticks his hands in his pockets, tipping his head with a condescending look in his eyes. "You're not even going to try and lie your way out of this, say you're tutoring someone at eleven o'clock on a well-known party night this side of campus?"

I stare without a word and his lips thin.

"I take it you haven't been online or on campus today," he continues, inquisition heavy in his tone. "If you had, I don't think you'd be here right now, then again, I thought you were smarter than this period. Guess I was wrong."

Panic swells in my chest and I have to fight myself not to pull my phone up again.

"Did you come here looking for me?"

"I came here to check on my athlete," he snaps. "I've been calling Tobias all day, and he hasn't picked up once." He glares. "Do you have something to do with that?"

"I was with Milo," I rush out. "He showed up this morning to surprise me."

He raises his chin, doing his best to decipher if I'm being honest since five seconds ago, I refused to tell him anything. "I got Tobias's grade check-in today, his GPA is almost at a three." He stands tall. "You're done, Meyer."

"There's three weeks of school left. He still needs help—"

"He's got a hint of cushion in his problem class, thanks to your ... dedication. He'll be fine," he snaps. "He'll be removed from your schedule by the time you sign in tomorrow, and I'll be refilling it with others."

A sharp pain knocks against my ribs, and my next words leave me before I have time to think them through. "You can take him off my schedule all you want ..."

He raises a brow. "Don't do something you'll regret, and you will regret it. Don't forget you're no longer on scholarship, Meyer. Think of Bailey."

"Every move I make I'm thinking of her."

"Your actions say differently. Do I need to remind

you I can make all this go away? Not just the job—"

"How can you be like this to me?" I cut him off, my panic morphing into something else. "I'm just trying to get through school so I can take care of myself and my daughter. Why are you making it so much harder than it has to be?"

"Don't put this on me."

"I won't need you forever, you know." I don't mean to whisper. "And then what?"

He's quiet for a moment, but when he speaks, he's just as callous as ever. "You have one stipulation and that's to steer clear of my athletes, *especially* Tobias."

"Then *why* am I in your department? Why do you assign your athletes to me? Why did you assign *him* to me?"

"Again. Do not put this on me." Anger shades his features, and he takes a quick look around before turning back to me. "Do as I said and everything will be fine."

"It's not that simple."

"Make it that simple."

My eyes begin to burn, but I won't cry.

Not yet.

The moment he disappears into the night, I lift my phone up with shaky palms. I know right where to go based on his comments, and open the student app.

I don't even have to click on the news tab, because this article made it onto the main page, as did the photo accompanying it.

My heart drops to my feet as I stare at the three of us, and my phone falls to the grass as I bring my hands up to cover my eyes. I can't hide from that.

Make it that simple, he said.

In other words, end it and quick.

Palms fall to my shoulders, and the soft touch has my heart clenching. His hands glide down, wrapping me up from behind and then his lips are on my neck, my jaw, my ear. "You saw the picture?"

I nod, my head falling against his chest, eyes locked to the lit-up screen wedged in the grass at my feet.

"We look good together, us three."

Tears prick at the back of my eyes, and again, I nod.

We do.

"You upset, baby? I didn't get the chance yet, but I planned on asking Coach Reid to help us out," he says, and those tears swell, threatening to spill over. "He might be able to get them to back off us. I know if I ask, he'll do whatever he can—"

The tears fall. I swiftly reach up, haul his lips to mine, and cut off his thought, allowing all common sense to escape me, knowing it's a cruel notion, but unable to hold back all the same.

Tobias groans, his hand flying up to grip my face, but it quickly disappears into my hair, and I spin, the need to get closer to him overwhelming, heartrending.

As if we're completely in tune with one another, his arm comes down the moment I jump up, my legs wrapping around him as his firm hold tightens.

"Baby ..." he pants, his kiss deep and devastatingly perfect.

My body aches with conflicting emotions, twisting and turning at an insufferable rate.

Dread and desire.

Fear and comfort.

Disgrace and devotion.

Yet still I whisper, "Take me home."

And he does, but much to my surprise, he kisses me good night at my door, with a heartfelt promise of a tomorrow.

Little does he know, come tomorrow, my mind will be clear, and my orders followed.

I'm at the mercy of a man who doesn't deserve to be called one, and there's not a thing I can do about it.

CHAPTER 26

Tobias

I've been out of the house since five fifteen this morning, and I won't be home until around seven, being today's a double header. I planned on dropping a coffee off for Meyer on my way to warmups, but that didn't happen. After class this morning, Coach said he needed me to come by so we could go over some game film, even though we covered most at our last meeting. If it helps secure the win, though, I'm all for it and he knows that.

My call to Meyer goes straight to voice mail, so I send her a quick text, letting her know I'll bring dinner tonight so she doesn't fill herself up on cereal or peanut butter, some of the only items she seems to keep stocked in her house.

At my locker, I toss my shit inside, quickly dress out, and just before I push my locker closed, my phone dings.

My Tutor Girl: I have to work tonight.

Damn, that sucks.

I start to tell her I'll be there when she gets off when another text comes through.

My Tutor Girl: Bianca is picking me up.

That's a bummer, but no big deal. I'm glad she figured out a ride rather than walking home like before.

Me: I'll come over after.

My Tutor Girl: I have to be up really early. Sorry.

I frown at the message.

Sorry. As in, I can't come over, sorry?

A hint of annoyance flares in my gut, but I shake it off.

I'll just go to her work tonight, have dinner with her the way I can. She'll be happy with that.

Yeah, that'll work.

I hit the field with my team, hanging around in the dugout while they warm up since I'm not pitching tonight – my pitch counts being saved for the next series, being this team is ranked last in the league. It makes for a long ass day, but it's good to see the second and third string guys come together with the rest of the team and do what needs done to pull out the win. Coach was smart though and left X and Neo on the field to keep things tight and hold our runs allowed number at its record low.

By the time the second game ends, everyone is beat, the sun shining heavier now that we're deep into May. It never gets too hot here, but we are on a turf field enclosed by a shit ton of metal, so it's hot. I'm not beat though, I'm pumped.

I skip the showers, quickly change back into my street clothes, and slip out without a word.

"Tobias."

I screech to a stop, backpedaling until I can see into Coach Reid's office.

"What up, Coach?"

He frowns, just now setting his clipboard down, his keys still in his left hand as he lowers onto the edge of the desk. "You skipped showers?"

"Didn't play. Figured I'm good until I get home." I shrug, glancing up at the clock on his wall.

His eyes narrow. "Why the rush, I was going to offer to take the team out for dinner."

"Hey, they deserve it, but uh, did you need me for something? 'Cause, if not, I'm gonna run."

He stares at me a moment, a slow nod following. "You go ahead. See you tomorrow."

"Tomorrow, Coach."

I'm out the door, and a few minutes later, walking into the diner, but Meyer is nowhere to be found.

The chick cleaning the tables sees me coming and tries to beeline away, but I catch up to her. "Hey, is Meyer here?"

She sighs, shaking her head. "If Meyer were here, I would be off already."

"O-kay... so she went home early?"

"She didn't show up, playboy." She tosses a dish into her bin and yanks it off the table. "Better luck next time."

Worry slams into me, and I hurry out the door, trying to call her on the way to her house, but it doesn't even ring. Her voice mail picks it up instantly.

"*Fuck.*"

I pick up speed, getting to her apartment in record time.

No one answers the door after my first knock, so I tap my knuckles a little harder, and then the lock clicks on the other side.

Meyer slowly pulls it open and the air whooshes from my lungs, right out of me.

"Shit, thank god." I dart forward. "I thought—"

I freeze after a single step when I realize she has the door drawn closed, nothing but her face and a fraction of her body showing. No part of her is crossed over the threshold of her entryway.

"What's wrong?"

"Nothing, I'm tired."

"That why you're not at work?"

Her eyes pop a bit. "Yeah, I ... I'm not feeling well."

"I can go get some soup or something? 7UP, maybe some ginger ale?" Unease whirls in my gut and I don't know why. "Or I could stay, wake up with Bailey tonight so you can rest?"

She scowls and her eyes drop to the floor. "Bianca's coming over to help. She was here earlier, so if I'm sick, she's already been exposed. It's just ... easier. Besides, you have a game tomorrow."

"I don't have a game until Monday."

"Right," she whispers, still not looking up. "I should go lie down."

A sudden weight falls over me. "Tomorrow then?"

"I-I'm going to my brother's."

My head tugs back. "What?"

"Yeah, he bought us train tickets. We leave in the morning so ..."

"You're going for the night?"

"For the weekend."

"I leave for Nashville Monday, we've got a double, and finish out the series Tuesday, we won't be home until later that night. Then I turn around for another Wednesday evening."

"Yeah, I saw. Good luck."

Good luck?

"Are you okay?"

Her eyes crease and she nods, unable or unwilling to meet my eyes.

"Is this about the picture? I told you, I'll ask Coach to take it down."

Her leg begins to bounce, and a shaky laugh escapes her.

"Baby, what—"

"I hear Bailey, I have to go."

My shoulders fall, but I manage to nod. She said she's not feeling well, so all I can do is take her word for it. "Okay, Tutor Girl. I'll see you Sunday night, maybe?"

Her smile is close-lipped, and then she's closing the door, leaving me on the other side.

Tension pulls at my muscles, but I stretch through it.

Only it all comes back when not fifteen minutes later, on my way home from picking up a plate from the taco truck downtown, I spot Bianca walking across campus with Cooper, headed in the opposite direction of Meyer's place.

By the time Friday night rolls around, I convince myself Meyer doesn't want me to feel obligated to stay with her when she isn't feeling well, so she told me Bianca was going to be there to help out even though that wasn't the truth.

But then when I texted her to make sure she made it to Milo's okay, and all I got back was a quick, one worded 'yes', I started to trip. It got worse when Saturday's good night text went unanswered.

If I knew where Milo lived, I might have driven there right then, and offered to be their ride back tonight, but I don't, which is why I've been parked at the edge of the school property, directly in front of the street that leads to Meyer's apartment's alleyway since noon.

Hours have gone by, and now the sun has fully set, and still no sign of her, so I try her phone once more with no luck.

Pushing to my feet, I climb inside my truck and do the only thing I can.

I head home, pack for Nashville and climb into bed, but sleep doesn't come.

Before I know it, my alarm's going off and exhaustion is in full effect.

My body aches, but I throw myself into the shower, and by the time I'm climbing out, Echo is ready and waiting in the kitchen, a protein shake in hand.

"You look like shit, brother."

"I feel like shit, my man." I take the shake, toss a few Vitamin Waters into the bag I'll take onto the plane with me, and off we fucking go.

I'm going to have to put my headphones in and blast my music to hide the fact that I'm not exactly in the game.

Coach would have my ass for taking my eye off the prize.

But the prize is looking a hell of a lot different nowadays.

Meyer

The last few days have been stressful, the only bit of relief was the fact that I knew Tobias was hours away, so I didn't have to deal with all that came with him being near. I had hoped he would ease up while he was gone, but that was me trying to convince myself of something I knew was far from true. I wasn't simply some girl to him.

I was more.

Which is why it hurt like hell when, like clockwork, every day he would text me.

He wasn't angry or inquisitive. He was sweet and silly.

Told me to tell Bailey things as if she understood or asked questions about what we were doing and how she was. Questions that went unanswered and as a result, they began to shift.

Flirt went to worry, worry to frustration, and that's when anger set in.

The last one I read was four simple words that about killed me.

'What the fuck, Meyer?' he had sent, and after that, I stopped opening them.

But it's Tuesday now, the day he gets back, and my nerves are high.

I'm on my third student of the day when Tobias's fifth text comes through.

I should have known better than to ignore them all, because moments after my phone vibrates on the desk beside me, something tells me to look up, and as I do, all the air leaves my lungs.

Tobias is charging up the front steps of the library.

My throat clogs, and I shoot to my feet, shoving my things in my bag in a panic.

"I'm so sorry, I have an emergency. I'll email you." I dash away, head around the back side of the bookshelves and sneak out the way he came in.

My palms begin to sweat, and I rush around the side of the building, following along the wheelchair path that leads to the child development center. I slip inside and rush into the bathroom, locking myself in an open breastfeeding room. I drop into the rocking chair, my hands coming up to cover my face.

My lips tremble, tears springing into my eyes and heating my cheeks on their way down.

I take a deep breath, blowing it out. *I can't do this.*

I shake my head, staring off into space.

I'm not sure how long I sit there, but when my phone vibrates in my front pocket, I jolt.

With a heavy heart, I pull it out, afraid to look to the screen, but as I do, I find it's not a text from Tobias, but an email from the admissions office at the University of Florida.

A strange numbness slips over me and I lick my lips.

It's with shaky hands that I open it up, and as I read over the acceptance letter, it's as if my insides crack wide open, creating a gaping hole in its wake.

It's painful and deep and suddenly, it's hard to breathe.

I push to my feet, fighting for air I can't seem to find, but then I look to the changing table in the corner, and I think of Bailey.

Of the future we can have rather than the one we can't.

It's torturous to push away thoughts that consume me, to let go of the hope I so recklessly allowed, but it's like I said before.

Reality is as sad as it is serene.

I step out of the room, splashing water on my face and bracing on the counter for a deep breath.

Once I have Bailey all checked out, I rush home, praying Tobias isn't standing on my front porch when we arrive.

Too bad for me, he is.

Shit.

CHAPTER 27

Tobias

Meyer's face falls, and she freezes where she stands.

Anger flares, and I push off the doorframe, but all the pressure in my body washes away as she approaches.

I didn't realize how badly I needed to see her and Bailey. To see with my own eyes that they're okay, but as I realize they're just fine, which deep down I knew all along, the tension returns.

"What the fuck, Meyer?" My shoulders hang, my tone beaten, even to my own ears.

She pinches her lips closed, slipping past me and unlocking her door.

Helpless, I watch as she gently rolls Bailey's stroller inside the apartment.

Slowly, she faces me, and it's not hard to see it's the last thing she wants to do.

A sharp pain punches my gut and I stretch my torso to ease it.

"What's going on?"

"Nothing," she says quickly. "I've been busy."

"Too busy to pick up the phone?" I step closer.

"I don't have a lot of time right now."

"Not even for me?"

A shaky breath flies from her lips and she looks everywhere but at me. "My schedule's jam-packed and—"

"Am I not on your schedule, ma?"

"No, actually. You're not ..."

I was joking, but the finality in her tone stirs something inside me and my muscles grow tight. "What?"

Slowly, her head lifts. "You're not on my schedule anymore, Tobias. Your grades are up. You'll go back to working with your team during study hall hours. That should be enough to get you through finals."

"All right ..." I draw, unease making my pulse pick up. "Whatever, fine, it doesn't matter, but tell me when I can see you? I can come early or late. Walk you to class or to drop off Bay. Whatever works for you, I'm there."

Meyer's eyes cloud and she looks away.

"Baby, what's wrong?" I step forward, but her words have me jerking to a stop.

"You're not my student anymore, Tobias." Her voice cracks, and I'm too fucking stuck to register what she's saying until she's closed the door in my face.

My chest grows tight, the rest of my body following as I force my feet to slide backward. With each step, my confusion grows and by the time I reach my truck, still running, idle in the space where I parked it in my rush, my chaotic mind grows frustrated.

I'm not her student anymore, she said. Well, so

fucking what?

I'm her man.

She's my girl.

And Bay ...

I swallow, stumbling a bit as I drag myself into the driver's seat.

I'm not sure what just happened, but I know something's not right.

She's pulling away, *pushing* me away and I don't understand why.

She's ...

I ...

My frustration bleeds into anger and I'm far past pissed as I reach Coach's house, a two-story home a couple blocks from campus.

There're a few cars out front, but I don't care. I bang my fist on the door, and I don't stop.

It doesn't take long for him to open the door, and as he does, over his shoulder, I spot the rest of the coaching staff sitting around a card table, cigar smoke filling the place.

"Why am I off her schedule?"

He steps out, closing the door behind him. "Son—"

"Why am I off her fucking schedule?! You need to force her to put me back!"

"*You need* to calm down."

"I can't! Give her back to me!"

His head tugs back, his frown deepening. "Give her back ... son, she was your tutor, nothing more."

Before I can think, before I even know what I'm doing, my fist flies, connecting clean across his jaw.

His head snaps to the side and I snap the fuck out of it.

My face falls, and I dart toward him. "Coach, I—"

He jerks away, flinging my hands off him. "Go home."

"Fuck!" I shout, running my hands along my head and spinning to face him again. "I'm sorry, I didn't mean—"

"I said go home. I don't want to see you until it's time to take the field tomorrow." He glares, spitting blood to the side. "Find somewhere else to dress out."

"Yes, Coach." I swallow, a familiar feeling surging inside me, making my temples throb and body heavy.

Regret is a motherfucker, and that motherfucker knows me well.

The ball leaves my hand with a hiss, and Echo's knee drops to the dirt as he slides right to snag it.

"*Ball two,*" the ump calls out.

Echo's throwback has more heat on it than normal, but I ignore it.

Jaw clenched tight, I point my left foot forward, leaning over until my shoulders are parallel with my knee. Ready to pitch from the stretch, I look right to left, letting the bastards on first and third know I haven't forgotten about them.

Echo calls for a curve, but I shake it off, as I do his

next, until he gives me what I want.

A fast ball.

With a deep breath, my nostrils flare and I wind back, releasing a fucking cannon, but this time, Echo's glove hits the dirt.

Ball low.

Fuck!

I grind my teeth together, stretching the cords of my neck and get set again.

Again, Echo tries for the curve, but I jerk my head and his chin lowers.

He's getting pissed, but I don't care.

My game, my ball, my fucking pitch.

I release on a hiss, and once again, the umpire calls out a ball, and the motherfucker walks to first.

My first official walk of the season.

My head is fucking screaming on the inside, but I pull at everything I've got to hold it in, simply stepping off the mound and pointing at the big belly bastard.

Don't fuck with me, blue. Not today.

The man just shakes his head, and when I turn mine, I spot Coach coming out onto the field.

Fuck!

He steps up, meeting my eye with a strain in his own. "You need off this field?"

"No."

"You sure, 'cause—"

"I said no, Coach. Let me finish."

"Bases are loaded, and you have one out."

"I know what I have and what I don't."

He opens his mouth, but remembers the cameras are on us and gives a brisk nod. "Do your fucking job, son."

Rolling my shoulders, I adjust my hat, look across the field and then face my boy.

Echo nods, slaps his glove and drops into position, so I do the same.

We're near the bottom of their lineup, a kid from Kentucky with a batting average below 230. Sitting him down will be cake.

Echo doesn't let up, and drops two fingers, so I nod, giving in.

Curve it is.

I send the fucker, but I know the second it leaves my palm, I'm fucked. That baby's coming around too soon, showing itself, and I watch in disgust as the punk's grip tightens around the thick leather.

The ball connects with the bat in the perfect fucking spot at the perfect fucking time.

His swing is hard and solid and he doesn't drop his shoulders or his head, that boy sends it ... right over the goddamn wall.

Grand fucking slam.

I throw my mitt into the dirt, kicking it away while all four fuckers round the bases to home plate.

Echo comes out to talk to me, but I give him my back, spinning the other way when he jerks at my collar, forcing me to face him.

I don't know why, but I shove the guy hard enough to send him lurching back and then the umpire is in my space, shouting something, but I can't hear.

My ears are ringing, the sun is beaming and the

next thing I know, I've got the ump's chest plate in my hand.

I tug him forward, all to send him tumbling onto his ass.

My coaches and half the team are on the field now, but I know what's coming.

The umpire gives the signal, and I'm ejected from the game.

Coach Reid grips my shirt, but I yank away, unable to look at him as I charge toward the tunnel and into the locker room.

Inside, I tear my jersey from my body, my hat already long gone, and bend at the knee.

I fucking scream, shoot up and start tearing shit off the wall, throwing anything I can grab and reveling in the sound of the clacking metal on metal, but it's not loud enough to drown out the pain.

The fucking confusion.

The ache I never wanted to feel but do.

This is worse, so fucking much worse, than when my parents turned their backs on me my senior year.

Worse than when I realized I'd never live up to my brother in their eyes.

Worse than when I thought I'd never again set foot on a field as part of a team.

I feel weak, like a pussy.

Like a little bitch.

'Cause, fuck me, I'm pretty sure my heart is actually breaking.

Straight up tearing into little pieces inside my body and ripping every blood vessel open with its end.

My body slides along the lockers until my ass hits the floor, my chin slamming into my chest.

I couldn't handle any of those things and I really can't handle this.

Meyer

I'm on my knees in front of the TV when my name is called.

It takes effort, but I look away from the screen, finding Bianca standing there, her bag slung over one arm.

"Oh, chica." Tears well in her eyes instantly and she rushes over, falling onto the floor beside me. "I knew you were watching the game."

I lean into her, shaking my head, but sensation evades me. I can't feel her arms as they wrap around me and I have no clue what she's whispering into my hair.

He just broke on the field, right there for all to see, Tobias lost it.

It's all my fault.

"No honey, it's not your fault."

I pull in a choppy breath. "It is." I sway, fighting back tears. "I knew what would happen, I knew he was more than what everyone saw. I felt something that night months ago. I told ... I told him I couldn't tutor him. I should have fought him harder. I should have fought myself harder."

I shouldn't have fallen in love with him.

But I did, knowing all along nothing could ever come of it.

To allow Tobias to love me would be selfish, because I would be taking away someone else he loves, and that's wrong.

He doesn't deserve to feel betrayed by everyone in his life, and I know that's exactly what would happen, so it's my job to make sure it doesn't.

Because there's no other option, and since there can be no winner here, I'll happily be the bad guy if it saves him the least bit of sorrow.

No matter what, we both lose a little.

I just have to make sure he loses less than me.

I swipe at my face, and pull myself free of Bianca's hold, slowly pushing to my feet.

"Girly, what are you doing?" she whispers, watching as I pull my sweater over my head and smooth my loose strands of hair back.

"Getting ready."

"For what?"

There's a heavy knock at the door moments later and her eyes crinkle.

My lips twitch and I nod, and with a shaky breath and strength I don't feel, I pull the door open, revealing Tobias on the other side.

"Tutor Girl ..."

CHAPTER 28

Tobias

I stumble, falling into a person, or maybe it's a tree? I laugh, push on it, but it doesn't move.

Tree it is.

I take another drink from the bottle and walk over to the cages. Slipping inside, I set the bottle down by the door and flick the switches, the gears kicking on and whistling around me.

Grabbing a bat, I step up to the red X made of tape on the ground and get into my stance.

The first ball whips by and I chuckle, wobbling back a bit before I get ready again.

I swing, but miss and stagger forward, catching myself on the metal chain links.

A ball releases, blasting against my ribs, and I lurch forward.

"Fuck." My hand falls to my ribs, but my body jerks when I'm slammed in the chest, the wind knocked out of me, sending me stumbling back against the fence.

Gasping, I lean over, slapping at the buttons on the wall, but before I'm able to push the off switch, another comes flying forward, nailing me in the jaw and my body slumps, crashing to the floor with my back up against the cage.

"What are you doing here, Tobias?"

"I wanted to see you. I needed to see you."

"You shouldn't have come."

I wince, a ball connecting with my chin.

"Why? Everything was good. We're good."

"Don't make this something it wasn't."

Another ball sends my head snapping into the chain links behind me, and I begin to cough, blood spitting into the air.

"I don't know what that's supposed to mean, but it's bullshit. I know you want me. I know what you feel. Stop this, whatever you're doing, quit."

There's a hard impact against my brow, then something warm is gliding down my face.

"I need you to leave, Tobias, and please, don't come back."

"Baby, just ... just tell me what I did, and I'll fix it. I'll change it. Ma, I'll be anything you want me to be if you just let me be yours ..."

Meyer laughs, but it sounds more like a cry. Don't cry, baby. Don't cry ...

"Is that a joke? I saw you on the field, you lost your mind. I can't have someone who acts that way around me or ... or my daughter."

I lurch forward, my eyes beginning to roll into my head.

Everything fucking aches.

"I would never do anything that put her in danger. Her or you. Meyer, I love—"

"Get away from my house, Tobias, or I'll call the police and tell them you're harassing me."

I groan, my body slammed with a ball again, but I have no idea where I'm hit.

Everything fucking aches, but nothing could possibly sting more than the last words Meyer spoke to me before she slammed the door in my face.

"You're nothing."

I hear a crack, and then I'm choking on something thick and warm.

Everything goes black.

I might lie there, passed out on the floor, for days, I don't know. All I do know is when my eyes peel open, I'm hunched over on the turf-covered cement of the batting cage. It's dark, my body is burning, and I'm covered in my own blood.

Reaching up, I accidentally touch my nose, wincing.

"Fuck," I groan.

A deep hum rings in my ears and I look up, finding the pitching machine is still on, but the bucket's empty.

I look around at all the balls surrounding me, and it's easy to know what happened: the thing whooped my ass. My chest rumbles as I pull myself to my feet, turn the shit off, and make a mental note to come clean this mess before anyone else has a chance to see it.

Dragging my ass through the back of the locker rooms, I slip into the shower. The water burns, but I welcome the pain.

Only when I'm stepping out do I look in the mirror, confirming what I already know. My nose is broken.

Pointer-finger knuckle wrapped tight around the bridge of my nose, I press my thumb to the opposite side. I use my other for stability, gritting my teeth as I snap it back into place. It begins to pour some more, but this time, I'm ready, having done this a time or two before, and pinch the thing with a torn towel I had ready.

I drop onto the bench, leaning my head against the locker, and the second I do, all the pain comes back, and it's got nothing to do with the bruises covering my body.

I can't believe the fucked-up place I've put myself in.

No fucking duh a woman, a beautiful, kindhearted, strong as fuck woman with a beautiful, precious baby girl doesn't want me. Why would she?

I'm a fuckup.

I don't think, I act.

The last few days have been a perfect example of what a piece of shit I can be.

I can't believe I hit the only person I've been able to seamlessly depend on, the one person who didn't leave me when they were done with me, who didn't chew me up and spit me out.

The one fucking person who has stood by me, picked me up when I fell and put me back on track when my wheels fucking broke.

He could hardly look me in the eye yesterday.

Again ... why the fuck would he?

I'm a fuckup.

He knows it, my parents know it.

Meyer must have realized it now, too.

With a heavy exhale, I close my eyes ... and lift the bottle to my lips.

It's five to seven when I'm finally dragging my ass into the locker room as the team's filing out.

"Uh-oh, golden boy's late." Some second-string punk spits, but when I turn to look at him, he's already gone, so I push forward.

Echo's finishing tying his shoes when I step inside.

"What up, man?" I mumble, my head fucking pounding.

"Fuck you, bro. You're fuckin up." He shoulder checks me on his way out, sending me stumbling a bit.

I drop onto the bench and kick my slides off, lazily tearing my sneakers from my locker and tugging them onto my feet.

Neo comes from the back, dropping onto the bench beside me with a sigh.

I scoff. "You too?"

"I'm still out of it, man." He sets his shit down, tugging his hoodie over his head. "I fucked up, took some Molly, washed it down with liquor like a dumbass."

"Damn, man, and I thought I was the jackass."

"You were, but you weren't alone." He grins, but it falls off quickly.

Holding my breath, I manage to stand again and

walk over to the dispenser for a quick cup of water.

"Aye, bring me one, yeah?"

Nodding, I fill up another and walk it over.

Neo opens up his palm and sitting inside them are two familiar blue pills. He sees me looking and scoffs. "Coach Reid to the rescue."

A frown pulls at my brows. "Rehydrating?"

"More like flushes your system." He tosses them in his mouth, downing the water, and climbs to his feet. "Two more tonight and I'll be good."

Unease slips over me. "What do you mean?"

"Remember how I tested dirty in preseason last year?" He pulls his joggers off over his shoes, his gym shorts already on underneath. "Coach said if I act a fool like that again, let him know and he'd do what he could, so I told him first thing this morning and he gave me these." He turns to me, tossing his hat into the locker. "Didn't want to, and he reamed my ass, but I can't test dirty again, man."

Neo slaps my shoulder, and if I weren't in my head, I might wince from the shot the pitching machine got me with there, but all I can think of is the night after the Cal Poly game.

How I don't remember drinking much and the pills he gave me the next day.

The same blue pills.

"Cruz, let's go, or it'll be even worse for us."

Knowing he's right, I follow him out and onto the practice field.

Like we could have figured, the team's standing there, waiting for the last two fuckers to show before they're allowed to start.

There is no one person's fuckup.

You fuck up, you fuck your whole team, and Coach hits us hard.

He starts us off with short track runs, then base sprints, but when he feels we aren't giving our all, we're called to the fence and sent for a three mile, no man left behind, run around campus.

But he's not done.

We get five seconds to breathe before he orders five laps around the field.

Two and a half in and I'm bent over a tin trash can, puking my guts out.

My body is slick with sweat and every fucking inch of me is sore.

I haven't slept, I haven't eaten, and haven't shaved. I can hardly lift my fucking limbs, let alone stand on the heated turf and throw a damn ball.

"Nobody breaks off into position drills until laps are finished as a team."

I glare at the fucking trash can, sticking my finger down my throat to force more liquor out, but I'm heaving up nothing. Tugging my shirt over my head, I wipe my face, my free hand falling to my hips as I try to catch my breath.

"Let's go!" Coach blows his whistle, but I simply look over my shoulder at him.

He lowers his clipboard, eyeing me. "You got a problem, son?"

When I do nothing but spit to the side, he starts walking toward me.

My head is fucking pounding and it hurts to breathe.

I'm thinking all kinds of crazy shit and I'm probably falling down a rabbit hole that I've imagined. All I know is I'm pissed off at everything and everyone, and I don't have the mental capacity for this shit right now.

So I shoulder past the man.

Fuck this.

"Tobias ... Tobias!"

I don't acknowledge him and I don't go back into the locker room.

I abandon all my shit and walk off the field, straight out the gate, his eyes burning into my back all the way.

I go home, shower, and collapse in bed.

All I wanted four months ago was to end the year with a winning season and go pro.

Now, all I want is to look Meyer in the eye and hear her say she wants me, that I'm worth it. That I'm worth more. That she believes in me, chooses me, and knows in her heart I can be what she needs, what Bailey needs.

But that's not going to happen, because I've been reminded of what I have been told time and time again

I'm not good enough.

I'm not worthy.

I wish I could see Bailey, kiss her chubby little cheeks, and make her understand I'm not leaving her, but her mama is leaving me.

All I know is I can't go back to before they were mine.

The guy the world has seen over the last few days is who I am now.

This is the new me.

The me who isn't wanted by her.

I fall asleep, knowing it's all downhill from here.

CHAPTER 29

Meyer

"Bailey." I lean over to grab the apple piece she snatched off of my plate, but she's already got the thing pulled to her mouth.

Her eyes go wide, and she tightens her little muscles in an attempt to hold on to it.

"Okay, okay. Hang on." I pry it from her fingers, checking the ends to make sure no part of it will break off and turn it, letting her run her swollen gums across it. It doesn't take long for it to soften, and I have to take it away.

She throws herself back on her blanket, and begins to fake cry, something she's recently discovered helps her get what she wants.

"Bailey, baby girl. Stop." I pick her up, but she bends her back, and if I didn't have a good hold on her, she might have just fallen out of my arms. "It's okay, mama. Shh."

Bouncing my upper body, I pat her little butt, offering her Binky and slowly she starts to calm, but I can't.

She's been increasingly testy the last few days and

I can't help but feel like I'm at fault.

They say babies can sense stress, and I've been nothing but a basket case.

She's sleeping less, as am I, and it's not good for her.

It's not good for either of us.

How can me doing what's right by her feel so wrong when I look at her?

I run my palm over her soft hair, and slowly she settles against me.

Tears spring into my eyes and I look to the ceiling to stop them. I should place her in her bed, but I can't bring myself to move. I just want to hold her a little longer.

But then there's a knock on my door.

My breath lodges in my throat and I tense, begrudgingly easing Bailey down on her play pad beneath me.

A second knock comes, and I push to my feet, my pulse beating wildly.

Bianca has a key, so she wouldn't knock.

There's only one other person it could be, and I haven't laid eyes on him since I looked into his and lied my ass off.

The hairs on the back of my neck stand as I reach for the handle, but even then I pause, wondering if he'll give up and go away, but then a third knock follows and so I tug the door open.

My heart falls to my feet as I look up into a completely different pair of blue eyes.

"Where is he?" *Coach Reid* snaps. "Where is Tobias?"

My shoulders lift, and I shake my head. "I don't

know—"

"No *lie*," he seethes, attempting to sidestep me into my house, but I snap out of it and slide with him.

I jerk out the door, tugging it closed behind me. "What the hell do you think you're doing?"

He tugs back, brow raised. "Am I not allowed in your home?"

"No." A humorless laugh leaves me. "You're not."

"I'm not, yet he is?"

My spine straightens and he narrows his eyes.

"You know nothing. You sit back and revel in the fact that I'm stuck under your thumb, the same way you tried to get Milo there."

"Guess your brother is smarter than you are."

"Not so easily manipulated is more like it."

"Don't blame your shitty decisions on me," he snaps back. "We both know you repeatedly make them. I agreed to pay for your classes when you lost your scholarship after you got pregnant. Don't fuck that up by fucking my star player!"

My organs shrivel inside me, and I look away. "I hate you."

"Look ... sweetheart, I don't want to do this right now, just tell me if he's in there."

I bite into my cheek. "I haven't seen him, not since I 'made it simple.'"

He cocks his head, and I'm sure he's going to call me a liar, but he doesn't. The opposite, in fact.

The man nods. "I guess that makes sense."

A frown creeps over me, and I want to ask him what he means, but I don't want to give him the satisfaction of having the upper hand yet again.

Turns out I don't have to because he always has it.

His understanding expression quickly morphs into one of constraint. "He slept through a game, missed two practices and four days' worth of classes."

Oh my god.

"They worked on research papers in history, and now he's a draft behind. His final's due by Wednesday."

A sharp pain zings down my spine.

And there it is, the reason for his constraint, for his sharing this information with me.

I shake my head.

He nods his.

"No."

"Meyer, yes."

"There's no way."

"You will fix it."

"No."

"I didn't give you an option."

"I can't."

"I said fix it!" he screams.

I jump and his hands come up as he takes a calming breath.

"I'm ..." He blows a harsh breath out his nose to calm himself. "I'm sorry, but Meyer, you will do this."

"I won't. I can't be near him."

He opens his mouth, but promptly clamps it shut as he narrows his eyes on me. "You fell for the kid ... like actually fell for him, as if it could ever happen for you two."

My jaw clenches, but I say nothing, and he laughs,

but it's mocking.

He lifts his hat, then slowly puts it back on. "You'll work with him the next two days. Do that, and I'll transfer you back into your old department. Don't do it and he fails, loses eligibility—"

"And you lose your championship."

His eyes narrow. "Yeah, you're right, but think of the boy, huh? Since you've been loose with your morals, yet again, put yourself in his shoes. You have the chance to help him, and it'll be on your conscience if you don't."

Tears form in my eyes without permission. "This will do more harm than good, you have to know that. It might help you through this final stretch, but what happens to him after that?"

"That will be his problem."

"He trusts you."

"And he lost that when he let a girl get in the way of his game."

"Some people are human on the inside, not machines."

"Some people are stupid." He walks backward. "I'll tell him where to be and when."

"What if he doesn't show?"

His feet halt where he stands, his tone one of resentment. "We both know he will."

I look away and then he's gone.

And because I seem to be drawn to pain, I go inside, open my computer, and go straight to the university newspaper page.

My heart drops as I read over the articles from the last week, every one of them blasting Tobias and documenting his 'downward spiral' as they're calling it.

There are shots of him fighting on the field, walking into the bar, and even one of him passed out on the courtyard picnic table.

My chest grows tight, it's as if a sheath of anguish is suffocating me from the inside out.

I did this.

I stole his happy and if I don't do what's being asked of me, I'll be responsible for stealing his future. He has no idea the man he admires is a malicious asshole who'll destroy him if he's wronged. Nothing is more important to Tobias than this next step, then accomplishing the goal he set out to make, to achieve what so many have sworn he couldn't.

Tobias is made up of dirt and sweat, of the game, and without it, he'll be lost.

It's his life, his future.

I can't let it slip away.

I have to help him, no matter how much it breaks me in return.

My stomach is in my throat, my heart is at my feet, and my mind is as muddled as ever.

I knew, just as the man who sent him knew, that he would show up today.

It's a sick kind of torture, but a necessary one.

I've had my laptop open and notes out on the picnic

table for the last ten minutes. I've tried to speak, to engage in work-related conversation, but Tobias has yet to say a word.

He hasn't opened his bag.

In fact, I'm not even sure he *brought* his bag.

The man has yet to move.

But he's staring.

His eyes are searing my skin, making my nerves dance on end and my muscles tight at every angle.

Clearing my throat, I try not to fidget or shake as I turn my laptop toward him, but his hands fly forward, and I yank mine back just in time for him to slam the screen closed.

My eyes jump to his and his glare sharpens.

"Are you for real right now?" he snaps, his palms tightening into a fist on the tabletop.

He stares, the anger in his gaze fighting to hold still, but dissolving with each passing second. He's waiting for me to respond, to say something, anything, I imagine, but I couldn't speak if I tried.

Because now that I've looked up, finally meeting his deep blue eyes, my insides liquify. Everything stings, burns like a festering open wound a sharp point is being pressed into.

He has dark circles that only come from lack of sleep, his normal scruff is five times sharper, and he might have even lost a few pounds. But none of those compare to the lost look in his eyes.

The confusion.

The hurt.

The hate?

"Talk to me." His forearms clench. "Talk to me ..."

"Tobias, please."

"Don't. Don't Tobias me." He jerks forward, reaching for my hand, but I pull it back, placing it in my lap and the ache in his gaze reflects the feeling in my chest. "Why are you doing this?"

"Stop."

"I won't. I'm fucking not." He shoots to his feet, stepping around the table, slowly dropping to his knee beside me, forcing us eye to eye.

My pulse pounds against my temple, in my throat. Everywhere. All over, and it only gets stronger when his knuckle comes up, squeezing my lungs and bringing my gaze to his.

A harsh, choppy hiss slips past my lips and I clamp them shut.

"Talk to me." He frowns.

"You should go."

"I said I'm not, so stop trying."

My resolve is cracking, so I jerk free, shoot to my feet, and shove my things in my bag, but he stops me, so I let it all go and take off.

"Meyer!" he shouts, dashing after me, but his voice grows farther away. "Damn it, Meyer. Hold on!"

I pick up the pace, thankful the place we met is on the edge of campus and all I have to do is make it across the yard, through the alleyway and into my front door.

His footsteps thump behind me, so I start to run.

I forget to look down the road before I cross and scream when a car comes close to hitting me, having to swerve out of the way as I dash into the street.

"Fuck! *Meyer!*"

Tears stream down my face and my body shakes, but I keep running.

I hear him shout something at the driver, as if it was their fault, and what sounds like a fist against a hood, but I don't look back.

I'm at my front door a minute later, reaching out and gripping the knob, and then his large palm comes down over mine, freezing me there.

My bag is tossed at my feet, and he grips my upper arm, jerking me around with a gentle force.

"What's the matter with you?" he nearly shouts. "You almost got hit!"

"Go."

"Stop telling me to go."

"I can't ..." My chest heaves. "Please, I can't."

"Can't what?" he asks, and the longer he stares, the more his shoulders fall. "Can't what, baby?"

"Leave!" I scream, my cheeks warm with my own tears and Tobias jerks away from me, his eyes roaming my face as he backs up, giving me the space I'm demanding but don't really want.

"What's really going on, Meyer?"

His tone is so soft, my cries are no longer silent, but breaking through my throat.

He opens his mouth to speak, but the door at my back creaks as he does, and Bianca meets my eyes, a question in hers.

Should she stay or go?

My lip twitches, and I nod, so she slips out, squeezing my arm with worry in her gaze.

It's okay, B. Go.

She nods back, climbs into her car and pulls away.

We both watch her go, needing that free second to breathe, but then her taillights are out of sight, and all that's left is us.

Tobias rubs at the scruff on his jaw, slowly looking to me.

"I don't want you here." I manage to keep my voice from breaking. "Please go."

"I don't get it," he mutters, defeat weighting every part of him down. "What did I do? I've replayed every minute I've spent with you over and over again and I don't get it. Was it the article? Or maybe the party? I only wanted to show you off to my friends. If you weren't ready for that you should have told me. I just ... I thought you were comfortable with us and that you might have needed a night out with people your age, that maybe you'd enjoy it, but I don't need that," he rushes. "I don't. I can give up all that."

"Tobias, please."

"I know I fucked up, I-I know I'm not someone who deserves you." He looks away, self-loathing drawing his features tight and making him pace. "But I thought, with you I thought maybe I was ... god, I am just a fucking jackass."

I don't mean to, but my body moves one step toward him, and it's a move he doesn't miss.

His gaze slices to mine, and I think he's stopped breathing.

I should move backward, heed the warnings whispering in my head by reclaiming the space between us, but the broken man in front of me drowns out the voices, freezing me in place.

His jaw clenches, his fingers twitching at his sides and slowly, very, *very* slowly, he inches toward me.

My hands plaster themselves on the door, and I'm not sure I'm breathing.

He starts to say something but is cut off by Bailey's soft cry from inside.

A burning sense of relief shoots through me and I spin, rushing for her room, but it was a false alarm.

She was searching for her Binky, and she found it, her eyes still closed and her breathing once again soft.

I hang my head in my hands, tears pricking my eyes and slipping from the edges as I try not to make a sound, praying he's gone when I walk out of the room.

He's not, and what's worse.

He's inside, standing right outside her room, the weight of the world resting on his wide shoulders.

I close Bailey's door and he steps closer.

I shuffle to the side, desperate for air that isn't infused with his scent, but he catches me by the arm, holding me back.

"Tobias."

"Tutor Girl," he rasps, swallowing as he shuffles closer.

God, he's such a beautifully broken man.

Misery blanketing his features, and hopefulness lining his eyes, he reaches up to touch my face, wincing as I wince.

Shaking as I shake.

"Don't make this harder."

"Don't deny me when you want me."

My muscles twist, a tornado whirling in my abdomen as the caution sirens blare in my head. My hand shoots up, latching onto his wrist and I clench my eyes closed.

"Please," he breathes, the heat of his body nearer. "Baby, please."

My nostrils flare with a fraught, rocky inhale. "You don't understand ... I can't."

He'll never allow this ...

"Please," he begs, his lips skating along mine, they're so close.

"I can't."

He'll destroy my entire world ...

"I'm losing my mind. I'm fucking fried. I can't think, eat, sleep." His hands begin to tremble. "Tell me you don't feel the same and I'll walk away, right now." He shifts closer. "Say the word, baby, and I'm gone. I swear, just ... say it. Tell me you don't love me back."

I shake my head, my eyes opening, locking onto his as I crack from the inside out, my words repeated, but this time as a tender confession. "I can't."

DIRTY CURVE

CHAPTER 30

Tobias

I crash my lips to hers, my hands instantly threading into her hair and yanking her closer, as close as fucking possible.

I'm fucking dying. Suffocating, my lungs are so starved, and only she's got the air I need.

My body's fucking shaking, desperate for anything she's willing to give and if the way she climbs me tells me anything, she's ready to give a lot.

Take it all, Tutor Girl. It's already yours.

I'm not sure if I groan or sigh, but fuck me, my airways open, filling with her scent and sending my insides dancing. Every nerve in my body is awake, ready.

Fucking needy.

But only for her.

Cupping her ass, I swing us around, carrying her into the living room and setting her on the edge of the dresser.

Her elbows knock into the TV screen as she

frantically tears at my shirt, throwing her arms up so I can rip hers from her body and I do, but before I go for her bra, I cup her face in my hands, pausing us both.

Her wild eyes snap to mine and goddamn if my dick doesn't swell more, ten times harder.

She's on fucking fire, a hunger in her gaze I've never seen, a need in her touch that's unmatched.

"I need to make sure you understand this isn't what I'm after. This isn't what I want from you." I stare deep into her eyes, looking beyond the surface, raring for her to read me correctly. "I want you. All of you and everything that comes with you. Good, bad, fucked. I want it. Every bit of it."

Her lower lip begins to tremble, so I take it between my teeth, gently biting at her.

I got you. Your fears and your troubles.

I got you ...

"I want you, I want *inside* you, but if I'm only promised one place, this is where I want it to be." I press my knuckles into her chest, over her heart. "Right fucking here, you understand what I'm saying?"

She chokes on her words, tears building in her eyes, and fear grips me like a vise, twisting at my muscles and creating a knot in my throat.

"I was awful to you." Her voice is strangled.

"I can take it."

"Tobias—" She attempts to lean away, but I hold firm.

Gripping the back of her head, I hold her eyes to mine.

"Do you love me?"

"It's not that simple."

"Do. You. Love. Me?"

Her body grows lax, her shaky fingers leaving my neck, pausing over my left pec. She presses there.

"Baby," I prompt.

And she finally says, "Yes."

That's it.

That's all.

Mine.

Lifting her from the dresser, I slowly set her on her feet, her deep brown eyes wide and locked on me as I use the backs of my fingers to ease the straps of her bra down her shoulders. I lean forward, kissing her collarbone as my palms glide around her ribs, but I'm met with a stretchy material.

Meyer chuckles as I pull back, and the smirk she hits me with has me groaning and yanking her to me.

"What is this sorcery?"

Her tongue slips between her teeth and she gently pushes me away.

The only reason I go is because the look in her eye is straight fire.

She eases me backward until my knees meet the metal of the fold-out bed, so I lower my ass onto it, adjusting my dick in my jeans.

Her fingers slide along her skin, coming together between her breasts, and only then do I notice the little clip there. She unsnaps it, her breasts falling from the thin material, they're full and round, sitting high and inviting. Her nipples are a soft, dusty pink.

She slips closer, and my palms find her hips, gliding

up and over her ribs, but I pause beneath the hollow of her breasts.

"Tell me, Ma," I rasp. "Are your nipples a sweet spot, too, or are they too sensitive?"

"I don't know, hotshot, are they?" she teases, desire thickening her tone.

I groan, scoot over the edge more and tug her to me. "Time to find out."

"Soft," she rasps, her chest rising and falling rapidly, anticipation making her anxious.

The edge of my tongue starts at the fullest part of her breast, and I lick my way up.

Instantly, her nipple grows taut, peaking from my touch, and so I close my lips around it, swirling and tasting, but I don't suck. Not tonight, anyway.

Meyer's head falls to one side with a low moan, her fingers gliding along the back of my head.

To be fair, I show her left breast the same love, and her body twitches.

"Sweet spot it is."

Meyer jerks her head up, smashing her lips to mine.

Her kiss is needy, and I know the wait is just as fucking excruciating for her as it is for me.

"Are you bare for me?" I nip her lips, my fingers curling into her leggings, and her thighs clench, her body trembling as I push them down to her knees. She pants into my mouth, and I hold her eyes as I slide my hand between her legs. Not until the tip of my finger is aligned with her opening, do I allow my touch to meet her heat.

Meyer's gasp mixes with my groan and I push up, sliding forward and coating my fingers with her arousal.

Her eyelids flutter, but she never takes them off mine, and I don't look away until my knuckles brush her clit. Her whimper has me aching, and the fingertips biting into my shoulders send a shock wave through my body, straight to my fucking groin.

Finally, I drop my eyes, and just as I thought. "Bare."

"Taste."

My eyes snap to hers, and I groan, lifting my fingers to my lips, like I had already intended to do, but apparently not quick enough for my girl. I don't taste though. Not yet.

I push to my feet, staring down at her as I cup her neck with one hand, the other held an inch away from my mouth.

Slowly, I drag my knuckle along my bottom lip, and then align them with hers. It's torturous, tasting her by scent and not sucking every bit of her off me, but she wants to play. So we'll play. "You want me to taste you, hm?" I skate my bottom lip along hers. "You first."

I expect her to hesitate, but she doesn't. She pulls my lip into her mouth, and my baby bites.

A bone-deep rumble makes its way up my chest and I crash my mouth with hers, pressing firmly and seeking out any bit of her flavor that's left.

Desperation crawls up my spine when Meyer's moans grow louder. Every muscle in my body tightens, my cock strains, and my girl knows it.

Her hands work my jeans open, and I gladly kick them off, pushing my boxers down with them.

Her eyes fall, her lips parting, as she squeezes her thighs shut.

"Grab me."

She doesn't waver. Her fingers wrap around my

shaft, squeezing, and slowly she pumps me in her palm. My abs constrict and she lowers to her knees, her eyes snapping up to mine as she pulls the head of my dick into her mouth.

She sucks, scraping me with her teeth and grinning around me when I hiss.

"Oh, you think that's funny?" I pull back, tug her to her feet, spin us and nudge her back until her ass falls to where mine once was.

Together we crawl up the springy mattress until her head meets a pillow. She lowers onto her back, her sneaky little hand slides between us again, and she grips me, running the tip of her thumb over bulging veins.

I flex in her palm, and she licks her lips, releasing me.

I pull back, align my hips and glide my cock along her slit

"Fuck," I grunt, adding some pressure, and my biceps clench.

Desperate for a hint of her, I allow the head to slip inside

My body fucking burns, her chest is heaving, and I can't wait any longer.

"Open up for me, baby."

Her legs spread a little wider, I push in a little farther, and then she looks me directly in the eye.

A deep rumble vibrates up my throat, and she flexes around me, her back arching off the bed, her neck begging to be sucked on. Licked.

I bite instead, and my baby moans beneath me.

I'm inside her in the next second, the heat of her cunt boiling the blood in my veins, and my body takes over.

With slow, full thrusts, I rock into her.

She gasps into the air around us, and I push a little deeper, my head falling into the crook of her neck.

"I've been dying for this," she admits with a low, torrid tone.

My muscles flex around her. "How long?"

Her hands fall to my bare back, and she lifts her knees higher. "Long."

I bite her collarbone and she whimpers, twitching around me and my cock swells even more.

She likes.

Her hold on me tightens, but I don't give her more.

I pull all the way out and my baby pouts. "How. Long?" I run the pads of my thumbs over her nipples, and she pants, gripping the ends of my hair in an attempt to pull, but I hold firm.

"Months, Tobias," she swallows, lifting her hips in search of some relief. "Months."

I groan, kiss the spot on her skin I bruised with my teeth, and drive back inside.

This time, when she grips my face, I let her drag my mouth to hers.

Meyer shoves her tongue into my mouth, and I kiss her back just as hard.

My blood pressure is through the fucking roof, my need to come right there with it, but only when she's ready.

So, I sit up, press her knees to the mattress and lift

her ass off of it.

I slide my cock out slowly, and push in faster, harder, my right hand coming down over her clit, left stretching forward to grip her peaked nipple.

She dances against me, her eyes hooded and holding mine, and when I hit the spot, deep in-fucking-side her, her neck stretches, her whimper frenzied.

Still, she doesn't look away, and something shifts.

Everything shifts.

I release her, blindly reaching behind me to grip the edge of the comforter, and I pull it up over us, barricading us inside. I lower over her, bringing us chest to chest, skin to skin, eye to perfect, beautiful eyes.

"Meyer," I whisper, dropping my forehead to hers and her lips curve into the softest of smiles.

She brings her legs up, locking them around my hips, and lifts her chin the slightest bit, skimming her mouth along mine. "Tobias," she whispers back.

I need you, that's what we've just said.

That's what this means.

I love you.

I fuck my baby slow and steady, and I don't stop until she's biting into her lip to keep from crying out, but I want it. All of it.

So, I press my mouth to hers, and she moans into me, her body vibrating under me, and then she's coming around me.

Her pussy pulses, gripping me like a custom-fitted sleeve, and I growl, my hand tethering into her hair.

"Come for me," she begs, and I growl into her mouth.

"Okay, baby." I drive into her as deep as I can, and I give her what she wants.

My cum pours into her, mixing with her own.

Her fingers glide along my back. "You're shaking."

"You feel good, like mine." I press deeper, jerking inside her.

My grunt is chest deep and her lips part. "Kiss me."

I do, and her hands wrap around my neck.

I've never felt more satisfied than I do in this moment, with my girl slick and satiated in my arms.

Desperate for more, yes, but satisfied.

It doesn't make much sense, yet it makes perfect fucking sense.

No amount of this girl will ever be enough.

I'll forever want more.

Need more.

Crave more.

Of her.

Of this.

Of us.

That's never going to change. I knew it weeks, maybe even months ago.

Meyer belongs to me.

Period.

Stretching my legs, my lips curve into a smile, the heat of Meyer's body making it real easy to peel my eyes open. She's still in a deep sleep, her naked back bare to me, her long brown hair spilling over the pillow and half in my face.

I bury my face in her neck, kissing her there and she stirs, but no more than a flicker of a smile in her sleep. As sneakily as possible, I climb from the bed, doing my best not to actually wake her.

Bay hasn't woken up yet, and from what I know, this might be a first, her sleeping in past sunrise.

It's a quarter to six, so a little later than I would normally wake, but before last night, I hadn't slept much at all. When I did, it was sleeping off stupidity, not actual sleep.

Today, though, I'm refreshed as fuck, feeling good, but also guilty as shit.

I've fucked off my team lately, gave half, maybe even less than half of myself and that's bullshit.

I need to get back at it, but before that, I need a quick run, my body is weighted with toxins that need to be released.

In the kitchen, I quietly pour a glass of water and pull the marker off the dry erase board, writing her a quick note, knowing she'll likely wake up before I get back.

Our clothes are all over the place, something I realize when I go in search of mine, finding one shoe under the bed, the other near the back door.

I grin.

No clue how that happened.

Moving a few things around, I hunt for my shirt, finally spotting it in the small gap between the couch and the end table. I pull it free, wincing when her bag tips over, half the shit falling out.

My eyes dart to the bed and while she stirs, she doesn't wake, and I make a mental note to move this thing when I get back to grab what fell behind it. In the meantime, I pick up what I can reach. Her wallet in hand, I go to set it on top, but my fingers brush along the clear plastic on the opposite side. Curious, I flip it over to look. Inside the protective screen, framed in pleather, is her ID.

I look over her photo, grinning at how, even here, her famous bun is in place, and then my eyes are pulled right.

Every single part of me locks up. The air in my lungs evaporates, and I'd swear the blood in my body has even stopped flowing by the way my organs seem to shrivel, fold over, and twist.

Meyer's last name isn't Sanders, like she said.

It's Reid.

Coach Reid isn't just her boss.

He's her fucking father.

CHAPTER 31

Meyer

The soft click of the door closing has my eyes fluttering open and I'm instantly struck with memories of last night.

Of the irresistible charge of desire that darkened Tobias's eyes.

Of the rough texture of his hands as they ran over every inch of my body.

Of how, even after our second round, it wasn't enough.

He needed more.

Wanted more.

My fingers lift, running along my neck, the spot he refused to neglect for more than five seconds. Be it his hands, his chin, his tongue ... he kept coming back for more, lighting the sensitive spot on fire with any and every move he made.

Not once was his focus on himself. It was all me, all night, and when he fell asleep beside me, all I could think was how perfectly he fit there.

Rolling onto my back, my arm falls to the now empty space and my lips curl. The heat of his body is still there, as is the indent in the pillow.

An unexpected sense of comfort washes over me, but it's short-lived, because in the next second, I push up onto my elbow, and the first thing I spot ... my wallet.

No.

My chest caves and I can't breathe. It's as if metal is seeping into my lungs and hardening by the second.

No, no no ...

I scramble off the bed, falling onto my knees as the blankets tether around me and lift my wallet toward my face.

My driver's license.

It's gone.

Dashing around the room, I search for my phone, tearing it from the charger and quickly dialing his number.

It rings once and goes to voice mail.

"Shit!" I hiss, trying again, but this time, there is no ring.

In a panic, I try the man I know he went to see, but the line just keeps ringing.

I call Bianca to see if she can come sit with Bailey, so I can find him before he finds *him.*

"Hi, I'm busy!" Her voice mail picks up. "Leave a message and if you're lucky, I'll call you back."

Damn it.

My heart cries and I fall onto my butt again, gripping my legs as I look to the ceiling, praying I didn't put myself into a situation I'll regret for the rest of my life.

It's with that thought in mind that I open the long

since ignored acceptance letter from UOF and click on the link provided.

Tobias

Pushing through the doors, I head straight for Coach's office, and to say he's surprised to see me is an understatement.

His head snaps up from his notebook and he slowly sets his pen down. "Tobias."

"I, uh" —I lick my lips, rubbing at the back of my head— "I went by your house. Your car wasn't out front, so I came here."

Creases form along his face. "Couldn't sleep with the big game coming so soon."

I nod, jerking around so I'm facing away from him, and let my eyes roam across the photos on the wall, not one featuring a beautiful brown-headed girl. They're all coaches and athletes and MLB stars. His life's work; his life's focus.

"What'd you give me?"

"What are we talking about exactly?"

"That night after the Cal Poly game." I don't turn, but my eyes cut to his. "What'd you give me, Coach?"

Slowly, he eases back in his leather chair. "Son—"

"Neo told me what those pills were, the ones you gave him. The ones you put in my hand that next morning when I couldn't remember shit, not even drinking a second bottle of beer."

"I don't know what you're talking about."

"Okay." I nod, tossing Meyer's ID on the desktop. "What do you know about that?"

The man visibly stiffens, and I know his mind's whirling, trying to figure out the best thing to say, but he delays by licking his lips.

Finally, he meets my eye, the truth written within them. "Tobias—"

"I don't get it." I shake my head. "You've spent the last three fucking years building me up at every turn. Bailing me out around every fucking corner. You lit the fucking path and drug me through it. I thought that meant you trusted me. Respected me. That I was worth something in your eyes."

He cocks his head. "And you thought right. I've done nothing to make you assume otherwise."

I grip the edge of his desk, leaning forward so my face is aligned with his.

"If that's true, look me in my eye and tell me you're not the reason Meyer's been doing everything she can to push me away."

The vein in his jaw flexes. "My relationship with her has nothing to do with my relationship with you."

"So long as her and I don't have one, right? Because I'm good enough to lead your team, but I'm not good enough to love your daughter?"

"Watch yourself," he says slowly.

"Why? Because it's the truth?"

Coach Reid licks his lips again.

"Tobias," he speaks with caution. "You've been my priority for years, you know this. She's—"

"Don't." I shake my head and push off the desk, now staring down at him. "Whatever you're going to say, just don't. I don't want to hear how I'm more important than your flesh and fucking blood, because that's bullshit."

"It wasn't bullshit when you benefited from it, now was it?"

"I didn't know!" I shout. "If I had, I would have turned around and given everything I've ever gotten from you to her. No question. It's no wonder she didn't tell me about you, nobody wants to claim what they're ashamed of."

"Don't stand here and act like you're an honorable man, Tobias."

"It's not about being honorable, Coach. It's about human decency, something we give to strangers on the street, but what decency have you shown her?"

"More than you realize, it seems."

"Just like with me and her, right?"

His eyes narrow.

"Come on, Coach, you know what I mean. How, after you convinced her to walk away from me, you *realized* she meant more to me *than it seemed*?"

"There was no convincing, Tobias. You were taking all her time." He watches me closely. "Which meant she had less for others. She needed to drop you to make back her normal income."

"You told me to take all her time!" I shout. "You said she made more when she was with me!"

His eyes narrow and he yanks his head back as he realizes, "You started failing on purpose ..."

"No fucking duh!" I whip around, running my hands down my face.

I stole her time, which stole part of her livelihood, which took from Bailey.

Fuck, man.

I took from Bailey.

"Son ..."

A scoffing laugh leaves me, and my chin falls to my chest. "I'm not your son."

Slowly, I face the man I've looked up to for the last three years, the man I hoped to one day become, someone who gives you hope when you have none, who holds your fucking head up when the weight of the world is dragging it down, and suddenly, I don't even recognize him.

He has no photos on his wall of Meyer.

Has never spoken of her.

Never even hinted about having a family.

All he cares about is his job, his career.

Baseball isn't just all he has, it's all he is.

I wanted to be him.

I will never be a damn thing like him.

"I'm not your son," I repeat. "And I don't want to be treated like one by a coward of a man who looks after his team more than he does his own family." Shame settles over me. "She's struggling, has little to nothing, and she doesn't even complain. You could do so much more for her and instead you waste it on me? Give me a house and truck and leave her to fend for herself *and* her daughter?"

"Who do you think covers that girl's tuition, huh?"

"She has a perfect GPA. She can do that without you."

"Shows how much you know."

"So fucking tell me!"

"It's not your concern. Focus on that nine-million-dollar contract coming your way, thanks to what I've offered you." He pushes to his feet. "Everything I've done, I did to make sure you'd get to where you are now. All those times I covered for your ass and got you out of trouble. The times I carried your ass out of bars or got rid of your company for you."

"I didn't ask you to do all that."

"Yeah, you did, Tobias. Own that."

"This isn't the same thing."

"It's exactly the same." He glares, and then something flashes in his eyes. "But I take it she never got around to telling you about the night I picked her up off your doorstep, did she?"

My face falls, the weight of a dozen boulders falling onto my chest.

He shakes his head. "Yeah, I didn't think so. I'm not the only one hiding parts of my life. The girl is trouble, Tobias, she's a natural born liar, and I'm trying to keep you away from that. The last thing you need is a leech."

"What do you mean?" I swallow, and when he doesn't say anything, I dart forward, grip him by the shirt and throw him into the shelves beside us. "I said what does that mean?! Are you saying I was with her before?! That I don't remember her?!"

I could never forget her. I wouldn't.

"Why do you think she didn't want to tutor you, *Playboy*?" Coach Reid shoves my hands off of him, standing tall. "Memories can be a bitch."

I stagger backward, searching my mind and coming

up empty.

"Bailey ..." My gaze falls to the floor and I run my hand over my head. "She ... is she ..."

Blue eyes.

I look up, struck by the gobsmacked expression on my coach's face.

He eyes me, his head tipping more and more to the side, the creases framing his brows deepening, and then the man laughs.

A full, unexpected, incredulous laugh that has my pulse picking up even more.

"Well, I'll be fucking damned. You really are a clueless son of a bitch." He shakes his head. "Get out of here and get your ass in check."

"Fuck you," I spit. "*Fuck. You.*"

I walk out, my body tingling. Full fucking rage brewing in my chest, and a million other emotions whirling with it.

"If you think you're going to play house with my daughter and I'm going to allow it, you're wrong. I own you for six more weeks, kid."

"School's out in three."

"And our season will continue to the end of June. Don't act like you don't understand what I'm saying. You made me a deal!"

I whip around, my fist coming down on the wall an inch from his face like a hammer. "I got you to the top. We're in the world series and on track for the championship game," I seethe.

"Now you'll get me my protégé," he says coldly. "You'll go back to your house that I pay for, take a fucking shower, and pack your fucking bag. You'll be at the gate in time to get on the bus. You will dominate these next few games and we'll be on our way to the big game. I'll get my banner, my program-grown god, and you'll get your contract." He creeps closer. "And after that, you'll be gone, nothing but a memory to me *and* Meyer."

It fucking stings, his quick disregard, but not more than it disgusts me.

"The fact that you believe me to be such a man is proof you don't know me at all." I shake my head, taking backward steps away from him. "I might have had a falling out with my parents, but my dad was a good man, and he taught me better than to leave the people I love. And I love her. I love them both."

With that, I push out the double doors and into the tunnel, but the bastard's footsteps follow.

"Stay away from her, Tobias!" he shouts. "You'll only hurt her in the end, and you know it. All those girls on the road, the fame you've been chasing. How many times have you said all you needed was the freedom to do whatever you wanted in the world? You could never let all that go!"

I cut him a quick look over my shoulder, and while I'm not sure what mine conveys, his face falls as I say, "Watch me."

For the last hour, I've been wearing a hole into my

rug, pacing the short stretch of my living room without pause, when suddenly, there's a soft tap at my front door.

My hands fly to my chest, and I freeze where I stand.

The minutes have passed abysmally slow as I wait on pins and needles for Tobias to get back, because I knew he would be, but now that he's on the other side of the door, I don't know if I can open it.

I'm scared.

I don't know what to say to him and I have no idea what he's about to say to me.

But to make things worse, the tiny hint of hope I've held on to that maybe he didn't go off the wall, that maybe he simply went for a run to gather his thoughts, suddenly seems like an utterly naïve thought.

This is Tobias I'm talking about, and he's anything, if not direct.

God, he deserves the same respect.

So, I drag in as much air as my starving lungs will allow and pull the door open.

His eyes are on his feet, and when he does look, his focus moves over my shoulder.

He can't even look at me.

Stepping back, he follows, quietly closing the door behind him and then we're in the living room.

I bite at my lip as he pulls his bottom one between his teeth, squinting out at the back patio.

"Is it true ..." His voice is hesitant.

"Tobias—"

"Is it true, Meyer?"

"Please tell me you didn't go to him."

That gets his attention, and he snaps his head my way, his brows nearly touching in the center. "Of course, I did."

"Oh my god." My hands cup my mouth, tears springing in my eyes as I lower myself onto the bed.

Tobias darts toward me. "I told him I don't fucking care. About any of it. I just want you. Both of you."

"You don't understand." The tears fall.

"What, that you lied to me?"

My head jerks up, the pain in his gaze mirroring my own. "I didn't."

"A lie by omission is the same thing, Tutor Girl," he rasps, dropping to his knees before me. He grabs my hand in his.

I close my eyes, a soft smile covering my lips. God, how selfish can I be?

I'm sitting here so focused on my own life that's about to tumble all around me when he had a bomb dropped on him this morning.

This is a lot for him, too.

My eyes open to find him waiting, with a look of tenderness that makes me want to cry for an entirely different reason.

"Tobias." I cup his cheek and my heart wrenches when he leans into my palm, his lips grazing my wrist. "This is why I refused to tutor you in the beginning, or ... *tried* to refuse."

"Why, baby?" His lips graze my wrist, his tired eyes locked on mine.

"Because as much as I pretended otherwise, I knew where it would lead. I knew what being around you meant for me ... which is why I was kind of hoping, but also not, that you'd be a jerk."

His chuckle is low, kind of sad, and I feel the ache deep in my bones.

"I didn't want to cause problems for you or get us into a spotlight we couldn't get out of, that he'd see, and have it hurt us both in the end."

"I deserved to know," he says simply.

"Yeah," I whisper. "You did, but you love him, and I didn't want to be the reason you looked at him differently."

"But this wasn't about him, Meyer." He frowns, his tone soft but firm. "This is my life and I never should have missed any part of hers. I love her, like I imagine a father loves a daughter and I didn't even know she was mine."

My vocal cords shrivel, my throat running dry. "What?"

He pushes to his feet, lowering onto the edge of the mattress beside me. "I mean it. I do."

I shoot to my feet, shaking my head. "What are you trying to say to me right now?"

He flies to his feet, anger making its way into his eyes. "I'm saying I love my daughter and I want to be here for her. That I will be here for her."

"Holy shit," I croak, on the verge of hyperventilating.

"I told your dad he can't stop this. He can't stand in our way."

My hand comes up to my mouth, tears spring and threaten to drown me. "Oh, my god ... Tobias."

He comes to me, gripping my face with a rough tenderness, desperation drowning out the blue of his eyes.

"Tobias—"

"I know what he held over your head. He told me about the tuition, about us. I'm pissed, yeah, maybe more than pissed, but ... but it's okay. I'm willing to forget everything if it means having you."

Defeat engulfs me, the ache in my chest doubling as I stare at the man in front of me.

I lift my hands, laying them over his, and gently remove his palms from my face. "You have it all wrong."

I back away, and he reaches for me, but I shake my head, turning to pull a file from the drawer.

Handing it over to him, I watch as his eyes are drawn to the header of the very first page, a muddled expression casting a shadow over his handsome face.

"Custody ... I don't ..." He shakes his head.

"Tobias, Thomas Reid isn't my father." I swallow. "He's my husband."

CHAPTER 32

Tobias

The file slips from my fingertips, every paper inside it falling to the floor.

I feel like I've been sucker punched, right in the gut, in the temple, in the fucking chest.

An hour ago, I was confused, angry, and then I thought Bailey was mine, and somehow, through that anger and confusion, everything felt good. Better than.

I suddenly had all the things I didn't know I wanted, but in the moment of supposed realization, couldn't imagine life without. Now here I am, staring into the eyes of her mama and all I'm consumed with is loss.

How can sixty minutes' worth of knowledge ache like a fucking lifetime of having something that's suddenly been torn away?

I can't breathe.

"I'm so sorry," she rasps. "I–"

She cuts off when I hold a hand up, turning away from her 'cause I need a fucking minute. I take several steps away willing my pulse to calm, my mind to chill, and my body to stop fucking shaking., but it doesn't work.

Husband. She said husband.

My hand comes up to swipe at my face, and I glance at her over my shoulder. "You're fucking married?" my brows climb. "You're someone's wife. Someone *else's* wife."

Her shoulders wing forward, and she shrinks into herself.

"I might be married to the man, but I'm not his wife, Tobias," she whispers, her tone thick with shame.

"Oh, come on, Meyer." I whip around to face her. "Don't bull shit me, not right now."

I'm angry, frustrated, but most of all I'm aching.

Everything inside me stings.

To know she loved before me, that she gave all of herself to a man that isn't me, that she technically belongs to someone else, someone I too loved, has me feeling wrecked. Betrayed.

I never knew a heart could truly ache. I thought that was something people said.

I was wrong.

It's real.

It's fucked.

"Tobias," she pleads, her tone as shattered as I feel. "I can promise you, whatever is going through your mind right now is nothing like the reality of the situation."

"You could have told me. You *should* have fucking told me."

She nods, tears pooling in her eyes. "I wanted to."

"That's not enough."

"I know, I—" she swallows her excuse, and nods again. "I know."

I look away from her, my head shaking as I try to understand, to process this.

It was one thing when I thought he was her father. I didn't feel an ounce of betrayal, and I think that's because the man was a great one to me, or I had thought. He filled the small gap my own left open when I decided to follow my dream. Knowing coach Reid did that for me and disregarded her redirected my anger. I was hurt for her, pissed for her, now I'm kind of pissed at her, a bit hurt by her.

The woman I fell in love with is married. She's not free to love me back.

She's not free to allow me to love her daughter.

Coach Reid's... daughter.

I swallow, speaking that fact in my own mind has my ribs twisting, it's as if some supernatural being has reached inside my body, grabbed hold and refuses to let go.

My eyes fall to the floor briefly, but then I do a double take.

Custody papers...

Why would she have these? She has Bailey already. She's her mom. That's her daughter.

Bending, I pick up a few of the forms now scattered around me feet, skimming over a few lines but I don't understand what it's saying.

And then I see the name next to the word 'petitioner', and it's not Meyer's printed there.

My skin prickles, my chest caving, and I shake my head.

A strong sense of dread washes over me, and my throat begins to clog as I force my eyes up to hers. "Baby..."

A softness sweeps over her features, and she gives a small, sad, side smile.

No...

I don't have to ask, she tells me.

"Thomas had those drawn up. He, um," her voice cracks. "He has a way of making himself clear, wants to make sure I know he's not one to bluff."

My stomach falls to my feet. "He threatened you ...with her?"

A small laugh leaves her, but it's more of a cry, and her eyes flick to ceiling. Once they come back to me, the anguish within them burns through me.

I can't take it.

I stand, go to her, and take her in my arms.

Her soft cries shake her body, and I squeeze her tighter.

"It's okay," I tell her, running my hands through her long brown hair. "I won't let him do this to you."

"There's nothing you can do," she breathes.

"Yes, there is. I can hire the best lawyer out there. I'll spend everything I have coming. I'll fucking give him everything. I don't care. I won't allow him to hurt you, to take her."

She shakes her head, looking up at me with those big, brown eyes. "Tobias..."

"I'm doing this for you."

Her palms fall to my chest. "He and I, we have an agreement." She gasps through her tears. "He put it all in a contract that I had no choice but to sign."

The despair in her gaze is suffocating, but I manage to ask, "what's in the contract Meyer?" I'm almost to fucking afraid to find out.

"It says if I tell anyone about him and me, about our marriage or the fact that we have a child together, I'm agreeing to surrender all rights to Bailey over to him. And if I get caught up with any of his athletes, I'm agreeing to the same thing."

My face falls, my body growing numb.

Being with me will hurt that baby girl.

I feel fucking sick.

I feel like beating the fuck out of that piece of shit.

Meyer's palms slide a little higher. "Do you know why he did that?"

Clenching my jaw, I give a hard shake of my head, gently kissing hers when a tear slips from the corner of her eye.

Meyer's smiles a broken one. "Because I told you."

My body grows stiff. "Meyer."

She nods in answer.

"So that part was true? Me and you ... so how do you know she's not my—" The words fly from me instantly, but the look in her eye has them ceasing just as fast. I speak through the knot in my gut. "You were already pregnant when we met."

"Yeah," she whispers.

"What happened?" My shoulders fall. "I need to know everything. Tell me everything."

Meyer nods, pulls in a deep, shattered breath, and takes me back in time.

Fifteen Months Earlier

Meyer

Music of all genres blares from every direction, adding to the chaotic scene that is Ruckus Row on a Friday night. The entire place is lit up from one end to the next, laughter and chatter loud in the cold night air.

Glancing around, I tug at the hem of my Avix University sweater, making sure it reaches well below my waistline, as if there was anything to hide.

There is, but nobody will know that for another couple months, if what I read online was true.

Please let it be true.

"Found it!" Bianca calls from behind me.

Forcing a smile, I turn toward her right as she's closing the back door of her new boyfriend, Cooper's car.

She waves her phone in her hand. "Right between the seats, just like I said it would be."

"What would he do without you?"

"Spend a lot of time with lotion, that's for sure."

A laugh leaves me and Bianca smirks, slipping her arm through mine.

"Don't think I'm buying that fake smile for a second." She shakes me, and we face each other. "I'm not sure what your insistence on coming out tonight was about and even *though we both know you'll tell me soon enough, that's not the point. The point, however, is that we can leave right now. I mean, I do have the man's keys. We could take that bad boy for a quick spin." She lifts a brow, but I know what she's doing, and I love her for it.*

She's right, though. I came here for a reason and that is to forget, to let go of my new reality, and be the girl I was a week ago, before those two blue lines change everything. At least for a couple hours.

"And skip out on a frat party? Are you crazy?" I play my role.

"Aww, chica, you're so cute." She leads us through the few people gathered near the porch, and an underclassman at the door pulls it open for us, allowing us inside. "It's a team house party, not a frat party, but trust me, there will be plenty of Sharks in the sea, if you know what I mean, all you gotta do is smile, and let the frenzy begin."

My lungs expand with a full inhale, and I glance around the room.

"Or maybe all you have to do is stand there looking pretty."

Frowning, I look to her and she dips her head slightly.

"Girl, don't look, but the great white of this bitch is staring this way."

My head snaps forward.

"Oh, my god! What did I say?" She laughs, dragging me to the side.

"Sorry." I chuckle. "I don't see anyone anyway."

"That's because he's smooth. You'll see him when he wants you to know he's looking, but honey, he's looking."

Right then, Cooper rushes up, annoyance clear in his dark gaze. "Sorry, but I've gotta go. Dumbass freshman fucker needs a bailout downtown."

Bianca shakes her head. "You can't drive."

"And he can't fight so ..." Another two guys walk up behind him, making me laugh.

I turn to Bianca, pulling my arm free of hers.

She shakes her head, but I'm already nodding mine.

"Go. I'll be here when you get back."

"I'm not leaving you here." She frowns.

"Half of my dorm is here somewhere," I remind her. "I'm fine."

"This could take a hot minute, Meyer." Coop winces.

"You guys, seriously stop."

"But I'm your wing woman." Bianca stomps.

"B, go."

Cooper doesn't let her protest again but drags her out the door and then it's just me.

Roaming the room, I say hi to a few people I recognize, and engage in light conversation when I'm drug into one by a girl with purple hair and breath that smells of a good time.

Every step I take, though, I'm keenly aware of the shadow that follows.

Curious, I leave the crowded living areas, cross the threshold into the kitchen, and like I thought it might, that shadow comes closer, blanketing my body from behind.

I reach for the handle on the sliding door, but another's hand falls just above mine, holding it in place.

I look up and over my shoulder, finding a black hat pulled low and a smirk too deep to be honorable. His eyes are probably worse, full of innuendo, but I can't see them behind the dark bill he's hid them under.

The guy is so tall, towers over me with ease, and smells of sun and sea breeze, of summer nights. His scent is fresh and inviting.

And then the beast speaks, and I can feel the gravelly tone down to my toes.

Yeah, this man's a scorned girl's weakness.

Or best friend.

Probably the first.

When that smirk of his grows, I blink, blush, and squint, remembering right then he had spoken, but what I don't remember is hearing a word.

"Sorry ... what?"

His chuckle is low. "I said, hi."

"Hi," I deadpan, tipping my head slightly. "You've been following me around all night, and 'hi' is the best you've got?"

"So, you did know I was tailing you."

"You're ... kind of hard to miss."

"I never miss." He grins.

"Okay ..." I chuckle, and this time, when I go to step out the back door, he lets me.

As I thought he might, he follows.

"If you knew I was watching you, why didn't you call me out?" He stumbles slightly, laughing at himself when his arm darts out to grip the patio post.

I fight a grin. "I figured if you had something to say" —I turn to face him, leaning against the fence edge— "you'd get to it eventually."

"What if I wanted to say I think you're gorgeous?"

"Then I guess you'd have to repeat it to someone else, because that's not a line that would work on me."

He pulls his bottom lip between his teeth, his smile wide. "Yeah, and what line would?"

I smother my own smile, dropping my gaze to the grass for a moment. When I look up, it's only with my eyes, and I give a small shrug. "How about a real one?"

"A real one." He tests the thought out. "'Cause you're gorgeous isn't real enough for you, all right," he teases, and then he reaches up, spinning his hat backward on his head, finally revealing his full face to me.

I'm struck, my words, if I had any, clogging my throat as riveting, ocean-blue eyes meet mine. My pulse leaps in my chest as recognition sets in.

This is what Bianca meant when she said the great white.

This is Tobias Cruz, Avix University's new superstar pitcher. I recognize him from the posters.

He's supposed to be this major party boy, but if that's true, why is he out here with me instead of in there with the rest of his crew?

Tobias starts walking farther out in the yard, and when I don't move, he pauses, glancing at me over his shoulder. "You comin'?"

"To the darkest corner of a house that isn't mine with a complete stranger? No." I laugh. "I don't think so."

He turns, now walking backward so he can face me.

"Except I'm not a stranger. You know my name, that's why you haven't asked for it, and about you not thinking so ..." He cocks his head, his words slurred, "I get the feeling you didn't come here tonight to think, but go ahead, gorgeous girl, correct me if I'm wrong."

I run my tongue along my teeth and this time, my grin breaks free. "You're not wrong, but I'd have to be blind not to recognize you from the posters, so that's not very fair."

"Forget all that." He shrugs. "What about the last part ..." He trails off, a curious gleam in his crazy blue eyes.

Something pulls at my muscles, but I manage to answer. "You're not wrong about that either."

"Then there it is." He holds his arms out wide in playful banter. "That was a whole lot of real. Do I get lucky now?" His smile couldn't be wider.

Laughter escapes me and he joins in, jerking his chin.

"Come on, gorgeous girl. Take a walk with me."

He might just be the last person I should be walking with tonight, but it's not like he knows this or ever will. It might be a really bad decision to join him, but I've made a crap ton of those lately, so what's one more?

I'm here for me tonight, so I'm not going to allow the thoughts of others into my headspace.

So, I accept his offer, falling in line beside him, and we keep toward the farthest point of the back yard.

At the fence's edge, he drops down onto the grass, so I follow, and slowly my eyes adjust to the darkness around us.

Tobias takes a slow drink from the bottle in his hand, and his shoulders seem to fall. It's as if he too has a lot on his mind, but his way of forgetting his problems for a while is to focus on mine. He studies me. "So, you came here to forget something, but you're stone cold sober."

I scoff, looking off. "Trust me, I wish I weren't."

"Let's hear why."

My head snaps toward his and he lifts his brows expectantly.

"I'm drunk, you're sober. I'm hot, you're gorgeous. Clearly you should tell me some dirt."

"That makes no sense."

"Not much does in college." His lips curve.

Okay, fair enough. "You first."

"Pshh." He shifts so he can lean his elbows on his bent knees. "What's there to tell? All my dirt is right there for all to see." His eyes find mine. "Media loves trouble."

"How much trouble can a guy who hangs out outside of parties really get into?" I tease.

His grin tells me I was right to have sensed his sarcasm, to understand it for what it was.

"Exactly." He gives a hard jerk of his chin. "I like you."

"You don't know me."

"Don't need to." He shakes his head. "Thinkin' I want to, yeah, but I already like you regardless."

"Yeah?" I lean toward him. "And what is it you like exactly?"

I expect him to have to think, to search for something good to say that won't sound made up on the spot, but he doesn't take a moment to think.

The man speaks without a single second's hesitation.

"I like that you ignored me instead of coming to me. I like that you knew I was watching and didn't do a damn thing to make sure I kept on. I like that you tried to escape me, and I like that you didn't want to walk with me." His grin comes out again then. "I mean, I like it more that you did, but ..." He laughs, and I bite my inner lip to keep from grinning. "I like that you walked around all night on your own, that you didn't need a gang of girls to stand beside to make you feel better or secure, and I like that you're the *only girl here in a hoodie and jeans."*

I roll my eyes playfully. "I doubt that."

"Don't." He laughs, but then his features morph into something a little deeper, more thrilling. "But most of all, I like that you asked me to tell you something."

My throat begins to itch and I'm forced to clear it. "Yet you told me nothing."

"I was still deciding if you were playing games or not."

"And now?"

"Now I know you aren't."

"All because I wanted to talk?"

"Most girls have no interest in talking to me." He stares me dead in the eye, and I stare right back.

It's odd, his words of choice lead me to assume they're spoken from a place of conceit, as if he's bragging about his escapades, but his tone doesn't quite match.

It's almost as if he disapproves of them and their choices.

In himself and his choices.

Call it a hunch, I guess.

Or naïve thinking.

"Tell me your name," he says then.

My smile is small. "Meyer."

"Meyer. I like it."

"Of course, you do, you're drunk," I tease.

"Maybe. Still like it though." He nods and then looks out over the yard. "So why you here tonight, Meyer?"

I take a deep breath, and when I open my mouth, a dejected laugh comes out. "To forget," I say before I rethink it. "I came here tonight to forget."

He looks to me again and I'm not sure what I expected, but what he does say isn't it.

"Don't we all in some way?" He squints at the bottle in his hands. "To forget the shitty week we had or the test that's coming up, the argument with our friends or ... shitty home visit with our family."

"The craptastic reality we somehow found ourselves in."

He grins and looks to me. "Exactly. We can bust our asses, but at the end of the day we're what the world makes of us. Expectation is a bitch, huh?"

"I'd drink to that."

He offers me the bottle, but I laugh it off with a shake of my head.

"What if I don't want to be what's expected?" I ask, more to myself but looking to him. "What if I want to blow statistics out of the water and become more? What if I want to be the success story?"

Tobias gauges me for a long moment. Maybe even a full minute before he nods his head.

"Then I'd say you and me got a lot in common, gorgeous girl." His voice is thick with emotion, and his eyes ...

I have to look away.

There's something brewing within them, something I recognize.

Something I feel deep in my gut, more so the last few days than ever.

Longing.

A desolate sense of solitude.

And maybe it makes no sense.

I have friends, he has friends, yet here we are, two strangers at a party, sitting alone in the dark having a conversation that feels more intimate than anything has in a long, long time.

"I want to help you," Tobias says quietly.

I turn back to him, and while it takes him a second, he looks to me, a burning sense of determination in his gaze.

"Help me how?"

"Forget," he says with direct intent.

"Forget."

I press my palms more firmly into the ground, and he nods, more to himself than me.

"Whatever it is you came here to forget, I want to make that happen. I can make that happen, but I want to be able to do it again tomorrow, and again after that." His eyes fall to my lips, and my stomach flips. "Tell me I can."

The muscles in my core grow taut and it's getting hard to breathe.

It gets even harder when his large, coarse fingers glide along my jaw, leaving a trail of fire and goose bumps in their wake. His touch stretches farther until his hand is wrapped around the back of my neck.

Tobias pins me with his piercing blue eyes and suddenly I'm mush before him, free for the taking.

His ... for the taking.

He scoots his body closer, his lips now hovering an inch away from mine.

His eyes close, his grip tightening, his heated breath growing closer, and then I rush out, "I'm pregnant."

Every muscle in his body freezes, and those lids snap

right back open, narrowing more and more by the second.

"No lie," I whisper with a nod, even though he asked nothing.

He didn't have to, his eyes did it for him.

"I am, with a man who sucks, but I didn't know he sucked and now I do because when I told him, he got angry and accused me of lying, as if I would lie about that, and then I found out he's been fucking another girl my age and I meant nothing the whole time and now I—"

I gasp, my nervous rambling cut off when he slams his mouth into mine.

His lips are full, his kiss hard and deep, and when his tongue demands entrance, I give it with relief.

I kiss the man back, and it's a kiss like no other. He's not just kissing me to help me forget, he's kissing me because he wants to.

He wants to take over my thoughts and mind and body, and he wants me to let him.

I'm not sure I could hold back if I tried.

Every part of me wants every part of him.

He doesn't feel like a heated body and good time.

He feels like ... more.

It's as if I need him tonight. Not someone, but him, and as strange as it sounds, I think he needs me tonight too.

It makes no sense.

But maybe it's not supposed to.

I'm here to forget, to let go.

So, I push away all my inhibitions, and I do just that.

I let go of me and I get lost in him.

I don't wait for Tobias to lie me back like some fragile princess.

I grip him by the collar and tug him down on top of me.

He doesn't protest but settles between my legs.

"Let me take you to my room," he says, lips now grazing along the hollow of my neck. "I don't want anyone to see you like this."

My heart races, my mind right there with it. "Don't worry about me."

He pauses, his bloodshot blues hooded and pinning me in place. "Let me take you to my room."

He has no reason to care if I'm spotted beneath him like this, but it's clear as day he does. Why, I don't know, but I slip my hands between us and unbutton his jeans.

"Meyer ..."

He grinds against me, and my body breaks out in chills.

"If we move, I might walk away."

He groans, dropping his lips to my ear. He nips at the skin there and I shake beneath him. "Then don't fucking move, gorgeous girl."

A chuckle leaves me, and together we kick our shoes from our feet, lose our jeans, and then he's at my entrance.

His eyes snap to mine, and he kisses me hard, whispering against my mouth, "I'm gonna slide inside you now."

I bite his bottom lip, and he does exactly what he says.

He pushes all the way into me in one long, slow thrust.

Our moans mix, our breathing turning into short pants.

"You're so fucking soft." He moans, grinding his hips into mine, and I lift, willing him deeper.

Tobias gives me what I want, but he has an even better idea.

He flips us, sits up, and pulls me onto his lap, right down over his shaft.

He reaches farther this way, and I shiver against him.

He smirks, lifting his hat from his head and placing it backward on mine. His hands glide along my thighs until he reaches the hem of my hoodie. He tugs it down. "Now if anyone does spot us, they can't see any naked part of you."

My chuckle is husky and I roll my hips in response.

Tobias's tongue comes out, gliding along his bottom lip and he pulls it between his teeth, his eyes moving between mine.

And then he kisses me again.

We put in equal effort, thrusting and rolling and tilting our bodies for maximum pleasure. My nipples ache to be touched, and it's as if he senses it, his hands disappearing under my top and into my bra, where he massages me with a gentle roughness that has my head falling back.

I open my eyes, and a smile graces my lips.

I stare at the stars above, lost in the scent around me, in the feel of him inside me.

Both our bodies are slick with sweat, overheated, and when he flexes inside me, my pussy squeezes him back.

He grips my hair, tugging a bit so I face him, and my toes curl from the devilish look in his eye. Our touches grow frantic, electrifying.

Desperate.

We're right there, both of us.

I grip his face, kissing his lips and pulling his head down into my chest so I can whisper into his ear.

"I'm gonna come, Tobias ..."

"Fuck, gorgeous girl." He grunts, his thrusts growing wilder, and he takes my ass in his palms, squeezing. His cock swells inside me and I slip my arms under his, my fingers spanning along his back, and he blows a harsh breath against my skin.

We come, both our bodies going stiff, but still, he moves inside me, chasing – delivering – every last bit there is to offer, demanding a full-body orgasm from each of us.

The man gets what he wants, chills break out all over me, covering every inch of my body and I'm sure my heart is going to beat right out of my chest, it pounds so hard.

I'm panting, seeking a steady breath my body refuses, but there's a smile on my face.

This is what sex is supposed to feel like.

Raw and primitive, a full-body takeover. No thought, no plan, no holding back.

"Jesus fuck." He falls to his back, rolling and taking me with him.

His grin spreads, and he pushes up on his elbow, staring down at me. "Told you I liked you."

I laugh, hiding my face with my elbow when I begin to blush, not that he can see it out here.

Not that it could be differentiated from the flush my orgasm already brought to my cheeks.

He shifts around me, and I jolt when his palm wraps around my ankle.

Looking to him, I watch as he slides my underwear and jeans up my thighs, lifting my hips from the grass as he reaches the curve of my ass.

"Not trying to rush you away," he rasps, staring at me. "But it won't be long before someone comes looking for me."

I nod. "Yeah, me too." I think of Bianca.

His lips twitch and he hops to his feet in full-naked glory, tugging his own clothes on.

I expect him to reach for my hand and pull me to my feet, for us to head back inside or him to offer a drink to get me to go, but he doesn't do any of those things.

He drops right back down beside me, staring up at the sky as I am.

Tomorrow I'll be sore in all the right places, and I couldn't care less because tonight I'm satisfied.

Free.

I know it won't last long, my entire world is about to shift and I'm terrified, but life is unexpected, if nothing else, so tonight, I'm going to forget tomorrow and just ... lie here in the dark with a stranger.

We sit silently for a few minutes before I catch his head turning toward me in my peripheral.

"I've never done this before," I admit into the darkness, slowly looking to him. "Had a one-night stand."

"Don't start now." He frowns. "I said I wanted to do this tomorrow."

I fight back tears, forcing a small, tight-lipped smile.

He has no idea what he's saying, but I won't burst the bubble we're in, so when he pulls out his phone, presses some buttons and then asks for my number, I give it to him.

We sit there, not speaking for a few more minutes, and then my name is shouted by a painstakingly familiar voice.

The color drains from my face, and in what feels like slow motion, I push onto my elbows, hesitantly looking toward the sound.

Thomas stalks forward with quick steps.

His silhouette grows closer, the light behind him hiding his expression, and I try to swallow, but the knot in my throat holds strong.

"Shit," I breathe.

"Coach," Tobias calls.

My pulse pounds, knocking against my ribs at a dangerous rate.

"Yeah, son, I'm here."

Son?

"You don't want to go in the house, Coach. Team's not exactly following the no-drinking rule tonight." I can hear Tobias's grin, but I can't bring myself to look at him.

"Don't worry, I won't, just came to give your friend a ride, remember?" Thomas says.

My brows pull and I drop my gaze to the grass, but then Thomas's hand is in front of my face.

I don't have to look up to know he's insisting, so I slip mine into his, allowing him to pull me to my feet.

Embarrassed and suddenly ashamed, I can't look him in the eye, but I do Tobias.

He rubs at the back of his head, looking from me to his coach.

"He, uh, I guess he's gonna give you a ride home," he tells me.

All I can do is nod, and then I turn, following the man out of the side gate. I slip inside his car without a word, and I know instantly we're not going to my dorm.

We're going to his house.

Outside of it, he fills me in on why he showed up tonight and follows with promises of our future.

Subconsciously, my hand falls to my stomach, and I make one of my own to the little one growing inside me.

Everything is going to be okay now.

It's as if a weight is lifted in this moment as Thomas sparks hope where I had none left.

We'll be okay ...

Present Time

Tobias

I can't feel my legs, and I'm not even sure I'm breathing.

I feel dead inside. Sick.

Disgusted.

"Fuck ... Meyer ..." My voice is strained, and I can hardly look at her.

Tears pool in her eyes. "It's okay."

"Nothing about that is okay." I push my palms into

my eye sockets. "How could I be such a fuckup?"

"You were drunk, it happens." Her lips twitch, and she lifts a shoulder. "And I was angry, and anger turned into recklessness, I guess. I wanted to get back at him, stupidly thinking he would care, so I went out and there you were."

I swallow, grabbing her hand and pulling it to my lips. "I really spotted you right away?"

"From the doorway the second I walked inside." Her smile is sad. "You really were trashed." She chuckles, but it soothes out. "I was a hot mess, so we fit that night."

"We fit period, Tutor Girl." I swallow, a frustrating sense of satisfaction and sorrow firing through me at the same time. "I can't believe I was inside you when she was."

Meyer squeezes my hand. "Thomas, he ..."

Anger builds within me, creating a heated storm in my gut. "He told you I called him to ..." Fuck, I can hardly say it. "To clean up my mess, didn't he?"

She licks the tears from her lips. "Yeah, he did."

"I didn't. I wouldn't have done that to you. He's known for popping in randomly. It had to be random."

"I believe that now," she rasps, closing her eyes and leaning into my hand when I cup her jaw. "I didn't then. He told me you'd be too messed up to remember the next day. That that was what you did, got drunk and slept with whoever was in front of you, and then cut them loose. He told me to read the papers, and I'd learn all I needed to know. So, I did, and when you didn't call like you had said you would," she shrugs. "I fell for all his lies back then. I married him a week later, and realized a month after that, in doing so, he owned me. I lost my financial aid because he made too much money. Lost my scholarship because

I deferred a semester to have Bailey. He only wanted the marriage so he could cover his ass if people found out he fucked a student, and so he could hold my daughter over my head if I ever let it spill who her father was. It was a huge ploy, he even tried to sneak my brother into the contract, tried to force him onto the baseball team as a sub, when he had a starting position on his school's team."

"Piece of shit." I shake my head.

"I lost everything I had worked for, so when he shoved the contract at me, offering me a bit of relief, I took it. That man changed my entire life, in both good and bad ways," she says with a devastating hint of acceptance.

My forehead falls to hers, and she grips my wrists tightly.

"If he were to follow through with his threats of taking her, I ... she's my daughter, Tobias," she cries. "My everything, I can't even think about—"

"Shh, baby, I know," I whisper, doing my best to be the fucking rock here when really, I want to scream. "I know."

"You have to let me go," she whispers.

Not a chance.

Her eyes hit mine. "And you have to promise me you won't fall apart this time. You didn't work your ass off to lose everything."

You and Bailey are everything.

Meyer cries. "Maybe in time ..."

"Yeah, baby." Heat climbs up my throat, determination firing off my every nerve. "Maybe."

Definitely. Posi-fucking-tively.

"Tobias ..."

"Tutor Girl."

She presses her lips to mine, but it isn't soothing.

It aches.

It fucking stings.

It's her goodbye.

She's crazy if she thinks I'm okay with that or assumes I ever will be.

I won't, but I know she needs this.

She needs the security of knowing her little girl is safe and secure, and she can only be those things if I'm out of the picture, so I'll give her what she needs.

I'll let her go, walk away, and keep my word across the board.

It'll kill me, but the alternative would end me, just like it would her.

So, when she presses her mouth more firmly onto mine, I'm the one who pulls away.

With slow, weighted steps, I put space between us, dying a little inside as her lips begin to tremble, our fingers hooked together until our bodies are too far apart to touch, and they're forced to fall at our sides.

Her cries grow louder, and she slaps her palm over her mouth to hide the sound.

That almost gets me, but before I break, I force myself to spin away.

I walk out of Meyer's house, and I don't look back.

CHAPTER 33

Tobias

I drove around for hours after leaving Meyer's house. Hours, and it wasn't until I was a hundred miles out that I realized where I was going.

Now, it's after three in the morning, and I'm finally dragging myself out of my truck and up the short walkway to the front door, but I don't even get the chance to pull my key out, because my mom beat me to it.

She's standing on the dark porch, waiting for me, just like she said she would be when I called her from the road and told her everything that had happened.

She said to me, "Come home, baby" not knowing I already was.

As subconscious as the decision might have been, it was the right one. I need them right now, and that's confirmed the second I meet my mom's watery eyes.

Everything inside of me crumbles and I walk right into her open arms.

"Mom," I croak. "I love her. I can't lose her. I can't."

"Oh baby, I know," she cries, clenching me tight. "I know."

"I'm sorry I fucked up before." I swallow. "I should have been better. I was raised better."

"Honey, no stop it." Her voice shakes, and she gasps for air through her tears. "I'm sorry. I'm so, so sorry for everything. You're my baby, and I love you. Every part of you. I'm so sorry."

My dad steps up behind her, placing his hand on her shoulders, and she steps back, tears spilling from her eyes.

He gives a tight-lipped smile, nodding, and when he steps up, unsure, I move in to hug the man.

He clamps my back tight, slapping his hands a few times. "It's going to be okay, son."

"I don't know, Dad. I can't do this."

"Hey." He pulls back, gripping my shoulders and locking his eyes with mine. "You can do anything; do you hear me?" His grip tightens. "You're Tobias Cruz, a man of honor. Strong and determined. You never give up and you won't be starting now."

My eyes cloud and I look away. "How am I supposed to step back on that field when I know she's hurting alone?"

My dad pats at my cheek, drawing my eyes back to his.

"She's not hurting alone, son. You're hurting right there with her, even if you're not at her side, she knows it, and it would hurt her more to see you fail. You know this." He dips his chin, and I nod.

"And my coach? How am I supposed to perform for a man like him? I want to fucking kill him."

"Then kill him with the acts of a man, because lord knows you're ten times the one he could ever be."

I blow out a harsh breath, dropping my chin to my chest, but he lifts it.

"You..." My dad swallows, moisture building in his gaze. "Are *our* son, and you have become a man any father or mother would be honored to call theirs. You're going to show that bastard what that means. You're going to get back in that truck and you're going to go do what you were born for, son. You're going to show the world what you're made of, and then you're going to show him the same. And while you do, we'll be there. Me and your mama." He swallows, his voice cracking. "Whatever you need, whatever you want, whatever you do. We'll be right there. Always. No matter what."

They'll be there.

My parents.

They'll be here for me.

They believe in me.

They see me.

My jaw muscles twitch and I nod, looking from my mom to my dad.

I can do this.

For them.

For her.

For me.

I will fucking do this.

Meyer

I can do this, I repeat for the hundredth time in the short walk from my apartment to the athletic department, and while I'm not so sure I believe it, I *am* doing it.

I'm so done living under the thumb of another. I can't do it anymore.

The only thing he has over me is that prenup, but I made the sacrifice he demanded, one he used his own daughter as a pawn in. I gave up the man I love, so the man I married couldn't take my daughter from my arms.

But I won't give up anything else. Not my time, not my name, not my future.

I needed him this year. He knew it and I hated it, just like I'm sure he did.

Had I walked away when I realized what a piece of shit he truly was, I would have had to drop out of college because I could never afford to pay my own way, no matter how many part-time jobs I could find. Leaving him would have meant digging myself into a bigger whole, and Bailey deserved more. So, I took the little he offered and found the smallest bit of comfort in the fact that my daughter would have a safe place to call home. That, and the knowledge that within a few short years, years she wouldn't even remember, I would graduate with the tools I needed to provide for her on my own. We would be free of Thomas Reid, and she would never be exposed to the hate inside his heart.

Just like I'll never allow him to know the pain he's caused mine.

It was devastating when he painted me a promise of sunsets and delivered instead a thunderstorm of destruction, but that was nothing compared to the hollow ache inside of me now.

But even through the pain and longing, there's relief, and the guilt the sensation causes only brings more pain.

I don't need Thomas anymore.

So, it's with that thought I hold my head high and step into his office, knowing he's due out the door mere minutes from now.

His head jerks up and he flies from his seat, but the man freezes when I lift my hands as high as my chest and let the crappy laptop he gave me fall to the old wood with a loud slap.

"What the hell are you doin'?" He glares. "I know you saw the bus loading up out-front. You should be far away from here right now."

I take a deep breath, and say, "I quit."

His eyes narrow farther. "What do you mean you quit?"

"I mean, I'm done. With this job, with this school, with all of it."

"You're dropping out?"

"I'm transferring to Florida."

Shock overtakes his face, but he can't hide the hint of hope, and it's disgusting. Expected, but disgusting, nonetheless.

"What?" he asks slowly.

"Yep, and since you can probably access anything related to me, *husband,* I'll tell you." I nod. "I got a new scholarship, completely academic, so there's no need to report my spouse's income. Bailey gets a spot in the child development program, and they have family housing. We leave when school's out, and we won't be coming back."

His eyes narrow. "I won't be mailing checks across the country."

"I wouldn't accept them if you did."

"I won't be signing any divorce papers either."

"As if I could afford to file against you."

He licks his lips, his chin tipping slightly. "Is this about—"

"Don't," I rush, shaking my head, willing my tears not to show themselves. "Don't even think about finishing that sentence. You don't get to ask questions and I don't have to answer to you anymore. I know full well what that contract requires of me, but there isn't a thing in there that says I have to stick around and face you every day. So, I'm leaving and I'm taking *my* daughter with me. And before you try and throw it out there in spite, let me tell you now." I plant my hands on his desk and lean forward. "I know you don't care so go ahead and smile, wave ... laugh even. It makes no difference to me."

"You know this only got complicated when you started sniffing around my pitcher."

"No," I don't mean to whisper, but that's the way my voice comes out. "This got complicated when you manipulated me into marrying you for your own benefit."

"You took what I offered, did you not?"

"I was naïve and afraid, and you took advantage of that to save your own ass, but you had been doing that all along, right? So I shouldn't' have been surprised." I lift a shoulder, shaking my head at the vile man in front of me. "I should have realized that when after we met in the hall of the tutoring center, you started showing up, offering me rides home, but only on my late nights. Never in the daylight. If not then, definitely the night you kissed me in the parking lot in front of my dorm, but only after you rolled up your tinted windows. I should have saw right through you, but I was young and dumb." I push upright and he stares at me a moment, his hand coming up to rub at his jaw. "Good thing I'm not that girl anymore."

With a shake of my head, I turn for the door, but his words have me pausing.

"I don't hate you, Meyer," he says to my back. "You know that, right?"

Glancing over my shoulder, I meet his blue gaze. "I wish you did. You know that ... right?"

I don't wait for a response.

I walk away.

I expect a freeing feeling to follow, to sweep over me and lift my shoulders high, to ease the tension in my muscles and clear the haze in my mind.

But none of those things happen.

In fact, I feel heavier, weaker, but it has nothing to do with leaving that man behind, and everything to do with the one staring at me through the travel bus window straight ahead.

His head falls against the seat, and I feel the weight of it in my chest.

His lips tip up on one side the slightest bit as if he's saying *it's okay, Tutor Girl. Go.*

Among so many other things.

He's letting me know he's okay, that he understands.

He's showing me he's keeping his promise, that he's here, pushing through the way I asked him to. The way he has to.

Tears pool in my eyes, and I force my own smile.

I'm so proud of you, Tobias.

As if he can hear me, his features twist, but he nods and when I nod back, he closes his beautifully broken eyes.

A cry slips from me, but I do as he needs, as we both need.

I rush away as quickly as I can so he doesn't have to see it.

It's the hardest, longest walk I've ever taken.

Goodbye, my hotshot.

DIRTY CURVE

CHAPTER 34

Meyer

I'm lost in thought, staring across the room when Bianca steps up beside me.

"You okay?" Bianca asks.

I nod, a bittersweet feeling washing over me as I glance around the small space I've called home for the last year and a half.

"Just trying to figure out how I can hate a place I love so much." I look to her. "This is the only home Bay has ever known, where I brought her the day we were released from the hospital. It's where she said her first word. Rolled over and pulled herself up."

"It's where you fell in love ..." she adds.

My throat burns.

Where my heart broke at my own hand.

It's been almost a month now since Tobias and I have spoken, and it's passed in slow, torturous minutes.

Almost a month since I quit the tutoring center and put in my thirty-day notice on this place.

Almost a month and nothing feels easier yet, and I don't have much faith it ever will, but maybe one day.

Maybe in time ...

I swallow.

Over and over again, I tried to push everything out of my head, but I needed to know he was okay, and that he was doing what he promised by being the badass he is.

The man knocked his finals out of the park, scoring above a ninety on every single exam, and then came the big games.

I watched every one that was broadcasted, read every article that the school posted, and just this week, while I was packing up my living room, I sat on my bed, Bailey on my lap, witnessing him throw a curveball that secured the Avix Sharks the number one spot in the NCAA World Series Championship game.

He was an Ace, on and off the field.

I cried, proud of him, and I tried to sit through the interview that followed, but I couldn't make it past the first few questions. That's the day I unplugged the TV and disconnected the internet.

Thomas hasn't spoken a word to me in weeks either, not that I want him to, and while it comes as no surprise, it's still somehow mindboggling that a man could be told his daughter was being moved across country and not so much as bat a lash.

But then again, he was never much of a man and he never claimed her as his own.

"Whatcha thinking?" Bianca prompts.

"How I hate to leave this place, but I really can't wait to go." My eyes glide to Bianca's, my lips twitching. "Does that make any sense?"

"Yeah, chica. It does," she whispers.

The movers Bianca's grandfather hired for me step out of what has always been Bailey's bedroom.

"Careful." I jerk forward, but Bianca pulls me back.

"Let them do their job." She shakes me gently.

"Yeah." My shoulders fall, and I take one last look around.

Most of the stuff in here came with the place, but the few things that are mine, I want moved in one piece. The last thing I need is a new expense because these guys don't know how to go easy on a crib.

"I can't believe you won't be here with me next year," Bianca says, and when I look to her, she laughs off her tears, tugging me into a hug. "I'm going to miss you and Bay."

"Hey." I blink rapidly, trying not to think about that part yet. Being alone in Florida won't be easy, but peace of mind is worth the hardship that comes with it. "There's no crying on vacation."

She sniffles, then pushes me away, and swipes the back of her fingers beneath her eyes. "Bitch, vacation didn't start yet. You promised me a month, that's thirty days to the minute, and it doesn't start until we step *off* the plane, so stop trying to cut my time short." She bends down, lifting Bailey's car seat in her hands. "Now grab your purse, put the key on the counter, and let's go."

I do what she says and climb inside her car.

She pulls out of the parking lot, but as we get to the end of the alleyway that faces the front of the school, she hesitates, glancing to me. "The team leaves today. Last game before they get the chance to take it all."

My chest pinches, a mix of pain and pride swelling

within me. "They'll take it all," I breathe, looking at my best friend. "Turn the car, B. Vacation awaits."

Tears spring in her eyes, but she nods and curves the car left. "Damn straight it does."

Just like that, I leave Avix University, as well as all that it holds, behind.

Including a large part of myself.

My heart leaps into my throat and I scurry onto my knees, ever so slowly scooting along the warm sand in order to get closer to Bailey, who has yet to realize she's let go of the upside-down sand bucket that she's pulled herself up on.

She's tapping on the hard plastic top, looking out at the water no more than thirty feet in front of us. After every few slaps of her palms, her elbows bend and she holds her open hands up near her chest, nothing but the strength of her legs and support of her back keeping her standing.

You got this, baby girl.

"Holy shit!" Bianca muffles, a bag of chips hanging from her mouth, daiquiris in each hand.

Bailey jolts, falling to her bottom, and I drop onto mine with a huff.

"Damn you!" I smile, clapping for Bay when she looks my way. "Did Auntie B scare you?" I pick her up, kissing her chubby little cheeks. "What are you doing standing all by yourself, huh? Stop growing so fast."

Bianca bends over, letting the chips fall onto the lounge chair and I stand with Bailey, dusting her feet and bottom off before setting her into the playpen beside us.

Instantly, she forces her body to fall forward, and she uses the netting on the side to help herself stand. Her fingers wrap around the edge and then she's peeking at us over the edge.

We laugh, and I accept the drink Bianca offers.

"I can't believe it's been three weeks already." She sighs. "You sure we can't push it out another month? It's not like you have to go back for work."

"I know, but I want to get settled, get Bailey acclimated and meet with the child development center there. You should just come home with me. It's not Hawaii, but I mean it is Florida. Close enough, right?" I tease.

"Wrong!" she shouts, being overly dramatic. "So wrong, but you're insane if you think I'm not coming to help you get unpacked."

We cheers, taking slow, satisfied drinks from our glasses.

Bailey starts to cry then, and my eyes glide her way, but she's not looking at me.

Instantly, she drops herself onto her butt, her little lip poking out in a pout.

"Bay, what's wrong?"

I take a step toward her, but then the hairs on the back of my neck stand to attention, freezing me in place.

Bailey's hands lift, her palms opening and closing as she reaches out, waiting to be picked up. But not by me.

My baby girl doesn't have to wait long, because in

the next second a shadow falls over me, shifts beside me, and then there he is.

In shorts and a T-shirt, a black hat turned backward on his head, he pays me no mind, passing right by, and stopping directly in front of my little girl.

Bailey kicks her feet, and his soft chuckle sends chills down my spine.

My throat runs dry as he bends, lifting my daughter into his arms. He pulls her close to his chest, one arm wrapped around her, the other gripping her tiny hand.

Only after he breathes her in does the man turn to face me.

I'm pretty sure my mouth is hanging open, but nothing's coming out, and then he gives me something he hasn't in far too long.

His infamous smirk. "Hi, Tutor Girl."

A mix between a laugh and a cry escapes, and then he's in front of me.

My pulse is beating so wildly I'm sure you can see it through my skin and I tip my head back a little, not wanting to miss any part of him.

"Hi?" I trace every inch of his face. "You're standing in front of me, on a private beach in Hawaii, and hi is what you say to me?"

He smiles, releases Bailey's hand, and wraps his arm around my middle. He yanks me to him.

I want to push to my toes and kiss him.

I want to pass Bailey off to Bianca and disappear with him for a while.

I want to touch him, love him, keep him.

But worry swirls in my abdomen and it's enough

to keep my feet planted on the sand. "What are you doing here?"

A softness falls over him and his palm widens on my back. "I came for my girls."

The ease in his eyes has me squinting, and then the most tender of smiles polishes his full lips.

"You don't have to worry anymore, baby," he promises, his tone warm and devout. "She's all yours now."

My lungs expand, stretching my ribcage to its max, and I subconsciously place my hand on Bailey's back. "What?" I rasp.

"He relinquished his rights, all you have to do is file the papers, and it's over."

Moisture clouds my eyes; clogs my throat and I blink through the overwhelming emotions. "Show me."

"It's in my bag, but I swear to you, it's legit. My agent had the papers drafted himself. All he had to do was sign." A knowing smile tipping his lips.

"He just ... gave her up?"

"Yeah, baby, he did," he whispers, understanding while it's a thrilling moment, it's also heartbreaking in a way I can't quite explain.

Thomas signed. He gave up his daughter as if she were nothing.

She was never anything to him ... but she's *everything* to me, and Tobias knows that.

"The marriage?"

His eyes flash. "Got those papers, too. You're not his, never were, never will be."

My muscles go lax, and I shuffle closer to him. "Tobias—"

"I finished out the season," he interrupts, a seriousness overcoming him. "I did what I said I would, what I promised you, and then I did what I had to do."

"You didn't have to do anything for me."

"Yes, I did." His forehead falls to mine and he holds my eyes hostage. "You said in time, Tutor Girl. Well, time's up."

"Tobias." My voice cracks, gratefulness and reproach overwhelming me. "The draft, it's in five days."

"You've been paying attention, huh?"

My features soften and he winks, jerking his chin.

Both Bianca and I turn, looking out over our shoulders.

A solid fifty feet away stands a large group of familiar faces, Echo, his parents and my brother among them, as well as a man in a black suit.

The moment they realize we're staring, they scream and shout, throwing their hands into the air, making the three of us laugh.

My head snaps back to Tobias, who is already looking at me.

"The resort is giving us their conference room. Camera crew and my agent's team will be here in a few days to set up."

"But you've worked all your life for this. This is what you've always wanted, to step on that stage."

"Wanted," he stresses, tracing my lips with his thumb.

"This is a huge moment for you. Your career ..."

"My life." His lips press gently onto Bailey's temple. "My future." He grabs Bailey's hand once more. "My world."

Slowly, their palms fall to the place over his left pec, his eyes clear and focused on mine. "Nothing I could ever do and nowhere I could ever go will ever mean a damn thing if I don't have my girls to come home to. I want you by my side when the call comes, and I want you there every day after that."

"Tobias ..." My tears fall and he steps closer. You didn't have to do this. I would have come to you."

"I know, baby, and that's the beauty of this. Of us. You want for me what I want for you, but we'll talk about that later, 'cause it's been a long ass time, baby, and I'm gonna need you to kiss me now." I chuckle, and he licks his lips, his brows jumping as he looks deep into my eyes. "From here, no matter what happens, we work through it together. It's the three of us, now and forever."

Blindly passing my drink over to Bianca, I wrap my hand around his neck and pull his lips to mine, but I tug back the second before they touch.

His chest rumbles and my grin stretches as I whisper, "No lie?"

And then he claims my mouth as his own. Again.

Months ago, I had no clue what to call the Playboy Pitcher, the hotshot athlete of Avix U.

But now I do and it's my favorite label of all.

Mine.

THE END

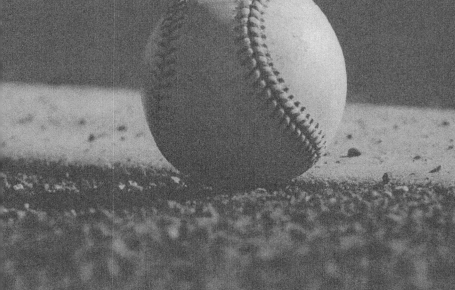

Avix Inquirer: Breaking News!

Head coach of the Avix Sharks baseball team, Thomas Reid, resigned today after allegations arose claiming he went against NCAA rules. While what exactly he was accused of was not released to the press, our extremely credible source tells us he broke the compensation rule and was using department funds to put a smile on his players' faces. Not only that, but he was also said to have slipped a little something into his players' drinks in a twisted game of manipulation. Allegedly, of course. Considering he bowed out after the best season of his career, I'd say there's no question to whether or not he's guilty. That man should have known better than to PLAY the BOY like that.

Well, that's a wrap for us at the Inquirer.

See you next school year, Sharks!

EP|LOGUE

Two Years Later

Tobias

Echo pops to his feet, glancing back at the umpire before jogging his way to me.

The batter shakes his head, stepping away from the plate, gripping the barrel of his bat with a hilarious amount of anger.

I jerk my chin as he approaches the mound, and my boy grins.

He lifts his glove up to hide his lips. "Just needed a quick stretch." He laughs, glancing around at the sold-out stadium. "Fuck, son, this shit's wild."

"Told you you'd like the new view."

"Aye, it only took me two seasons to get here." Echo shows his smirk. "You think the man who signed my check is happy now?"

"Not yet." I cut a quick glance toward the visiting teams dugout. "We promised him a Championship."

"That we did." E lowers his chin, looking me dead in the eye. "We gonna give it to him?"

Thrill fires down my spine, making the hairs on the

back of my neck stand.

This is fucking it.

This is the pinnacle of the game.

Of my game.

I've already got the world to go home too, now it's time to bring home the dream.

I lift a single brow. "You gonna give me what I want?"

"You gonna let me choose where we go for dinner tonight?" he counters.

A quick laugh escapes and I nod at my best friend. "Let me end this shit quick, and you got it."

"Curveball it is my man." He slaps my sleeve, moving back to his spot.

I stretch my neck, spinning the ball in my palm, and flick my eyes up to the seats right behind the batter's box, where my family sits watching.

When I signed my contract, my agent secured me a box at the top, a private suite cased in with glass, and AC, but Meyer has yet to take advantage of the perk. She wants to be in the exact spot I first told her I wanted her. And so far, for every home game we've had, she has been, weather be damned. She's got Milo to thank for that one. He loves the damn box and goes into babysitter mode quick so long as he has access to it. It's a sweet trade, and the man never misses a game either. Meyer wasn't kidding when she said he wants to be there for her. The semester after she moved here, he was right behind her, and I couldn't have been more thankful.

My job takes me all over, so knowing she has him when I'm gone makes this job possible. He's a huge part of the reason I'm able to perform the way I do, because I know, no matter what, my girl has someone looking out for her.

The move to Florida has been good to us, and the Miami Marlins have been, too.

They treat me well, and the press surrounding my name nowadays is nothing but an honor.

They talk about the game and my future in it, wagering it'll be a long one right here in Sun Life Stadium.

I'm a damn angel in their eyes, and with my next six pitches, I'll be their fucking God, too.

With one last look at my wife, I get myself set.

I take a deep breath, and then it's on.

I'm about to win The World fucking Series.

Meyer

When I was little and imagined my life, I saw me and Milo living next door to each other, our mom in a small house on the back of one of our places. I hoped to meet a man who would come home and want to kiss me like the couples did in the movies. He'd set his briefcase on the table near the door and untie his tie as he made his way to me.

I'd have dinner waiting and our kids would be well mannered and excited to talk to us about their day.

But here I am, a year out of college and my life is nothing like I pictured.

It's so much more.

Yes, Milo lives twenty miles away, but that's nothing on a Florida highway, and I see him no less than three out of seven days of the week. And while my mom can't be with us, I like to think she's near, that her ashes rode the waves off the coast of California to Miami's shoreline, as if she found her way to us.

I did find the man, or more, he found me, but he doesn't own a briefcase and complains when he has to wear a tie.

But he does wear a black baseball hat pulled low like no other.

He kisses me when he gets home, and everywhere else for that matter.

I don't have dinner ready when he gets home because my man likes to be a part of every aspect of our lives, and meals are no different. As for well-mannered children, well, I'm not even sure what that means.

I have a toddler, and she acts like a toddler, as she should. She cries if she's upset and laughs when she's entertained. Smiles when she's happy and pouts when she's sad.

Bailey is sweet and kindhearted, and the most precious thing, and not just to me, but to her daddy too.

And Tobias *is* her daddy, in every single way that counts.

I couldn't imagine a better man or father if I tried. I'm unconvinced one exists.

Pushing to my feet, I slide my fingers through the chain linked fence as he gets set for the very last throw of the season, the pitch that will light the fire of the young man inside him and solidify everything he hoped was true but wasn't so sure of at different stages in his life.

He has it in him.

He's capable and enough.

He's so much more than enough.

As if he can hear my thoughts, Tobias lifts his chin the slightest bit, allowing me to see his eyes beneath the bill of his hat.

Suddenly, person after person, row after row jumps to stand, and my eyes float from one side to the other, teal and black blanketing the place at every angle. The echo of the crowd vibrates from all around me, the faith they have in their pitcher bringing tears to my eyes and my favorite smirk to Tobias's lips.

He isn't even nervous, not in the least bit.

He's ready for this, worked his ass off to get right here right now.

"Come on, hotshot. Make this your dirtiest curve yet."

He does just that.

The pitch is thrown, and the crowd is celebrating before the umpire has even made the call.

The Miami Marlins win the World Series on their home field.

Before I even have time to look behind me, security is at my side, ushering me down and through the small opening that leads to the field – no doubt in my mind Tobias gave them strict instructions to do exactly this.

He's already halfway to me, his glove in the dirt, and then I'm in his arms.

Tobias swings us around, kissing me hard on the lips as he lowers me to my feet and grips my cheeks with both hands.

"How'd I do, Tutor Girl?" He grins, sweat beading along his brow.

"I'd say you aced it, hotshot."

"Damn fuckin' straight." He smashes his lips to mine again, glancing up at the suite, where Bianca and Milo are being escorted from, Bailey in his arms.

A few guys come up, his coach hot on their tail, congratulating and hugging Tobias.

I use the moment to slip my hand into my purse, my stomach erupting with butterflies as I do.

The men are approached by a few others in suits, and my husband turns back to me, pulling me against him, and as he does, he feels the toy now smashed between our bodies.

With a small frown, he pulls back, laughing when he sees the little baseball in my palm.

"Holy shit, you brough it." He takes it in his hand, tossing it up and catching it in his palm.

"No." I shake my head. "I *bought* it."

He frowns, and then he looks to the ball again. "This...this is new." His eyes dart up to mine.

"Yeah," I nod. "It is. Bailey's still learning to share so..."

In that instant, the toy is forgotten. It falls to our feet and he grips my face once again, but this time, to hold me still. "Baby...are we pregnant?"

A mix between a cry and a laugh escapes me and I nod. "Yeah, we are."

"Oh my—" he cuts himself off, and shouts into the air. Bending, he lifts me up, his arms tight around my knees, and starts jogging.

Laughing, I hold on for dear life, and he runs right for the reporter section, cutting off the interview they were getting with the head coach.

They're all more than happy to turn their mics to the man of the hour.

But he doesn't let them speak, at least not yet.

He lowers me beside him, leans into the microphone and announces to the millions of people watching, "Tonight is one of the best nights of my life!" he shouts, getting the crowd riled up again. "We just won the game of all games and my gorgeous wife has just told me that we're expecting baby number two!"

Tears fall from my eyes, and I burry my face in his chest, his arms closing tight around me as the fans go wild, happy for the man they've come to love.

Happy for us both.

"Bailey!" He shouts then, and I look over my shoulder to find the others have finally made it.

I let go of him, and Bianca pretty much jumps on me, squealing and clapping like a crazy person, and Milo steps in next.

Bailey is already in her daddy's arms and that's exactly where she stays as he gives interview after interview right there on that field.

I stand back, watching the two most important people in my life, my palm resting on the third.

Tobias's reaction to the news was more than I hoped it would be. I knew he would be thrilled, we've been trying for eight months now, but I hadn't even paused to wonder what his excitement would feel like from my side.

I didn't have that before and I have no words for

the feelings sweeping over me.

Every part of me, from deep within my core to the tips of my fingers is aglow. It's as if I'm standing on air. The weight of my body has eluded me and I'm afraid if I try and speak, a jumbled mess of words is all that will come out.

I couldn't ask for more in this lifetime, not when I've already been so blessed.

It took a lot for us to get here. We had our ups and downs, but looking back, there isn't a moment I regret. Not a single second of it.

Because if we went back and took away the bad, there would be no good left standing.

All the hurt and hardships lead us to this very moment in one way or another. Neither of us would be who we are today without the path it took us to get here.

Unyielding love and support, that's what we have.

That's what our lives will be full of for years to come.

"Mommy!"

I blink, looking down to find Bailey running toward me, her baseball cap hiding half of her face. Smiling, lift it up so I can get a good look at her. "Bailey Bay!"

"Are you ready?" she says, her R sounding more like a W and blue eyes wide with excitement.

I bend, so we're more eye level and put my hands on her little hips. "Ready for what, pumpkin?"

"Daddy said we're getting a baby!" she pulls away, running a few steps away, all to run right back. "Let's go find him!"

I laugh, pushing to my feet, let her take my hand,

and lead me where she wishes, knowing full well where she's taking me.

Right to Tobias's side.

My little daddy's girl.

Tobias pulls me into him, whispering dirty promises of what the night holds into my ear.

My husband keeps every single one.

AVIX INQUIRER!

Attention, Sharks!
In this special, print only edition of the inquirer we're sharing some major news! Avix Universities very own Playboy Pitcher is a playboy no more!
But we knew that, didn't we?
Last time we reported on the stud that is Tobias Cruz, it was to break the hearts of dozens across campus with the news of his winter wedding! This time, we're delighted to help the happy couple announce the birth of their second child! We're told he and his mother are healthy and headed home as we speak!
So, on behalf of all of us here at AU, we want to say congratulations to Mr. and Mrs. Cruz on the birth of their son, Easton!
Yes, we see what you did there, Mr. Cruz, and we're all for it!
That's all we've got today!
Be sure to tune in next week ...
we've got a wild quarterback on our hands.
Until then, Sharks.

Quick Note from the Author

I cannot believe this book is in your hands!
I started this baby in 2017, but something held me back,
and I think it was the fact that in order to love Tobias,
you had to see every bit of who he was. In short? I was
afraid, but telling his story the way I saw it was the only
way I could write this book.
He's a young man. A college student. He had sooo much
growing to do and his path from beginning to end is one I
am immensely proud of.
Finishing and sharing this story with you feels truly
special to me. Thank you SO MUCH for reading.
These two have been with me for so long and it means
the world to me that you wanted to meet them.
I hope you loved Tobias and Meyer's story as much as I
enjoyed telling it.

More from the Author

Boys of Brayshaw

Trouble At Brayshaw

Reign Brayshaw

Be My Brayshaw

Break Me

Fake It Til You Break It

Fumbled Hearts

Defenseless Hearts

Wrong For Me

Baldy Behaved

Head over to: www.meaganbrandy.com/books

Stay Connected

My newsletter is the BEST way to stay in contact!
You'll get release dates, titles, and FUN first!
Sign up here: https://geni.us/BMMBNL

Be the FIRST in the know and meet new book friends in my Facebook readers group. This is a PRIVATE group. Only those in the group can see posts, comments, and the like!!

Search Facebook for: Meagan Brandy's Reader Group

Purchase EXCLUSIVE merchandise here:
https://www.teepublic.com/user/meaganbrandy

Find me here:
Amazon
Instagram
Facebook
Twitter
Pinterest
Bookbub
Goodreads

Acknowledgements

Thank you to my readers for for following me from one journey to the next. You make this dream possible!
To my man, I love you. I literally couldn't do this without you in my corner. Keep your ass there, k?!!

Melissa Teo! You keep me in check, order, line...all the things. You make this journey a smooth one and I appreciate every bit of work you do.

Serena and Veronica, busy schedules be damned, we always fall right back in place! Love having you on my team.

To my blogger and ARC girls! THANK YOU for helping spread the word and for your love for my books. You take this from a nine to a ten!

Danielle! Thank you for putting up with my repetitive questions and loving me even though I change my decisions on the daily LOL Happy to be a pat of Wildfire!
To my editors and proofreaders...one day I won't suck so bad at commas. Today is not that day!
AND THANK YOU TO ANY AND EVERY PERSON WHO PICKED UP THIS BOOK! You make my dreams come true.

xoxo
Meagan